About
John Ford...

About John Ford...

Lindsay Anderson

'Quand on veut respecter les hommes,
il faut oublier ce qu'ils sont et penser à
l'idéal qu'ils portent caché en eux, à
l'homme juste et noble, intelligent et
bon, fidèle et vrai — à tout ce que nous
appelons une âme.'
Amiel: *Journal*

Plexus, London

Anderson, Lindsay
      About John Ford.
      I. Ford, John, b. 1895
      I. Title
      791.43'0233'0924   PN1998.A3F/

      ISBN 0-85965-013-8
      ISBN 0-85965-014-6 Pbk

Made and printed in Great Britain by
Hillman Printers (Frome) Ltd

Cover design by Phil Gambrill
Cover: My Darling Clementine;
Henry Fonda as Wyatt Earp and Cathy Downs
as his "Lady Fair".
Page 1: She Wore A Yellow Ribbon.
Frontispiece: Young Mr. Lincoln: *Henry Fonda.*

To Lois
Remembering the Pioneers and
the Glenroyal, Shipley

and

To Gavin and Peter
Remembering Sequence, and
the Granada, Greenwich

Acknowledgements

I have many people to thank.

For memories frankly and generously shared: Harry Carey Jnr., Donal Donnelly, Henry Fonda and Robert Montgomery. The editor of 'Action' for permission to reprint recollections by John Carradine and Andy Devine. Miss Mary Astor for the passages from her unique memoir, *A Life on Film*.

Thanks to Mr. John Nichols for permission to reprint letters from Dudley Nichols; to Mrs. Jean Nugent, for allowing me to use a letter from her husband Frank Nugent; and Mrs. Dorris Johnson for permission to reproduce letters from Nunnally Johnson, from *The Letters of Nunnally Johnson*, published by Alfred A. Knopf, Inc. To my friend Kevin Brownlow double thanks, for his interview with Willis Goldbeck and for some rare stills from his collection.

Other friends who were generous with photographs are Dan Ford, Marilyn and Harry Carey, William Everson, Robert Parrish, Walter Hill and Paul Schrader. I am most grateful to the management of 20th Century Fox for allowing me access to their stills archive, and especially to Steve Newman for his efficient and enthusiastic help. At the British Film Institute, Anthony Smith helped with friendly interest and Michelle Snapes of the stills library with generous assistance. Similarly Wendy Dalton at the National Film Theatre, and Clyde Jeavons at the National Film Archive. Simon Crocker provided invaluable help and stills from the Kobal Collection. At the Museum of Modern Art, Charles Silver provided invaluable projections, advice and stimulus. Thanks also to Mary Corliss of M.O.M.A. stills library; and Sybille de Luze at the Cinémathèque Francaise; to Ann Gyory; and to Culver Pictures and the Bison Archive.

I have availed myself freely of the two best books about John Ford. I am hugely indebted to Dan Ford for his permission to quote from his fine — indispensable — biography *Pappy;* and to Robert Parrish for letting me quote from *Growing up in Hollywood*, which contains a unique portrait of Ford in action. Peter Bogdanovich's *John Ford* (Studio Vista) contains a very useful interview, and a finely detailed filmography.

The material in this book has been discussed over the years with more friends than I can mention or even remember: but I must make a friendly salute to Barbara Ford, Gene Moskowitz, Louis Marcorelles, Derek York — and Alex Jacobs, sadly gone ahead . . . Sandra Wake and Terry Porter put in endless labour and encouragement; and Kathy Burke needled, prompted and cajoled, and finally typed it all out. My sincere thanks.

Contents

John Ford; photograph by George Sidney

Preface

Sean Aloysius O'Feeney, born in Portland, Maine on February 1st, 1895, died in Palm Desert, California, on August 31st, 1973, was always a most contrary character. O'Feeney was how he signed his will, over thirty years before he died, but for most of his life he was known as John Ford. His father, who went under the name of John Feeney, and his mother were both Irish. Aggressive and defensive in about equal measure, he was gentle and irascible, bloody-minded and generous, courageous, uncompromising and endlessly evasive. He could be kind and he could be cruel. He was an artist, strictly professional, obstinately personal, with a profound sense of family, community and nation. He was fiercely anarchic. Very often he drank too much, but it rarely interfered with his work. He was probably the greatest film director working in the world's richest film making tradition, and at one time he was the most successful. He claimed that he cared nothing for the art of the cinema or for its aestheticians, that he never gave interviews and that he would far rather be doing other things than making films — like sailing boats or fighting the English in Ireland. None of these claims was true; yet none was wholly untrue. His pose enabled him at least to avoid the attentions of high-falutin' critics for the most of his life and to accept homage only when it gratified him. Towards the end of his career his work became less popular. Since his death he has been much written about: two biographies, at least five books of criticism, innumerable references in exactly the kind of theoretical works he most despised. I feel no need to apologise for adding to the list; but perhaps some explanation is in order.

This book is the record of an enthusiasm, an obsession, that has lasted for over thirty years. Its genesis has been a singular one, singularly protracted. The earliest writing in it dates from 1951, the year of my first meeting with Ford in Dublin, when he had finished location shooting on *The Quiet Man* in Galway and was on his way back to Hollywood to finish the picture in the studio. My account of this meeting was written for the last issue of *Sequence*, which I edited with Karel Reisz. By then, as will be apparent from the introduction which follows, I was well and truly Ford-intoxicated.

Sequence had started life in the immediate post-war years, as the magazine of the Oxford University Film Society. I became an editor with the second issue (the one with a still from *My Darling Clementine* on the cover): my friends Peter Ericsson, Gavin Lambert and I continued to edit it for most of its four-year existence as 'The Independent Film Quarterly'. A year or so before its demise, Gavin moved to the British Film Institute, to take over as their director of publications. An over-independent review of Ealing's tribute to the police force, *The Blue Lamp*, almost lost him his job as soon as he got there; but he survived to resuscitate the Institute's publishing activities and to edit their magazine *Sight and Sound* brilliantly until he moved on to Hollywood five years later. Towards the end of his time at the Institute, Gavin planned a series of monographs on great directors: he invited me to contribute one on John Ford. I laboured mightily and had almost got it finished when the money ran out and the series was abandoned. That essay forms the nucleus of this book.

Happily the B.F.I. recovered its financial stability; but by then the conduct of its publications was in the hands of another director-person, more responsive and more compliant than Gavin to the trends of critical fashion. A series of books did eventually appear, including two on Ford, but these approached his work from a point of view very different from mine.*

It is really my friends Sandra Wake and Terry Porter of Plexus who are responsible for this book. They had published the scripts of *If . . .* and *O Lucky Man!* and done surprisingly well with them. They suggested exhuming and resurrecting my essay on Ford. At first I was doubtful. Apart from being unsure about it, as one is bound to be unsure about something done twenty or more years ago, there was the question of completeness. Even without rewriting, there was a great deal to add. A quantity of films which I had been unable to see had become available in the years between: these would need to be discussed. And Ford had produced a good dozen more pictures before his career ended. These, too, would have to be written about, and with the more difficulty since they did not, in my judgement, represent his talent at its best and most creative. This was not a fashionable view. The consensus, in fact, of contemporary 'serious' criticism is quite to the contrary: *The Searchers* is now held to be his masterpiece, and the films which followed it — which I would consider clear evidence of decline — have secured Ford's admission to the vaults of *auteurism*. This diminution of John Ford from artist to *auteur*, the cutting down of him to current critical size, was perhaps the decisive factor in my resolve to complete and to publish. A *rappel a l'ordre*, so to speak.

I have rewritten very little of my original piece, only made a few minor notes and corrections. I have added some sections in which I have discussed films which were not available to me twenty-five years ago: these are printed in italic. And I have completed the critical story with a consideration of Ford's work in the last ten years of his career. So much for criticism. But John Ford the man is hardly separable from John Ford the artist. I was lucky enough to meet him a number of times and to enjoy a kind of friendship with him (I would not presume to use the word had he not written it himself); so I have fleshed out my critical exegesis with recollections of these encounters, and I have added contributions, in the form of conversations enjoyed and letters received, from a number of artists who worked with Ford and had unique opportunities to know and understand him — or at least part of him. Perhaps no one knew the whole of him. I have concerned myself anyway only with those aspects of his personality which I have judged relevant to his work.

Criticism is always a difficult business — to convey in words the personality of an artistic work, to define its essence and to interpret the experience it offers. Criticism of films is extraordinarily difficult. Film is such a complex, multifaceted medium, not to be analysed simply in terms of script, though writing may be a part of it, nor of ideas, though these may be its substance; not to be valued purely in terms of image, though that may be its basis; not to be fully enjoyed without appreciation of all (or some) of so many contributory arts — of movement and rhythm, of acting, of camerawork, of sound, music, design . . . Not to mention the recognition and appraisal of industrial, economic and social pressures almost inevitable in a medium so costly and so influential. And films are elusive in a more literal sense. They perish, they are destroyed. Of the thirty or forty films Jack Ford made in the first years of his career, only one survives, discovered comparatively recently in Czechoslovakia: you will have to go to Prague or to New York to see it. And when films do survive, they are often made inaccessible by the mindless bureaucracies of the industry or by the compulsive possessiveness of archivists: Miss Elaine Burrows of Britain's National Film Archive will some day perhaps finish checking her copy of *Four Sons* ('Some day . . .' as Rutledge says).

Even when one has been fortunate enough to see a film, one finds oneself often in frustrated need to refer to it when writing. Which is why critics of the highest repute can come up from time to time with such amazing howlers — as M. Jean

---

* The Cinema One series, published by Secker and Warburg in association with the B.F.I. The Ford books were *John Ford* by Joseph McBride and Michael Wilmington, and *The John Ford Movie Mystery* by Andrew Sarris.

Mitry with his imagined ending ('seen in Geneva . . .') to *The Grapes of Wrath*, or Mr. Andrew Sarris with his pregnant reflections of a mis-remembered conclusion to *Rio Grande*.

Television perhaps would offer the ideal medium for film criticism, or video-cassette coupled with the printed word — if only we were not so content to dedicate these genial inventions to the service of distraction, vulgar at worst, bland at best, relentlessly trivial. For how can we write persuasively without quotation; and how can the film critic quote? Words are imprecise, too subjective and can mislead. 'Stills' provide our most suggestive, most accurate means of evoking the look, the style, the imagery of a film. But stills can be inadequate or misleading, with composition that is nothing like the original, lighting that does not reproduce the texture of the original, and poses that fail completely to capture its subtleties of feeling and performance. Stills may be hard to come by too — particularly now that Hollywood has discovered the accumulating value of what it would formerly junk as worthless, and the studios have begun to render their treasures inaccessible behind new bureaucratic regulations, or by hideous over-pricing. The obvious solution is to take stills, where possible, from a print of the film itself. I have included a good number of such stills 'from the frame'; sometimes I have even photographed images on the screen during projection, illicitly no doubt. The quality of such stills is of course very variable. Even when the result is blurred and poorly exposed, though, some quality of atmosphere, some suggestion of style gets through. And with a poetic artist like Ford, style is the essence.

I suppose this is a book for specialists, meaning people who are specially interested in cinema, as they may also be specially interested in gardening, cooking, architecture or old cars. Not meaning (though not of course excluding) academics or film critics. In recent years, it seems to me film criticism — which is not the same as reviewing — has risked losing its proper sense of purpose. Under the twin deadly influences of sociology and aesthetics, critics have tended to write more and more as though criticism were an end in itself, comprehensible only to the academically elect, expressible only in its own hieratic jargon. 'It is the richness of the shifting relations between antinomies in Ford's work that makes him a great artist . . .' writes Peter Wollen. And, in amplification: 'In practice we will not find perfect symmetry, though as we have seen, in the case of Ford, some antinomies are completely reversed. Instead there will be a kind of torsion within the permutation group, within the matrix, a kind of exploration of certain possibilities, in which some antinomies are foregrounded, discarded and even inverted, whereas others remain stable and constant.'* This is film criticism busily engaged in disappearing up its own backside, with critics addressing themselves to (or against) each other, in a complicity of intellectual snobbery, instead of to the people who really matter — the 'common readers' of the cinema, who like films, are capable of being intelligent about them, and want to understand and enjoy them more. In this connection I think always of the words of Charlotte Bronte in her prefatory note to the edition of *Wuthering Heights* published after Emily's death. The true seer (or critic), she says, is one 'who can accurately read the Mene Mene Tekel Upharsin of an original mind; and who can say with confidence "This is the interpretation thereof!"' The function of the critic is to make clear, not to obfuscate; to interpret rather than to judge. John Ford had an original mind — 'vision' perhaps would be a better word — and it is for us who dare to play his critic to offer the interpretation thereof. I have addressed myself to those who can respond to his vision. I hope this book will help them to know better, to understand more clearly and to enjoy more fully the work of one of the great poets of humanity in our time.

---

* Peter Wollen: *Signs and Meaning in the Cinema*, pp. 102-104. (Secker and Warburg, in association with the British Film Institute, 1969).

My Darling Clementine: *Set for the dance on the church site.*

Introduction

When I was but thirteen or so
I went into a golden land.
Chimborazo, Cotapaxi
Took me by the hand.

In 1946 I was twenty-three. And my golden land was not conjured up by exotic place names, but by film titles — one in particular — by landscapes, by snatches of old tunes, and by the names, faces, personalities of certain actors. And by one name in particular. The best film director in the world? Who cared! Let others celebrate their Wylers, their Eisensteins, their Clairs. It was not even his own name as a matter of fact. Never mind: it had — like the name of one of his heroes — a 'ring to it'. His parents had not given it to him. Destiny had given it to him. John Ford.

At the beginning of the year, when I was still twenty-two (and he was fifty-one), the name did not mean so much to me. I had been infected by the cinema virus ever since childhood, but in a general, all-embracing way. Mostly American and British films: you did not see foreign films in those days, unless you were something of an intellectual and belonged to the Film Society. My favourite film stars in the thirties were Norma Shearer and Robert Montgomery. I had spent the last three years of the war in the army in India, where I had seen *The Maltese Falcon, Meet Me In St. Louis* and *Henry V*. I had all the conventional upper-middlebrow ideas about 'good cinema', 'realism' (good) and 'commercialism' (bad). Some of these ideas of course, were true, but they did not add up to a very knowledgeable understanding of the medium.

I returned to Britain at what was considered to be a time of vitality and promise for the British cinema. In London on one autumn weekend I could choose between David Lean's *Great Expectations* at the Gaumont and the ambitious Powell-Pressburger fantasy, *A Matter of Life and Death* at the Empire. These were the films, both enthusiastically hailed as evidence of the British film renaissance, which I should have seen. Instead I chose, and I'm not altogether sure why, Henry Fonda, Linda Darnell and Victor Mature in *My Darling Clementine* at the Odeon, Leicester Square.

I certainly could not have been much influenced in my choice by the reviews. The critics were generally disappointed that John Ford should have returned to Hollywood with anything as mundane as a Western. Westerns were unfashionable in those days. 'Horse Opera for the Carriage Trade', I remember, was the verdict of the trade paper, *Kine Weekly. The Times* critic spoke more dismissively: making facetious play of the fact that the story was set in Tombstone, he consigned the film to 'the graveyard of mediocrity'. It seemed to be agreed even by those who enjoyed it that there was nothing very distinguished about *My Darling Clementine*.

My own reaction was one of puzzlement. I was entranced by the film, but not in a patronising, I-love-Westerns kind of way. I found myself affected by it more powerfully and somehow more intimately than I had ever been affected by a film before. I did not know exactly why. In conventional, 'literary' terms there was nothing particularly remarkable about it: the genre was familiar; and so was the plot — in fact the story of Wyatt Earp and his brothers and Old Man Clanton and his sons had been filmed at least twice before. There was a special charm, perhaps, in the character of Clementine Carter, and a special lyricism that resulted from her motivating presence in the story. Fonda's performance had the extraordinary interior strength, the subtlety and the simplicity that belongs to the very finest screen acting. There was a particular warmth, a particular familiarity about the handling of the traditional atmosphere and the traditional themes. The images were masterly, the music perfectly evocative. But none of these easily identifiable excellences, singly or together, seemed really to explain the magic of the film. This emanated rather from a quality altogether more elusive and more profound, some kind of moral poetry. I knew of course that poetry could not be defined. But something impelled me to try. So I began to have some glimmerings of what is, after all, the essence of cinema: the language of style.

I was back at Oxford now, after three years in the wartime army. I had joined the University Film Society, seen some silent Russian and Swedish classics, and contributed — out of an almost total ignorance — an article about French films to their magazine. This had been launched early in the year and named *Sequence*. One of its editors was Peter Ericsson, to whom I communicated my enthusiasm for *My Darling Clementine*. Speedily he became as rabid a fan as I. 'Ford's in his Heaven' — a paraphrase from *Brave New World* — was the headline of a piece we wrote

My Darling Clementine. *Wyatt Earp and his "Lady Fair" open the dance on the church site; Henry Fonda and Cathy Downs.*

together for *Isis*, the University magazine. Peter, whose studies included philosophy, borrowed from Novalis and used to talk about 'the Ford-Intoxicated Man'. We saw *Clementine* in London and we saw it in Oxford. We went by bus to Headington, a village outside the city, and saw it again. I became an editor of *Sequence*, and when the second issue appeared Fonda and Cathy Downs were dancing on the cover. Fortunately I knew that I still did not know enough to write about him myself.

But I did know enough — or felt enough — to write to him. I can't now remember exactly what I said. But I received a reply, on Argosy Pictures notepaper. I have it still: a short letter, appreciative and courteous. 'It gives one's soul a fillip to hear such intelligent praise. Thank you.' The letter was typewritten, and Ford apologised. 'I am as yet unable to write longhand, due to a bathing accident at Omaha Beach.' It was signed rather grandly with a simple (left-handed?) 'Ford' in what looked like green crayon. In the letter he mentioned that he had just completed a picture in Mexico, *The Fugitive*, 'a very simple picture about a very simple man'. He asked me to see it when it played England, and give him my opinion of it. This was to bring our relationship to an abrupt, if temporary close.

I was naïf as well as enthusiastic, and perhaps self-righteous, too. I did write to Ford, and I told him, as respectfully as I could, that I did not feel *The Fugitive* was successful. Naturally, our correspondence ended. But even if I had not been naïf, the result would have been the same. For I could never have managed to pretend to admire *The Fugitive*, which seemed to me then as it seems now a mistaken film, forced in its conception and over-indulgent in its style. And no artist wants to hear

The Fugitive. *Dolores Del Rio and Henry Fonda.*

that kind of thing, however carefully expressed. I had to continue my discipleship without contact with the Master.

Peter and I finished with Oxford and came to London, bringing *Sequence* with us. Gavin Lambert, an old friend from Cheltenham days, became an editor. An admiration for Ford, which Gavin shared, though less insistently, became one of the hallmarks of the magazine. Those were days of excitement and discovery: many films had vanished during the war years or never reached Britain at all. There was no National Film Theatre and very little Film Society activity. *What's On* had to be searched scrupulously for oldies and rarities, showing on Sundays and in the remote suburbs. We discovered *The Prisoner of Shark Island* at the Blue Hall, Edgware Road, and we journeyed on the top of a bus to the Granada, Greenwich, to stare for the first time at *They Were Expendable*. So impressed were we indeed by this masterpiece, which had been all-but disregarded when it appeared a couple of years before, that we persuaded a puzzled M-G-M to show it to a puzzled audience of critics — although there were no plans to re-issue it. It even got a few polite reviews.

It was *They Were Expendable*, that most personal of epics, that enabled me to write for the first time about Ford with some confidence.* (By this time I had started making films myself, in an extremely modest and hesitant way.) I must have sent him a copy of my *Sequence* piece, but I never received an acknowledgement. Nor did I expect one. Apart from my early *faux pas* I knew that Ford disliked critics. Probably, too, my approach was too tiresomely analytical: and the piece contained, of course, further strictures on his famous collaborations with Dudley Nichols. In any case, even then I had the feeling that the artist is best known, or most likely to be understood, through his work. The piece did, however, bring me into contact with Ford's screenwriter on three of his most characteristic pictures: Nunnally Johnson, who had scripted *The Prisoner of Shark Island, The Grapes of Wrath* and *Tobacco Road*. Johnson was outraged by my enthusiasm for *She Wore a Yellow Ribbon* — a picture which he found full of cliches, with a perfunctory triangle-romance between John Agar, Harry Carey Jnr. and Joanne Dru which infuriated him by its careless surrender to commercial convention. What astonished me was the absolute lack of response I found in Nunnally Johnson to the creativity, the transforming power of Ford's direction. Was it possible that the screenwriter of *The Grapes of Wrath* could see nothing in the completed film beyond a straightforward putting-on-the-screen of the words and actions specified in the script? (This was not arrogance on Johnson's part: he claimed nothing for his own contribution either, beyond a faithful transposition of Steinbeck's book.) Yet so it was. By this very lack of perception, Nunnally Johnson made clearer to me the essential magic, the transforming power of style, the basis of screen poetry. And I realised for the first time that even people whose business is cinema — whether the making of films or (God save us!) the assessment of them — are often quite blind to this, the first essential of film communication.

In 1950 Ford came to Ireland to shoot locations for *The Quiet Man*. The idea of meeting him, of watching him work, fascinated me. But I knew my weakness for critical insistence and what it had led to once already. I was wary, too, of vulgar curiosity: would we after all learn much more about Hamlet by meeting Shakespeare? And I was (though this may have been an excuse) finishing off one of my industrial films, about belt conveyors. I hesitated. Finally I realised it was now or never. I got the address of *The Quiet Man* location in Galway from the London office of Republic Pictures, and I set off.

Sequence was not important enough to concern Republic Pictures greatly; and probably their London office was not anyway in very close touch with the shooting. When I got out of the train at Galway Station the platform was bare. I was not particularly surprised. It had hardly seemed likely that there would be anyone there to meet me, or that I would actually find myself in flesh-and-blood contact with that legendary world. I remember very little more than I later wrote in *Sequence*. I must have had a telephone number for the *Quiet Man* production office and from them I learned that shooting had finished the day before and the Unit had left for Dublin. They gave me a Dublin number. I rang and was told that Ford would be leaving for

---

* 'They Were Expendable' and John Ford'. *Sequence 11.*

the U.S. in a couple of days. I felt an idiot, but persisted. If I caught the train back across Ireland the next morning, would I still be able to see him? They would do their best. An hospitable lady recommended by the ticket office let me a room for the night, and the next morning I left Galway for Dublin. Ford had agreed to see me, and so we met for the first time that afternoon.

My account of this meeting was published in the last issue of *Sequence*: I called it, with some irony, 'The Quiet Man'. I gave as accurate an account as I could of an encounter which confirmed my hopes and expectations completely — in a way that such encounters with the great, alas, very often fail to do. I recognised Ford immediately: his deliberate perversity, his warmth, his taking one on, so to speak, as an equal. (Yet always as a superior too). I found nothing strange, nothing uncharacteristic of his work in the humour with which he tested one, the aggressiveness with which he shielded himself, the arrogance and the foxy intuition with which he waged war against the superficiality and the opportunism of the world. It surprised me recently, then on reflection amused me, to see that the American film critic Andrew Sarris, discovering Ford as an *auteur,* described this interview as 'especially disastrous' on the grounds that it demonstrated Ford's 'instinctive response to stylistic psychoanalysis'. Foolish as I may have been, stylistic psychoanalysis was the last thing I thought of attempting. I wanted to meet a great man; and I was lucky enough to do so.

The Quiet Man.

Escape from Hollywood. Ford on location in Galway for The Quiet Man.

Meeting in Dublin:
The Quiet Man

1950

'I'm a quiet, gentle person.'
John Ford

It is futile to attempt to envisage beforehand what places, people will be like. Inevitably, though, images form in the mind. They certainly had plenty of time to form in mine, for by the time I actually got to see John Ford I had crossed Ireland twice, trusting the telegram I had received to say that the *Quiet Man* unit would be shooting in Cong (in Ford's — or rather his father's — native Galway) till the end of the week. By the time I got there the unit had left. So back I crawled to Dublin, hoping to catch Ford before he flew off to America the next day.

A succession of slowly moving trains and buses had by this time lent to the journey a dream-like quality, not inappropriate to a pilgrimage to the source of a well-loved myth. About Ford himself I felt no temptation to speculate; as my last bus stopped and started its way through the Dublin suburbs I found that I had almost ceased to believe in his existence. What of the setting in which I should find him? I imagined something large, rather formidable; an aloof Georgian or nineteenth-century mansion staffed with a squad of retainers, furnished in mahogany, with soft carpets and tall, dark rooms. I was, anyway, quite unprepared for the trim, very contemporary little suburban home in front of which the conductor set me down; neat front lawn, paved path from the gate, aproned parlourmaid to open the front door. Voices and the clink of knives made it clear that supper was still in progress; I was shown into the front room. But I had scarcely time to sink into a chair and look around me when footsteps sounded outside, the door opened and Ford came in with a rush.

By-passing the stage of first impressions, we seemed to be plunged straight into familiarity. But let me try. A bulky man, craggy as you would expect, sandy hair thinned and face deeply lined. Eyes hidden behind dark-lensed spectacles. Informal in clothes as in manner; he wore an old sports coat and a pair of grubby grey flannels, his shirt was open at the neck. He flopped into an armchair, in which, as we talked, he shifted from position to position of relaxed comfort — legs crossed, then one up over the arm of the chair, then both. Speech forthright, with a matching ruggedness of vocabulary. Frank; responsive to frankness; a bit impatient, but ready to listen.

He was sorry to have missed me in Galway; they were behind schedule on the picture and, once finished, had no thought but to get away at once, back to Hollywood to polish off the interiors. He did not seem altogether happy about the experience. 'Something seemed to get into people down there. I guess it must have been the climate'. Had the rain held up shooting? 'No, the weather was all right — that softness is fine with Technicolor. But the unit seemed to go soft too; they

On location for The Iron Horse *(1924). Left: Township location. Right: Herbert 'Limby' Plews sounds Reveille. Far right: George O'Brien, Ford. (Snapshots by Harold Schuster.)*

started standing about looking at the scenery. I had to start watching for points of continuity — people looking out of windows, that sort of thing, which no one else noticed. Then, of course, our technicians work a lot faster than yours. It was really too big a job for one man to tackle on his own...I'm just going back to making Westerns.' He looked at me. 'Of course, you're one of the people who think it's a disgrace the way I keep turning out these Westerns.' I protested. 'Yes, you do. You've written that, haven't you? I'm sure I read that somewhere'. One other thing from that article had caught in his memory. 'And what was that you said about me being anti-British?' I told him. ('A true Irishman, Ford has no time for the English.') He laughed, but took pains to deny it. 'I've got more British than I have American friends...Of course, you must remember I'm Irish — we have a reputation to keep up.'

About here I made an attempt to pull myself together and be business-like. I asked if I might get my notebook (which I had left in the hall) and ask some questions. 'Carry on,' said Ford, but with a slight unease. 'I'm not a career man, you know,' he announced defensively. 'I don't suppose I've given more than four interviews in my life. And now two in an evening...' He did not speak as if the prospect attracted him. 'Christ,' he said, 'I hate pictures. When people ask me if I've seen some actress or other, I say "Not unless she was in *The Great Train Robbery* or *Birth of a Nation*. Then perhaps I've seen her. Otherwise, no."' I said: 'Why do you go on with them?' 'Well, I like *making* them of course...But it's no use asking me to talk about art...'

We chatted for a bit about Ford's early days in the cinema. How had he started directing? 'I just started,' he explained. (He had gone out to California at the age of nineteen, after three unprofitable weeks at the University of Maine, to work for his brother Francis — at that time an established star and director.) He began making Westerns in 1917, when he was twenty-two. 'I can't remember much about them, now,' he said. 'We made about one a week. I directed them and Harry Carey acted them. All those early ones were written by Carey and me — or stolen. We didn't really have scripts, just a rough continuity...' But he well remembered the making of *The Iron Horse*, his railroad epic of 1924. 'We went up there prepared for routine Hollywood weather — all sunshine and blue skies. We got out of the train in a blizzard and nearly froze to death...We lived in a circus train, had to dig our own latrines, build up a whole town around us. Saloons opened up; the saloon-girls moved in...The whole thing was very exciting.'

Suddenly we had skipped twenty years and were talking about *They Were Expendable*. Perhaps Ford's attitude towards this film so dumbfounded me that a whole tract of conversation was wiped from my memory. As a matter of fact, we were both dumbfounded. He was looking at me in extreme surprise. 'You really think that's a good picture?' He was amazed: 'I just can't believe that film's any good.' I was amazed. 'But — didn't you want to make it?' Ford snorted. 'I was ordered to do it. I wouldn't have done it at all if they hadn't agreed to make over my salary to the men in my unit.' (Naval, not film.) He added: 'I have never *actually* seen a

goddamned foot of that film.' I told him that horrified me. 'I'll use the same word,' he said, 'I was horrified to have to make it...' 'Didn't you feel at least that you were getting something into it even though you hadn't wanted to take it on?' He scorned the idea. 'Not a goddamned thing', he said, 'I didn't put a goddamned thing into that picture.' He had been pulled out of the front line to make it, had just lost thirteen men from his unit, and had to go back to Hollywood to direct a lot of actors who wouldn't even cut their hair to look like sailors. I said I found this particularly extraordinary because the film contains so much that needn't have been there if it had been made just as a chore. 'What, for instance?' I made example of the old boat-builder (played by Russell Simpson), who appears only in a few shots, yet emerges as a fully, and affectionately conceived person. Ford relented slightly: 'Yes, I liked that...' He shifted his ground: 'The trouble was, they cut the only bits I liked... Is that scene in the shell-hole still there, between the priest and the boy who says he's an atheist?' 'What priest?' I asked. 'Played by Wallace Ford.' 'There's no priest in the film at all.' This surprised him. I said I found it extraordinary that one could cut a whole (presumably integral) character from a story without leaving any trace. 'M-G-M could,' said Ford. I said: 'But *Expendable* runs two and a quarter hours as it is...' Ford said: 'I shot the picture to run an hour and forty minutes — it should have been cut down to that.' I said that this could not be done without ruining the film. 'I think I know more about making pictures than you do,' said Ford.

He asked me what the music was like; he said he had fierce arguments when the M-G-M music department had shown him the score they intended to put over it. 'But surely — it's full of just the tunes you always like to use in your pictures.' But Ford had found it too thickly orchestrated, too symphonic. 'I wanted almost no music in it at all — just in a very few places like "Red River Valley" over Russell Simpson's last scene. We played and recorded that as we shot it. Otherwise I didn't want any music; the picture was shot as a documentary, you know. No reflectors were used at any time, and we kept the interiors dark and realistic.' He asked if that last shot was still in, with the aeroplane flying out, and the Spanish rower silhouetted against the sky; and what music was over it. He seemed satisfied when I told him it was 'The Battle Hymn of the Republic'.

But chiefly Ford was amazed at the thought that anyone could find *They Were Expendable* an even tolerable picture. 'John Wayne had it run for him just recently — before he went back to the States. And afterwards he said to me: "You know, that's still a great picture." I though he was just trying to say something nice about it; but perhaps he really meant it.'

I asked him about the music in his pictures generally; how close was the relationship between himself and the musical director on the pictures he had made at Fox? 'Very close — we knew each other very well. I think you can say that I'm responsible for the faults or the qualities of the music we used in those pictures.' (Films like *Young Mr. Lincoln, The Grapes of Wrath, My Darling Clementine*.)

I tried to switch from the particular to a more general view: what was Ford's

21

bird's-eye view of his career; of that astonishing trail? Looking back, did he trace periods of exploration and discovery; the series of pictures he had made with Dudley Nichols, for instance, how did he now feel about them? Ford countered: 'What pictures did I make with Nichols?' 'Well... *The Long Voyage Home — The Fugitive — The Informer*.' 'Oh,' said Ford, 'so Nichols wrote *The Informer*, did he?' He resisted implacably, in fact, any attempt to analyse his motives in picking subjects. 'I take a script and I just do it.' Even when I suggested that there were some films (apart from *They Were Expendable*) that he must have undertaken with reluctance, I got nowhere. He had *enjoyed* making *Wee Willie Winkie*, and was charmed by Shirley Temple, now as then. The nearest he would come to discrimination was: 'Sometimes I get a story that interests me more than others...' Such as *The Quiet Man*, which he had wanted to do for ten years. 'It's the first love story I've ever tried. A mature love story.'

Singly, he would comment on films I mentioned. How did he feel now about *The Informer?* 'I don't think that's one of my best', said Ford. 'It's full of tricks. No, I think that comes quite a long way down the list.' His favourite is *Young Mr. Lincoln*: 'I've a copy of that at home, on 16mm. I run that quite often...' He thought. 'Now let me see...What other pictures have I got copies of? Not many... *The Lost Patrol* — I still enjoy that one; and I think I may have a copy of *Yellow Ribbon*.' He is fond of *How Green Was My Valley* and *The Fugitive*. ('I just enjoy myself looking at it.') With some trepidation I asked about a personal favourite — *My Darling Clementine*. 'I never saw it,' said Ford.

We talked for a bit about the Westerns to which he has devoted himself since *The Fugitive*. I asked if they had been undertaken primarily to make money. 'Oh, yes. I had to do something to put my company back on its feet after what we lost on that. And they've done it.' All these films, apparently, from *Apache* to *Rio Grande* have achieved commercial success — particularly (which surprised me) *The Three Godfathers*. Since Ford gave the impression of anticipating attack about them, I made the point that the objection was less to the fact that they were 'just Westerns', than to the carelessness with which, too often, they seemed to have been put together. I asked if it wasn't true that *Fort Apache* was shot deliberately in a hurry and under budget, as it appeared to be. 'Yes, it was,' Ford admitted; then scratched his head. 'Now what was that one about? Oh yes; that was a very concocted story. But very good box-office.' *She Wore a Yellow Ribbon*, he said, was made even quicker than *Fort Apache*; though it was a picture he liked. And so was *Wagonmaster*: 'I really tried to do something with that.' When I instanced crudities that seemed to me to disfigure some of these films, Ford countered with the familiar arguments of finance. 'I think you're being too demanding,' he said. 'These refinements cost money — and all the time there's that tremendous pressure of money on top of you. You do the best you can...And remember that with all these pictures I wasn't just working to pay off on *The Fugitive*, but to make enough for *The Quiet Man* as well. Of course, it'll probably lose the lot again; but that's the way it always goes.'

Another point Ford made about his recent Westerns, or rather about his reasons for making them, was more personal. Holding up his left hand he said: 'It looks all right, but it isn't.' Injuries inherited from the war give him, intermittently, a good deal of pain; they had put him out of action for a few days on *The Quiet Man*, and generally made studio shooting — in the glare and oppressive atmosphere of a sound stage — a penance. 'I was out in Korea before coming to Ireland — I made a documentary there called *This is Korea* — and oddly enough I never had a twinge. But out at Cong it really got me down.' He could even, as a result, envisage *The Quiet Man* being his last picture; at any rate, after it, he would have to take a good long rest.

In the end we talked for about an hour and a half, and I forgot all the questions I had meant to ask. I prepared to take my leave. But first Ford had a question he

The American epic. Top: defeat in the Philippines, 1941. Robert Montgomery and John Wayne as Brickley and Ryan in They Were Expendable. *Below: Mormon wagons roll westward in* Wagonmaster.

wanted to put to Maureen O'Hara in front of me. (I had not realised before that this was her family's home where Ford was staying.) 'Now, Maureen,' he said, 'have you ever heard me talk of a film called *They Were Expendable* — or have you ever seen it when we've had a show at the house?' 'No,' said Miss O'Hara, 'I haven't. 'You see?' Ford said. 'But we'll put it on when we get back. The kids will like the boats anyway.'

We shook hands, and Ford went out into the garden to talk. 'He's a great man,' said Miss O'Hara. 'And a wonderful director to work for. In other films you'll be just mediocre; then with him ...' I asked her how he did it. 'He seems to know just what's necessary to get a good performance from anyone; some people he'll be entirely gentle with, and with others he'll be a brute. But you don't mind because, when you see it on the screen, you realise why.' I asked her about the last scene of *Rio Grande*, Ford's most recent picture. The band plays "Dixie" as the cavalry rides past — Captain York's olive branch to his Southern wife, received by her not with tears or sentiment, but with mischief and a parasol provocatively twirled. 'Whose idea was that?' I asked. 'Oh, his,' she laughed, 'he told me to do that.'

Rio Grande: 'He told me to do that.' J. Carrol Naish, John Wayne, Maureen O'Hara.

As the foregoing has probably made plain, Ford is pretty well interview-proof. This is not to say that my hour and a half was not a memorable one, but it was not exactly rich in generalisations, personal pronouncements readily quotable to illustrate the views of John Ford on the film as an art. About other people's films he professed himself uninterested; and certainly it requires a stretch of the imagination to visualise him 'going to the cinema'. Of his own hundred-odd films he was quite willing to talk, or at least to answer questions; but he shied away from any invitation to generalise. They were like, as he spoke of them, stories that he has told, some with more care and enjoyment than others. Some he remembers, some he has all but forgotten; all are of the past. 'The best in this kind are but shadows.' At one point, when I broke off for a moment to refer to William Wootten's Index of his films, he reached over and took it from my hand. 'I suppose I ought to have one of these,' he said as he inspected it; but there was no conviction in his tone.

How far this impression of a first meeting corresponds with the truth, I am in no position to say. Any such talk has to be seen in its context: a director in mid-film, at the end of six trying weeks on location, somewhat wary perhaps at being thus pursued to an interview for the first time for a number of years. And at any time (one senses) Ford is a man who speaks by mood, from impulse rather than reflexion, and without much concern to qualify — he might very well contradict any of his statements the next day. For instance, it is obvious to anyone who knows his films that his attitude towards his craft has not been always as instinctive, as unconcerned with questions of style and subject, as it pleased him to make out. But in a single interview there was no opportunity of breaking past this firmly-held position.

There remained the man. It is natural that anecdotists should concentrate on his wild Irish temper, his fondness for horseplay, the violence of his conflicts with producers and high-stepping actresses; and there is no reason to suppose these stories exaggerated. (Ford has only to protest 'I'm a quiet, gentle person', for one to be quite sure they are not.) But besides the stampedes, the war parties, the knock-about fights, there are those quiet moments in his films, equally characteristic, of tenderness and insight; and these too his presence reflects. This was the Ford I found in Dublin — a man of fascinating contradictions; of authority in no way diminished by a complete rejection of apparatus; of instinctive personal warmth as likely to evidence itself in violence as in gentleness; confident of his powers, yet unpretentious about their achievement. A patriarchal figure, sitting among friends; it was easy to understand the devotion he inspires in those who work for him.

When Ford started talking in terms of his 'last picture', I had the impression that this was not necessarily serious — the momentary result of ill-health and fatigue rather than a real determination to bring his career to a close. And perhaps also a sense that yet another turning point had been reached? Today Ford stands apart, an isolated figure as well as a great one — and the isolation is different from the fierce independence which has characterised his whole career. It is not merely the penalty of remaining true to his own, at the moment unfashionable, vision; his recent pictures have not been consistently of the quality he can give us. The argument of commercial necessity in fact sounds in his mouth far more like the uneasy justification of one who feels himself in some degree guilty, than the callous admission of one who has problems of artistic conscience firmly behind him. It is not necessarily a question of subject; the fresh and vigorous poetry which his often repeated themes evoke from him is more to be valued than the artwork which has sometimes resulted from his tackling of more conventionally ambitious material. It is rather a question of seriousness.

A good deal would seem to hang on *The Quiet Man*, for its success or failure must affect Ford's attitude towards film making in the future. In any event it is difficult to believe that he will not continue at it for a while yet. 'I want to be a tugboat captain,' he says. But God made him a poet, and he must make the best of that.

Ford on a 1920s vacation off the Maine coast.

Postscript

My Dublin interview with Ford had an epilogue. By the time we had finished talking it was too late to return to London the same day so I took a hotel room for the night: I suppose I gave my telephone number to the publicity man who had arranged the interview.

In the morning, as I was packing my bag, there was a knock at my bedroom door. I was wanted on the 'phone. I was mystified: who on earth knew where I was? I went to the telephone. It was Ford.

'I want to thank you for going to all that trouble to come and see me,' he said. I was touched and amazed: it was for me to thank him. But Ford went on. 'You were quite right with some of those criticisms you made. Some of that stuff isn't up to standard.' I was humbled, as one is apt to be when people readily admit errors one has charged them with. I hoped I hadn't been too impertinent. 'No — no. It's easy to get careless. Particularly when the financial pressure is so great. But that's not a justification. Thank you for reminding me.' (By now I was speechless. Ford went on.) 'I'm going back now to finish *The Quiet Man*, and I promise you I'll do my best. I'll make it as good as I possibly can.'

I wished him good luck, and he thanked me again — then added, before he rang off: 'I'll see *Expendable*, and I'll let you know what I think.'

He kept his word. Some weeks later I received a telegram. It read: *HAVE SEEN EXPENDABLE. YOU WERE RIGHT. FORD.*

I carried this around with me for a long time, till my wallet was stolen. The police found it, but of course the money in it had gone. So had the telegram.

Escape from Hollywood. Ford on location in East Africa for Mogambo *(1952).*

Meeting at Elstree

1952

I was unlucky again when it came to my next meeting with Ford, a year later. I did manage to see him direct a couple of set-ups in a studio jungle, but nothing of any substance. The film was *Mogambo* and the studio was Elstree, where a few inserts and small interiors were being polished off after the bulk of the film had been shot on location in Kenya.

Ford had returned to Hollywood. He had finished *The Quiet Man* as promised, and had achieved with it one of the great successes of his career. He had followed it with another, modestly-budgeted picture for Republic called *The Sun Shines Bright*. This had not yet been shown in Britain, but I knew that it was Ford's own personal choice, and that it brought back to the screen the same Judge Priest whom Will Rodgers had played for him in the thirties in *Judge Priest* and *Steamboat Round the Bend*. Then Ford had accepted an assignment from M-G-M, a remake of their romantic melodrama of the thirties, *Red Dust*, which had starred Clark Gable, Jean Harlow and Mary Astor. In the long interview published by Peter Bogdanovich, Ford declared that he had never seen Victor Fleming's film, and one can very well believe this was so. Fleming's was a taut, tough, humorous romance, sharply and excellently played, shot on the stages and back-lots of Culver City. The new version was switched from Malaya to Africa, shot in colour, 'opened up' with picturesque Kenyan location scenes, and shots of wild animals captured by a second unit. This was the style of the early fifties, of Hollywood on the run from TV. *Mogambo*, like *Red Dust*, starred Clark Gable, but twenty years on. Ford was at pains to forestall any criticisms of lack of ambition. He repeated his phrase of a year back: 'You know I'm not a career man. I just like working with people.' He had invited me down to Elstree, where a corner of one of the stages had been filled with tropical under-growth and he was supervising some shots of Donald Sinden and Grace Kelly being terrified by gorillas. (The gorillas were absent. They had been shot by a second unit. I didn't get the impression that either of the actors had seen the gorillas. Or Ford either.)

The cameraman was still lighting. I stood back against the wall, as discreetly as I could, and watched as Ford paced moodily round the set. He gnawed compulsively at the corner of a crumpled handkerchief in his hand. Every now and then he stopped to have a word with a technician, a prop man, the sound man, the continuity girl, as they sat or stood waiting. The Commanding Officer was patrolling his lines.

It was the producer who had asked for two more close-ups. 'I said I didn't think they were necessary . . . That's all they know about. They're the only trick we've got. If you misuse your close-up, the whole story falls to pieces. Just a close-up of some fatuous face.' He moved off again restlessly, to see how the lighting was going, or to order a mattress for Grace Kelly, kneeling or lying on the hard studio floor.

'He's a very good technician,' the sound man said, 'If you do your stuff he's very good. If you alibi, he'll fall on you like a ton of bricks. He can't stand alibi-ing.' He emphasised Ford's liking for naturalness, for the impromptu. Gable had fluffed a line. 'He likes it like that. If a stumble sounds natural, he'll keep it.' Gable had made a spoonerism, 'Corch porridor'. Ford said "We'll keep it for the laugh".' (I wondered whether it would appear in the completed film.) Usually he used the first take: 'Sometimes we do three or four others. If they're not better *enough*, he'll say "Forget about them. Print the first."'

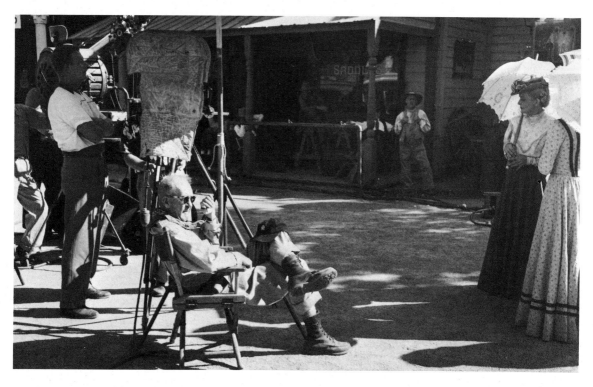

Ford shooting a scene for The Sun Shines Bright *on the Republic lot (1951).*

Ford let the odd personal reflection drop as he passed on his rounds. 'I'm a socialist,' he declared, apropos of what I can't remember. 'I believe in state ownership. I'm an anarchist.'

I hope I didn't remark that there might be a contradiction here. I think I was wise enough to keep my mouth shut. Ford went on a bit in this political vein. He told me proudly that he had been elected Union Shop Steward by the unit. This tickled him greatly. He called the teagirl over from her trolley. 'Who's our Shop Steward? Tell him...' He nodded across at me, as he strolled away.

The next time he came by, he was on to religion. 'You know I'm anti-clerical. I choose my church and my priest very carefully. I took my own priest across to Ireland for *The Quiet Man*. We had him down as Technical Adviser...'

He had some caustic comments to make about the African locations. 'You know the two things I hate the most: anti-racialism, and the English.' The Whites in Kenya disgusted him: 'Middle-class snobs, trying to be gents.' He told me how a white worker out there had stubbed out a cigarette on a little girl's hand. A member of the unit had knocked him down. I tried to look as though I believed him.

When it came to taking the shots, the work went quickly and authoritatively. No fuss. 'Very dramatic,' he remarked, dryly, as Donald Sinden blenched before the imaginary gorillas. 'Don't be dramatic. You're in close-up, you know. You don't need to do anything. Let the gorillas be dramatic.'

We lunched at a large round table in the studio restaurant. I am not sure who else was there, possibly the producer, whose name I see from the reference books was Sam Zimbalist — and that, besides the fact that he had asked Ford for two more close-ups, is all I know about him. But I do remember that another M-G-M producer, Gottfried Reinhart, had just flown in from Germany; and that Clark Gable had arrived from Hollywood, probably to do his dubbing (and perhaps to revoice 'Corch Porridor'). I sat next to Gable.

Ford, on the other side of the table, was in good form. He made everybody laugh by his mythic accounts of how he had persuaded Herbert Yates, head of Republic Pictures, to back *The Quiet Man*. 'I took him to the west of Ireland, to the most picturesque part of Connemara, and I showed him a little whitewashed cottage, with shutters and a thatched roof. "There it is," I told him, with the tears running down my cheeks, "the house where I was born..."' 'And was it?' asked Reinhart. 'Of course not. I was born in Maine. In Portland. But Yates started crying too."Alright," he said, "You can do *The Quiet Man*. For a million and a half".'

They asked Gable, who seemed an easy, undemonstrative man, how things were back home. He told them how he had got back from Kenya to find Hollywood shaken by the crisis in confidence and investment. He described in a shocked, almost awed way how the M-G-M studios at Culver City were empty, the huge stages shadowed and silent. The dark age of television had arrived. 'There's only one unit shooting in the whole place,' he said, 'and that's for some TV series.' Then he added, and it was like an epitaph: 'It's the end of an era.'

Ford gave me a lift back to London in his studio car, and we chatted more personally. He questioned me about my background, my parentage. He was interested to know that my father was an Army officer, that my parents had divorced, that I had been in the Army myself for three years during the war.

'Did you hate the Army?'

'Yes.'

'Probably a paternal hatred.'

He was interested, too, when I told him how my elder brother had refused to be a prefect at school, preferring to stay on for his last term undifferentiated from his friends by the responsibilities or the privileges of authority. Neither my brother nor I responded too easily to discipline — particularly not to be being disciplined by fools. My response was to individuals.

Judge William 'Billy' Priest, 1934 (Will Rogers in Judge Priest*) and 1952 (Charles Winninger in* The Sun Shines Bright*).*

'Yes,' said Ford, 'I had the same trouble.'

I asked him if he would like to have made the Navy his career. 'Yes, very much. I'd probably have written, too, as a sideline. 'Did he write bits of his scripts? 'Yes — the ones I like. *The Quiet Man...Stagecoach...*I like writing stories — children's stories. I've never had anything published.'

I talked on a bit about my wartime in India, about my film making attempts in Britain. (I had been directing documentaries of sorts for three or four years, but found myself still barred by the Union.) I did not talk about myself for the pleasure of it, but because I was trying to make our meeting a friendly one rather than an interview. (I have never written about it until now.) But I couldn't feel much response in Ford.

Earlier that day, on the studio floor, I had asked him about his latest picture, *The Sun Shines Bright*, of which I had only seen some bare, trade-press reports. He had rather played it down (perhaps because Republic had given him trouble with it). 'I didn't make it for the public, or for the critics. I made it the way I wanted it.' He mentioned that it was about a character I would never have heard of, Judge Priest.

'Oh, yes' I said, *'Steamboat Round the Bend...'*

Ford went on as if I hadn't spoken. 'It's got no names in it. I made it with a lot of small-part actors, unknowns...'

This seemed to me rather hard — not so say ungenerous to Jane Darwell, Charles Winninger, Stepin Fetchit, Aileen Whelan...I was happy to tell Ford that indeed his players were known, and fondly. But he, I immediately realised, did not wish to be told. Not unless he asked.

I returned from this meeting with a certain disappointment. I was egotistical, of course, and over-sensitive. I found that I resented being made to feel quite so firmly the limits of a relationship (paternal rejection?). I was not interested to meet Ford as a visiting journalist, or as a yessing disciple, oohing and aahing over stories which my commonsense told me were not true. (My Scottishness against his Irishness?) Also, I felt that Ford did not really like to be known.

I did not see Ford again before I had returned, two years later, to the challenge of writing about his films. The best way, probably, I could know him.

Hollywood pioneers, 1915. Francis Ford (left) directs Eddie Polo and Grace Cunard in a Universal serial, The Broken Coin. *Assistant Jack Ford stands right of camera.*

The Film Maker

1. Career Man

'I'm not a career man, you know.'
John Ford

Comme c'est curieux les noms
Martin Victor Hugo de son prénom
Bonaparte Napoleon de son prénom
Pourquoi comme ça et pas comme ça...

Jacques Prèvert

And even more curious is the case (not cited by Jacques Prèvert) of John Ford. When that name comes up on the credits, heralded as often as not by a resounding surge of music, backed by a rugged and romantic landscape of the West, it is impossible not to marvel at its aptness to the personality of the poet — four-square and solid, forceful and direct, with happy connotations of poetry and industry. Yet it was not Destiny that stumbled on the appropriate choice. John Ford was born Sean Aloysius Feeney, on February 1st, 1895, in Cape Elizabeth, Maine.

The family background is of more than ordinary importance. John Ford's — Sean Feeney's — parents were immigrants; his father was born in Galway, in the West of Ireland, and his mother came from the island of Arran. Sean was the youngest in a family of eleven. Beyond this, we can be sure of very little. For among the Irish traits that have remained influential in his character, Ford has delighted to indulge that fondness for mystification, that evasiveness, half mischievous, half poetic, which seems profoundly a part of the national temperament. Like many Celtic emigrants, and their descendants, he seems to have cherished the traditional habits of his forebears, sometimes to the point of exaggeration. But it is worth remembering that 'Irish' qualities are only an extension of Irish qualities. If they make reliance on Ford's own statement and anecdote somewhat risky, they are also the key to much that is fundamental in him as a man, and as an artist.

Disregarding, then, some latter-day suggestion that Ford was himself born among the green fields of Western Ireland, it seems safest to accept the facts as they have many times been stated in Hollywood press releases: that Sean Feeney arrived on this earth in Maine, in the United States of America. When he was still young, his family moved down the coast to Portland, and there he was able to indulge in his boyhood passion for sailing. Other facts are scanty. Whether Sean had any idea of becoming an artist seems doubtful. He wanted to be a sailor. But in spite of his enthusiasm, he failed on graduating from High School to win his appointment to the Naval College at Annapolis. Instead, at the age of nineteen, he went up to the University of Maine. His experience of higher education was, however, brief. Three weeks after his enrolment, he cut loose and made for Hollywood.

Hollywood in 1914 was far from being the established capital of the world's cinema. The year before, it was regarded as an unconventional step when Griffith chose to shoot an ambitious four-reeler, *Judith of Bethulia*, in California; and naturally he returned to the Biograph studios in New York for the winter. It was indeed only in 1913 that Hollywood — formerly a mere suburb of Los Angeles — was legally granted its independent existence. Its expansion, though, was brisk. 1913 was also the year in which Cecil B. de Mille arrived from New York to make *The Squaw Man*, and Charlie Chaplin started work in Hollywood. Pictures were getting longer. The standard ten-minute one-reeler (tailored to the length of the average Vaudeville turn) had been supplanted by the two-reeler, pioneered by Griffith. Now the enormous success of the Italian *Quo Vadis*, an epic of nine reels, was paving the way for films of more ambitious scope. In 1914 Griffith removed himself definitively to Hollywood and set to work on the independent production of *The Birth of a Nation*, in twelve reels. The language of cinema was being evolved.

Another innovation, less pregnant than these, 31

Early days in Maine. Left to right: family friend John Connelly, with Eddie, Francis and Sean (Jack).

Francis Ford and Grace Cunard at Universal.

was the production about this time of the first serial films. In 1912 Edison, in the perennial pursuit of a new commercial 'gimmick', had hit on the idea of releasing a film in a succession of monthly parts, to coincide with its publication as a serial in *The Lady's World*. The scheme prospered, and other serials followed. April 1914 saw the start of Pearl White's *Perils of Pauline*, and of another, less celebrated series, chronicling the adventures of *Lucille Love*. This was produced by Carl Laemmle's Universal Pictures, and starred Francis Ford and Grace Cunard.

Francis Ford was one of Sean Feeney's elder brothers. He had left home some years before, adopted a new name (in homage, M. Jean Mitry pleasantly suggests, to the English Elizabethan dramatist), and embarked on a career as an actor. He had worked in the theatre, in the cinema in New York, and finally, as both actor and director, in Hollywood. In July 1914, the Francis Ford Serial Company was established in Laemmle's newly opened Universal City studios, a quarter of an hour's drive out of Hollywood. Here, on the three large stages ('capable of accommodating thirty sets',) thirty pictures could be in production simultaneously. When Sean arrived from the East, he changed his name to his brother's (Sean naturally became John), and as Jack Ford was set to work as a prop boy, earning twelve dollars a week.

If the new world of the cinema was an exhilarating one, presenting to the bold and the farsighted a challenging vista of rich, virgin territory, it was one which demanded toughness as well as enterprise from its pioneers. There is no indication that Jack Ford's first years in Hollywood

were comfortably padded as a result of his brother's prominent position in the industry. The movies were growing up in a tradition of rough-and-tumble professionalism. Today's rigid distinctions between grades and techniques were as unknown as pussyfooting precautions or scruples in the hazardous shooting of the full-blooded action sequences. Jack was soon (whether by title or not) a stunt man. For scenes in his brother's films he dived off railway trains, chased and was chased in cars, was blown up on endless battlefields, and shot up in countless Western saloons. A characteristic anecdote, recounted by Frank Nugent,* tells how Jack 'found himself in Confederate uniform, dodging shot and shell on a half-acre of battleground. Frank was pitching the powder-bombs. He saved the last for a close-shot: it bounced off Jack's head and exploded just beneath his chin. "That was a close thing," Frank told him later, when the nurses began admitting visitors. "Another second, and audiences would have realised I was using a double."' Another story, that of Ford's first promotion to assistant director, catches something of the atmosphere of those vivid and hectic days:

'Ford's first year in Hollywood ended in a blaze of glory. The company was shooting a circus sequence, to be climaxed by the inevitable fire in the Big Top. As the tent had been rented for the

* In an article 'Hollywood's Favourite Rebel' published in the *Saturday Evening Post*, 1947. Further quotations are from the same article.

occasion, Laemmle warned everyone to treat it with respect. A spare flap of canvas would be ignited at a safe distance from the tent walls; a standby crew with buckets of water would douse the flames the second the action had been shot. It was John's job, as prop boy, to provide the water buckets... He was up at dawn on the morning of the big scene. When the company arrived, he was standing guard over a platoon of red-painted fire buckets. The torch was put to the kerosene-soaked canvas flap: it flamed beautifully.

"Fine!" yelled the director, "Now douse it!"

'The fire brigade swung the buckets. There was a roaring explosion as the gasoline they contained hit the burning canvas and turned the circus tent into an inferno. "Don't stop — keep cranking!" yelled Ford. The camera-man numbly did as he was told. John went into hiding: he didn't have to be told that he was fired. Two days later Laemmle hired him back as an assistant director.'

The first documented allusion to Ford as assistant director is in the Motion Picture News Directory for October 21st, 1916. Within a year, he was directing.

The pace at which Jack Ford set about the business of making films was less remarkable in those days than it would be now: it presaged the concentration and unremitting professional activity that was to mark his whole career in the cinema. He started on Westerns. This was a genre already firmly established in popularity. As has often been observed, the development of the West was America's epic; and before even the historical process was complete, its heroes and traditions were passing into mythology. And, since this was the twentieth century, the Western saga found its fullest poetic expression not in literature, but in the youngest, most popular of the arts. In the films of Griffith and Ince, as well as those of a number of lesser directors, heroes like 'Brorco Billy' Anderson, Tom Mix and William S. Hart, were all celebrating, and perpetuating, the myth of the Cowboy. In 1917, Jack Ford was set to work by Carl Laemmle on a series featuring a new hero — Black Billy — played by Harry Carey, a rugged, likeable actor, already a popular leading player, who was to become under Ford's direction one of the brightest stars of the early Western sky. (The phrase was Ford's, from the epigraph to the film he dedicated to Carey's memory over thirty years later.)

The films poured out. The titles of many of them have almost certainly been lost, but from those still on record, we know that in his first year Ford directed at least eight two-reelers, one in three reels, and three in five reels. With titles like *Cactus, My Pal* (Ford's first recorded picture), *Straight*

Top: *Harry Carey—Cheyenne Harry in* Straight Shooting. *Above:* Straight Shooting, *the Outlaws' stronghold.*

Shooting, Wild Women, A Fight for Love, A Gun-fighting Gentleman. All of these featured Carey. The only exception was an early two-reeler, *The Scrapper,* in which the pugnacious hero, Buck the Scrapper, was played by Jack Ford himself.

One regrets the disappearance of these films (they all seem to have vanished into limbo) not merely for their historical interest. For surely pictures made with that youthful, unselfconscious hustle must have reflected and preserved some of the gusto that went into their making. Much of the shooting was impromptu. 'We didn't really have scripts,' Ford has said, 'just a rough continuity.' And Dudley Nichols has recorded how Harry Carey 'would tell me funny stories of how Ford and he worked up their stories, and then shot them "during the balance of the week". Improvising, mostly, as they shot. The old trick was to get one story and shoot it at various studios in succession, using new titles and different actors. I think Ford once told me

he shot one story about ten times — and no one knew the difference. They were funny, energetic, catch-as-catch-can days for "the movies".' But alas, until at least the days of the 'Super Western' — films like *The Covered Wagon* and Ford's own *The Iron Horse* — the Western tradition was not honoured with much serious critical interest. What enduring qualities were possessed by these primitive efforts it is therefore impossible to say. But one can see, from the reviews they obtained in the contemporary press, that in comparison at least with other films of the same school, they showed in bud a number of the felicities of style that were to distinguish Ford's mature work. 'Jack Ford again demonstrates his happy faculty for getting all outdoors into the scenes ... The plot is not particularly new, but there are pleasing touches which give it a fresh appeal' (*Bucking Broadway*), 'The lighting effects and the photography are so good as to bring out special comment' (*The Scarlet Drop*), 'Two remarkable things are Carey's rise to real acting power, and director Ford's marvellous river locations and absolutely incomparable photography' (*The Outcasts of Poker Flat*). And Ford's work at this early stage showed another inclination he was never to lose — that of working continuously with familiar and congenial collaborators. The partnership with Harry Carey was of course the most constant, but there were also the writers George Hively and Eugene Lewis; actors like J. Farrell MacDonald, Vester Pegg and Mollie Malone; and the cameramen Jack Brown and George Schneidermann. No doubt most of these associations began as a result of studio contracts; their continuance clearly witnesses Ford's partiality for the tried and the familiar in his professional relationships.

It is the more unfortunate that these films have largely disappeared because with them has vanished our opportunity to watch a developing style. Jean Mitry's comments* (written presumably from memory) are of interest. 'A robust simplicity' is the term he uses to characterise Ford's early manner — 'almost a style' — which he describes as consisting of 'hacking away the inessentials, in order to enclose the movement of the film in a violent, dynamic continuity, each image like a blow from a clenched fist ...' Such, apparently was the effect at the time of such films as *Desperate Trails* and *The Outcasts of Poker Flat*.

* In *John Ford*, Editions Universitaires, Paris 1954.

The Just Pals *unit — Ford's first picture for Fox (1920). Ford in white shirt, centre, with George E. Stone between his knees, and Buck Jones, centre front.*

[The sections in italics which follow are additions to the original text, written when films which had previously been thought lost were made available for viewing in the late 1970s.]
The Ford enthusiast of today — 1981 — is luckier than I was twenty-five years ago, when his first pictures could only be written about from hearsay. Some time in the 'sixties one print of one film from those 'funny, energetic, catch-as-catch-can days' was discovered in an archive in Czechoslovakia: in it we can now see Jack Ford and Harry Carey working together in that first friendly collaboration which neither of them would ever forget, having fun and creating entertainment with a vivacity and a feeling which still communicate themselves through images sometimes scratched, sometimes faded.
This one surviving film is Straight Shooting, *a Universal picture of 1917, and the first with which Carey and Ford broke out of two-reeler production into 'features': its five reels run about fifty minutes. No doubt the story-line is representative of its genre, with a plot based on the classic conflict between ruthless cattlemen and stubborn home-*

steaders, which has served as the mainspring for thousands of Western stories since — but which Ford, strangely enough, never used in the Westerns of his maturity. It is zestful, light-hearted stuff, always on the move, always good to look at, with a fresh spontaneity in the familiar sentiments.
The story of Straight Shooting *is an odd mixture of simplicity and complication — perhaps because George Hively (who was credited as scenarist on most of the longer Ford-Carey pictures) had some spinning out to do to fill the five reels. The homesteaders are archetypical: old Sweetwater Sims, with his patriarchal beard, his upstanding son Ted and his pretty daughter Joan, farm the smallholding that stands in the way of mustachioed 'Duke' Lee and his herds. Joan's suitor, Sam (a charmingly modest early appearance by Hoot Gibson) works as a ranch hand for Lee: their romance is threatened when Ted is treacherously shot down by one of Lee's henchmen. Enter Cheyenne Harry (Harry Carey making his characteristic entry with a boyish grin, popping like a mischievous Jack-in-the-Box out of the hollow tree*

36

Straight Shooting

Ford told Bogdanovich — and the influence of the Master is strong in the handling of montage (the climactic fight and rescue) and the tender purity of sentiment. Molly Malone as the innocently spirited, sweetly sensitive heroine could well be sister to Mae Marsh in Birth of a Nation — in which Ford always claimed to have performed as one of the white-sheeted riders of the Ku Klux Klan. (And in film after film, long after her official retirement, Miss Marsh continued to appear in little roles in John Ford pictures.)

Harry Carey, of the level gaze and the open grin, is a powerful presence in Straight Shooting; and it is easy to sense his authority and genial influence. His disarming first appearance is characteristic, but Cheyenne Harry can be dangerous as well as affable, sensitive as well as tough. He undertakes to deal with old Sims casually enough. But when he sees father and daughter and young Sam grieving over the dead boy's grave, his eyes mist over — the image blurring with a nice subjectivity — and he turns back. This does not make Harry a sentimental hero: there is a formidable, steely side to him too, and when he goes into a shoot-out we know who is going to win. This combination of chivalry with strength is one which will characterise many a Ford hero to come; Will Rogers has it in quite a different key, and both Fonda and Wayne can suggest the same ambiguity. We can feel Ford, in this early exercise, learning from Carey what he was later to teach.

Straight Shooting is an entirely modest film, but it conveys unmistakably Jack Ford's natural warmth, that sense of the truthfulness of each moment, the individuality of each character, which would always disinguish his best work. Familiar situations are brought alive by the sheer conviction of their imagining. The boy Ted is dead: the place which his sister has laid for him at the supper table is still there as she numbly starts to clear the dishes. As she moves to take up his clean knife and fork, his unused plate, she suddenly feels her heart twisted by the sense of his presence and his loss. The moment is beautifully observed, touchingly true. Elsewhere the curse of melodrama will be suddenly lifted by humour. During the slam-bang siege which gives the story its climax, one of the outlaws spots a promising-looking jar up on a shelf. As the bullets continue to ricochet around, he lifts it down, puts in his finger, licks it, and finds the taste good. Glancing round to see that he is unobserved, he stows the jar stealthily under his coat — and returns to the fight. To Ford, men were always liable to behave like boys grown big; it is part of the peculiar innocence of his vision.

on which a lawman has just hammered a notice offering a reward for his capture): he is contracted by the cattlemen to finish off the Sims family. But Harry is moved by the old man's grief, and switches sides. He shoots Lee's henchman in a mainstreet duel, and persuades a friendly outlaw to ride in with his gang and relieve the besieged farmers. Will Harry stay, to replace the murdered son? Or will he leave Joan to her devoted Sam, and ride away?

'Harry Carey tutored me in the early years...' Ford told Peter Bogdanovich, 'and the only thing I always had was an eye for composition — I don't know where I got it — and that's all I did have.' It was not all he had; but certainly he had it. From start to finish, Straight Shooting shows the shaping hand, the original eye of the born film maker, with compositions either handsomely framed for pictorial effect, or sensitively chosen to express character and feeling. At the same time, key 'dramatic' scenes tend to be staged with traditional silent movie theatricality, shot flat-on with the formal groupings and gestures of melodrama. But — 'Griffith was the one who made it an art...' as

Images from Straight Shooting *show Ford's style, in cutting and composition, already characteristic and eloquent. Above: Sweetwater Sims, with daughter Molly and hired hand Sam, mourns over his son's grave. Harry watches and understands.*

The end of Straight Shooting *is odd: in fact there seem to be two endings. In the first Harry, the loner who has wistfully felt the attraction of Joan Sims, resists the old man's urging that he should stay on with them as one of the family. 'Me a farmer? No — I belong on the range.' But he is tempted in spite of himself: 'Give me a day to think it over.' So he sits by himself on a rock, pondering, till he is interrupted by Sam, who loves the girl too, and he accepts his solitary destiny: 'I'm leaving Joan to you. Bless you — and goodbye.' This leads to a wry little scene, played with a subtle mixture of emotions, in which Joan, all expectation, opens the door of the hut, hoping that it is Harry come to claim her, and finds it is only staunch, good-hearted Sam. And Sam senses her disappointment. The feelings of boy and girl, both fond, both hurt, are touchingly unresolved. But Cheyenne Harry is not after all to be the first Ford hero to ride away alone — at least not in this print of* Straight Shooting. *Another title mysteriously follows: 'At sunset he gives her his answer.' And the film fades out with Harry and Joan in unexplained embrace. Was this an alternative ending? Did some executive insist on a happy fade-out? It doesn't really matter. A sense of 'as-you-like-it' quite fits the impromptu charm of the whole picture.*

This sense of carefree improvisation, this exuberant story-telling pleasure, gives Straight Shooting *an unmistakably personal quality: one regrets the more sharply the loss of all those other Ford-Carey adventures. Jack Ford's next surviving film dates from three years later, when he had moved from Universal to Fox, and left his collaboration with Harry Carey behind him.* Just Pals *is its name, with Buck Jones as the amiable, small-town idler who befriends a footloose orphan and finds himself involved in an amazing succession of adventures before he can walk away into happiness with the village schoolteacher. There is charm, humour and a great deal of free-wheeling energy in the picture; but because there is so much more story, the tone is less intimate, less somehow characteristic. Ford is becoming the useful all-rounder, ready to do a capable job with almost any story, the professional without pretensions.*

At the start of Just Pals *the Griffithian atmosphere is strong. The time is 1920, but the tranquil images of the small-town scene seem to evoke a period twenty or thirty years before: and so do the dramatic conventions of exploited innocence, mustachioed villainy and bashful, devoted heroism. This is the mythic America of popular legend ('The Town of Nowalk, on the borderline of Wyoming and Nebraska') with its traditional humours and*

Above: A moment of theatre. Sam, the cattlemen's messenger, is ordered from the Sims' home. Above right: Showdown. Below: Sam (Hoot Gibson) realises that Molly's feelings are for Harry. Harry decides to leave alone — the Harry Carey gesture, used in homage by John Wayne at the end of The Searchers.

traditional intrigues.

The film starts as a gentle comedy of sentiment, with Buck Jones, as the town bum, Bim ('the idol of its youth and the bane of its elders') — another sensitive, manly, boyish hero, yearning shyly for the pretty schoolmistress and befriending the ragged little fugitive chased off a passing train. Melodrama takes over as the plot sprouts an amazing profusion of themes, all pursued with irresistible conviction, in typical early silent movie style: mistaken identity, imposture, embezzlement, a bank robbery, a horseback pursuit, attempted suicide and abduction ... All this before Bim and the schoolmistress can find each other, and the prying village gossip can stick his head out of the hollow tree for the fade out — a good idea is worth repeating, as Ford knew even then.

If in Just Pals we seem to feel its director's touch less intimately than we do in Straight Shooting, it is still recognisably a personal work, characteristic in its humanity. For all the artifice of its plotting, the way people behave is real; feelings are experienced, not just represented, and in this way the stereotypes are brought to life. Its vigour and the outrageous twists and turns of its story may be typical of its period; but its comedy, always characterful, usually disrespectful, is Jack Ford's. Often we can feel the carefree haste of the shooting, with daylight shots cut obviously into night sequences and generally not too much bother about continuity or a lucid narrative. Then the style will switch, the images will become graceful, poetic. Charles Silver compares the picture with 'such affecting evocations of rural America' as Griffith's True Heart Susie or A Romance of Happy Valley, released the year before.* He adds: 'The Ford film exhibits some of the same brilliance at being simultaneously naturalistic and poetic ... Somehow these two men share an ineffable genius for baring their souls and moving us by the way they photograph a tree or shade a landscape.' Ford's poetic maturity was many years and many pictures away, but his first two surviving films make clear the way he was to go.

* Charles Silver: 'The Apprenticeship of John Ford', *American Film*, May 1976.

Just Pals. *Buck Jones as Bim, the town loafer. ('Just watching people makes Bim tired.') and George E. Stone as the little vagrant he adopts. Helen Ferguson is the schoolteacher Bim idolises and finally wins. And for a fadeout the town gossip surprises Mary and her rehabilitated Bim with Harry's hollow tree trick from Straight Shooting.*

Shooting The Iron Horse: *George Schneiderman, Burnett Guffey and John Ford.*

In 1920 came Jack Ford's first attempt at a non-Western subject; *The Prince from Avenue 'A'*, a comedy, significantly, of Irish life in New York, with the boxer, Gentleman Jim Corbett, in the leading role. In 1922 he made his most ambitious film to date, *Cameo Kirby*, with John Gilbert as a romantic Southern gambler. For this, he changed his name on the credits, assuming for the first time the formal dignity of John Ford.

'Ford had just seen the first great German and Swedish films of the post-war period,' writes Mitry. 'He understood what it was possible for him to draw from their expressionist style, moderating their excess and applying their method to a more immediate and realistic world. The plastic image was a complete revelation to him.' It would be interesting to know on what precise grounds this is based. For while it is possible that *Cameo Kirby* would lend support to M. Mitry's contentions, it is certain that, seen today, his great film of 1924 — his fiftieth film, and his most celebrated achievement in the silent cinema — betrays no appreciable influence from the German or the Swedish cinemas. *The Iron Horse* is a film of developed style — of 'robust simplicity' still, but with at the same time a fine sense of dramatic composition (expressive

rather than expressionist) and the kind of exciting imagination that can bring into sharp and vivid focus the intimate personal gesture as well as the far-reaching historical event. This story of the building of America's first transcontinental railroad presented Ford with his greatest opportunity to date. The picture was planned at first for a four-week schedule, but (in Frank Nugent's words):

'The troupe had barely made camp in the Nevada Sierras, between Pyramid Lake and Reno, when a blizzard struck. Ford decided it was easier to change the script than the weather, and began shooting. The first blizzard was followed by a second and a third; temperatures of 20-below were common. At the end of the allotted month, the producer ordered their return . . . Ford sent his railroad builders out into the drifts to lay another mile of track.

'They laid three miles, built three shack towns, and hauled their vintage iron horse over the spine of the Sierras . . . This was five weeks after the first recall order; it had been repeated, on a rising note of outrage, at weekly and then daily intervals. The producer . . . relented when he saw the film they had shot. One day's footage had been overexposed. "That must have been the day the sun came out", said Ford.'

Three Bad Men: *Tom Santschi, George O'Brien, J. Farrell McDonald, Frank Campeau, Olive Borden.*

The Iron Horse, with its theme of enterprise, and achievement, its open-air locations, and its setting in a vigorous, pioneering past, proved exactly the subject to stimulate Ford's talent to its best advantage. Designed by its producers (Fox) as a riposte to *The Covered Wagon,* which James Cruze had directed for Paramount the year before, the film won a great popular success in America, costing 280,000 dollars, and grossing over three millions. The young John Ford was established as one of the leading directors in the industry — a reputation he was never to lose.

The success, however, was not immediately repeated. In his following films, Ford relapsed again into the trough of commercial production. His next picture, for instance, *Hearts of Oak,* was a melodrama in which 'an old sea captain heroically goes to his death in the Arctic so that his two young wards might find happiness'. Yet here again it is interesting to find reviewers drawing attention to the exceptional qualities of the handling: 'Packed with realistic scenes of storms at sea, wonderful views of the Arctic, fine shots of the New England coast . . .' The fashion in Hollywood now was for greater sophistication, both of style and subject, than could come naturally to Ford: of his remaining films of the silent period only two were exceptional — *Three Bad Men,* in 1926, and *Four Sons,* a pacifist drama set in Germany, in 1928. The first of these, a story of three chivalrous outlaws who take part in

the gold rush of 1877, is described by Jean Mitry as Ford's silent masterpiece, reminiscent in its poetic climate of the best films of Thomas Ince. 'The originality is less in the subject, than in the three characters who set the key, the climate, the colour of the story. The film is certainly an epic, but a picaresque epic, in which the heroes never take their heroism seriously.'

In *Three Bad Men* it is clear that once again the vigour and cameraderie of a pioneering subject had evoked from Ford a response that lifted the picture to a level far above that which he was able to achieve with the conventional scripts, melodramas and sentimental comedies which were more frequently his lot in these years. By contrast, Mitry describes *Four Sons* as another film whose handling testifies to the influence on Ford of European conceptions of film making, with compositions verging on the formal and sets designed in a style half way between realism and expressionism. This 'Sternbergian' side of Ford was one that was to play an important part in his development, enriching his style, but also tending to corrupt it, resulting at times in a rather lifeless aestheticism. It is interesting to remark, too, that the theme of this story — a family divided and disintegrated by the pressure of external events — was one that Ford had used in previous silent films, and that was to reappear in his later work, always charged with particular feeling and signifance.

Probably it was inevitable, writing at a time when the 'commercial' and the 'creative' are so often at odds, and when most of Ford's early films seemed anyway to have disappeared, that I should have dismissed the bulk of his silent work with superior scorn ('the trough of commercialism'), reserving commendation for more celebrated achievements, like The Iron Horse and Three Bad Men, in genres that were to become peculiarly his own. But now that a good handful of those missing films can be seen — and enjoyed as well as examined — it becomes clear that really it was not like that at all.

John Ford, silent movie maker, was not the victim of commerce. He was happy in the role of popular story-teller, providing entertainment for a vast, avid, uncritical and innocent (artistically at any rate) audience. He did not need to tell us this: we can sense his enjoyment in the vitality of the work. He was telling his stories in a language that came to him naturally. It had only been invented ten years or so before; he and his contemporaries were developing it, with relish and flair. Questions of style, conscious aesthetic aims, would come later.

He seemed able to turn his hand to pretty well anything, and no doubt he was proud, as a practising professional, to do so. He could manage the spectacular effect as well as the intimate human touch, adventure as well as romance; he was strong on comedy. Of course in some territories he was more at ease than in others. He was not particularly happy with urban sophistication, or with psychological complexity. It would not be true to say he was better with doing than with feeling, but he was perhaps more comfortable with his heroes than with his heroines. In Straight Shooting, the developing West, with its empty spaces to ride in and its freedom of choice and action, obviously nourished his warm, anarchic soul. So did the innocent humour of Just Pals. His big assignment for 1923, three years later, provided a marked contrast in pretension — and becoming John Ford for the occasion was rather like putting on a coat and tie. Cameo Kirby is named for its hero, an honourable but misjudged gentleman gambler, suspected of murdering the father of the girl he grows to love. Ford executed the starchy romance expertly enough; but clearly the elegant mansions and estates of the Southern gentry offered him little ease. Nor did John Gilbert have quite the sensitive

Top: Action *(1921). J. Farrell McDonald, Hoot Gibson, Clara Horton. Centre:* The Face on the Bar-Room Floor. *Henry B. Walthall, Ruth Clifford. Bottom:* Hoodman Blind. *David Butler (right).*

The Iron Horse. *Left: construction teams at work. Right: Western and Union Pacific lines come together. J. Farrell McDonald and George O'Brien greet their friendly rivals with joy.*

directness or the moral sensibility which even then characterised the Ford hero.

It was surely with relish that he returned to the plains and mountains passes of the West for the epic adventure of The Iron Horse, his first essay on the American theme, and his first salute to Lincoln, the leader whose quirky, common-folk genius compounded so sympathetically with his own. The film is encumbered with a conventional story of crookery and vengeance: the young Pony Express rider manages to thwart the greedy land-owner who is scheming to delay and exploit the construction of the transcontinental railroad, and at the same time avenges his father's murder and wins the hand of his childhood sweetheart ... There is no sign that Ford questioned this claptrap and sometimes tiresome plot, which he plays out with proper, full-blooded conviction. But the distinctive strength of The Iron Horse is in its poetic sense of history, its vision of the building of a nation by uniting a continent, the dream of great men realised by the courage and skill, the suffering and the labour of a multitude of ordinary folk. There is tremendous vigour still in its lusty fresco of creation: the turbulence of the construction towns, roughnecks and girls in bars and brothels, rough justice in Judge Haller's combined court-room and saloon, the humour of the labouring men, the savagery of the hostile Indians, locomotives manhandled over all-but impossible terrain, whole townships uprooted and transported to follow the men as the railroad pushes further into the West. A nation stretches and grows before our eyes, like those speeded-up films of vegetation uncurling, reaching out, pushing up irresistibly into maturity. And the epic theme is brought to life not by the platitudes of official record, nor by the over-emphatic gestures of melodrama, but by the ever-present sense that the whole massive design is built up out of countless unique, individual lives. There is

a sense here of human singularity that seems to have been part of Ford's artistic soul from the start, and that would always give his stories a special kind of warmth and reality — a face picked out in a crowd, one woman's grief bringing to life a world of tragedies, one death evoking the loss of many. The night before the ceremony of completion, Davy, the young hero, goes out alone to the last stretch of track where the Union and Western Pacific roads have joined. He stands alone that night and sees the consummation of his father's dream.' As the young man stands — sits — feels the last join of the rails, we enter into the fullness of his feelings. The passage recalls Harry's solitary decision at the end of Straight Shooting — and looks forward to many a future Ford hero and heroine who will make us feel the significance of a moment as they withdraw into a silent, self-communing confrontation with destiny.

The Iron Horse brought John Ford distinction, but it did not make him a career man. The next year he was back on the Fox production line with four films, all 'programme pictures', not exactly in the trough of commercialism but certainly on its broad, well-frequented highway. His first production for 1925, Lightnin', was adapted from a play — as had been Hearts of Oak, the picture which had immediately followed The Iron Horse the year before. Lightnin', which can still be seen at the Museum of Modern Art, New York, is a whimsical, often stagey comedy, of a quirky elderly couple — she runs a hotel, split eccentrically in two by the California-Nebraska stateline, and he keeps bees and hides his whisky in the hives — whose tolerant acceptance of each other is disrupted and their marriage almost destroyed by a couple of big city swindlers. The tale meanders agreeably: its theatricality does not seem to have irked Ford particularly, and his amused affection for cantankerous old age — fifteen years before Tobacco Road

The Iron Horse. 'He Stands Alone that Night...'

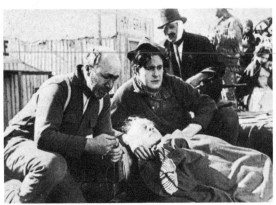

Left: The Iron Horse. *Aftermath of an Indian raid on the line. The wounded and dying are brought back to the base camp: Ford at his most simple and humanely eloquent.*

— *gives the picture a pleasant glow of sentiment, and even from time to time a hint of deeper feeling.*

His next release, Kentucky Pride, *took Ford out of the studio again for a horse-racing romance, conventional in its melodrama of the aristocratic Southern family ruined by gambling debts and saved by a favourite foal (its birth, subjectively presented, starts the picture) that grows up to win the Kentucky Derby. But the convention is still lively, with nothing jaded or perfunctory in the handling. There is warmth in the sentiment and an infectious enjoyment in the rough-and-tumble comedy, most of it in the hands of J. Farrell MacDonald, whose flagrantly 'Irish' whimsicality and quizzically raised eyebrow seemed to figure in all Ford's films at this time.*

These were not pretentious pictures; all of them were plainly assignments, picked for obvious popular qualities and clearly accepted by Ford with sometimes greater, sometimes lesser enthusiasm, but never with resentment. And it is remarkable how he was able to colour them in the making, giving them the attributes of his own personality, his own warmth of sentiment and sense of fun, his own allegiances and ideals. The Shamrock Handicap *in 1926 is another horse-racing romance, and one which offered Ford some particularly sympathetic chances. For this is a story that starts and ends in Ireland, ('Old Erin' as the title puts it, 'Where the Horn of the Hunter is oft heard on the Hill'), whence the young jockey-hero comes to America and manages to restore the fallen fortunes of his old Master ('Sir Miles O'Hara, the Last of his Line') by riding Rosaleen to victory in the Shamrock Handicap.*

Ireland, of course, and his Irish ancestry were always powerfully a part of Ford's sense of the world and of himself. Dan Ford tells us how in 1921, the year after his marriage and six months or so after the birth of his son, he journeyed alone to Ireland, making the crossing from Liverpool on the boat that was carrying Michael Collins and Arthur Griffith back to Dublin with Lloyd George's peace proposals, and spending a couple of weeks in Galway, searching out his relatives (some of them in hiding from the British), closely watched by the Black and Tans.[*] In his films, though, Ireland was mostly a fairy-tale

---

[*] Dan Ford, *Pappy,* pp 23-4. The story of travelling on the same boat as Collins and Griffith is, of course, typical Ford — *poetically true, no doubt.*

Top: a theatrical adaptation, Lightnin' *(1925). Millie (Madge Bellamy) confronts Lightnin' (Jay Hunt) and his drinking pal. Above: J. Farrell McDonald and his quizzical eyebrows in a racetrack scene from* Kentucky Pride *(1925).*

place, a land of comedy and idyll — an indication of how happily in the early stages of his career at least, Ford conformed to the role of popular entertainer. In later years, it is true, he was to make some unsuccessful attempts to tackle themes of violence and political struggle. But now, as in his beautiful The Quiet Man *twenty-five years later, he was content to accept the Hollywood tradition of romantic-pastoral Erin. 'Aie,' begins* The Shamrock Handicap, *'But Ireland's the fair place . . .' And there is great charm in the softly-diffused vision, with its*

47

Riley the Cop. *Louise Fazenda, J. Farrell McDonald.*

kindly, impoverished squire, its raggetty shepherd lads, its little girl with her offering of oatcakes (graciously accepted) in place of the rent her mother cannot afford to pay, and the dark-haired colleen under the trees, with a flock of sheep straying gently away into the sunlit valley...

Two years later came Hangman's House, set again in Ireland — 'Such a little place to be so greatly loved' — with another exciting horse race (our first glimpse of John Wayne in the Ford canon, as an over-excited spectator smashing up the fencing), a Celtic Cross in the square and a more dramatic key. And again the note of emigrant longing in Victor McLaglen's farewell, as he returns to the Foreign Legion after avenging the death of his betrayed sister: 'I'm going back to the brown desert...but I'm taking the green place with me in my heart.'

Irishness with a different accent runs through Riley the Cop, one of Ford's last silent pictures, though released in 1928 with a soundtrack of music and effects. J. Farrell MacDonald, inevitably, is the kindly neighbourhood cop whose philosophy is that 'You can tell a good cop by the arrests he doesn't make', and whose tranquil round of street baseball with the kids and on-duty snacks in the bakery kitchen is disrupted when he is sent off to Germany to fetch back a local lad suspected of robbery. ('Why couldn't the lad be arrested in Ireland?') The comedy is delightful — affable and Chaplinesque at the start, broadly farcical when MacDonald finds himself romantically pursued in a Munich beer-garden by a manic Louise Fazenda. Ford was never more Irish than when he was exploiting with gusto his

countrymen's talent for self-mocking farce.

Even where his stories and characters had no particularly Irish connotations, Ford still usually continued to give them heroes of sympathetic Celtic charm. George O'Brien, the camera assistant whom he had introduced to stardom in The Iron Horse, contributed his forthright appeal and handsome physique to a succession of action-packed romances, from The Fighting Heart in 1925 ('A prizefighter is swept to Broadway; love brings him back to mainstreet. Three of the most thrilling fights ever screened.' Photoplay) to The Blue Eagle (1926: Rival gang leaders continue their feud in the Navy), Salute (1929: Army-Navy football rivalry) and The Seas Beneath (1931: Wartime adventures with America's 'Mystery Ships'). Victor McLaglen, a rolling stone Irishman from South Africa, ex-British Army officer and Heavyweight Champion of the British Empire, made his first Fordian appearance in The Fighting Heart, and went on to the sentimentalism of Mother Machree (1928), the drama of Hangman's House and the comedy of Strong Boy (1929), as a brawny, genial railway porter ambitious to rise to higher things. These were all popular pictures, not pretentious, certainly not critically remarked. But their vigour, affability and unhesitant romanticism were all characteristic; and they were good practice.

Two more ambitious productions survive from this period which show Ford working at fuller stretch. In 1926 he returned to the Western epic with Three Bad Men — more anecdotal than The Iron Horse, with the Dakota land rush of the seventies serving as background to the tale of three 'Wanted' ruffians who befriend a fatherless girl and the young pioneer who loves her. (George O'Brien again, as Dan O'Malley — 'All the way from Ireland'). Loyal and tender-hearted for all their villainy, the Three Musketeers watch over the young couple like solicitous nannies, and end up sacrificing themselves to save them from a corrupt Sheriff and his gang. As in The Iron Horse, the scenes of endurance and endeavour are full of vigour, as the wagons move Westward across the plains: then the rush itself, with the massive line-up of wagons, carts, carriages, vehicles of every kind stretching away into the distance, down to a lonely eccentric on a penny-farthing bicycle, all racketing off in frantic competition at the crack of the starter's pistol. (This memorable sequence features a famous shot — the baby left carelessly in the path of the advancing

The Shamrock Handicap (1926). *In the middle distance: Janet Gaynor, Leslie Fenton.*

THE FILM MAKER

49

hooves, snatched away to safety at the last minute — an idea, according to Dan Ford, of Harry Carey's, which Ford had long searched for an excuse to try.) *Much of* **Three Bad Men**, *with spectacle and melodrama continually leavened by humour, is early Ford at his best; yet the film was not a great success. Perhaps the central situation was too simple, or too familiar, to support the epic claim. In any case, the public responded with much greater enthusiasm to* **Four Sons** *two years later, the First World War story of a German mother and her three sons who die in battle, and the one who survives, an emigrant to the United States, where she herself finds a haven after the long tragedy of war is over.*

Adapted from a novel by I. A. R. Wylie, **Four Sons** *is a frankly sentimental story, and much of it today is dated: the operetta-style Bavaria where Frau Bernle, the archetypal* mutterchen, *lives with her four fine sons: the familiar stereotypes of Postman, Burgomaster, Innkeeper and arrogant Army officer: the contrived battlefield climax in which the emigrant son, now an American soldier, finds his brother dying of wounds in a shellhole and recognises him just in time to kiss him farewell... But there is genuine sentiment here as well as sentimentality, and charm as well as story-telling skill: the warmth of family affection and the tragedy of separation are truly felt and so, unmistakably, is Ford's reverence for the enduring mother-love of a simple woman. 'I read the story by Wylie in some magazine and had them buy it', Ford told Bogdanovich. One is not surprised that this should be one of the films for which he had a special personal feeling. The Irish heart of Ford always softened at the thought of home, of family and of a mother's self-sacrificing love — themes that are no less true for having been so often celebrated in platitude. This is the necessary obverse of the world of action, adventure and cameraderie which characterise films like* **The Iron Horse** *and* **Three Bad Men**. *And of course Ford, who seemed to find it so hard to make a happy family of his own to replace the one he had lost — or imagined — was always equally responsive to themes of separation, loss, splitting apart. There are touches of this feeling in* **Straight Shooting**; *it is the essence of* **Four Sons**; *and it will give depth and resonance to many a masterpiece to come.*

To shoot background scenes for **Four Sons** *Ford*

Top: **The Blue Eagle** *(1926). George O'Brien confronts William Russell.   Centre:* **Three Bad Men**. *Tom Santschi, Olive Borden. Left:* **Strong Boy** *(1929). Victor McLaglen, Leatrice Joy, Clyde Cook, Slim Summerville.*

Four Sons: *Margaret Mann as Frau Bernle in happy days — James Hall, Charles Morton, George Meeker, Francis X. Bushman Jnr., as the sons.*

went to Bavaria in 1927. On this visit he met F. W. Murnau, who had just signed a contract with Fox, and made contact with a number of his contemporaries in Berlin, and with their work. Some of the results of these meetings can be seen in the picture: indeed the battle scenes in Four Sons *are said to have been shot on the sets built at Fox for* Sunrise, *which Murnau came to Hollywood to make the next year. An awareness of camera, and a skill with composition and lighting, was part of Ford's instinctive gift; but there seems little doubt that the example of Murnau and his colleagues inspired him to a richer, more conscious conception of style. At times in* Four Sons *the influence is strong, with movements that recall German camera handling and lighting effects that verge on the expressionistic. There were examples of this kind of thing in earlier pictures: in* The Shamrock Handicap, *with its romantically diffused Erin, and in the nightmarish chiaroscuro of the villain's death in* Three Bad Men, *which Charles Silver suggests may well have derived from* Nosferatu. *But in* Four Sons *the tendency is more consistent; and in following films like* Hangman's House *and even* Riley The Cop *(where*

we discover runaway Davey imprisoned in a handsomely expressionistic Munich prison cell — an oddly powerful image for a comedy) shows a reaching out towards greater visual sophistication.

Charles Silver, discussing Ford's early works, remarks: 'Judged by the dramatic standards of The Gold Rush, The Marriage Circle, Isn't Life Wonderful?, The Navigator *or* The Big Parade, Ford *(save for his evident craftsmanship) might have been dismissed in the mid-twenties as a very minor director indeed.' 'Very minor indeed' is perhaps severe, but essentially this is true. Ford took time to find himself as an artist: early on he hardly seemed to feel the need. But the films he produced so spontaneously are far from worthless. Even in the less distinguished among them there is almost always a strong, attractive personality, one which it is a pleasure to meet. It is a personality which wears, so to speak, its beliefs on its sleeve, simple beliefs in friendship and family; there is a warmth of humane conviction, and a sympathy with the humble and disreputable, complemented by an impatient scorn for the grand and the hypocritical. And there is a pervasive humour that ranges from the delicate to*

Above: Riley the Cop. *Riley (J. Farrell McDonald) rescues Davy (David Rollins) from the Munich gaol.*
Below: Four Sons. *Brother finds brother on the battlefield.*

the boisterous, always there to dispel the threat of sentimentalism or presumption. These are not minor virtues.

To those who have grown up in the era of sound, silent cinema often seems unsophisticated. Much of it is, though often by standards of sophistication that are not especially admirable. It is easy to forget that this was not really a naturalistic medium, and was not taken to be such either by its audiences or by the artists who worked in it. It was a medium for fairy tale, for myth, poetry for the market place. John

Ford's formation in silent cinema gave him expertise and a narrative mastery that became second nature to him. And it gave him more. It gave him the understanding that a film director is a man who creates worlds, or rather a world, and that film is in this sense poetic. It was to be his great achievement that after being, like everyone else, sidetracked by the introduction of sound, and the need to make 'realistic' dialogue films, he found his way back again to myth, to poetry.

2

The coming of sound provoked from John Ford no protest, no statement of aesthetic principle or position. Instead, as one would expect, he took the step forward in his stride. He was now in an assured position in Hollywood, a director professionally much admired and highly valued by his studio, known to have a particular flair for subjects of action and the out-of-doors, but dependably proficient in the handling of any kind of story. At times, no doubt producers found him difficult to handle, but never in the manner of a Stroheim or a Flaherty: his ambitions remained, so to speak, *within* the framework of the industry. The heartbreaking dichotomy of the cinema as art, and the cinema as industry, had not yet claimed him as victim. His first shot at a sound picture was a four-reeler, all-talkie version of a one-act play, *Napoleon's Barber*; his second, *Black Watch,* was an adventure story of the Indian North-West frontier. Both seem to have been fairly routine productions, using the new technique with competence rather than daring. (In between these first two sound films, it is worth noting that Ford directed a couple of silent quickies, the second of which marked the beginning of an important association, with the cameraman Joseph August.) It was not until 1929 that Ford entered into another partnership that was to have a great influence on his development, and to result later in the thirties in the first films which brought him decisively into the ranks of directors critically accepted as artists in their own right. This was with the writer Dudley Nichols.

'I landed in Hollywood in June, 1929. I had earlier finished ten years journalism in New York (reporting, drama criticism, music criticism, columning, one year on a roving assignment in Europe) and had cut my journalistic ties to go on with fiction and other writing ... Winfield Sheehan, then executive head of Fox films, talked me into coming to Hollywood. Sound had arrived and writers were needed. I knew nothing about film and told him so. I had seen one film I remembered and liked, Ford's *The Iron Horse*. So I arrived rather tentatively and experimentally, intending to leave if I found it dissatisfying. Fortunately Sheehan assigned me to work with Ford ...'*

It is natural that film makers who had grown up in the silent cinema, and who had devoted themselves to learning the art of story-telling as far as possible through image alone, should have felt themselves at a disadvantage when 'movies' were replaced by photographed plays. The problem for a director of individuality was not merely to find a writer, but to find a writer whose mind worked sympathetically, whose responses were congenial. From the start, Ford and Nichols worked well together and Ford seems to have spared no effort to make the collaboration a success —

'. . . . Fortunately Sheehan assigned me to work with Ford. I liked him. I am part Irish, and we got on. I told him I had not the slightest idea how to write a film script. I had been in the Navy during the war, overseas two years, and we decided on a submarine story. I told him I could write a play, not a script. In his humorous way he asked if I could

---

* From a letter to the author. All the following quotations from Mr. Nichols are taken from the same source. For the full text of these letters, see page 237.

write a play in fifty or sixty scenes. Sure. So I did. It was never a script. Then I went on the sets and watched him break it down into filmscript as he shot. I went to rushes, cutting rooms, etc., and began to grasp what it was all about. But I must say I was baffled for many months by the way Ford could see everything through a camera — and I could not . . . Working with Ford closely I fell in love with the cinema . . .'

This first film on which Ford and Nichols worked together was *Men Without Women*, a story about fourteen sailors entombed in a crippled submarine. It is evident that in this Ford found again (and at last) a subject to which he could give something of himself: the film at any rate was a critical success, which evidenced considerably more daring in its technique than anything in Ford's previous sound work. Mr. Nichols writes:

'It was remarkable in many ways. They believed long dolly shots could not be made with the sound camera. He did it — one long shot down a whole street, with men carrying microphones on fishpoles overhead. And there were 'many astonishing pictorial things in it. I remember, when I started the "script", I told Ford I feared I would imagine and write scenes which could not be photographed. "You write it", he said, "and I'll get it on film." Well, he did. Even put the camera in a glass box and took it on a dive on the submarine. It is old hat now. Not then.'

Ford's partnership with Nichols was not, however, maintained consistently. After another picture together, *Born Reckless* ('Which was, I believe, the first American gangster melodrama in sound-film'), Ford branched away into a succession of miscellaneous assignments. The end of 1931 saw the release of *Arrowsmith* (adapted by Sidney Howard from the novel by Sinclair Lewis) — a great success for its director, and perhaps his most popular film since *The Iron Horse*. And another that sounds interesting is *Doctor Bull* (1933), from a novel by James Gould Cozzens, with Will Rogers as a country doctor in a small Connecticut town. Most of these pictures have disappeared from view.

*Top: Writer and director: Dudley Nichols and John Ford. Between 1930 (*Men Without Women*) and 1935 (*The Informer*) Nichols contributed to eight Ford pictures. Centre: Getting the camera out of the studio. Ford (centre) watches cameraman Joe August (left) prepare for an underwater shoot on* Men Without Women. *Left: Ford's first picture with Will Rogers, Dr. Bull, co-scripted by Nichols. Andy Devine (right).*

Men Without Women. *Dudley Nichols' first script for Ford. Left to right: Harry Tenbrook, Stuart Erwin, Kenneth McKenna, Warren Hymer, Paul Page, J. Farrell McDonald.*

Now that his work of this period can be more easily seen, one can follow more clearly Ford's development through the first half-dozen years of sound — and appreciate more clearly the underlying conflict between artistic ambition on the one hand, and on the other a ready, all-purpose professionalism. This he would justify by a continual playing-down of creative pretension, an insistence that he was to be considered 'merely' a craftsman (whose success could be proved by results at the box-office), rather than anything as dubious, and as vulnerable to criticism, as an artist.

In his late silent films, Ford was working much more deliberately than in his carefree early years, with a camera style often elaborate, richly textured, emphatically expressive. Most of these films were photographed by George Schneidermann, who had lit almost all his twenties pictures for Fox, from Just Pals *in 1920 to* Four Sons *and* Hangman's House *in 1928. But for* Strong Boy, *his last silent in 1929, Ford found himself with another cameraman, one whom he had worked with only once before, in* Lightnin'. *This was Joseph H. August, raised in the business by Thomas Ince and W. S. Hart, and already, it would seem, an accomplished stylist in his own right. His second film for Ford,* The Black Watch, *was a military adventure story adapted from a popular novel* King of the Khyber Rifles. *Shot as a silent,*

The Black Watch *was overtaken by the introduction of sound, and had dramatic scenes added, under the direction of the English actor (also playing the Colonel of the Regiment), Lumsden Hare. The combination of Ford's camera-eye with August's voluptuous lighting gives the film a remarkable visual distinction: strikingly chiaroscuro, boldly dramatic in its compositions, strongly dramatic in atmosphere.* The Black Watch *is indeed well worth preserving, though partly, it must be admitted, for the rich absurdity of its stiff upper-lip regimentals, and its romantic scenes between a wonderfully sensuous Myrna Loy and an endearingly clumsy Victor McLaglen, all fists and thumbs as the dashing Scottish(!) officer ordered away from his regiment on a secret mission to the North West Frontier ('You speak the Indian dialects like a native'), where the mysterious Yasmini is inciting her fanatical hordes to sweep down into India through the Khyber Pass. The story takes place during the First World War. Since the officers of his regiment are just celebrating their last dinner in the Mess before leaving for France, Captain King (McLaglen) naturally finds himself suspected of cowardice when he announces that he will not be coming with them. Not till he returns on New Year's Eve, his mission accomplished, to hear 'Auld Lang Syne' (in a characteristically Irish high tenor) by his baby*

Top: The Black Watch *(1929). Myrna Loy as Yasmini captivates Captain King (Victor McLaglen). Centre:* Born Reckless *(1930). Edmund Lowe. Bottom:* Up the River *(1930). Tracy and Bogart made their Hollywood debuts in this film.*

brother Davy in a wheelchair, is he accepted back with honour by his brother-officers.

Much of the stilted theatricality of The Black Watch *is clearly due to the poker-stiff Lumsden Hare, assigned to handle the dialogue scenes on the assumption that Ford would not be able to direct actors who actually spoke. But some of the artificiality is Ford's. The self-consciousness of the style, the formality of the groupings and the near-expressionism of the lighting (with a lot of mist, diffusion and shooting against light) all play against spontaneity, naturalness and humour. There is an impressively staged scene of the regiment's departure for France which is split amazingly between a genuine virtuosity of imagery, and a falsity of sentiment and stereotyped characterisation that is pure operatta. It is as though in Ford the conscious artistic impulse pulled one way, and instinctive talent another. The divergent impulses were not to be reconciled for almost another ten years, when he found his way at last to the splendid poetic maturity of the late thirties.*

For The Black Watch, *and for* Strong Boy *before it, Ford found himself with a new and congenial writer, James Kevin McGuinness, an Irishman, ex-publicist and (in Dan Ford's words) 'contact man for the Catholic Church'. McGuinness worked again for Ford, as dialoguist, on his next picture,* Salute, *a genial football romance, set in the Naval Academy of Annapolis — a continuation of the long special relationship between Ford and the Navy. For this, footballers were supplied from his College contacts by the young John Wayne, still known by his birth name of Marion Morrison, now working regularly as prop man and general assistant around Fox. (And on* Salute, *too, Morrison's bumptious fellow-student Wardell Bond — 'a 220-pound tackle with thick lips and big ears, whose only baggage was a bottle of bootleg gin'* — became an actor and staunch prop of the Ford stock company.) McGuinness is also credited with the story for Ford's next, the submarine drama* Men Without Women, *though the script of this was provided by another writer, one who was to contribute even more to Ford's development and achievement over the next decade — Dudley Nichols.*

---

* Dan Ford: *Pappy*, 1979, Prentice-Hall, Inc, New Jersey.

We may guess that James McGuinness did not attempt to influence or re-shape John Ford; but Dudley Nichols was made of different stuff. Ex-Navy, ex-liberal journalist, he was a man of formed artistic ambitions and decided liberal views. The first films of the partnership were, as we have seen, essentially commercial assignments on which Nichols was chiefly occupied with learning the craft of dramatic writing for the screen. Men Without Women, unfortunately, is hard to find today, but its successor, Born Reckless, is a fine old mess, half gangster melodrama, half roistering Army comedy, with one opening shot of night in the city that shows what Ford could do, in terms of composition and atmosphere, when he tried. (George Schneidermann lit this film, but all the others around this time were photographed by Joe August.) Up The River, which introduced Spencer Tracy and Humphrey Bogart to the screen, is more successful in its outrageous way — a prison drama revamped into comedy to escape from the shadow of M-G-M's successful The Big House. There is not too much bother with continuity in this one, but some recognisable Ford touches of slapstick and sentiment; the handling is fast and free and the comedy of bad men behaving like naughty boys is artlessly disarming.

Ford did not immediately commit himself to collaboration with Nichols: he was not to desert the commercial highway so soon. His second film in 1931 was a straight theatrical adaptation, from a sentimental Broadway comedy success, The Brat. Once again, after a vivid and stylish opening — a police round-up of prostitutes and a session in a New York night court — this lapses into straightforward reproduction as the pompous playwright takes a spirited, disrespectful waif into his stuffy household, so that he can study 'a Rose in the Gutter'. The playing is competent, there is a swing in the stage-set garden, swans on the pond and a windmill. J. Farrell MacDonald is the butler and there is a look-in for Ward Bond. The nicest moment is provided by Victor McLaglen as a well-muscled artist's model, beating himself despairingly at the sight of a Vorticist drawing of his torso. Then economic difficulties at Fox took Ford away for his next three pictures. Arrowsmith was a reputable success for Sam Goldwyn, and Airmail (for Universal) introduced him to another writer, the ex-Navy Frank Wead, who was to become a friend, the author of one of his greatest films and himself the subject of a late Ford picture, The Wings of Eagles. These two (which I have not managed to see) were followed by Flesh, a romantic essay in comedy-

pathos for M-G-M, starring Wallace Beery as a simple-minded German wrestler, infatuated with an ex-convict girl who is already involved with a ruthless swindler. There is some nice, rather touching comedy in this, some hard knocks at American show-biz opportunism, and a first-rate unsentimental performance by Karen Morley: finally, though, the picture slides into melodrama, sentimentalism and the Big Fight. (Moss Hart's dialogue conveys the style: 'Mama and I have bet all our savings on the big fight.' 'There's something I've got to tell you'. 'No — no — not now, darling.') It was only after this that Ford returned to Fox, to work again on a film dialogued by Dudley Nichols. Pilgrimage (1933) was another 'Mother' story by I. A. R. Wylie, following sad, over-possessive Hannah Jessop to the battlefields of France, together with a group of Gold Star Mothers, to visit her son's grave. It is inevitably a sentimental picture, but one with a certain sober power, distinguished by touches of imagination and sympathy that show again how Ford, for all his toughness, would always respond to the pathos and inspiration of motherly love.

None of all this activity would lead one to expect the artistic deliberation, the symbolism and style of a picture like The Informer: Ford's career at this time, indeed, recalls rather the unpretentious, wide-ranging professionalism of his work in the early and mid-twenties. He could still turn his hand to pretty well anything, and he was quite happy to — provided the terms were good. He was a 'money director', as he boasted to Sol Wurtzel of Fox, the man for 'a good commercial picture'. One may guess at a defensiveness behind the aggressiveness, a creative uncertainty that needed to be screened by an assumption of philistinism. Perhaps he was shielding himself from the challenge of Dudley Nichols when he told his agent he was 'a journeyman director, a traffic cop in front of the camera, but the best traffic cop in Hollywood'. This was certainly not the whole of his ambition, however much he liked to pretend that it was. Nor, we may guess, was it just the 'traffic cop' side of Ford's talent that prompted Sol Wurtzel to assign him in 1933 to direct Fox's top box-office star, Will Rogers. This was the start of a relationship that soon showed itself to be a special one: Ford and Rogers did three pictures together during the next three years, and whether or not Ford thought of them as journeyman work, Dr. Bull, Judge Priest and Steamboat Round The Bend turned out to be pictures of exceptional success (not just commercially) in the perspective of his career. Films of 57

Flesh (1932). Ford with Wallace Beery as Polokai, the simple German wrestler, and other members of the cast.

particular charm, particular intimacy, they point forward as clearly as any of his work up to this time to the poetic achievement of his maturity.

Will Rogers was not exactly an actor; he was an original, a skilled performer who came to the movies with a personality already formed: friendly, idiosyncratic and appealing. Born in 1879, his ancestry was said to be part Irish, part Cherokee Indian. He had been a ranch hand in his youth, then twirled ropes in various Wild West shows, moving on to Vaudeville shows in which he developed his gift for homely, sardonic comment on politics and the ways of the world. He was in musical comedy on Broadway and had a silent movie career of modest success. It was only with sound that he could achieve stardom, for his was a personality that needed the power and the charm of words to express itself with full effect.

It was not a twentieth century personality. Rogers came out of the West, not out of the Big City; he deliberately evoked the wisdom of the saloon, the crackerbarrel, the front porch. His was the sagacity of peasant tradition, sceptical of modern ways and facile ideas of progress. The three films Ford made with him were all from stories set in the past: Dr. Bull, from a novel by James Gould Cozzens, in a small provincial town in the twenties; Judge Priest, from stories by Irvin S. Cobb, in the 19th-century post-Civil War South; and Steamboat Round The Bend on the Mississippi of the same period. (Dudley Nichols worked on the scripts of the last two, together with Lamar Trotti, who five years later was to give Ford Young Mr. Lincoln; but they do not seem to have been assignments to which he attached much importance.) Naturally, since they were all chosen as vehicles for Will Rogers, the stories have a world in common. They are all comedies, strong in sentiment: their values are the values of community, and their themes crystallise communal values too. Dr. Bull struggles against prejudice and vested interest to save his town from a typhoid epidemic. Judge Priest sees to it that local prejudice and mean-mindedness do not victimise a proudly secretive

Top right: Will Rogers as Dr John Pearly with Francis Ford in Steamboat Round the Bend. *Right:* Judge Priest: *Will Rogers and Hattie McDaniel; Anita Louise; Henry B. Walthall tells his story of Civil War heroism; Francis Ford as the disrespectful jury member.*

58

Steamboat Round the Bend *(1935). The New Moses (Berton Churchill) leads his disciples into baptism.*

outsider. *Dr. John Pearly in* Steamboat Round The Bend, *who spends his time sailing up and down the Mississippi in his river boat, peddling patent medicine and exhibiting his collection of historic waxworks, wins the steamboat race — and sacrifices his precious collection as well as his entire stock of strength-giving Pocahontas mixture — to save his nephew from an unjust hanging.*

The world of these films is lyrical as well as comic; there are hymns and songs and a parade at the end of Judge Priest *which evokes pride in a common past as well as comradeship in the present. The style is light, with a relaxation that matches Rogers' own habit of wry throwaway. All three films are photographed by George Schneidermann, with images that are high-keyed, unstressed, romantic in a delicate way quite different from the emphatic, sometimes portentous manner of Joe August. There is a scene in* Judge Priest *which perfectly evokes the casual, sly, poetic humour of the style. The Judge is writing a letter. Aunt Dilsey (Hattie McDaniels), his faithful, fussy black housekeeper, is hovering around inquisitively with a duster. She is singing a spiritual, covering her curiosity. The Judge, perfectly aware of her manoeuvre, joins in full-throatedly*

from time to time; but she does not get to see the letter. It is a little scene, surely improvised, that evokes perfectly the humour, the mutual affection and the hierarchic consent on which their relationship is based: it is funny and it is warm. The 'democracy' of this world is not, of course, egalitarian, nor is its sense of destiny at all grand. Meanness, intolerance, injustice, pomposity — these are the evils against which, from day to day, a man must stand.

Judge Priest is perhaps the first of Ford's heroes to carry on a living, conversational relationship with his dear departed. He talks to his dead wife's picture in the manner of the lonely, the sight of his nephew and his girl walking together on a moonlit lawn conjures up the ghosts of his own youth, and he carries his stool out to sit and chat in the evening by his wife's grave. Abrasive and warm-hearted, wise without sophistication, serious with humour — one can understand how this character struck sympathetic chords in John Ford. Did he find echoes here of his early mentor and friend Harry Carey (they were almost exactly the same age, Rogers the younger by a year)? The men had much in common: the same modesty, the same pride, the same dogged honesty. Even the same pleasant, craggy looks, with the same undapper cowlick that tended to fall across the forehead. Carey of course was an actor, while Rogers was a humorist; but both brought an unmistakable and inimitable integrity to their performances. Perhaps most significantly, both conveyed without effort the idea that they were men of justice. Rogers' comedy, in fact, was always that of a moralist, concerned with what was right and wrong, certain and steadfast in his choices. Ford's nature was the same. And although for a time his poet's progress seemed to take him along a rather different path, this was the way to which he would return.

Judge Priest *(David Landau, Will Rogers). Like many a Ford hero to come, the Judge likes to sit and share thoughts at a dear one's grave.*

The next year brought Ford and Nichols together again:

'I was working at Fox again, when Ford, who had gone to RKO to make a modest film from Philip McDonald's war novel *Patrol*, called me, in some urgency. He was to start shooting in about ten days — and had no script. What had been done he considered a mess and unshootable. Eager to help, I got leave from Fox and we sat down together with the novel, taking a fresh concept and starting from scratch. I wrote, and Ford would spend part of the time with me. The script was finished in eight days, very long days I must say . . .'

From this script Ford made *The Lost Patrol*, and won with it considerable critical, and reasonable box-office success. During their work together on it he had broached to Nichols the idea of filming Liam O'Flaherty's novel *The Informer*, but since he was unable to get any producer or studio to back it, they proceeded no further with the project. Instead Ford made his second Will Rogers feature, *Judge Priest* (on the script of which Nichols collaborated with Lamar Trotti, a young newspaperman new to Hollywood), which he followed with a speedy and very successful comedy, *The Whole Town's Talking*. This story of a timid clerk who finds that he is the double of a ruthless killer on the run from the police (Edward G. Robinson in a double role) was written by Jo Swerling and Robert Riskin — later Capra's regular collaborator. Like *The Lost Patrol*, it drew

Left: The Informer. *Ford and Victor McLaglen watch the shooting.*

considerable critical attention on its director. And, propitiously, it was at this time that Ford had the good fortune to encounter Cliff Reid, a producer at RKO, who had the vision and the courage to back his project against considerable resistance from the studio, for a film of *The Informer.* Nichols agreed to work on the script for a figure considerably lower than his usual fee, and Ford's arrangement was for a percentage of the takings. The film was from the start a labour of love.

Whatever one's estimation of *The Informer* today, there is no disputing the historical importance of the film, or its impact on contemporary critics. As Theodore Huff wrote (what he says is no longer true but it well expresses critical opinion of fifteen or so years back): 'Nearly every list of "ten best pictures of all time" includes this film. Many consider it the greatest talking picture ever made in America. It is as much a landmark in the history of the sound film as *The Birth of a Nation* is in the silent era.' The extraordinary impression created by *The Informer* must be attributed in part at least to the contrast it presented to characteristic Hollywood productions of the time. A deliberate aesthetic experiment, it was above all a film of precise and pre-determined style; and the style was one that ran quite contrary to the predominantly naturalist tradition of American cinema. Dudley Nichols' own account of the preparation of the picture is of great interest.

'I had just completed a script for de Mille, when Ford and Cliff Reid called me with enthusiasm. They had obtained approval to film *The Informer,* against much studio resistance...I wrote the script at white heat in a phenomenally short time, and there never was another draft — the only script I can remember in which there were never any changes or revisions or further drafts. I had of course been mulling the story for a long time, and was full of it, had been gathering ideas as to how to do it. I had a few talks with Ford beforehand, but nothing specific was discussed. Then we had one fruitful session together with Max Steiner, who was to write the music; Van Polglase, who was to do the sets; Joe August the cameraman; and a couple of technicians. This, to my mind, is the proper way to approach a film production — and it is, alas, the only time in 25 years I have known it to be done: a group discussion before a line of the script is written.'

Summing up the intention of *The Informer,* Nichols writes that '... stylized symbolism was the key to the whole thing. I brought to the script, and Ford brought to the direction of this film everything I had learned and all that he knew. Never since have I been able to work so freely or experimentally.' It is not surprising that a film made with such devotion to a completely unorthodox conception should have filled its producers with alarm. 'Even after the preview the RKO head looked disgruntled and said "We should never have made it!" Ford and I walked out from the preview past glum faces...' And at first it looked as though the RKO head was right. First shown to the world at the huge Radio City Music Hall in New York, *The Informer* (to quote *Variety*) 'opened poorly and never recovered'. It lasted a week. Yet, on its release through the country, the miracle somehow occurred: critics noticed the picture favourably, and the news spread by word-of-mouth. The film returned again to New York, and this time achieved great success. When the Academy awards were announced at the end of the year, *The Informer* captured four of them: Ford won his first Oscar for his direction, and Nichols for his screenplay. Victor McLaglen was voted the best actor of the year for his performance as Gypo Nolan and Max Steiner's score was voted the year's best film music.

The Informer. *Gypo (Victor McLaglen) tempted to betray his friend for the price of a passage to America.*

3

'John Ford: Incontestably the *maître* of the American sound cinema since his outstanding trio of 1934/5 — *The Lost Patrol, The Whole Town's Talking, The Informer...*' This entry from Henri Colpi's *Le Cinéma et Ses Hommes* shows the impact made by Ford's work at this time, and the new eminence in world cinema which it was beginning to earn him. Yet three further busy years were to elapse, and eight films, before circumstances again combined with such favour. *The Informer* marked no clear way ahead. The RKO Front Office was no doubt relieved by its financial success (a very low-budget production, it must comfortably have recouped its costs), as well as by the concomitant prestige — but they showed no eagerness to repeat the experiment. Immediately after it, Ford returned to Fox, where he directed two stories of nineteenth-century America, *Steamboat Round the Bend*, and *The Prisoner of Shark Island*. The first was scripted by Nichols in collaboration with Lamar Trotti; the second, the story of Dr. Samuel Mudd, a country doctor unjustly condemned to life imprisonment for participation in the murder of Lincoln, was the work of a writer new to Ford, Nunnally Johnson.

At the time, however, Ford was clearly more interested in the style of film-making represented by *The Informer*, and by his collaboration with Dudley Nichols. In an interview given when he was making his next picture, *Mary of Scotland*, for RKO (from a script by Nichols), he made no allusion to his films for Fox, but concentrated rather on his

The Lost Patrol. *Billy Bevan, Victor McLaglen, Reginald Denny, Boris Karloff.*

battle for the right to experiment: 'They've got to turn over picture-making into the hands that know it. Combination of author and director running the works: that's the ideal. Like Dudley Nichols and me. Or Riskin and Capra . . .' But for all the honours that had been heaped upon them, the partners were finding no easy road forward. 'We did *The Informer*. Does that make it any easier to go ahead with O'Casey's *The Plough and The Stars*? Not for a second. They *may* let us do it as a reward for being good boys. Meanwhile we're fighting to have the Abbey Players imported intact, and we're fighting the censors and fighting the so-called financial wizards at every point.'* These fights were lost. RKO's price for the Abbey Players turned out to be the starring of Barbara Stanwyck, and the romantic aspects of the story were disproportionately emphasised to 'Front Office' dictation.

But the failure of *The Plough and the Stars* could not be blamed wholly on the RKO front office. The fight to bring the Abbey Players to Hollywood was won — Barry Fitzgerald plays his brilliant Fluther, cocky, characteristic and outrageous; Denis O'Dea shows he must have been an excellent Covey in the theatre, and Eileen Crowe presents a formidable front as Bessie Burgess. (F. J. McCormick, unfortunately, is wasted as a very diminished Brennan). It is true that Nora Clitheroe's scenes are given too much emphasis, and disastrously, since she has little to do but whine; but Barbara Stanwyck acts the part very adequately — she is certainly better than Heather Angel in *The Informer* — though she is not well directed. The film's failure would seem to be largely the fault of Ford himself and his determination to turn O'Casey's ironic tragedy into a romantic and sentimental celebration of the struggle for Irish independence. Scenes from the play, shredded and theatrically performed, alternate with 'heroic' IRA parades and stagey tableaux in the beleaguered Post Office. Yet another conflicting strand is provided by extensive documentary sequences, with banal commentary, of the Troubles

---

* *John Ford: Fighting Irish* — Emanuel Eisenburg — New Theatre, April, 1936. Another passage in the same interview gives Ford's description of the conditions under which he and his contemporaries were at this time directing pictures at 'four of the major studios'. 'The director arrives at nine in the morning. He has not only never been consulted about the script to see whether he likes it or feels fitted to handle it, but he may not even know what the full story is about. They hand him two pages of straight dialogue or finally calculated action. Within an hour or less he is expected to go to work and complete the assignment the same day, all the participants and equipment being prepared for him without any say or choice on his part. When he leaves at night, he has literally no idea what the next day's work will be . . .'

Above: The Plough and the Stars *(1936). Una O'Connor, Eileen Crowe, Barbara Stanwyck, Preston Foster, Barry Fitzgerald. Right:* Mary of Scotland *(1936): Katherine Hepburn.*

and after, including even a speech by de Valera. The real lesson of *The Plough and the Stars* was that Ford's Irishness would always be a thing of romance and fantasy, and could never encompass the political and social realities of twentieth-century Ireland. That is why *The Quiet Man* succeeds — as a poetic comedy, a fairy tale.

It is reported that Ford refused ever to view the completed version of *The Plough and the Stars*. Returning to Fox, he was assigned to direct Shirley Temple in a free adaption of Kipling's *Wee Willie Winkie*. He followed this with *The Hurricane*, a spectacular romance for Samuel Goldwyn. His production for 1938 consisted of two further undistinguished programme pictures for Fox.

Ford's recovery from this creative nadir was characteristic in its brilliance, its unexpectedness, and its rejection of compromise. There was no intermediate period of re-ascent. Early in 1939 he directed *Stagecoach* for Walter Wanger, an independent producer. Returning to Fox he made *Young Mr. Lincoln*, and followed that with *Drums*

65

Stagecoach: the stage and its cavalry escort cross Monument Valley. Ford's first use of his best-known, best-loved location on the Arizona-Utah border.

Along the Mohawk. January, 1940, saw the release of *The Grapes of Wrath*. These four films appeared, one after the other, in a period of just under a year — surely one of the most extraordinary creative achievements in the history of the cinema. It is not merely that they were successful, or that they offered Ford the opportunity to express himself that had been denied him since *The Informer* or *The Prisoner of Shark Island*. Though driven underground, his talent had continued to develop during these dismal years: it became suddenly clear that it had reached a new maturity. The style was surer, and the feeling more intense, more wholly personal. The one informed the other, and produced great film art.

These films may be said to have constituted for Ford a rediscovery of America. For the first time since *Shark Island, Stagecoach* took him out into the open air of America's past, and the winds that blew there proved invigorating. Dudley Nichols wrote the script, from a short story by Ernest Haycox called *Stage to Lordsburg* — the account of an adventurous trip by stage through the Apache country of New Mexico in the eighties. By contrast, the film which followed differed in almost every respect, except for its equally vivid evocation of a far period of American history. Where *Stagecoach* gallops magnificently, *Young Mr. Lincoln* (whose script was the work of Lamar Trotti) advances with a leisurely grace; where the first distributes its attention equally round a chance group of accentuated characters, the second concentrates chiefly on a single, heroic figure; and where the earlier film has the vigorous appeal of masterly prose narrative, its successor has a quieter and deeper-reaching quality of poetry.

In both these two films, Ford used for the first time actors who were to play often for him in later years — and their difference strikingly epitomises the difference between the films themselves. *Stagecoach* introduced the rugged and unassuming personality of John Wayne, a friendly player who

Right top: Drums Along the Mohawk *(1939).* Ward Bond, Henry Fonda. *Right:* Young Mr. Lincoln *(1939).*

Ford's two most memorable hero-figures both first appeared for him in 1939. Above: Henry Fonda as the young Lincoln. Right: John Wayne as the Ringo Kid. The Yang and the Yin of Ford's poetic soul?

had started as one of Ford's prop-men, and who had starred formerly without much distinction in a number of 'B' Westerns; the young Abraham Lincoln was played by Henry Fonda, an already experienced actor of the most sensitive kind, with a strength and a simplicity of style that matched — one might almost say providentially — those very qualities in Ford's own personality as an artist. This partnership was an immediate success, and continued for three pictures in a row. In Ford's next assignment, *Drums Along the Mohawk,* Fonda appeared as a young settler trying to build a home for himself and his wife in the backwoods of New England at the time of the war of Independence. In the hands of any other director, this episodic story — adapted from a best-selling novel — would probably have been just another romantic period adventure; but shooting in Technicolor for the first time, with plentiful open-air locations, Ford managed to give it depth as well as vividness, moments of tenderness and courage as well as the traditional excitements of Indian chases and attacks. Next, with Fonda as Tom Joad, came *The Grapes of Wrath.*

If its immediate predecessors had shown the development of Ford's gift, both in technical command and in maturity of feeling, it was *The Grapes of Wrath* that proved its consummation. Adapted by Nunnally Johnson from John Steinbeck's book, the script outlined, forcefully and unsparingly, the slow disintegration of a farmer's family, evicted from their land in the dust-bowl of Oklahoma, trekking West in pursuit of employment and self-preservation. Even if the adaptation was more liberal-reformist than radical, the film still told its story with an honesty quite exceptional in a Hollywood film. The realism was matched by Gregg Toland's photography. Powerful and austere (though never inelegant), this was characterised by a subtle sobriety of tone and a consistent grandeur of composition which expressed perfectly Ford's heroic conception. For it is the epic style with which Ford developed the narrative, and his passionate,

The Grapes of Wrath. Top: Tom and Casey cross a dawn skyline to the Joad homestead. Centre left: Casey (John Carradine) tells Tom (Fonda) of his loss of faith. Right and bottom left: the journey West. Right: Tom and Ma (Jane Darwell) survey the Californian Promised Land.

The Long Voyage Home. *The seamen return to their ship at the end of the story, for another voyage. A characteristic Toland image, fatefully chiaroscuro.*

abrasive, tender human commitment, that gives the film its greatness. It is a film of monumental stature, in which the small, infinitely significant details of human suffering and aspiration were yet never lost. Every character has the definition of reality; and, in the forefront, the Tom Joad of Fonda, Jane Darwell's Ma, and John Carradine's Casey, personify all three in their different ways man's inarticulate groping towards social justice and solidarity.

The conviction with which he managed to express this idea in the film of *The Grapes of Wrath* showed unmistakably the fundamental nature and direction of Ford as an artist.

The success of *The Grapes of Wrath*, which in America at least was as popular commercially as it was critically, had the happy result of decisively establishing its director amongst the *grands seigneurs* of the industry. The further films made by Ford before the war interrupted his career were all ventures of artistic ambition, and all distinguished for their polished virtuosity of handling. The first, *The Long Voyage Home,* was made for Walter Wanger as an Argosy Production — a title which presumably implied a particular interest in the film on Ford's part, since it was the name under which he and Merian C. Cooper formed their own production company after the war. Photographed again by Gregg Toland, the film was written by Dudley

Nichols from a sequence of plays by Eugene O'Neill, centred on the relationships and adventures of a group of sailors on a tramp steamer in wartime. Though superficially a realistic subject, *The Long Voyage Home* proved in many ways a return to the familiar Ford-Nichols style of some years back, shot throughout in a virtuoso, heavy-contrast lighting style, and in its final sequences abandoning realism

Tobacco Road *(1941). Elizabeth Patterson, Marjorie Rambeau, Charley Grapewin.*

How Green Was My Valley. *Mr. Morgan and Huw (Donald Crisp and Roddy McDowell)
in the idyllic valley of childhood.*

altogether for the kind of poetic symbolism employed in *The Informer.* Returning after this to Fox, Ford executed a quick turnabout, and made *Tobacco Road,* a markedly idiosyncratic version of the Erskine Caldwell novel, adapted by Nunnally Johnson via the sensationally successful Broadway stage production. This was America again, with a story whose lusty humour and touching sentiment sprang directly from the sympathetic familiarity of its setting and theme — in contrast to the film which followed it, which set Ford the impossible task of recreating on the Fox lot, with a mingled cast of English, American and Irish players, a mining village in early twentieth-century Wales. *How Green Was My Valley* was a 'prestige' commercial picture (which Ford took over from William Wyler in the early stages of preparation), produced in the most lavish style and directed with decorative but rather 'applied' mastery. It is typical that this film won more 'Oscars' (a total of six, including one for its direction) than any other in Ford's career.

It was at this high point that Ford's progress in Hollywood was interrupted by the war, and there came a break in his work as a film maker for which

Ford at Midway, June 1942, holding the 16mm camera with which he filmed the Japanese attack, material edited by Bob Parrish into The Battle of Midway.

he was not unprepared (or even perhaps ungrateful). Frank Nugent writes:

'As early as 1939, Ford was certain the United States would be drawn into the struggle, and he began to urge the importance of a motion picture unit which could be used for reconnaissance, combat photography and documentaries . . . He took the plan to some Navy friends. The best they could do was to assure him of their personal interest; officially it was turned down. Undiscouraged, Ford set about recruiting his volunteers from among Hollywood's cameramen, sound men and editors. They had no status — only the possibility that the Navy might take them in as reservists if it so elected. They had no equipment, so Ford borrowed it from the studios. They needed drill masters, so ex-marine Jack Pennick and old-

time Chief Boatswain's mate Ben Grotzky, a veteran of thirty years in the Navy, were brought in to whip the volunteers into some semblance of military order . . .

'By midsummer of '41, the Navy decided to accept the group as a reserve unit, and ordered it to Washington. There it was broken up into combat camera teams. Ensign Ray Kellogg took a small group to Iceland; his detail was one of the first Navy units to see action in the North Atlantic. When Pearl Harbour was hit, members of the unit were serving in every quarter of the globe. Cameramen from Field Photo filmed the Japanese surprise attack; others serving with the famous Navy Patrol Wing Ten, brought back some of the first pictures of the defence of the Philippines . . . The Navy belatedly started to organise similar teams. So did the Army and the Army Air Forces.

They Were Expendable: *the end of the 34 boat. Marshall Thompson, Arthur Walsh, John Wayne carrying Harry Tenbrook.*

When Brigadier General Donovan was put in charge of the O.S.S., he asked that the Ford unit be transferred to his branch. Thereafter it was to be the official eye of the American high command.'

From 1941 to 1944 Ford served with the Navy, finishing with the rank of Captain (he later attained the rank of Admiral). Since for much of the time he was engaged on secret work, it is impossible to chronicle his activities with accuracy: it is evident, however, that he grabbed his chance of action and naval experience with the zest of one for whom the service had never lost its glamour — and who had been forced to wait nearly thirty years for an opportunity to take a share in it. He was in the Battle of Midway, filming the action; he shot the Navy's part in the raid on Tokyo by the Doolittle squadron; he took part in the raids on Marcus Island and Wotje, led elements of his command in the invasion of North Africa, flew the 'Hump' several times, and filmed the Normandy landing at Omaha Beach on D-day. The material shot by Ford on these expeditions went mostly into the common pool of material, for use by newsreels and official organisations; but there survives one documentary that was shot at least partly by him and made wholly under his jealous supervision — The Battle of Midway (1942). Edited by Robert Parrish, the film

carries the voices of such habitual Ford players as Fonda and Jane Darwell, speaking a text that was almost completely the work of Ford himself.

War service took Ford away from the making of films for some three years at a time when his powers were at their height. One would regret this interruption more had it not led directly to the making of a masterpiece. In 1944 he was released by the Navy to return to Hollywood to produce, for purposes of propaganda, a version of W. L. Whites' They Were Expendable — a plain and unassuming reportage of the part played in the first days of war in the Pacific by a single squadron of Motor Torpedo Boats. Ford undertook the assignment reluctantly; the war was not yet won, and he had no desire to quit the field where members of his own unit were still in action. But, however great his reluctance, it is clear from the result that the subject and theme of They Were Expendable stirred and inspired him as he had not been since The Grapes of Wrath. The film he made, which was shot for him by his old associate Joseph August with a sober eloquence of style which forewent completely the earlier photographic mannerisms of mist and backlight, had from beginning to end the vividness and force of profound personal experience, the sincerity and purpose of a dedicated work. As if to signal this, 73

My Darling
Clementine. *Wyatt
Earp (Henry Fonda)
invites Clementine
(Cathy Downs) to
church.*

Ford's credit carried his rank as well as his name: Captain, U.S.N.R. So did that of his author (Cmdr. Frank Wead), his cameraman (Lt. Cmdr. Joseph August), his second unit director (Capt. James Havens) and his leading actor (Cmdr. Robert Montgomery): all of them had served with the Navy, and Montgomery had commanded a squadron of P.T. boats in the Pacific. Although designed as a work of propaganda, the film's intentions were much higher and more serious than that term might imply: its values and its faith were those of *The Grapes of Wrath* — love and brotherhood, loyalty, the spirit of endurance that can wring victory from defeat. The war was still being fought when Ford started shooting *They Were Expendable*; yet he was somehow able to transcend the immediacy of its experience completely. Nothing, perhaps, that he ever did showed more clearly his creative genius than his ability to give this film the poetic authority of emotion recollected, detached, transformed into art.

By the time *They Were Expendable* was released, the war was over; it was received with respect, but it had missed its moment, and neither critics nor public were in the mood to appreciate the greatness of the achievement. In 1946 Ford reluctantly bid farewell to the Navy and returned to the profession of motion picture director. As if to get his hand in to the routine of commercial production again, the first story he undertook was a Western, for his home studio of Twentieth Century-Fox. (He had not made a Western since *Stagecoach* in 1939.) *My Darling Clementine* was a new version of a story filmed

already at least twice — 'Wyatt Earp, Frontier Marshal' — based on the duel between that legendary hero of the West and the notorious Clanton family, in the remote mining township of Tombstone. But the film proved much more than a remake. With Fonda playing Earp, in one of his most original and endearing characterisations, Ford produced a rich and elegiac picture, as freshly evocative as ever, enlivened by a deep and serious sympathy with the values and code of behaviour of its vanished world. The success of the film did not however reconcile him to the idea of returning to his former position at Fox, to work under Zanuck's nagging supervision, restricted by studio policy in his choice of subject and players. A desire for independence was in the air, felt commonly by a number of prominent Hollywood directors, returning from their war experience in the world outside with eyes more open than before. Just as Wyler, Capra and Stevens banded together to form their own Liberty Films, Ford extricated himself from his contract with Fox, and joined forces with the veteran producer and open-spaces director Merian C. Cooper. Together they set up an independent producing company, Argosy Pictures, to release films through RKO Radio, the company for which Ford had made *The Informer* twelve years before.

My Darling Clementine: *Sunday morning sequence. Marshal Earp has his hair cut and escorts Clementine Carter to the meeting where the townsfolk celebrate the founding of Tombstone's first church with a 'dang-blasted good dance'.*

The Fugitive (1947). Henry Fonda, J. Carroll Naish.

4

Liberty proved intoxicating: Ford had no inclination to play safe. For his first venture as an independent producer-director, he undertook a version of Graham Greene's novel *The Power and the Glory,* for which he renewed his old association with Dudley Nichols. Mr Nichols describes the adaptation of this difficult subject.

'This project we had talked about for years, but no studio would back it. Now Ford was independent, with Merian Cooper, and he wanted to do it. I said I was sure it would not make any profit, but I was eager to script it. We soon realised it was impossible to script the Graham Greene novel (*The Labyrinthine Way* it was called here), on account of censorship. His novel was of a guilty priest, and we could have no such guilty priest. It was a wonderful tale, I thought, and after I had worked at its impossible problems for a while, I suggested writing an allegory of the Passion Play, in modern terms, laid in Mexico, using as much of Greene's story as we dared. Ford liked the idea. I did a long draft but was dissatisfied — on the point of throwing it over. Yet Ford showed enthusiasm, and he came to my office at RKO for about a week or ten days, and from what I had written, and from the novel, and from our own ideas, we redictated the script.'

The work of adaptation over, Ford moved with a small unit and six or seven actors (headed by Henry Fonda) to Mexico, where he allied himself with a group of Mexican film makers. These included the director Emilio Fernandez, who became Ford's associate producer, and his cameraman, Gabriel Figueroa — who have been together responsible for a number of picturesque, visually lush Mexican film romances. The actors Pedro Armendariz and Dolores del Rio (both of whom had worked frequently for Fernandez) were cast for leading roles, and small parts and extras were cast from native talent.

As Dudley Nichols had forecast, *The Fugitive* (as the film was finally named) was a commercial failure; nor, however, did it achieve much success of any other kind. Taking full advantage of his hard-won freedom from Front-Office control, Ford shot it with absolute self-indulgence, departing considerably from the script where the fancy took him. He turned out a long, ponderous film, whose slowness of pace was unsupported by any true dynamism of conception. Superbly photographed in a style of unrestrained opulence, its atmosphere was suffocatingly 'arty'; and the actors were either poor or (in Fonda's case) plainly uncomfortable in their roles. It was a discouraging debut for the Argosy Picture Corporation.

Ford has never admitted to regretting *The Fugitive,* but its considerable financial loss turned him decisively away from this style of film making, and it marked the end of his association with Dudley Nichols. Instead, he set to work to recoup his losses, with a succession of pictures of sure commercial appeal. He turned back to American history, to the Frontier, to the West.

Fort Apache: *outpost life. Contrasting commanders, Colonel Thursday (Henry Fonda) and Captain York (John Wayne) take the salute from a party of recruits.*

This new approach, and the need to build up a film making team without the resources of a major studio to draw on, brought Ford in the succeeding years a number of new associates, and deprived him of others. Up to now the actor most closely linked with his best work had been Henry Fonda. But this remarkable collaboration was drawing to an end: in the films which followed, John Wayne took over the role of the Ford hero. New writers appeared. Nichols apart, the scenarists who had been responsible for some of his most notable films were under contract to Fox, and no longer available to Ford even if he had wished to use them. The majority of his Argosy productions were scripted by Lawrence Stallings, a veteran writer of long and varied experience, and by Frank Nugent, a newcomer to the industry, who had formerly been film critic on the *New York Times*. In his colour films, Ford worked regularly with a cameraman new to him, Winton Hoch; though several of his black and white pictures in these years were photo-graphed by Bert Glennon, who had been his cameraman on *Shark Island, Stagecoach, Young Mr Lincoln* and *Drums Along the Mohawk*.

The genesis of the first film in this series, *Fort Apache*, is described by Frank Nugent:

'I had known Ford slightly when I was motion picture critic of the *New York Times*. Our paths crossed again when I did the *Saturday Evening Post* article on him in 1947. After the article was finished, I dropped in to see him one day, and he started talking about a picture he had in mind. "The cavalry. In all Westerns, the cavalry rides in to the rescue of the beleaguered wagon train or whatever, and then it rides off again. I've been thinking about it — what it was like at a cavalry post, remote, people with their own personal problems, over everything the threat of Indians, of death ..." I said it sounded great. And then he knocked me right off my seat by asking how I'd like to write it for him. When I stumbled and stammered, he grinned and said he thought it would be fun. He gave me a list of about fifty books to read — memoirs, novels,

Left: She Wore a Yellow Ribbon *(1949). Captain Brittles and Sergeant Quincannon (Wayne and McLaglen). Right:* Three Godfathers *(1948). Right to left: John Wayne, Harry Carey Jnr., Pedro Armendariz.*

anything about the period. Later he sent me down into the old Apache country to nose around, get the smell and the feel of the land. I got an anthropology graduate at the university of Arizona as a guide, and we drove around — out to the ruins of Fort Bowie, and through Apache Pass where there are still the markers "Killed by Apaches", and the dates. When I got back, Ford asked me if I thought I had enough research. I said yes. "Good," he said, "Now just forget everything you've read, and we'll start writing a movie".*

Despite the care that went into the preparation and writing of *Fort Apache* (the inspiration of which was a short story, *Massacre*, by James Warner Bellah), it did not turn out a very satisfactory film. There are many points of interest in the conception, with a concluding irony that tempers the romance, but the shooting was rushed — it was completed in three weeks, and 700,000 dollars under schedule, and it evidently suffered as a result. Archie Stout's photography was far below Ford's usual standard, and the casting was weak, with several of the subordinate characters poorly played and Fonda unhappily miscast as the martinet Colonel Thursday. The story only really became effective towards its close, with a magnificently staged Indian attack, and the massacre of an outnumbered, ill-led detachment of cavalry. A similar lifelessness marked Ford's next Western, a remake in colour of the Peter B. Kyne tale, *The Three Godfathers,* which he dedicated to the memory of his old friend Harry Carey — 'Bright Star of the Early Western Sky'. The film was finely shot, with some remarkable scenes set in the same Death Valley that Stroheim had used for the climax of *Greed*; but its sentimentality and the rather clumsy Biblical parallels of the final sequences, made its last impression a disappointing one.

'. . . In such a context fine images, with their reminiscences of great things past, only further emphasise the tragic decay of a noble talent.'** So wrote a too-quick despairer on the appearance of *The Three Godfathers.* The disappointment was premature: even a cursory examination of Ford's career to date should have suggested the possibility

of the heartening resurgence that almost immediately followed. Adapted from another story of the cavalry by Bellah, also scripted by Nugent and Stallings, *She Wore a Yellow Ribbon* formed in many ways a companion piece to *Fort Apache:* but with the distinction that what was merely conceived in the first film, was realised in the second. Shot again in Technicolor (and again by Hoch who won an Academy Award for his work on it), the picture was one of continual visual delight, extremely well acted (including a most surprising performance from John Wayne as the elderly captain of cavalry), and alive all through with humour, vigour of handling, and bold romantic panache. After an interlude for a single picture at Fox *(When Willie Comes Marching Home* — an amusing, Sturges-type comedy, capably done), Ford made another Western for his own company — *Wagonmaster* — of equally outstanding poetic quality. Unfortunately this lyrical celebration of a hazardous trek west by a Mormon wagon train in the eighteen eighties was prevented by its lack of star players from achieving a wide commercial release; as a result it received almost no critical attention. Outside Britain, it seems never to have been shown in Europe at all.

After *Wagonmaster,* Argosy's connexion with RKO-Radio came to an end. Rejoining the Navy for a spell, Ford made a short documentary, *This is Korea,* on the American Navy's part in the Korean war. This has never, unfortunately, been distributed outside the United States. Meanwhile a new agreement was negotiated for Argosy: its films were now to be handled by Republic Pictures — a relatively small, independent company, whose prosperity was firmly based on a steady output of comedies and Westerns starring such popular favourites as Gene Autry, Roy Rogers and Judy

---

* From a letter to the author. All further quotations from Mr. Nugent are from the same source: for the full text see p. 242

** From an ill-considered review in *Sequence* by the author.

79

Wagonmaster (1950). Travis and Sandy lead the way with Elder Wiggs (Ben Johnson, Ward Bond, Harry Carey Jnr.)

Rio Grande (1950). J. Carroll Naish, John Wayne.

Canova. In recent years, however, a number of distinguished directors (Lang, Welles, Borzage, Milestone) had made single, modestly-budgeted films at Republic; and Ford could presumably expect a greater degree of independence there than he would be likely to obtain at one of the major studios.

The first picture made by Ford and Cooper for release under this contract was another cavalry subject, *Rio Grande*, of less sustained quality than *She Wore a Yellow Ribbon*, though with the same comfortable ease of atmosphere, and a warmth and a rough-hewn vigour of its own. Ford seems indeed to have shot *Rio Grande* with enjoyment, but cheaply and at speed, with his attention straying to the future. For this film was to consolidate his position for a more risky enterprise, and one into which Herbert Yates, the czar of Republic, needed some cajoling — the shooting in Technicolor, chiefly on Irish locations, of *The Quiet Man*, an adaptation of a story by Maurice Walsh which it had long been Ford's ambition to film.

The elements in this tale which made so strong an appeal to Ford are not hard to find. Ireland itself, to begin with; a rich mingling in the story of farce and

The Quiet Man *(1952). Francis Ford, John Wayne, Maureen O'Hara, Barry Fitzgerald.*

fancy, humour and feeling; a setting sufficiently remote from the actual to permit the creation within it of a mythic, personally imagined world; and a central figure, an Irish-American returning with hungry affection to the land of his fathers. And with the pull of these familiar things went the challenge of a new theme: Ford had never managed to tell a love story with much degree of success, and in general the subject was one he had avoided. Now the omens were propitious; and the event conformed. The sunlit geniality of his picture, its authentic quality of romance, its combination of a lusty, benevolent humour with the greatest delicacy of feeling, made it probably — and deservedly — the most widely-loved film of his career.

The outstanding success, on every level, of *The Quiet Man* was in a sense a grand justification of these latter years of independence, of Ford's decision to cut himself off, at least as far as his serious work was concerned, from the resources of the major studios. For if this was a period of sustained commercial success — probably none of his films since *The Fugitive* had lost money — it was equally marked by a wide variation in the quality of his

work. His erratic progress after *The Quiet Man* illustrates this. At the end of 1951, Ford returned to Fox for a single picture — a new version of *What Price Glory?* the bitter, wisecracking war play by Maxwell Anderson and Lawrence Stallings, first filmed by Raoul Walsh in 1926. The rowdy farce and the wry militarism of this obviously appealed to Ford, and there is a good deal that is recognisably personal in his film; but it is far from successful in combining its oddly-assorted elements. The knock-about lacks charm, and the serious side of the story is hopelessly dated. The intrusion of two musical numbers adds a final touch of the bizarre to this strange picture. Critics were understandably confused when, after *The Quiet Man* they found themselves confronted with a film like *What Price Glory?* —which, in turn, was succeeded by a couple as disparate as *The Sun Shines Bright* and *Mogambo*.

The first of these was made by Ford at Republic again, early in 1952: a modestly budgeted production in which he could afford to be as personally indulgent, in story and treatment, as he liked. Pieced together from a suite of three stories by Irvin S.

The Sun Shines Bright. *Ford's idyll of the South, a feudal harmony and content. Lucy Lee (Arleen Whelan) arrives to teach at the village school.*

Cobb, this was a return to nineteenth-century America, with the same Judge Priest whom Will Rogers had played for Ford nearly twenty years before — but this time a Judge Priest at the end of his career, standing for election for the last time. The film is autumnal, leisurely and meandering. Its nobility is unassuming, its affirmation gentle and relaxed, tinged with regret. These qualities only emphasised Ford's estrangement from the Hollywood of the time; its themes of humanity and reconciliation seemed distinctly old-fashioned, its simplicity seemed naïf. When M-G-M engaged Ford to direct *Mogambo*, the commission offered him an escape, as well as the agreeable opportunity to spend some months on location in East Africa. A typical Hollywood extravaganza, tailored to the requirements of Clark Gable and Ava Gardner, the result was distinguished from a hundred other similar films only by its superior camera sense, and by the sly — sometimes charming — humour with which the director made clear his small regard for the romantic complications of the story.

5

'I'm not a career man', Ford has always been quick to protest. But it is an Irish remark, and it means in fact the precise opposite of what it would seem. Ford is not a 'career man' only in the sense that he has never set the dignity of his career above its straightforward professional pursuit. He has not been concerned to establish his title to the name of artist, and then to live up to it. He has preferred to establish himself as a professional, believing above all in the importance of continuing to make films — survival by seeming acquiescence. For all his scorn and conflict with producers, he has always seen himself as part of the industry, not as its opponent. This is part principle, and part, no doubt, a matter of temperament: Ford likes to work. He enjoys making films. And finally the important thing is the use to which he has managed to turn his acquiescence: the astonishing fact that he has been able somehow to preserve his poetic talent unalloyed, continually developing, and to exercise it purely and freshly whenever the opportunity has arrived. This is the explanation of a sequence of films so apparently illogical as *The Quiet Man, What Price Glory?, The Sun Shines Bright* and *Mogambo.*

It is also the explanation of *The Long Gray Line.* After a break in activity of over a year (during which he underwent a serious operation on his left eye), Ford signed to direct a film for Columbia Pictures. This was an adaptation of the best-selling autobiography of an Irish physical-training instructor at West Point, an unwieldy chronicle that spread over three generations and two wars, shot (as contemporary fashion dictated) in colour and CinemaScope. The script itself precluded the possibility of a satisfactory result. Ford surrounded himself with as many of his familiar actors as possible, played up the humorous, sentimental and (above all) the Irish elements in the story, and set out to produce a simple-minded, popular film. In this he may have succeeded; but unfortunately too much in *The Long Gray Line* comes too near the personal world of Ford's own, poetic films for one to be able to accept it with indulgence. Reminiscences of *They Were Expendable* and *The Quiet Man* emphasise the facility of the sentiments, the vulgarisation of Ford's own ideals which is at the heart of the picture.

The case of *The Long Gray Line* emphasises the difficulties that attend Ford's position in Hollywood today — the risks entailed in a policy of subscribing to the system and at the same time reacting against it. For there is no doubt that his vision is an unfashionable one. The values of Ford's work at its best are utterly in opposition to those of films like *On the Waterfront* or *The Blackboard Jungle* (to name two characteristic contemporary 'prestige' successes); while it is significant that the studio for which he worked for so long, and where he was fifteen years ago directing *The Grapes of Wrath* and *Tobacco Road,* now dedicates its resources to 'spectacular' productions in CinemaScope — *The Robe, The Egyptian, Untamed.*

In such a situation compromise is almost inevitable for any director who is not content to spend three years of inactivity for every year he works. The question only remains whether such compromise is significant. In Ford's case there seems little reason to suppose so.

For someone who is 'not a career man', Ford has come a long way: that is the least that can be said for the principle of professionalism that has guided him. In the history of the American cinema, which has been so full of slow or sudden deaths, no other creative director has survived so long the perils of the Hollywood jungle.

She Wore a Yellow Ribbon. *The Cavalry dismounted: 'Only a cold page in the history book...'*

John Ford with his friend William Collier (seated centre), uncredited writer on The Seas Beneath.

2. Artist

'Since the beginning of his career Ford has directed 104 films, of which 90, at least, are mediocre. And it should be realised that his better works owe a great deal to their scenarists, or to the originals from which they have been adapted. This director, whom many would claim to be America's finest, is above all a perfect craftsman, a technician trained by 30 years practice, but who often mistakes technical ability for the art of the film. From many points of view, he is the American Duvivier . . .'

Georges Sadoul, in *Les Lettres Francaises*.

'Because he once gave us *The Grapes of Wrath*, and a couple of more than reasonable movies in the Western tradition, we have got into the habit of expecting from John Ford more than he is able, or even willing to give. Mr. Ford has been consistently and unfairly overestimated.'

Richard Winnington in *The News Chronicle*.

'. . . . I hate pictures . . . Well, I like *making* them of course . . . But it's no use asking me to talk about art.'

John Ford, reported in *Sequence 14*.

On what terms, then, is Ford to be considered as a poet? It must be acknowledged at the outset that we are not dealing with an artist solely and wholly responsible for any of his work. This of course is true of almost any poet in the cinema; but it is less true of directors like Eisenstein, Vigo, Flaherty or Chaplin, who conveniently fulfil the academic postulate that the true *cinéaste* should write his own films, than it is of Ford, who has never, since he made *The Scrapper* in 1917, been credited as his own script writer.

Ford's films had all to be written before they could be directed: this truth is not too elementary to deserve stating. Working with him in varying degrees of collaboration — sometimes very closely, sometimes hardly at all — his writers deserve their credit. But it remains none the less fundamental that the peculiar distinction of these films, their greatness, where that word is applicable — rests in their style. Poetry, declared Housman, is not the thing said, but the way of saying it. Or perhaps more exactly: Poetry is created when the way of saying *becomes* the thing said. In the cinema the only artist

with the power to effect this vital fusion is the director.

Anyway, it is always better to start from fact, and work inwards to theory, rather than vice versa. Ford has made 111 films (perhaps more), of which 25 at least are relatively often to be seen. The surest way of establishing his rank as a creative artist is to examine these, and to endeavour to distil from them any constant poetic personality they may evidence, through whatever differing combinations of writers, producers, cameramen and players.

The variety of this work is considerable — the result, as we have seen, of Ford's choice to work always firstly as a professional craftsman. No doubt it was a misunderstanding of this attitude, as well as an insufficient acquaintance with his best films, which led Sadoul so absurdly to bracket Ford with Duvivier. (There is no excuse for the gratuitous assumption that he 'mistakes' his commercial exercises for works of art.) Obviously any serious examination can start only after pictures like *Four Men and a Prayer*, *Wee Willie Winkie* and *When Willie Comes Marching Home* have been put on one side.

2

Even a cursory glance at what we may call Ford's self-expressive work in the cinema shows him to be to some extent a split personality. Frank Nugent quotes his comments on style. 'He despises (his word) directors' touches. "I try to make people forget they're in a theatre", he says. "I don't want them to be conscious of a camera or a screen. I want them to feel that what they're seeing is real".' One can see that this attitude — without being pressed to the logical conclusion of a style deliberately styleless, as in the case of Rossellini — is reflected in the general sobriety of camera technique in pictures like *They Were Expendable* and *The Quiet Man*. But there is a whole group of films by Ford in which unconsciousness of the camera is hardly possible; in which the photographic style is emphasised almost to the point where it becomes an end instead of a means (he has remarked of *The Fugitive*: 'I just enjoy myself looking at it'); and in which the 'reality' of what goes on on the screen has no connection with its 'realism'. The most remarkable of these films are those which he has made with the collaboration of Dudley Nichols.

The consistency would be less remarkable had the initiation of these films been entirely the work of Nichols. It would certainly simplify matters if one were able to regard Ford (as one has at times been tempted to do) as the simple, intuitive poet, enticed from time to time into a lotus-land of aestheticism by the sophisticated theories of a beguiling writer; but this would be far less than just. Of the three most notable efforts made by Ford and Nichols in this style, two at least originated with Ford (*The Informer* and *The Fugitive*); and the third, *The Long Voyage Home*, seems from its subject, very likely to have done so. His pugnacious Irish-ness (in the film of *The Informer* the Communist organisation of the book is characteristically replaced by the I.R.A., and the Irish police by the British soldiery); his love of the sea; his Catholic faith — these elements in his character explain the appeal of such stories for Ford. It is only reasonable to suppose that their shared qualities of style sprang at least to some extent from his own delight in photographic research, and from his own susceptibility to a certain aesthetic manner. But there is no doubt at all that, in these tendencies, Ford was encouraged by Nichols' belief in the nature and function of the 'artistic lie'.

'Hollywood', Nichols has justly observed, with some justice, 'has been half destroyed by its dead-set at "realism" — making everything appear exactly as it does to the average man, or to a goat, instead of sifting it through the feelings of the artist.' And he goes on to describe the conscious opposition to this attitude which found expression in his films with Ford. '*The Informer* was not realism at all, but a search for the truth through the use of the artistic lie.' This is the approach that is evident also in *The Fugitive* and (less consistently) in *The Long Voyage Home*, both films whose worlds are for the most part deliberately non-realist in conception. Speaking of *The Informer*, Nichols continues 'You sense in this film "a deliberate and devoted stylistic experiment", and you are correct. Ford and I felt that way from the beginning. By this time our two minds worked as one . . . I believe honestly, though I may be mistaken, that it was I who pushed this idea of stylization hardest.' The Dublin sets of *The Informer* were purposely abstracted from life; with effects of light, contrast and design heightened to accentuate the inner drama of Gypo's treachery and punishment. The S.S. Glencairn of *The Long Voyage Home* is similarly isolated — there is only one shot in the film of the ship actually at sail — and

the final sequences of the story takes place in a London as stylized as the Dublin of *The Informer*. *The Fugitive* is shot in settings realistic enough, but which are again lit in such a manner as to disguise their realism; and the whole film is given an atmosphere expressly divorced from identifiable place or time. ('The following photoplay', begins the spoken introduction, 'is timeless . . .')

These films may all be said to take deliberate aim at significance. At first glance, their subjects appear diverse. But if we take into account other films scripted by Nichols for Ford, there emerges a significant fondness for one particular situation: the group, generally of men, thrown together by duty or by hazard, brought face to face with the great finalities of love and death (*Men Without Women, The Lost Patrol, The Long Voyage Home, Stagecoach*). One can see, in the repeated variations on this theme, the essential bias of what Nichols refers to as the 'search for truth' which was the aim of *The Informer* — a repeated attempt, by viewing a collection of characters *sub specie aeternitatis*, to disclose and illuminate some fundamental attributes of the nature of man, and while *The Informer* and *The Fugitive* do not conform to this pattern, each has the similar objective of penetrating beneath appearances, the first to lay bare the spirit of the brutish and baffled betrayer of his friend, and the second to give expression to man's irrational but persistent capacity for religious faith.

Elevation of aim, seriousness of purpose — these are estimable qualities in any artist, and nowhere more so than in the American cinema. It is all the more sad to be forced to the conclusion that an objective survey of the Ford-Nichols corpus reveals, in the perspective of time, a succession of more or less distinguished failures. Their early exercises on the studio production line are not really relevant, nor are Nichols' contributions to the Will Rogers films which he obviously did not take seriously. Of the collaborators' minor works, *The Lost Patrol* now appears crudely melodramatic, *Mary of Scotland* a pretentious essay in the historical-dramatic (with some admittedly impressive effects of lighting and art direction), and *The Hurricane* a picturesque romance, with an extraordinary spectacle as its climax, and a vitality of handling which brings the novelettish situation fitfully to life. Of the still

Top: The Informer. *Right:* The Long Voyage Home. *Deep-focus and heavy-contrast 'expressionism' in Toland's lighting. Yank (Ward Bond) dies, watched by Smitty and Olsen (Ian Hunter, John Wayne); attempted escape.*

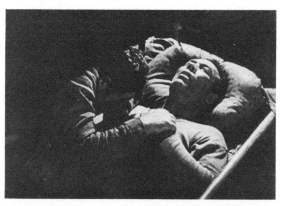

The Informer. *Gypo attends the wake of Frankie McPhillip.*

considerable films, *Stagecoach* stands somewhat apart from the others, and will be considered later; there remain a rather gloomily consanguineous, trio, *The Informer, The Long Voyage Home* and *The Fugitive.*

Of these, the most elaborately or at least consistently worked is probably the first, with its style of formal groupings and (for a film of its place and period) extraordinarily venturesome, expressionist lighting. The influence of the German cinema seems to be conscious; it is certainly strong. The visual continuity, so much praised in the past for its refusal to rely on dialogue, has today rather the painstaking explicitness of a silent film striving to tell its story without the aid of titles — an impression strengthened by Max Steiner's blatant, imitative music.* The scenario's chief merit is its conciseness and compression, rather than its striving to translate every subtlety and implication into literally equivalent images; the film is strongest when it is nearest the book. In this connection it is worth noting that the last scene of all, which has often been condemned as sentimental melodrama — and which Ford himself has apologised for, as a concession to the producers — in fact follows O'Flaherty's description exactly. It is the shooting of it that is at fault — whereby Gypo's conception of the scene becomes that of the film, and objectivity is lost; nor, of course, does Steiner's absolving choir do anything to redeem the error. There is great unevenness in the characterisation: the romance between the leader of the 'Organisation' and the sister of the betrayed man is extremely unconvincing, tritely written and flatly presented by Ford; and indeed much of the acting is weakly theatrical in style. Perhaps the film's greatest, and certainly its most enduring strength is the performance of

* Steiner's misguided contributions to both *The Lost Patrol* and *The Informer* were acutely characterised by the French composer, Maurice Jaubert, himself responsible for such masterly scores as those for *Zero de Conduite* and *L'Atalante,* and for the pre-war films of Carne. 'In *The Lost Patrol* — otherwise an admirable film — the director was apparently alarmed by the silence of the desert in which the story was laid. He might well have realised the dramatic possibilities of silence, but instead he assaulted the ear, without a moment's pause, with a gratuitous orchestral accompaniment which nearly destroyed the reality of the images. Another attitude was well illustrated in *The Informer,* where music was used to imitate the noise of coins falling, and even the gurgling of beer in a man's throat. This is not merely puerile, but a misconception of what music is . . .' *(World Film News,* July, 1936).

The Long Voyage Home. *Ward Bond, Thomas Mitchell and bumboat women.*

Victor McLaglen as Gypo, a lost and lumbering animal, the helpless victim of his uncomprehended instincts — lust and love, generosity and greed, loyalty and treachery all fatally muddled into one. Yet even of this it may be observed that it is not fundamentally keyed to the formal style of the film at all; but, on the contrary, almost 'neo-realist' in its suggestion of actual behaviour — an impression which is borne out by Frank Nugent's account of Ford's methods with McLaglen during the shooting of the picture. 'Ford literally double-crossed him into his Academy award performance. He browbeat him until Gypo's truculent expression couldn't come off. At the close of a long day's shooting, he suggested a quick run-through, of a scene scheduled for the next morning. 'It's only a rehearsal,' Ford assured McLaglen, and then signalled the camera-man and the sound man. . . McLaglen groped his way through the scene trying to catch his cues . . . It played as Ford had known it would.'*

There are similar variations of approach in *The Long Voyage Home*. The script of this was

fashioned by Nichols from a sequence of four one-act plays by Eugene O'Neill, each comprising a different episode in the wartime voyage of the S.S. *Glencairn*, a cargo tramp sailing from the Caribbean to London. The crew carouse with native bumboat women; in an American port a load of ammunition is put aboard, and one of the crew tries to jump ship; a storm in the Atlantic dislodges the ship's anchor and a man is killed; another is suspected of spying by his mates; and finally, in London, one member of the crew breaks away to leave the sea for good, a couple of others are shanghaied on to another ship, and the rest return to the *Glencairn* for the return trip. 'For them', in the words of the final title, 'the Long Voyage never ends.' Such a story offers itself readily for poetic treatment in the Ford-Nichols style, but again the most successful portions of the film are those in which the handling is most straight-forward, and the conception least overtly symbolic: the wild carouse at the start, the comradeship and suspense of the fo'c'stle scenes, the storm and burial at sea, the slow return of the men at the end. In these the playing is vigorous and natural, the feeling is unforced, and Toland's monumental images manage powerfully to convey both the immediate atmos-phere on the cramped and harried little ship, and the

* There are many versions of this story — see also the interview with Donal Donnelly, page 229. All emphasise poor McLaglen's incapacity and the wily ruthlessness of Ford.

89

The Fugitive: *Henry Fonda as the Whisky Priest, glorified.*

sense of allegory behind its voyaging. Elsewhere the material is unsound, and the film rings correspondingly false. Not even Ford can make acceptable the dated melodrama of the episode in which 'Smitty' — the gentleman-ranker who has left his family for the bottle — is taken for a spy, and has to endure his shipmates' open reading of his wife's letters; and when, in the next reel, he is machine-gunned by an enemy plane, one is hard put to stomach the fluttering tarpaulin which dissolves into a Union Jack over his fallen body. More gravely — since it invalidates the poetic heart of the film —the switch to a non-realist, symbolic manner once the sailors are ashore in England jars badly against the best of what has gone before; and in spite of the memorable performance of Mildred Natwick as a frightened prostitute, the last episode fails to persuade. A particular focus of incredulity is provided by the 'pimp' — a characteristic Nichols fate-symbol — played in irritating stage Cockney by J. M. Kerrigan,

the Irish actor who had performed much the same function in *The Informer,* as the toadie who attends Gypo throughout his brief, ecstatic reign.

The emphasis on purely pictorial effect (in itself always suspect), which is evident in both these films, is even more marked in *The Fugitive* — and with even less relevance to the picture's theme. On Gabriel Figueroa's work for Ford, a French writer[*] has commented: 'His aesthetic of the cinema, magnificently sensual . . . falls something short of interior radiation when it is Divine love that is the subject.' The over-luscious images are frequently vulgar in their sentimental appeal: a lame child in a church doorway holding a lighted candle; shadows of men with arms outstretched, crucifixwise; virginal figures reverentially haloed. What the effect of Ford's divagations from the script during shooting may have been, it is of course impossible to

[*] Amedee Ayfre: *Dieu au Cinema* Presse Universitaire de France, 1953.

90

say; but it is unlikely to have been beneficial. The film is almost totally without impetus, moving on a level of facile religious symbolism from one self-conscious tableau to another, while the actors play independently — as is always the case when there is no commonly-comprehended conception to subscribe to. Thus Fonda, as the fugitive priest, stumbles through the film with an air of earnest, but confused naturalism; Dolores del Rio's 'Maria Dolores' preserves throughout the statuesque complacency of a holy postcard; and J. Carroll Naish seizes with exhibitionist relish on every opportunity for overplaying (and they are not few) provided him by the Judas-role of the Police Informer. The film has not even the last merit of honesty: as so often in works of spiritual-political propaganda, every question is begged from the start. As he hears the sound of the shot which puts to death (as he imagines) the last priest in the country, the police officer — atheist and priest-hunter — is seen to finger the sign of the Cross surreptitiously over his heart.

The finally disappointing effect of these films cannot be explained by any assertion of the 'fundamental realism' of the medium. (In the short history of the cinema, experiments in stylisation as varied as Melies' *Trip to the Moon*, Vigo's *Zero de Conduite*, or Eisenstein's *Ivan the Terrible* have fully established its capacity to give expression to the poetically-imagined world as vividly as any other form of art.) It is in their particular worlds that these films are deficient — in a lack of consistency and intensity in their conception. Too often their symbolism is merely banal, inspired, one feels, rather by a belief in the necessity to create symbols, than by an irresistible poetic impulse to do so. To take a single instance: the blind man who appears only once in the novel of *The Informer,* and who fulfils his dramatic function there without strain, is

The Informer. *Katie (Margot Grahame), Ford-Nichols' Magdalene of the streets.*

enlarged in the film into a symbol of glaring obviousness, presented in a manner so portentous as to destroy the possibility of his existence on any level *but* the symbolic. Non-realism in style is not — must not be — synonymous with unreality. These worlds are unreal.

The Informer

3

'Je n'aime la merveille', wrote Alain-Fournier, *'que lorsqu'lle est étroitement insérée dans la réalité.'* One knows better than to ask for statements of aesthetic creed from Ford, but if the other side of what we have called his split personality were gifted with the power of critical self-expression — or with the readiness to declare itself — such is precisely the kind of statement one would expect it to make. During the span of years between *The Informer* and *The Fugitive*, Ford was, as we have seen, producing another series of films (apart from his purely commercial assignments), entirely different in atmosphere and approach. These were not films which came unexpectedly from his talent: they related closely to the pioneering tales of his youth, to the genre pieces he was producing with Will Rogers in the thirties. They were films which he seems generally not to have initiated himself, but which he was able, with increasing authority, to stamp with his own vision, and make speak with his own voice. Unlike the three pictures with Nichols (which take place in Dublin, on a British tramp-steamer, and in a mythical country of the imagination), these are all American subjects, with stories which pass in a context of reality, closely and literally observed. This 'reality' gives substance to what is 'marvellous' in the films — that is to say, what is poetic. The first of them, or at least the earliest that can now be seen, is *The Prisoner of Shark Island*, made shortly after *The Informer*, and released in 1936.

The film starts in Washington, on April 9th, 1865. Peace has been signed, and the Civil War is ended; the people are celebrating with bonfires and dancing in the streets. Shots of the jubilant crowds silhouetted before the flames are accompanied by the sturdy thump of bands which play the Northern march, "Rally Round the Flag". A procession gets under way, heading for the White House; from a high angle we see the cheerful mob crossing a dark, empty square, torches bobbing, a high-stepping couple hilariously leading the way. Before the White House, they come to a halt. A window opens and out on to the balcony steps the President — a weary, bowed figure, an old shawl round his shoulders. He addresses the hushed crowd with gentle words of thanksgiving and reconciliation, ending, '. . . I ask the band to play "Dixie".' There is a moment of silence, as people look at each other in surprise and

The Prisoner of Shark Island. *Warner Baxter, Harry Carey, Ernest Whitman.*

momentary hesitation; they then burst spontaneously into cheers, the band strikes up, and the crowd joins in with the words of the unofficial anthem of the South . . . There could be no better introduction to the other Ford. For all its distance from us in time and space, here is a world made immediately vivid; recreated for us with gusto, an enlivening sympathy, and a simple generosity of emotion; above all bathed in an idealizing light — illuminating in this instance the person of Lincoln — more apt to show what men can be, and should be, than what, to the superficial observation of every day, they actually are.

Written by Nunnally Johnson, *The Prisoner of Shark Island* tells the true story of Dr. Samuel Mudd, a country physician in Maryland, an innocent victim of the policy of political expediency pursued by the American government after Lincoln's death; its theme is this man's persistent courage and integrity in the face of the bitterest injustice. The prologue shows Lincoln in Washington, his public appearance at a performance of *The American Cousin*, and his murder. Booth, his fanatical assassin, is wounded, and breaks his flight at the house of Mudd, who sets his leg for him. The incident is discovered, and, together with half a dozen other suspects, Mudd is tried by a military court for complicity in Lincoln's murder. The judges have been instructed beforehand that, with public opinion in its present inflamed state, the accused must be found guilty. Some are executed; Mudd is sentenced to life imprisonment on the island prison (its name comes from the shark-infested moat which surrounds it) on the Dry Tortugas. With the help of his wife, he makes a daring attempt to escape and seek a retrial; but at the very moment of success he is caught, taken back, and thrown into solitary confinement. When an epidemic of yellow fever breaks out on the island, the governor is forced to ask Mudd for his help; his ungrudging service is instrumental in securing him a pardon.

In theme as well as in style, *The Prisoner of Shark Island* is a film with many points of interest. It is openly patriotic, but its patriotism is of that rarer kind (particularly in the cinema) that does not flinch at criticism. From this point of view its spokesman is the Governor of the prison — an upright man, fair-minded as well as strict (and played, incidentally, by Harry Carey, Ford's old friend and mentor, with the same manly simplicity that brought him such popularity in those early Westerns). Convinced finally of Mudd's innocence, he tells him that he will fight to secure him a pardon '. . . because I do love the flag I serve, and because I

93

The Prisoner of Shark Island. *Accused of complicity in Lincoln's assassination, the prisoners are brought hooded into court. Political expediency demands their condemnation.*

am jealous of its honour.' The film too, in the same unrhetorical manner, loves the flag it serves, and is jealous of its honour. If the ideal spirit of the nation is evoked in the revered figure of Lincoln, and in the national songs that echo through the picture, the other face of democracy and of government is no less feelingly depicted in the opportunist carpet-baggers; the mob calling vengefully for blood; the harsh and inhuman Attorney General who dictates to his judges that they shall find the accused guilty ('. . . with no pedantic regard for the customary laws of evidence') before the trial has even begun. Whether in anger or affirmation, the film's statement is constantly humane: the 'suspects' are shuffled into court, manacled and hooded, to be thrust down one after another in the dock, and brought blinking and dishevelled, like frightened animals, face to face with their implacable accusers . . . In the prison hospital, as Mudd smashes the windows to let out the foetid air, a gaunt, tattered figure rises in the background, bathing himself in the clean wind that comes sweeping

through the ward. These are glimpses that have the force and implication of true symbols — for this world is a real one; the people are real. There is no attempt to keep the story on a permanent level of symbolism; in the relaxed scenes at Mudd's Maryland home (the exteriors are all shot on location), and in characters like Buck, his devoted Negro servant, and his peppery old father-in-law, there is a popular, earthy humour that gives a solid backing to the more highly dramatic episodes. When Buck, who has followed his master to prison, remarks with a musing sigh — 'Maryland sure seems a long way away . . .' — there is a reality in the situation, and in the memory, that gives the moment a sudden, surprising depth of emotion. Just as this is a pointer forward to one of the most characteristic virtues of Ford's developed style —the ability to crystallise in a word or a silence a whole range of underlying feelings; so the character of Mudd himself is the first in a line of recognisably fraternal heroes — a good man in no spectacular sense, conscientious in his work, a kindly master and a loving husband and father; plunged by chance into nightmare, and humanly tempted to bitterness. But his courage prevails. He remains faithful to his ideals, and true to himself — a humble and persistent Mr. Standfast.

The qualities of *The Prisoner of Shark Island* at its best are remarkable; one would not claim that they are consistent. One is used to thinking of Ford as already a fully-equipped craftsman by the time he came to make *The Informer*; but there are passages in *Shark Island* (particularly in the domestic scenes) which show that he had not yet entirely mastered the art of shooting a conversation piece. These scenes are in fact marked by a certain, rather engaging primitivism, accentuated by the playing of Gloria Stuart as Mudd's wife — a charming, flaxen-haired girl, but lacking somewhat the sturdy flesh-and-blood of the majority of the other characters. And where Ford's control is firm (which is during most of the film), the handling varies interestingly, at times maintaining a quite naturalistic style, and at others employing effects that recall the more mannered experiments of *The Informer*. Here and there the set designs are purposely distorted, and there is occasional use of shadow effects, simplified backings and formal grouping of characters. At times the lighting is strongly chiaroscuro, giving an almost formal quality to some of the shots of Mudd in his cell, and accentuating the difference between the idyllic Maryland countryside, and the ugly world of courtroom and prison.

Effective though such contrasts can be, they are liable to break the unity of feeling in a film. By the time Ford came to make *Stagecoach*, three years later, he had achieved a degree of control which enabled him to make his effects within a consistent and homogeneous style. *Stagecoach* stands apart from the other films in this group as being the only one scripted by Dudley Nichols (and also the only one, apart from *They Were Expendable* in 1945, not produced at 20th Century Fox); similarly, it differs from the other surviving films made by Ford with Nichols in that it is the only one to take place in an American setting. It is an adventure story, adapted from a *Saturday Evening Post* story, *Stage to Lordsburg*, by Ernest Haycox. In the turbulent eighties a stagecoach sets out with Cavalry escort to

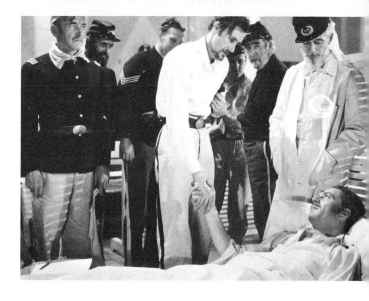

The Prisoner of Shark Island. *Top: execution. Centre: Dr. Mudd (Warner Baxter) makes his bid for escape. Bottom: Mudd's heroism is acknowledged by his gaolers after he has saved the prison from epidemic. The centre group includes Jack Pennick, John Carradine and Francis Ford. Left stands Harry Carey, Ford's old patron and friend, as the Prison Governor.*

Stagecoach: *the chase.*

cross the Apache territory in Utah-New Mexico, *en route* for Lordsburg. Half way through the journey, the stage loses its escort, but the majority of the passengers vote to continue. On the last lap, they are attacked by an Indian war-party; there is a wild, prolonged chase; ammunition is exhausted, and the Indians are closing in when the sound of bugles is heard, blowing the 'Charge'. The Cavalry have ridden out from Lordsburg, and the stage is saved. In writing the screen play of *Stagecoach,* Nichols does not seem to have been tempted to enlarge the symbolic possibilities of the story: briskly constructed and incisively characterised, the script sticks to events, and Ford's direction urges these forward with terrific zest. From the first scenes in the little Western town, with the dusty stagecoach drawn up outside the one 'Hotel' in the place, the rakish gamblers at their tables, and the resentful prostitute being hustled down the street under the virtuous eye of the Ladies' Watch Committee, the observation of place and people is continually acute. The good-hearted prostitute, the young outlaw being taken in for trial, the romantic Southern gambler, the snobbish army wife, the drunken doctor and the timid commercial traveller — none of these is profoundly drawn, but each is presented

with a sharpness, an eye for the detail and interplay of personality, which gives continual colour and variety to the steadily mounting tension of the action.

In *Stagecoach,* it is above all the action which counts. In this sense, it is not a poetic film. It is not concerned to achieve existence on anything but this single level; its excellence is the excellence of masterly narrative prose, taut, dynamic, and irresistibly holding. These virtues are of course characteristic of Ford — the swinging rhythm, the broad landscapes, the hectic excitement of the chase across the flats — but the very urgency of the drive leaves little room for the more intimate revelations of style. The contrast with Ford's next film, *Young Mr. Lincoln,* could hardly be more marked.

Written by Lamar Trotti, a Southern newspaperman who had started his work in Hollywood writing with Dudley Nichols (they collaborated on *Judge Priest* and *Steamboat Round The Bend), Young Mr. Lincoln* is essentially an imaginative portrait of Lincoln in his early years — as the youthful New Salem storekeeper, and as the uncouth lawyer of Springfield five or six years later. Its slender story is worked from a basis of fact: the tragic romance with Ann Rutledge, the meeting with Mary Todd, and the embryonic rivalry with Stephen Douglas. The crucial trial for murder of two innocent boys, which

Young Mr. Lincoln. *Abe (Henry Fonda) rides into Springfield to start practising law.*

Young Mr. Lincoln. *Solomon prepares to give judgement (Henry Fonda, Russell Simpson, Charles Halton).*

forms the dramatic centre of the film, is drawn from a real case — though one which took place at a later period in Lincoln's life. It is not a plot that relies much on action. Apart from the single main episode, the incidents are small ones, and their significance implied rather than directly stated. All through the film the movement is leisurely, the mood poetic. It is recognisable that the subject sounded in Ford the same chords of response that had given such a quality of emotion to *The Prisoner of Shark Island.*

The reason is not elusive. The story of Dr. Mudd was one that could have borne a number of emphases: Ford responded to the moral one, and placed at the heart of his picture an ideal of human conduct. In Lincoln he was offered a hero who could — indeed, who must — represent the same ideal with even greater force. The difficulty of the task can hardly be overestimated; for while it is relatively simple to show courage in action, and integrity threatened by corruption, it is less simple to show these qualities simply *existing,* to reveal, through a man's slightest words and gestures, his inward virtue, and convincingly to suggest a future greatness. This is the achievement of *Young Mr. Lincoln.* In so far as it can be analysed at all, it can be said to be done by a style of extreme directness and simplicity, itself expressive of the very qualities that had to be shown as existing in its hero. The advance since *Shark Island* is even more evident here than in *Stagecoach.* Although every set-up of the camera is chosen with the utmost care, and many of the

images have a quite formal dignity of composition, so closely are they attuned to the dramatic intensity of the moment that there is no sense of stiffness, or even of deliberation, about them. The tempo of the film is slow, but never undynamic: it is charged everywhere with the sense of the importance and pleasure of everything we see, not merely in such moments of tension as Lincoln's speech from the prison steps to the attacking lynch-mob, or the passionate outburst in the courtroom by the mother of the accused boys, but also in passages of relaxation and sheer fun: the lively charm of Springfield's roistering Independence Day celebrations — the military parade, with the veterans of the War of Independence nodding from their antique barouche; the Pie Judging and the Rail Splitting Contest; and the Tug-of-War which Abe wins by tying his end of the rope to a buggy and whipping up the horse. These shifts of key, from farce to the gentlest comedy, from comedy to the most serious issues of life and death, are faultlessly managed, with no more jarring impression than we get from such variations in life in the behaviour of some sensitive and serious, but not unhumorous person we know. And over the film's 'present' falls constantly the shadow of Lincoln's future. It is impossible to be unaware that this is a great man.

With *Young Mr. Lincoln* Ford may be said to have achieved maturity as an artist. He had found, that is to say, his theme, and he was master of a technique fine enough to give worthy expression to it. And in

Young Mr. Lincoln. *Top: The brief idyll of Abe's love for Ann Rutledge (Henry Fonda and Pauleen Moore). Above: Independence Day celebrations at Springfield: Abe acts as pie taster.*

Young Mr. Lincoln: *Fonda's Lincoln. The hick lawyer becomes the man of Destiny.*

Henry Fonda he had found at the same time its most subtle and sympathetic interpreter. Ford's skill in the direction of actors had always been proverbial; he had acquired the reputation of being able, magician-like, to conjure good performances out of players whose acting elsewhere is seldom better than mediocre. This, however, is less the result of magic than of the acutest human response, an intuition of the natural quality of personality in a player, and the ability to use that quality in such a way as to make it equally apparent to the world. Poor actors, and those who are also unremarkable people (or people uncongenial to Ford), are likely to be as inadequate in his films as they are in anyone else's; the actors whom he used again and again, with such regularity that they came to be known familiarly as his 'Stock Company', are often those whose distinctive worth is simply not perceived by other directors, and would not be valued by them if it were.

Fonda's entry into this company provides a characteristic instance of Ford's flair for casting. Hesitant before the challenge of such a role, he had first refused the part of Lincoln; but Ford was insistent, and at last persuaded him to agree.* It was a choice marvellously justified by the result, and it led to the further films in which Fonda was to play for Ford with a similar closeness of understanding and identity of aim. This sympathy is not surprising. For if one examines the creative personality of the actor, one finds it clearly complementary to that of the director — as each reveals himself in his best work. In Fonda as in Ford there is the same rare combination of sensibility with authority, gentleness with strength; the same openness of feeling; and the same compulsive integrity that reveals itself with a directness so seemingly simple that it is easy to overlook the artistry that such revelation, such simplicity demand. *'Une dose égale de pureté, honnêteté et de droiture,'* is how a French critic has attempted to describe the talent of Fonda — *'le plus solide et le plus simple de l'ecran americain'.*** They are words which may be applied with equal fitness to these films of Ford which gave Fonda his most golden opportunities in a long and brilliant career.

* Fonda tells this story himself, in a series run by the *Saturday Evening Post* in which actors were asked which of their films they had most enjoyed making. Fonda chose *Young Mr. Lincoln.* For his own account of the casting and his experience of the film, see pp. 218.
** Jean-Georges Auriol: 'L'Ami Fonda'. (*Revue du Cinéma,* July, 1948).

They Were Expendable

4

If it is ever permissible to divide an artist's creative life (which has probably seemed to him a constant and unbroken struggle) into neatly docketed periods, the years between 1939 and 1945 may be said to form a particularly rich and cohesive one in Ford's career. From *Young Mr. Lincoln* his progress was triumphant and prolific. In the following seven years — three of which were taken up with service in the Navy — he made seven further pictures of the finest quality, all works of high style, five of them drawing their inspiration directly from American themes. Two of these were set, like *Lincoln,* in a romanticised, or at least an affectionately idealised past: *Drums Along the Mohawk* (1939) from Walter Edmunds' novel about the settlers of Upper New York State at the time of the War of Independence, and *My Darling Clementine* (1946) with its retelling of the legend of Wyatt Earp in the far West of the 1870s. The others were contemporary subjects: *The Grapes of Wrath* (1940) from John Steinbeck's novel; *Tobacco Road* (1941), an adaptation of Erskine Caldwell's savage farce of poor whites on the burnt-out tobacco lands of the South; and *They Were Expendable,* derived from W. L. White's documentary account of motor torpedo boats operating in the Pacific in World War II. (Possibly one would class with these *The Battle of Midway,* the documentary assembled and supervised by Ford in 1942, were one now able to see it.)* The two subjects which came from outside the American tradition were the O'Neill-Nichols *The Long Voyage Home* and the best-selling *How Green Was My Valley* — both works of powerful feeling, both somewhat flawed by 'literary' pretension or sentimentalism. The themes of common humanity which are implicit in all these stories were clearly inspiring to Ford's now mature poetic imagination, and that imagination everywhere suffuses and irradiates the films he made of them. Amongst them *They Were Expendable* occupies a special place. Its subject — the ethos and dedication of men at war — makes it distinctly unfashionable (and therefore underestimated) as a work of mid-twentieth century art. But its deeply personal inspiration, crystallising so many of Ford's most intimate convictions and aspirations, gives it a uniquely revealing, uniquely affective power.

It is strange, in view of this, to think how reluctant Ford was to undertake *They Were Expendable.* The book, which had been a best-seller in 1942, was bought by M-G-M: James Kevin McGuinness was put in charge of production, and he engaged another old friend of Ford's, Frank Wead, to write the screenplay. Both of them felt that there was only one possible director for the project, and they flew to Washington in 1943 to persuade Ford to

---

* *The Battle of Midway* can now be seen, at the Museum of Modern Art. Its subject was certainly 'contemporary', but it is more to be admired for the extraordinary conviction and virtuosity with which its vivid, scrappy material is used to dramatise the Ford heroic myth, than as a documentary picture of war. Robert Parrish, in *Growing Up In Hollywood,* tells the inside story in fascinating detail: how Ford hi-jacked the eight cans of 16-millimetre material whose shooting he had supervised during the Japanese attack on Midway Island — how he set Parrish to work in secret, editing a picture 'for the mothers of America' — enlisted Dudley Nichols and James Kevin McGuinness (informing neither of the other's participation) to write commentary and lines for Fonda, Darwell, Irving Pichel and Donald Crisp — and won the backing of Roosevelt by cutting in a five-foot close-up of his son which he'd been carrying around in his pocket. No, the film is not a documentary classic; yes, it is an extremely skilful (and heart-felt) manipulation of patriotic sentiment. 'When the lights came up, Mrs. Roosevelt was crying. The President turned to Admiral Leahy and said, "I want every mother in America to see this picture".' It won the Academy Award for best short subject in 1942. Parrish sums up: 'I saw a number of women actually sobbing, and most of them looked like mothers.' As usual, Ford achieved his objective.   (1980)

They Were Expendable: *casualty*.

take it on. But the war was still being fought, and he was enjoying it; he was reluctant, too, to abandon his commitment to the Navy for what might seem a cushy job back in Hollywood. It took another full year, and service in the Far East and in Europe, before a heaven-sent coincidence changed his mind. Shortly before D-Day, Ford met John Bulkeley (his name was changed to Brickley for the film) at Claridges Hotel in London. (He was still in bed, but 'insisted on getting up and saluting the Medal of Honour winner — even though he was stark naked'.)* Then, during the Normandy landings, he spent five days and nights aboard Bulkeley's P.T. boat. He grew to admire the man, to see him as an undemonstrative hero after his own heart. He realised he had to make the film.

The script which Wead and Ford finally produced had very little in common with traditional Hollywood pictures of men at war. There are no 'Why We Fight' speeches, almost no allusions to 'back home', and no special acts of heroism. A few conventional sparks of rivalry are struck between Brickley (Robert Montgomery) and Ryan (John Wayne), his friend and second-in-command — only to be immediately snuffed out, in the name of common sense, realism and mutual respect. As is proper with a work in the epic style, the characters are seen as part of the theme, not so much subordinate to it as emanations of it. They are not as a result any less 'real' or any less individual. The crew members of *They Were Expendable* are not picked out by conventional dramaturgic methods of conflict or sentimental recollection; but each is none the less accorded a sharp independence of personality, proudly or humorously distinct, from the boy whom Brickley spots shivering under a blanket after the Squadron's quarters have been destroyed in the first Japanese raid ('Wet?' 'No sir,

just scared.' 'You haven't got a monopoly on that'), to Andy Andrews, skipper of the 33 boat, dying in hospital and playing cheerful for his friends.

At the start of the film, the ambition and elevation of the work is clearly announced. Two solemn opening titles act as preface. The first runs: 'Today the guns are silent. A great tragedy has ended. A great victory has been won . . . I speak for the thousands of silent lips, forever stilled among the jungles and in the deep waters of the Pacific, which marked the way. Douglas MacArthur, General of the Army.' And the second sets time and place: 'Manila Bay. In the Year of Our Lord Nineteen Hundred and Forty-One.' There follows a prologue, and introduction to the story's protagonist: Motor Torpedo Boat Squadron Three of the U.S. Navy . . . Led by its Commander, Lieutenant Brickley, the Squadron is showing its keen, shapely paces in Manila Bay before the appraising eye of its Admiral; after the exercise the Admiral makes a perfunctory inspection, and leaves with a few politely disparaging remarks. The sequence closes with Brickley alone on the quay, eyeing his boat with speculation. With a minimum of words the main threads of the story have been drawn: its element, the sea; the P.T. boats, graceful and dangerous weapons of war; official doubts of their worth (they are 'expendable'); Brickley's quality as an officer, his faith in his boats, his deep and undemonstrative feeling for the Squadron — contrasted with the careless impetuosity of Ryan. That evening, as officers and men are dancing and drinking at the Services Club, the music is interrupted by the announcement of the Japanese attack on Pearl Harbour. Later, the Admiral announces to his staff that war has been declared.

The war is soon a reality. Next day, enemy bombers attack in force and reduce the Squadron's

* Dan Ford, *Pappy*, p.194.

They Were Expendable. *Top: a last visit. Right: The hospital tunnel.*

They Were Expendable. *Sandy (Donna Reed) visits the squadron for dinner.*

base to a shambles. But in spite of rumours that a Japanese task force is in the vicinity, Brickley is ordered to stand by for messenger trips. It is not till after the fall of Manila that the Squadron's first real opportunity comes — an attack on a Japanese cruiser, sunk with the loss of one boat. Further actions follow, and further losses. Ryan is injured and sent, protesting, to sick-bay, where he meets an Army nurse. With humorous, touching formality she is entertained at dinner by the officers of the Squadron. The Commander of one of the boats is wounded and dies in the hospital. All the time the enemy presses nearer. At last, the Admiral sends for Brickley and orders him to stand by: his boats are to carry 'certain key personnel' south to Mindanao, *en route* for Australia. His spare crews must dwindle into soldiers, reinforcing the Army on Bataan. So, with the first of a series of farewells, the break-up of the Squadron begins. Carrying the Admiral and his staff, the Commander-in-Chief (MacArthur) and his family, the boats make off for Mindanao, while the two redundant crews stand watching them leave, then silently form up and march off down the long avenue of palms to Bataan.

Losing one boat on the way, Brickley arrives at Mindanao with only three. He is refused permission to return to Bataan for his men, and is surrendered by his Admiral to the Army. An accident cripples two further boats, which have to be towed to a shipyard on the coast, still working under the tough old trader who has spent his life building it up. One of these is ready in time for Brickley and Ryan to go out on a last attack against a Japanese cruiser. On their return, the boats are separated. Ryan's is attacked from the air and blows up; two of his crew die with it. As he and his men sit silently in a bar, after burying their dead, they hear a radio announcement of the fall of Bataan. This presages the ultimate defeat. Making contact again with Brickley, Ryan finds the last boat being hauled away on a truck, turned over to run errands for the Army. Directionless and exhausted, what remains of the Squadron marches off, to lose itself in the confusion of defeat. Brickley, Ryan and two junior officers are ordered back to Australia in the one plane that remains. As night falls, the remnants of the

Squadron straggle away down the deserted beach, while over their heads the last plane soars out to Australia, and MacArthur's words come up to fill the screen: 'We shall return'.

The sweep is epic, its rhythm cumulative. The three fine battle-scenes are vigorously staged, but otherwise the story unfolds at an expansive, leisurely pace. Ford has shown no great concern for clarity of development; maps are used only once, to cover the flight south to Mindanào, and the continuity of action is not always clear. Yet the occasional obscurity hardly matters at all. The essential continuity of approach is preserved without a lapse. It is grounded in absolute authenticity of atmosphere and behaviour. There is no trace of what servicemen know as 'bull'. When war is announced, the news is taken gravely, but without surprise: there are no propagandist allusions to its causes, its purpose, or its consequences. The Japanese are neither discussed nor execrated; they are simply the enemy, anonymous and invisible. Tensions and relationships within the American forces are similarly convincing — between officers and men, between the Navy and the Army.

'Authenticity' does not imply a ruthless or objective realism. *They Were Expendable* is a film with a viewpoint, a purpose. It sets out not merely to relate but to pay tribute to the courage and traditions of service, of the fighting men who are its heroes. Its

They Were Expendable. *Brickley and the Admiral (Robert Montgomery, Charles Trowbridge): 'Listen son. You and I are professionals. If the manager says "Sacrifice", we lay down a bunt and let somebody else hit the home runs ... Our job is to lay down that sacrifice. That's what we were trained for, and that's what we'll do. Understand?' 'Yes, sir. Thank you.'*

theme is put into words by the Admiral when he explains to Brickley the reasons for their inactivity at the beginning of the campaign: 'Listen, son. You and I are professionals. If the manager says "sacrifice", we lay down a bunt and let somebody else hit the home runs ... Our job is to lay down that sacrifice. That's what we were trained for, and that's what we'll do.' Its characters are shown in the light of this sacrifice, ennobled by 'the ideal which they carry within them' — not through words, but through image after image of conscious dignity: Sandy, the Army nurse, assisting at an endless series of operations as casualties pour into the hospital on Corregidor; the men of the Squadron watching with astonished pride as their Commander-in-Chief boards the leading P.T. boat.

In spite of its emotional unity, the mood of the film is never montonous. It is frequently varied with humour, of a fond, colloquial kind: the young ensign who finds himself continually carried away by the dignity of his position; the seaman who offends every canon of discipline by asking for MacArthur's autograph (one may sense a further humour in the readiness with which the General grants it); the submarine captain who is blackmailed into surrendering half his torpedoes by an allusion to his performance, in former years, as Tess of the d'Urbevilles at the Academy ('And does your crew know?'). Just as true are the moments of serious emotion: Brickley saying goodbye to the men who have to go to Bataan, and leaving his speech incomplete, unable to bring himself to utter hopes he knows cannot be fulfilled; or the visit of the officers of the Squadron to the friend they know is dying, each side rising to the occasion with pathetic, transparently pretence jocularity. The film is full of such moments of emotion, expressed in a word or

They Were Expendable. *Top: 'Chief Bo's'n's Mate Mulcahey, take over.' Brickley says goodbye to his crew (John Wayne, Ward Bond, Robert Montgomery.) Above: Donna Reed as Sandy.*

two, an inflection, a silent pause.

This underemphasis is saved from any taint of theatricality by the consistent sincerity and power of feeling which pervades the film. Clearly the feeling communicated itself to Ford's collaborators, however little he was prepared in later days to give them (or himself or the picture) credit. He claimed that he had wanted almost no music at all — 'just in a very few places, like Red River Valley over Russell Simpson's last scene'. But it would be difficult to imagine They Were Expendable without Herbert Stothart's elaborate, evocative score, true to the Fordian tradition of popular quotation ("Anchors Aweigh", "The Battle Hymn of the Republic", locker-room choruses) and supplying a fine original theme of its own, imaginatively varied in mood and tempo throughout the picture, first as a confident chorus over the titles, then echoing, sometimes grandly sometimes sadly, all down the long chronicle of struggle and dissolution.

Talking later about the film — which he seems never to have quite forgiven for taking him away from the war — Ford was as little inclined to be generous to his actors, 'who wouldn't even cut their hair to look like sailors'. The comment is characteristically grumpy and demonstrably unjust.

In fact the film is cast and played beautifully, by a company of actors wholly in tune with its style, direct, truthful and unadorned, accepting disaster as a matter of fact, yet never afraid to take the moment of feeling full-face. This is not naturalism: weakness and vulgarity are not part of the picture. Only so can characters rooted in an unpretentious reality assume a dignity and stature of quite a different order. Donna Reed as Sandy, the attractive, devoted Navy nurse, becomes, as she assists the surgeon through the operations, torch held steady as the bombs fall around, the image of unwavering humane devotion. The men of the squadron, servicemen of the most ordinary kind, are transformed into exemplars of the archetypal man-at-arms, steadfast to the end, as they watch their Commander disembark from his launch and stride the jetty to the P.T. boat which will carry him to Australia; or as they bid farewell to their Captain, under orders to leave them to face a leaderless defeat. There is a rare combination here of emotion and restraint, and these are the qualities, conveyed with the most delicate subtlety, which give such distinction to Robert Montgomery's Brickley — a central performance which identifies itself so completely with the film that it can easily pass unnoticed by audiences (and critics) who have learned to equate acting with the pyrotechnics of personality. In some ways Ford's choice of Montgomery was surprising; for years the actor had been struggling with M-G-M for the right to exercise his talent in more worthy material than the endless succession of high society dramas and comedies to which his 'sophisticated' personality condemned him. Once or twice he had succeeded, with brilliant results (*Night Must Fall, The Earl of Chicago*), but not often. Now, for Ford, he achieved a perfectly selfless portrait of leadership, quietly authoritative, deeply reserved, with a wry humour that balances and humanises an unwavering devotion to duty. We are shown nothing of Brickley beyond what the occasion demands; we know nothing of his private life, his home or his family; he is the Commander and must keep his feelings to himself. Only at the end, when Ryan senses his friend's isolation, his bitter regret at having to desert his men, and silently puts his arm round his shoulders, are we allowed to share for a moment a

They Were Expendable. *Top: Last survivors of the squadron — expendable ... Centre: Ryan and Brickley fly out to Australia: 'We're going back to do a job' (John Wayne, Robert Montgomery). Bottom: The remnants of the squadron march away to Bataan: 'We're in the Army now ...'*

They Were Expendable. *The war is going badly; the squadron loses two boats; the survivors must be assigned to duties with the Army defending Bataan. Brickley (Robert Montgomery) says farewell: 'You're a swell bunch. I'm glad to have been able to serve with you. I'd like to be able to tell you that we were going out to bring back help, but that wouldn't be the truth. We're going down the line to do a job, and you're going to Bataan with the Army. That isn't what you've been trained for, but they need your help. You older men with longer service records, take care of the kids. Maybe... That's all. God bless you.'*

whole inner world of powerful feeling.

Just before shooting ended on *They Were Expendable*, Ford fell from a camera scaffolding, fractured a leg, and ended up in hospital. The scenes that remained to be shot were mostly battle inserts, and these were directed by Robert Montgomery. Ford returned to the service as soon as he could; but fortunately the war was ending and although he sent a detachment of his Field Photo Unit to Europe, where they set to work researching evidence for use in the Nuremberg trials, he himself remained in

Washington, making frequent visits to Los Angeles where his picture was being put together. He liked later to pretend that he knew nothing of its eventual shape or length, but the masterly construction of the final version, the slow cumulative rhythm so different from the dynamic pacing of a conventional Hollywood war picture, show unmistakably the guiding sensibility of Ford himself. This is the kind of material which could so easily be ruined by impatient handling, but the editing of *They Were Expendable* is as delicate and as firm throughout as the shooting. Close-ups, affectionate or noble, are held at leisure; long-shots are sustained long after their narrative role has been performed. A marginal figure is suddenly dwelt on, lovingly enlarged to fill the centre of the screen. Informed with heightened emotion, a single shot, unexpectedly interposed — a ragged line of men marching into nowhere, one of them playing a bugle-call on his harmonica — assumes a deeper significance than is given it by its function in the story. This is one of the properties of poetry. *They Were Expendable* is a heroic poem.

5

Peace, we are told, has its victories 'no less renown'd than war'. This alas is not always true; but it is true that some poets have always been inspired by the heroism of common humanity just as powerfully as by the heroism of fighting men. Such, for all his attraction to the service, is the case with Ford, and particularly during this most richly productive period of his career. Each in its own way and with its own emphasis, his films from *Young Mr. Lincoln* in 1939 to *My Darling Clementine* in 1945, present a variation on a constant theme.

The theme, first and last is human. These stories are full of action, battles and chases, gunfights, celebrations and slapstick humour; but they exist always for and because of and in terms of the characters. Ford never uses people simply to justify happenings or to illustrate themes. His human allegiance is unqualified; the value *per se* of the human creature is a truth he holds to be self-evident,

and his characters, presented always as ends in themselves, have a habit of suddenly taking on the stature of heroes.

This is true not only in obvious instances like that of the dispossessed wanderers of *The Grapes of Wrath,* or the sailors of *They Were Expendable,* who are left at the end of the campaign to meet death or captivity with spirit still unbroken. Time after time, Ford will halt the progress of these films to concentrate on a face or an attitude, not with the glancing stroke of one who makes an apt marginal observation, but with a deliberate enlargement of the detail until it seems to carry for that moment the whole weight and intention of the picture. In *They Were Expendable* the quite subordinate character of the old trader who has spent all his life building up his post, and who refuses to desert it to the Japanese ('I've worked forty years for this, son; if I leave it they'll have to carry me out'), is last seen in a wordless shot, sitting on the steps of his shack. He shifts his keg of whisky to his side, lays his shotgun across his knees, and waits. And the film waits with

Drums Along the Mohawk. *Settlers in the Mohawk Valley work together to clear the land for cultivation.*

him, till the scene dissolves to the river, with night falling, and the image fades. Without a word, and with a minimum of action, a comment has been made, a resonance sounded. The first sequence of *My Darling Clementine* ends with a held shot that similarly illuminates. The four Earp brothers, driving their cattle to California, have finished supper on the trail. Three of them mount and ride off to spend the evening in Tombstone, leaving their youngest brother to watch the herd. The boy watches them ride away, calling their names: 'Goodnight Wyatt — Goodnight Morg — Goodnight Virge . . .' They have disappeared, but still he stands there, the camera lingering on his face. Shots such as these are true film poetry, not pre-planned in the script or on the drawing board, not juggled together in the cutting room, but created at that stage where the process must be at its most intense, when the director is most immediately and intimately in contact with his material — the camera, the actors, and the situation.

The skill with which these moments of significant pause are integrated into the narrative shows more than a masterly technical grasp: more fundamentally, it is the result of a sureness of aim, an uncompromising consistency of viewpoint that

Ford's Song of America, like Whitman's, has humanity as its most persistent theme, shown always with respect and love. Above: 'Granpa' (Russell Simpson) in They Were Expendable. *Top right: Mrs. Clay and her sons' wives (Alice Brady, Doris Bowden, Arleen Whelan) in* Young Mr. Lincoln; *the Youngest Seaman in* They Were Expendable; *centre right: an anonymous black woman from* Drums along the Mohawk, *an Italian railroad worker from* The Iron Horse, *and (bottom) young James Earp in* My Darling Clementine — *'Each singing what belongs to him or her and to none else'.*

enables Ford, without betrayal or self-contradiction, to alternate mood and accent in the most daring fashion. In the long trial scene in *Young Mr. Lincoln,* the prosecuting counsel's cliché-packed, histrionic declamations are presented with the heightened emphasis of farce; yet the direct cuts to the two accused boys, or to the agonised face of their mother, or to Lincoln himself, stern and anxious for all his homespun humour, 'come off' without a jar. An even more striking example is the whole of *Tobacco Road,* which for the extraordinary balance and control of its continual variations of mood — wistfully elegiac and wildly slapstick, cruelly satirical and tenderly sentimental — constitutes perhaps the most sheerly virtuoso performance of Ford's career.

Tobacco Road. *Jeeter and Ada set out for the poorhouse.*

Young Mr. Lincoln. *The fulfilment of men and women together in Ford's world is contrasted always with the ultimate solitariness of us all.*

Without a highly accomplished technique, effects of such subtlety would be impossible; but style is more than technique, and these films are poetic by virtue of their style. It is not that this ever obtrudes itself, breaking into or away from the narrative. Ford remains always a story-teller. In contrast with other poetic film makers — Dovzhenko, for instance, with whose lyric vision his own has not a few qualities in common — he never goes outside the immediate dramatic context to find his symbols. It is rather a question of intensity within the flow of the drama. Constantly the images are charged with an emotional force so strong that, while continuing to perform a quite straightforward narrative function, they acquire as it were a second dimension of existence and meaning: what they are saying becomes inseparable from the way they are saying it. In the last reel of *Tobacco Road,* as Jeeter and Ada are being driven (as they think) to the poor farm, a succession of sustained close-ups on their tired, defeated faces conveys not only this, but also, through this, the pathos of decrepit and abandoned

old age, and, on a deeper level still, the eternal riddle of human transience. This powerful use of close-up, as affirmation or silently to reveal an inner state, is characteristic in Ford. Its stylistic complement are the long-shots which relate his men and women to the world about them. Two silhouetted figures cross the dark crest of a hill against a cold early morning sky; a column of soldiers marches off into the distance; an old truck chugs persistently on, up the broad, far-stretching highway; a man on horseback rides away, and away... The films are full of far views and slow departures, stoically setting the gloried figure of man — 'the brave, the mighty, and the wise' — in his mortal perspective.

Every poet is to some extent occupied in creating in his work his own, particular image of the world; and, for all his sense of the uniqueness of men, Ford's world is far from being bounded by the individual. His vision is rounded by its emphasis on the relations of men with one another and with the world in which they find themselves; on life lived in community; on all the hazards and rewards of 113

Fonda as the young Lincoln (left) and, seven years later, as Clementine's Wyatt Earp. The dance and the awkward movements are unmistakably the same.

physical existence. The scenes of action in these films thus become something more than mere occasions for excitement: they reflect a philosophy that finds virtue in activity, seeing struggle as a necessary element in life: the Protestant (rather than Catholic) ethic at its most congenial.

Ford is never happier than when he is telling a story that illustrates these principles in their most direct and simple terms: all his excursions into America's past are fired by a kindling sympathy with the idea of life in a pioneering community, in the tough, disorderly mining township of Tombstone in *My Darling Clementine,* or amongst the hardy settlers of *Drums Along the Mohawk,* who have the natural perils of country and climate to contend with, as well as the savagery of Indian marauders and the British enemy. In such stories the disasters of war and the threats of lawlessness serve to throw into relief the necessary ideals of love and comradeship — which find their expression not only in acts of sacrifice and mutual aid, but in the scenes of celebration and conviviality, of dances, processions and games, which none of these films, with the exception of *Tobacco Road,* is without. (It is no coincidence that the jig to which young Mr. Lincoln clumsily steers Mary Todd round a

Springfield ballroom, is the same as that to which Sheriff Earp takes the floor with Clementine Carter, to dance on a sunny Sunday morning, on the site of the first church in Tombstone.) Just as, on the individual plane, Ford's intense feeling for the dignity of the humblest of his characters gives them from time to time a heroic enlargement, so, in the sphere of action, their deeds, conflicts and relationships acquire a corresponding poetic power of suggestion, bearing witness to the general theme — the theme of the good life. Hardihood and enterprise are qualities of this life, and also love.

The ideal of love which arouses the deepest response in Ford, and which has certainly inspired his most eloquent passages of poetry, is not that most habitual to Hollywood: none of these films can adequately be described as a 'love story'. Even where there is a hero with a heroine to win or to lose, it is not the emotional progress of their relationship that gives the picture its heart. This is by no means to say that Ford's heroines are nothing more than obligatory ciphers. They are always individuals in their own right, people of spirit and resolution as well as charm: Lana Martin (in *Drums Along the Mohawk*) accepts with courage and good humour the hard lot of a pioneer's wife; Clementine is a determined girl, though quiet; and Sandy, the nurse

Top: Tobacco Road. *Jeeter and Ada face failure and the Poor Farm (Charley Grapewin and Elizabeth Patterson).*
Right: She Wore a Yellow Ribbon.

in *They Were Expendable,* does her job with strictness as well as sweetness, with a moral devotion that is made to seem as important as love. Ford is not interested to stress the specifically sexual elements in the relationships between his men and women; he is content to leave temperamental and sensual intimacies and conflicts largely unexplored. Instead the emphasis is on woman as the helpmate of man, as wife and mother — the ministering angel rather than the coy and uncertain mistress. (Even Clementine has been trained as a nurse.) The great and most significant relationships are those of family and community, of comradeship, of the shared struggle for survival; the bitterest wrongs are those of social and economic injustice, of the persecution or exploitation of men by men. 'I will plant companionship thick as trees along all the rivers of America...' The democratic vision of these films recalls that of an earlier, equally warm-blooded American poet — Walt Whitman.

Values like these cannot be asserted without moments of anger. 'What the Hell else does a man live for?' Ford had said in 1936 to an interviewer who had asked him whether he believed, as a director, in including in his pictures his point of view about 'things that bothered him'. And he quoted as an example an anti-lynching plea that he had put into *Judge Priest,* but which had been cut out of the finished film, for reasons of space. 'It was one of the most scorching things you ever heard.' He was to wait until 1952, when he inserted the same episode into *The Sun Shines Bright,* for an opportunity to get the sequence realised; but the same fierce sentiment is evident often elsewhere in his work: in the bitter trial scenes in *The Prisoner of Shark Island*; in the attempted lynching in *Young Mr. Lincoln*; and in the numerous incidents of exploitation and thuggery in *The Grapes of Wrath.* That the last impression of these pictures is never one of denial or defeat is not the result of compromise or false resolution. The wrongs are countered and the anger purged by the passionate affirmation of the opposite ideal, of human solidarity. Settlers and brothers; the family and the unit; the mother who refuses to betray one of her sons to justice to save the life of the other; the commander struggling to preserve the unity of his squadron; Ma Joad fighting to keep the family together — these are the persistent symbols. Disintegration is the tragedy: the derelict, hopeless

The men ride away: the women wait and hope. Such farewells are a constant motif in Ford's tales. Top: The Iron Horse. *Centre:* Drums Along the Mohawk. *Bottom:* Wyatt Earp rides West in My Darling Clementine.

The Grapes of Wrath. *Henry Fonda, Jane Darwell, Dorris Bowdon, Russell Simpson.*

community of share-croppers left withering on the exhausted, infertile tobacco lands; the farmer's family uprooted and splitting into fragments; the Motor Torpedo Boat squadron dwindling away man by man and boat by boat, until all that remains is a handful of men wandering down a deserted beach. Such stories would legitimately — one might think inevitably — end without hope; but for Ford acceptance of defeat seems not to be possible. Instead, each time, the music shifts into the major key, the beat is resumed, and the last images state positively: the living pathos of Jeeter Lester; the resurgence of hope in Ma Joad; and, over the heads of the men who were expendable, the plane soaring out, the struggle continued, the words *'We Shall Return'*.

She Wore a Yellow Ribbon. The column has arrived too late: the post is destroyed. Captain Brittles faces the failure of his last mission (Joanne Dru, John Wayne).

3. Independence:
Freedom and Its Price

But there is always a last departure. Now, when we see Wyatt Earp take leave of Clementine, to ride away and away, down the winding road from Tombstone, we know that he was never to return. In this particularly sustained farewell, did Ford have any thought of a last salute of his own to the years that were ending? For with it a period did end; another stage was completed; and the poet pushed forward into new territory.

The 'independence' to which Ford progressed in 1947 was of course relative; but it was sufficient to mark his work distinctively. Liberty had its price: production for Argosy had to be undertaken under more immediate and probably severer economic pressure than direction for Fox. Gone were the days when Ford, behind schedule, could magnificently dismiss Front Office protests by tearing ten pages out of the script and innocently asking whether they wanted it done well or quickly. But with the limitation came a gain: as his own producer, Ford's influence on the conception of his films, on the choice of subjects and preparation of scripts no less than on the actual shooting, became far greater than it had ever been before. So strong and so consistent is the personality informing the best of his work at Fox, that it is easy to forget that Ford had been used to directing scripts conceived and written without necessary reference to him. This even includes such films as *The Prisoner of Shark Island, The Grapes of Wrath* and *Tobacco Road,* as Nunnally Johnson's own account makes clear:

'If memory serves, Ford was not assigned to the three pictures I did with him. I wrote the scripts without thought of the director to do them, and they were offered to him by Zanuck, who selected all the directors for my pictures in those days. All were accepted in the form offered, and I can't remember that Ford ever said anything one way or the other about them. Nor can I remember his ever altering or rewriting any of the scripts on the set. It was always on the set, I might add, that he made all his contributions to the picture. These were in the

staging of the scenes, the shaping of the characters, and his wonderful use of the camera. In any case, the pictures he did with me were, for good or bad, completely faithful to the text of the script.'

A description by Kenneth MacGowan (its producer) of the genesis of *Young Mr. Lincoln* makes the same point: the idea had been Lamar Trotti's, and on the strength of his treatment Zanuck had commissioned a script. 'After seeing the final script, Ford consented to do it. Only four lines were cut out of the entire script.'*

That so many of those pictures made for Fox should have achieved such intense personal and poetic qualities is a considerable tribute to the production flair of Darryl Zanuck. It was none the less natural that on returning to Hollywood after the war, Ford should have wanted to exercise greater control over his work — a control approximating, in fact, to that he had enjoyed on the films he had made with Dudley Nichols.

But those days too were over. *The Fugitive* was the last film Ford made with Nichols, and even on that he broke very loose from the script during shooting. For good or ill, he was determined now to make his own mistakes — and win his own victories. Mr. Nichols has already been quoted on the closeness of his early collaboration with Ford: 'I went on the sets and watched him break it (the screenplay) down into filmscript as he shot. I went to rushes, cutting rooms, etc., and began to grasp what it was all about.' In significant contrast to this is Frank Nugent's account of writing for the Ford of later years (he worked on nine of Ford's films after *Fort Apache*); 'Once the script is finished, the writer had better keep out of his way. On occasions he will invite you to visit the set; if he has not invited you, you enter at considerable risk — and then are advised to remain in the background. The finished

---

* 'The Seventh Muse in San Francisco', by Albert Johnson. *Sight and Sound*, Vol. 24, Nos 3 & 4, 1955.

Fort Apache. *George O'Brien, Henry Fonda, Ward Bond.*

picture is Ford's, never the writer's . . .' And this strict creative control, it is interesting to note, now extends over the way the films are written, as well as the way they are put on the screen:

'Ford works very, very closely with the writer or writers. I don't think it would be entirely true to say that he sees his story in its entirety when he begins —although he sometimes pretends to. Sometimes he is groping, like a musician who has a theme but doesn't quite know how to develop it . . . then if I come up with the next notes, and they're what he wanted, he beams and says that's right, that's what he was trying to get over. He has a fine ear for dialogue, and a lot of it is his own — like Barry Fitzgerald's wonderful line in *The Quiet Man:* "It's a fine, soft night so I think I'll go and talk a little treason with me comrades".'

Inevitably, these changed relationships, economic as well as creative, were reflected in a change of style. Common to all Ford's pictures after *My Darling Clementine* is a quality which can best be described as 'relaxed'. The values are the same; but the tone has modulated, the personality has become even more unmistakably clear. Frank Nugent remarks how Ford refuses to preview his pictures: 'No sneak previews, to test audience reaction. He makes them his own way, to suit himself.' And recognisably, from *The Fugitive* to *The Sun Shines Bright,* Ford's Argosy productions all have an

obstinate, take-it-or-leave-it air to them, that shows itself sometimes in an even wilful neglect of the accepted rules of narrative. 'Ford detests exposition', is another of Nugent's illuminating remarks: *She Wore A Yellow Ribbon, The Quiet Man, The Sun Shines Bright* — all these show signs that passages of exposition which most directors would spend time over have been impatiently shrugged aside. A tussle that occurred between writers and director on *She Wore A Yellow Ribbon* seems to have been characteristic:

'Stallings and I (Mr. Nugent writes) both fought with him over *Yellow Ribbon,* where he eliminated what was to us a key scene: an explanation of Brittles' mission when he initially sets out. It had always been a tough scene to write, because it had to be expository — and Ford detests exposition. We trimmed it to the bone, and Ford reluctantly accepted it at long last — then threw it out after shooting it.'

Ford, in fact, has been chiefly interested in stories during these latter years as excuses — as pretexts — for making poetry.

The return to the West after the failure of *The Fugitive* was immediately prompted by the need to strengthen the finances of his company; but there is no doubt that *Fort Apache,* and its Cavalry theme, represented more to Ford than an opportunity for an easy raid on the box-office. A return to the past was inevitable: for the poetic image of the world which had always been the essential inspiration of his work was becoming harder and harder to express in terms of the present-day. *The Fugitive* had taken a problem whose circumstances were contemporary (however 'timeless' its implications), and failed to represent them honestly. The passionate, unsectarian liberalism of *The Grapes Of Wrath* was no longer feasible, even if Ford's inclination had led him that way: when for instance he was signed by Fox in 1949 to make a contemporary social subject, this turned out to be *Pinky,* a heavily-compromised film in the post-war 'Negro' cycle (scripted, incidentally, by Dudley Nichols). Ford shot on this for a few days, then abandoned the attempt, with the excuse of a 'broken leg'. The picture was taken over, much more suitably, by Elia Kazan, while Ford switched instead to a slapstick war comedy, *When Willie Comes Marching Home,* whose relevance to contemporary reality was safely remote. The same is

Top: The Long Voyage Home. (*Jack Pennick, Ward Bond, John Qualen, Thomas Mitchell*). *Right:* She Wore a Yellow Ribbon. '*Goodbye is a word we don't use in the cavalry . . .*' (*Joanne Dru, John Wayne, Mildred Natwick*).

The price of freedom. Ford, with Maureen O'Hara and John Wayne, attends a première of Rio Grande. *Herbert Yates, Republic's answer to Zanuck, stands left.*

true of his other commercial assignments during these years — the peculiar *What Price Glory?*; the engaging, escapist *Mogambo*; the sentimental *Long Gray Line*; and the ill-fated *Mr. Roberts*.

Inevitably, by this deliberate side-stepping of disputed contemporary issues, Ford incurred the censure of critics who demand that an artist should participate directly in the conflicts of his time. We may doubt, however, if such objections are as valid as the instinct of the poet himself — who must go where his feeling takes him. As Yeats wrote, when challenged by similar demands: 'We have no gift to set a statesman right':

> *He has had enough of meddling who can please*
> *A young girl in the indolence of her youth,*
> *Or an old man upon a winter's night.*

On this question, Ford took the way of Yeats. The series of productions for his own company which comprise his creative achievement during these years (an achievement no less considerable than those of any other period in his career) were even further removed than his commercial assignments from current political conflicts and the oppressive materialism of twentieth-century civilisation. And

that this return to the past took the form at first of a fascination with nineteenth-century *military* life, is also indicative that this was no mere cynical retreat to the commercial security of the Western. There can be no doubt of the importance to Ford of his wartime service with the Navy, nor of the imaginative stimulus to him of the experience of war — the quickened sense of community among fighting men, moral ends limited and made sharply manifest, physical action as fulfilment of part of man's essential nature, the charged atmosphere of tragedy . . . all these things, to Ford, had been of deep significance.

Such a fascination with the one-time profession of arms, with the theme of the "Happy Warrior", would in itself oblige a return to the past — for such sentiments, in an age of atom-bomb and hydrogen bomb warfare, have lost their validity. 'Listen, son', says the Admiral in *They Were Expendable*, 'You and I are professionals . . .' Ford's attitude to war is that of a professional soldier, not that of a militarist; and the soldiers whom his films invite us to respect are men who have freely chosen to serve their country in its armed forces. And just as this attitude is the key to *They Were Expendable,* so it is also the key to Ford's post-war Cavalry pictures — *Fort Apache*, *She Wore A Yellow Ribbon* and *Rio Grande*.

Presumably as a result of commercial pressure, these give the impression of having been rapidly shot. This makes for an unevenness in their accomplishment that sometimes jars. *Fort Apache* in particular suffers from a heaviness of touch — especially in the staging of the comedy — and an unusual number of inadequate performances. Alone of these films, in fact, it is more interesting in its conception and for its implications than as a realised work of art. Its central character, Colonel Thursday, is a thinly disguised representation of Colonel Custer, that reckless and ambitious officer whose resentment at having been by-passed for promotion, combined with a ruthless appetite for personal glory, betrayed him and his command into the historic disaster of the Little Big Horn. A fine subject — for any director but Ford, whose heroes are made of better stuff than Custer, and whose warmest feeling is not aroused by such infirm and contradictory personalities. Nor was Henry Fonda, with his gift for integrity, the actor for the part. With their almost documentary quality of reconstruction, the earlier scenes of life on the dusty little frontier fort have considerable interest for the light they throw on a long-neglected and very important Western community; and the most successful characters in these sequences are not the neurotic, dissatisfied Thursday, nor his pretty daughter (played by Shirley Temple), but the good soldiers, Captain York (John Wayne), Sergeant O'Rourke (Ward Bond) and O'Rourke's long-suffering wife. But it is not till its last half-hour that the film rises to its subject, in the magnificent scenes of fighting, with the Indian hordes sweeping time after time through the trapped cavalrymen, and Thursday achieving dignity only in his hour of failure and death. The film finishes remarkably: York holds honourable parley with the Indians — the justice of whose action is undisputed — and avoids further bloodshed. Nor will he besmirch the name of his commander. 'He must have been a great man —and a great commander', comments a journalist, intent on laying the foundations of a heroic myth. 'No man died more gallantly', replies York. There is irony here, of course. The journalists' hero was foolish and vain, and dishonourable in his treatment of the Indians. But York's evasion permits the necessary lie: the irony is of less account than the tradition. At the end Ford leaves us in no doubt where our sympathies and our respect should lie. The image dissolves to a Cavalry troop, riding out on another

Fort Apache

patrol. A voice speaks over them: 'They'll fight over cards and rot-gut whiskey, but they'll share the last drop in the canteen . . . The regular army, now and fifty years from now . . .'

Again the reference to 'Regulars' is specific. Ford's homespun heroes are the rough, tough men of the Cavalry — 'The dog-faced soldiers, the regulars, the fifty cents-a-day professionals', to quote from the similar closing dedication of *She Wore a Yellow Ribbon*. The lines, indeed, so characteristic in tone, so precise in their tribute, deserve quotation in full. 'So here they are', the narrator sums up, as the Cavalry go past, pennants flying, uniforms worn and stained, hats jauntily angled:

> 'So here they are — the dog-faced soldiers, the regulars, the fifty cents-a-day professionals, riding the outposts of a nation. From Fort Reno to Fort Apache, from Sheridan to Stark, they were all the same, men in dirty shirt blue, and only a cold page in the history books to mark their passage. But wherever they rode, and whatever they fought for — that place became the United States.'

Names of Forts and Battles, of Indian tribes and Cavalry commanders, the flag of Custer's Fighting Seventh, and the ringing calls of attack and retreat — these stir Ford, one feels, with the same emotion as that avowed by Sir Philip Sidney in his famous confession — 'Certainly I must confess mine own barbarousness, I never heard the old song of Percy and Douglas, that I found not my heart moved more than with a trumpet'. This is the power to move of these films at their best. By a combination of realism and poetry, the cold pages of the history books are lit up: the world of the Cavalry outpost at this crucial moment of American history — a time of advancing frontiers, of continual menace from hostile Indians, the irresistible and painful growth of a nation — this hazardous world is evoked with a vividness of everyday detail which somehow intensifies the admiration for the human effort and self-sacrifice on which it was founded. 'Wherever they rode, and whatever they fought for . . .' Ford's attitude is not one that kicks against history. He selects those aspects of it that he can use, and he accepts it all, accepts also the tragic events that were, no less than the generous acts of heroism, a part of the total,

Rio Grande: opening sequence. Captain York leads a patrol back to camp; wives wait anxiously; wounded are dragged on stretchers; the doctor ministers.

inevitable process — the creation of the American nation. 'That place became the United States.'

The 'relaxation' in the style of these films differentiates them somewhat from Ford's previous work. The craftsmanship is no less masterly, but it is less punctilious, more impatient. The strokes are bolder, the formal concern less in evidence. The only serious criterion now seems to be the artist's own pleasure, with sometimes a few comic or romantic concessions thrown to the undiscriminating public, like poor scraps to yelping dogs. If the result is undeniably a loss of poetic tension — none of these films has quite the concentration or the sustained elevation of style of, say, *They Were Expendable* or *Tobacco Road* — it represents at the same time a gain in another direction. The work is more colloquial in tone, more humorous in its view of life, and more approachable. It is no longer the drama that signifies, so much as the feeling behind it; and only those sequences interest Ford which give him an opportunity to express his feeling. It is in this connection that his impatience with exposition becomes understandable: 'The feeling gives importance to the action and situation, and not the action and situation to the feeling.'

The quotation is from Wordsworth's preface to *Lyrical Ballads*; and in these late films of Ford, both the ballad and the lyrical elements are strong. As in all ballads, the poetry is easily assimilable, recounting stories based in familiar history, appealing to emotions traditional and popularly shared. And in a literal sense, the films are lyric, too. An unfailingly evocative, dramatic use of popular musical themes has always characterised Ford's sound-tracks, from the sophisticated arrangements of *Stagecoach* to the simple revivalist hymns of *Tobacco Road* and the 'Red River Valley' played on set by Dan Borzage's lonely concertina in *The Grapes of Wrath* and *They Were Expendable*. In his films for his own company, this interplay of action and music is more pronounced: the columns of cavalry, the wagon trains, the galloping riders move across their vast Western landscapes to tunes whose compulsive beat reinforces the zest, exhilaration and spaciousness of the images; dances and sing-songs are enjoyed for their own sakes; moments of quiet feeling, of meditation or of death are given a special tenderness by the songs which softly accompany them.

The joys of physical existence, of a hard life in the open air; the refreshment of communal pleasures; the ideals of loyalty, of love and comradeship — such things make up the feeling of these films. As emphatically as ever, human beings are at the centre

of them, and many are the memorable characters they create: John Wayne's Captain York (a Colonel in *Rio Grande*), strict, sensitive, unwavering in his devotion to the army; or — surely the best performance of his career — his elderly, shy, endearing Captain Nathan Brittles, who had been 'a lad in blue jeans and barefoot when he left his Daddy's farm to join the Army', and now sees with sadness the day of his retirement approaching. (Like an earlier Ford hero, Captain Brittles likes to take his stool out to his wife's grave in the evening, and talk over the day's news with her: the poetry of living is not dead for him.) The jovial, richly absurd Sergeant Quincannon (played by Victor McLaglen) blarneys his way through all three stories; there is the gauche and eager Harry Carey (son of Ford's old friend); and Ben Johnson, the soft-spoken, sharp-eyed Tyree, with his gallantry, his wry humour, and his untouchable reserve. This is a man's world, of course, yet women have their important part to play in it: flirtatious sisters and nieces, stoical army wives — Maureen O'Hara as the beautiful, spirited Mrs. York; Irene Rich in *Fort Apache*; and Mildred Natwick, jaunty, tender and indomitable as the Colonel's lady in *She Wore A Yellow Ribbon*.

To make films which are so dedicated to a military tradition as these are, and yet not to make them militaristic, is an extraordinary achievement. Yet none of these stories can be called aggressive. In *Fort Apache*, Colonel Thursday, who insults the Apache leader as a 'recalcitrant swine', is shown to be an arrogant and embittered man, and a bad soldier: the good soldier is the one who comes to terms with the Indians, and who respects them. In *Rio Grande* it is the Indians who attack: the Cavalry foray is made to rescue the women and children, who have been carried off by the marauders. And the whole plot of *She Wore A Yellow Ribbon* (this is a circumstance which seems to have passed generally unremarked)* turns generally on the necessity for *avoiding* war: Captain Brittles' triumph is to have won his victory without a shot fired and without a man lost on either side.

This pacific (not pacifist) theme is common in

* Jean Mitry, for instance (Vol. II, p.88) writes of the 'spectacular destruction of the Indian camp'. In fact, the essential point of Brittles' manoeuvre (of stampeding the braves' horses) is that such destruction is averted.

Wagonmaster. *The leaders of the Mormon train make assurance of peace and friendship to a party of wary Indians. (Ward Bond, Ben Johnson, Harry Carey Jnr. standing left.)*

fact to all these films — in the mature spirit of Brittles' pow-wow with Chief Pony-That-Walks. 'We are too old for war,' says the old Indian, urging his White friend to leave the young to their folly, and join him in hunting the Buffalo and getting drunk. 'Yes,' replies Brittles. 'We are too old for war. But old men should stop wars.' The same attitude is reflected in *Wagonmaster* — a film which is not without its fatalities. Near the end of the story, when the bad men have been killed, Elder Wiggs turns to the wagonmaster who has saved his life, and says: 'I thought you never used a gun on a man.' 'I don't,' says Travis. 'Only on snakes.' And he flings his gun away onto the rocks. (The death of the bandits has in itself been a demonstration that those who live by the sword shall die by the sword: Uncle Shiloh Cleggs' last words are identical with those of the boy behind the counter at the bank, whom he has shot down in the first sequence of the film.)

Of all the films in this group, *Wagonmaster* is the most purely lyrical; and perhaps also the most original. 'Ford's script cutting,' Nugent notes ruefully, 'especially of dialogue — was rather harsh.'

This is not to say that the film is without conversation. Almost at the start, for instance, with a wonderful dramatic negligence, a long, relaxed dialogue scene is used to establish the mood and the situation — the slow, easy mood of a hot, sunny afternoon; the Mormons who need horses and guides to lead them on their trek; the young horse-traders who are looking forward rather to a spell of drinking and card-playing in town. It is a slow conversation, wary on both sides, but Ford expects us to take the West as we find it — he is not going to force the tempo for us: so the Mormon elders assess severely; a horse whinnies; and Travis (Ben Johnson) whittles his stick, pauses to consider, calls occasionally over his shoulder to a restless animal — 'Ho there! . . . Be gentle . . .!' But once the action gets under way, it is on movement and atmosphere that Ford concentrates, rather than on the development of any 'plot' — the community atmosphere of the township on the move, the stubborn progress of the wagon train across valleys and torrents and hills, with again a full and tuneful musical score to contribute to the lyricism of style. 127

Wagonmaster: *celebration (above) and confrontation (right). As the members of the wagon train dance their way through a Texas Star, they are interrupted by the violent menace of the Cleggs. Such unqualified confrontations of good and evil occur naturally in the mythic world of Ford.*

Absence of plot does not mean lack of incident or character: *Wagonmaster* is acted by a number of Ford's most likeable players, and there are a succession of encounters, cheerful, sinister or strange, as the Mormon pilgrims push on to their promised land. But once again, it is the feeling which gives importance to the action; and the feeling for these pioneers, for their courage and good faith, is all admiration and love.

This kind of poetry is not separable from its moral statement. Although Ford is a Catholic by religion, and certainly no scorner of the world, it is clear that there is much to him that is attractive as well as admirable in the Puritan ideal. The little Mormon world of *Wagonmaster* is shown with warmth — self-sufficient, disciplined and contented, moved by inspiring ideals of charity and labour. Ford himself is not exactly a part of this world (his relationship to it is very much that of the two affable horse traders); he can see humour in it as well, and he can relish contrasting human eccentricities. As the wagon train heads into the desert, miles out from the last township, the outriders prick up their ears at the casual strumming

of a guitar: they have come upon the stranded outfit of Dr. A. Loxley Hall, doctor, dentist and general quack, another fugitive from frontier justice. So Ford displays his fondness for human weakness and chicanery; for, of course, Dr. Hall is allowed to join the wagon train, with Miss Florrie, his faded but still elegant 'assistant', with his 'niece', Miss Denver, and with his amiable old driver, Mr. Peestrie, who loves to bang his drum while Sister Ledyard blows her come-to-meeting horn. Nor is all this mere farce; Dr. Hall, preposterously top-hatted among the rocky wastes, has still his shabby dignity and his pathos, as he insists on his right to shave even when water supplies are at their lowest, or when he reclines at night on his brass-knobbed bedstead, whisky tears brimming in his eyes, but not so drunk as to be forgetful of the betrayed hopes of a lifetime.

Further encounters enrich — even make specific — the theme. As the pilgrims celebrate one night in the middle of the desert, dancing their way through a 'Texas Star', there is a menacing interruption, and the music trails away as a haggard, desperate looking quintet (Old Man Cleggs and his four half-witted, murderous boys) slouch in to the firelight. The

sequence of close-ups with which Ford contrasts these shifty, essentially destructive desperadoes with his simple and courageous pioneers, whose goodness makes them vulnerable as well as strong, proclaims his faith as directly and unequivocally as possible. The opposition is an inevitable one, as old as life itself, but it must be met with a challenge, not a shrug: as young Abe Lincoln put himself between the Springfield lynch mob and their victims; as Wyatt Earp set out at sun-up with his brother Morg and Doc. Holliday to arrest Old Man Clanton for the murder of his two younger brothers; as Doctor

Samuel Mudd faced his corrupt accusers. This moral element is implicit throughout *Wagonmaster,* from its start in robbery and murder, to its end in peace, blessedness and joy.

Between films like these, which relate so essentially to the historic growth of America, and their successor, *The Quiet Man* (which was to be Ford's most resounding post-war success), there might at first seem to be a huge gap. *The Quiet Man* is an Irish story, more or less contemporary, told for much of its length in the broadest, most popular style of comedy. But it is not in this that its newness 129

Top: Rio Grande. *The tension between Captain York and his wife — North and South, duty and emotion, both passionate, both stubborn in their pride — prefigures the same clash of independent spirits, equally fiery, in* The Quiet Man *(above), with Maureen O'Hara and John Wayne.*

(for it does represent an innovation) lies. Ford's awareness of his Irish heritage has never, as we have seen, been less than acute. Apart from such attempts to recreate Ireland in Hollywood as *The Informer* and *The Plough and The Stars,* there has always been a place in his films for an Irish character player or two, or for a scene of Dublin music-hall knockabout — from the dentist's chair of *The Iron*

John Wayne with Ford (right), on location in County Galway for The Quiet Man. *Winton Hoch watches for sun through his pan glass (centre right).*

Horse to Victor McLaglen's epic bar-room brawl in *She Wore a Yellow Ribbon*. That he should long have been possessed with the idea of taking a unit on location to Ireland, to shoot a comedy among the green hills and meadows of Galway, is not in itself surprising.

But *The Quiet Man* is more than a comedy. Or rather it is truly a comedy — which is to say, considerably more than a farce. While still in the middle of its production, he described it as 'a love story — an adult love story', and though this aspect of the picture has been curiously little appreciated, it is certainly unique amongst Ford's films in owing its *raison d'être* to a love affair, in turning entirely upon the complexities of a relationship. 'Unique', though, must be qualified: Ford's previous picture to this was *Rio Grande,* and it is surely no coincidence that the plot element in that story of the American Cavalry on the New Mexican border in the 1870s also turned upon the conflict between a man and a woman who love each other, a husband and wife, estranged by real and fancied wrongs, brought together at last by circumstances which combine to defeat the woman's pride. Captain and Mrs. York are played in *Rio Grande* by John Wayne and Maureen O'Hara; and so are Sean Thornton and Mary Kate Danaher in *The Quiet Man.*

Although this is a story of two people in love, and although their situation is presented with subtlety, the method is dramatic rather than discursive and the dialogue carries little direct analysis of the problems involved. The approach, in fact, is again poetic. The love between Sean and Mary Kate is physical as well as temperamental, but Ford has eschewed the directly sensual close-ups of love-making which audiences today have been taught to expect: instead he has imaged their passion in the wind that sweeps over them as they embrace, in the thunder that breaks into their courtship in the churchyard, and in the rain that drenches down as they stand in each other's arms, wetting the girl's upturned face, and soaking the man's shirt so that it clings, transparent, to the flesh. Never, perhaps, has the delicacy, the essential *decorum* of Ford's style been more in evidence than in this film: his camera never sensationalises or draws too near — even in the climactic fight he is careful to stand at the proper distance, to keep the violence in its proper perspective.

Like *The Taming of the Shrew* (with which it has several points in common), *The Quiet Man* is a comedy of pride, of self-will. Sean returns to his native land with two resolves. First that, having once killed in the ring, he will never fight again; and second, that he will buy back the little cottage in which he was born, get himself a wife and raise a

Above: The Quiet Man. *'Here's a stick to beat the lovely lady.' Sean marches Mary Kate across the fields to see him fight her brother. (Maureen O'Hara, John Wayne.) Opposite: 'Pardon's the word to all': a Shakespearean spirit of reconciliation inspires Ford's late romances. (Top)* The Quiet Man. *Mary Kate, her dowry won, is happy to welcome her brother to her home. (Victor McLaglen, Maureen O'Hara, John Wayne.) (Below)* The Sun Shines Bright. *Little Billy Priest (Charles Winninger) is saluted by his neighbours' love and gratitude — and electoral victory.*

family. He finds the girl, but he has reckoned without her pride and her prejudices. When her brother withholds her rightful dowry — her precious furniture, and her equally precious gold sovereigns — Mary Kate refuses to sleep with her man until he has gone out and won her her dowry with his fists. 'Innocence' may seem an odd quality to find in an intrigue that turns on a wife's blackmailing refusal to sleep with her husband; but such is the purity of the comedy, and so forthright the handling of it, that Ford can even manage a joke about the wreck of the huge bed in which Sean and Mary Kate are imagined to have spent their wedding night ('Impetuous', breathes Michaleen O'Flynn, 'Impetuous! Homeric!') without a suspicion of slyness. As the humour is robust, the human understanding is wise. Ford shows us that his high-spirited couple cannot live together until both have been humbled, and both have won their victories. Sean grabs Mary Kate from the Dublin train in which she has tried to make her escape, and drags her a fairy-tale ten miles through woods and meadows to see him do her will at last, confront her brother and issue the decisive challenge. The fight itself is almost irrelevant, the

jolliest of codas, and the story ends in universal harmony: victor and vanquished sit down to table together, with the woman in her proud and rightful place at the stove — Catholics cheer Protestants — straggling romances are cheerfully tidied up — and the happy people of Innisfree make their bows to the world.

As we all know, there is no such place as Innisfree. Though nominally *The Quiet Man* is a contemporary film, there is only the occasional sight of a bicycle or a telephone to link it with this century — even the Bishop's motor car has a pre-1914 air to it. This is a fairy story, or at least a fable; and the lovable grotesques who act it out are no more to be criticised for being larger than life, than is its picture of Ireland for being a country forever green, forever fertile. Leisurely in rhythm (it is a real story-teller's film), rich in its humorous detail, unrepentantly digressive, this picture perhaps more than any other shows the relaxation and the ripeness which Ford's art has gained with the years.

For all its continuity of professional activity, Ford's career seems, creatively, to have fallen into a number of quite clearly defined bursts of

The Sun Shines Bright. *Independence Day celebrations climax with the traditional Ball. Black banjos accompany the military formation dance — hierarchy at its most gracious.*

achievement; and with *The Sun Shines Bright*, in 1952, yet another period comes to a close. There is even something of a dying fall about the picture — not in any falling-off of quality, but in the graceful nostalgia, the sense of old age and replete experience which is implicit in the subject. It was nearly twenty years since Ford had filmed *Judge Priest*, with Will Rogers as the genial, wry philosopher of Irvine Cobb's stories; but their charm had remained with him, and at last the time had come for a return to Fairfield County.

In 1934, Judge Priest was middle-aged — perhaps a little more — but still active, a wry, tender-hearted, companionable widower living alone with his Negro housekeeper and houseboy. In 1952, it is an old man we see, not quite so firm on his feet as before, an undeniable eccentric, still living alone, still with the same houseboy, the same friends, and still circuit judge. Election time has come, and he is standing for a third term (it will assuredly be his last) — against his traditional opponent, the brash and arrogant Horace K. Maydew, detestable Yankee.

To a certain extent the film is a comedy of manners; but these are manners that Ford loves, however humorously he may regard them. Of course, they are not the manners of today: that is the whole point. Ford is not concerned to graft the attitudes and conflicts of the modern world on to the past — to set contemporary statesmen right — but to conjure out of the past his poetic, idealised picture of a happy society. It is an ordered society, whose members are content with their places, where existence moves to a steady, human tempo, where justice is dispensed without regard to creed or colour, and where the arts of living are still uncorrupt, unstandardised and spontaneous. There is still room here for eccentricity: the intransigent allegiance with which the old Confederate soldiers honour their lost cause is 'They Won't Forget' in a comic key, with no harm in it. And the old enemies are here, too — of meanness, cupidity, violence and ambition. Another fable, in fact. And from the film's sunny, river-side beginning, with the steamboat churning up the river, the Calliope playing, and the crowds waiting on the Levee, to the Negroes' last, affectionate serenade to their Judge, the story moves on two levels — the homely yarn of how old Judge Priest got himself re-elected for a third time, and the fresh crystallisation of a poet's world, of harmony and pleasure, of moral affirmation and reward.

'I got to get my heart started again . . .' Such is

always Judge Priest's excuse as he turns again for reassurance to his jar of rye. Never, though, was there a heart which needed less prompting — and never one freer, either, from the self-satisfaction of the entirely disinterested. 'I'd do anything for you, Judge,' says the boy whom he has just saved from the lynch-mob. 'I know you would, boy,' the Judge answers, patting his hand absently, —'but you're too young to vote . . .' But where self-interest might conflict with duty, it does not occur to him to hesitate. The flag of the Confederacy must be preserved from dishonour; the Negro boy must be defended from the lynchers; and the prostitute must have her funeral.*

The scene of the funeral is a tour-de-force: the crunch of wheels on the stony roadway, the deliberate tread of the horses, which is all the sound in the little town as the plumed hearse goes by, the prostitutes grand and dignified in their carriage, and the little Judge, Bible in hand, following behind. A few people laugh (as a few people always will), but, in ones and twos, the procession is joined by the decent, kindly townsfolk, to the rage of the mean-spirited and the scandal of the hypocritical. But it is in the beautiful scene that follows, in the school-house that has been converted for the occasion into a church, that Ford most daringly and most openly shows his heart. In his own conversational way, Judge Priest retells the story of Christ and the woman taken in adultery — and those who laugh at his naivety must laugh also at the naivety of Christ. (What else is Ashby Corwin doing, when he sinks to his knees with his nursery prayer to 'Gentle Jesus', but humbly submitting to Christ's condition — 'Except you become as little children . . .'?) No scene in any of his films conveys more unmistakably Ford's belief in moral and emotional simplicity, his rejection of the world in so far as the world is represented by the pretentious, the orthodox and the established. (The service itself must be held in a schoolhouse and conducted by a Judge, because no Priest, we are told, would risk the scandal of conducting a prostitute's funeral, before a congregation which notably includes Madame and her girls.)

Looking round in this congregation, we realise, too, that the emotion is reinforced by memories which these people bring with them of so many past occasions. There, at the harmonium, is Jane Darwell, who as Sister Ledyard, blew the horn for 'Wagons West!' and who in earlier days personified

* A heavy cut imposed by the distributors (one complete reel out of the first four) has unfortunately obscured the point of the first of these episodes.

Top: Judge Priest *(1934). Will Rogers, Charley Grapewin, Robert Homans. Above:* The Sun Shines Bright *(1953). Robert Homans, Charles Winninger, Slim Pickens.*

the heroic spirit of Ma Joad. Lucy Lee, the dead prostitute's daughter, is Arleen Wheelan, a young wife in *Young Mr. Lincoln*, and Dr. Lake, her foster-father, is Russell Simpson, who was also Grandpa Joad, and who repaired the Squadron's last two boats in *They Were Expendable*. Judge Priest's clerk of the court is Robert Homans, who performed the same office for him twenty years before, who was there when young Mr. Lincoln saved the two Barratt boys, and who met the Joads with bad news on their way to California. Francis Ford, a genial, inarticulate old comrade in so many of these adventures, is there in his coon-skin cap — it is the last time we shall see that childlike, impertinent grin of his; and Mallie Cramp, the outcast, was driven as a girl from the little Welsh chapel in *How Green Was My Valley* by the viperish intolerance of the village elders. Only Judge Priest himself is a new face in this company. . . .

Meeting in London
1957

After I had met Ford on the set of *Mogambo* in 1952, I more or less reconciled myself to the idea that admiration was better from afar. His defensive barrier was so strong; and one of its effects was infallibly to make one say the wrong things, ask the wrong questions. Nothing seemed to come back from him. The pull of his personality was not diminished by this; but I did not like being made to feel like a journalist. And I lacked the confidence to behave like a friend, which he would probably have preferred.

Four years later he returned to Britain to direct a picture. In the time between I had continued to carry the flag. I had arranged a Ford season at the National Film Theatre: he had sent a courteous telegram regretting that he couldn't be there. And I had become something approaching a professional film maker myself — at least I had at long last been admitted to the union. I had achieved some success with a short film about deaf children which I had made in collaboration with my Oxford friend Guy Brenton, and with a documentary about the market in Covent Garden, *Every Day Except Christmas*. I continued to write occasionally about films; and the year before, a group of friends and I had launched the Free Cinema series of programmes at the National Film Theatre. I got the odd commission, for a talk or an interview, from BBC radio, usually from a friendly talks producer Richard Keene. It was he who precipitated my third meeting with the Old Man.

The film Ford came to London to make in the summer of 1957 was a crime thriller called *Gideon's Day,* based on the adventures of John Creasey's character, Inspector Gideon of Scotland Yard. It seemed a peculiar choice of subject, with Gideon being played by Jack Hawkins, classical representative of the firm-jawed English hero. (Years later, in his interview with Peter Bogdanovich, Ford remarked: 'I wanted to get away for a while, so I said I'd like to do a Scotland Yard thing and we went over and did it.' Which is more or less how the film turned out.) Richard Keene wanted an interview with Ford for his programme, and he asked me to do it. I could not resist the temptation.

We were to meet at Brown's Hotel, a cosy, unfashionable island of 'county' comfort in Mayfair: plump armchairs covered in flowered chintz, open fires, tea with buttered toast. Richard Keene came with me to carry the tape recorder and hold the microphone. We waited a short while in Ford's suite till he appeared with his crony and associate Lord Killanin, his fellow director in Four Provinces Films and later Chairman of the Olympic Games Committee, an affable, unassuming Anglo-Irish Peer.

Ford was jovial, though in some way he seemed diminished since I had seen him last. He was in his early sixties now and showing his age; he gave the impression of being not altogether firm on his feet. He wore smoked glasses and a black patch over his left eye. There was a cable waiting for him. He shoved his glasses up on his forehead and brought the cable-form close to his right eye, peering at the message like someone deciphering an ancient inscription. 'Back home,' he announced. The family had been on holiday in Honolulu.

He was in joshing mood, greeting me with off-hand familiarity and making jokes about my accent. He pretended he couldn't understand my 'Oxford English'. 'Will they understand him — you know — ordinary people?,' he asked Richard Keene, who obliged by smiling in an embarrassed way, not sure what was going on. I tried to begin, but Ford was not going to let a good joke drop. 'What's that? Sorry — it's difficult for me to get what you're saying . . .' He was winning: my smile was growing

Contrast in location. Top: Ford at home in Monument Valley, with Ward Bond and John Wayne, for The Searchers *(1956). Bottom: In England, a suburban location for* Gideon's Day, *with Jack Hawkins, and Freddie Young behind the camera.*

137

strained: I tried to get some kind of conversation going. How was he enjoying working in England — knowing how he felt about the English? He feigned indignation: he loved England, he had a great many very good English friends. I tried to ask him about the kind of films he most enjoyed making — the subjects he'd found for himself and the subjects he'd accepted as studio assignments. He denied everything. He had never chosen his own stories. No, the films he'd made since the war were no more 'his' than the ones he had made for Zanuck at Fox. No, there was no difference between getting a start in the old days, and setting out to be a movie-maker today. No, there was none of his films that he remembered with particular affection. Only the Westerns, all of them. And only because he enjoyed the life on location.

Ford's reputation with interviewers was of course legendary; now I could appreciate the legend at first hand. It was much worse than the first time we had met, when he had been gruff but friendly. His technique was brutal, ruthlessly destructive; by lying, by contradicting everything he'd ever said, by effecting not to understand the simplest question, he could reduce one to dispirited impotence. In this mood, the best journalist in the world could not have got anything out of him. I was not the best journalist in the world; and I was handicapped further by not really wanting to be a journalist anyway. In the end, Ford shrugged all my questions off and launched into a long account of shooting *The Iron Horse* in the snow. It should have been fascinating, but I found myself unable to listen. I could not rid myself of the feeling that he was telling me all this chiefly because I hadn't asked him about it.

Towards the end of our conversation, no doubt sensing my disgust as well as my defeat, Ford reversed direction again. He began to speak more warmly. He seemed anxious to make it clear that he remembered our earlier meetings: that I was a soldier's son, that I was born in India, that I had been in the Army in India during the war . . . By this time Richard Keene had surrendered, packed up his tape-recorder and stolen away. I don't believe the interview was ever broadcast.

There had not been much discussion of cinema in this conversation. I remember Ford saying how much he liked English actors; he expressed, apropos nothing, a particular admiration for the character actress Martita Hunt (she was not in *Gideon's Day* so I suppose he'd seen her in the theatre). Also, naturally, Jack Hawkins. I raised an eyebrow. 'He's a great actor,' Ford said, firmly. He had seen *The Admirable Crichton* (the film), which he praised as a piece of 'English social comedy'. Rightly or wrongly, I didn't find any of this very convincing.

I have no idea how the names of Eisenstein and *Ivan The Terrible* came into the conversation, maybe through some mention of the National Film Theatre. But I do remember that Ford had never seen the film — and remarked that he'd very much like to.

'We could get them to screen it for you, if you'd like.'

'Yeah — good idea.'

Then rashly I went further. Richard Keene had gone and Killanin had left the room, so there was no-one to embarrass me. I mentioned hesitantly that I had made a film, a documentary about Covent Garden Market called *Every Day Except Christmas*. I wondered if, by any chance, Ford would like to see it too. He was affable. 'Bring it along.'

Three or four days later, on a Monday afternoon, Ford turned up at the National Film Theatre, the faithful Killanin in attendance. I was touched to see that he was wearing a tie: I had never seen him before in anything but an open-necked shirt and a pullover. But there was no-one to greet him except myself and Alex Jacobs, colleague and publicist in our Free Cinema ventures. The only suggestion of occasion was provided by the NFT's Chief Projectionist, who hovered around us with a 16 mm. camera. This seemed to please the Old Man.

We went into the theatre and sat down near the front, because Ford needed to be close to the screen. I sat next to him, with Killanin on his other side and Alex in the row behind. We started with *Every Day Except Christmas*.

My film was a forty-minute portrait of the old Covent Garden market, impressionistic and personal, poetic rather than journalistic or informative. Its neglect of documented fact about wages or working conditions had, in fact, already incurred the disapproval of survivors of the Grierson school and exposed me to charges of sentimentalism and 'patronising the working classes'. Privately I considered that its unabashed sentiment and its traditionally-derived music were strongly Fordian. No wonder I was uneasy as the lights went down and the projection began.

Ford smoked, chewed gum and accompanied the film with a prosaic barrage of questions. Did we use lamps? (Minimally). Was 'God Save the Queen' the end of a broadcast programme? (Yes: I had used the Home Service closing announcement and final Anthem in Humphrey Jennings-style counterpoint to the lorry's journey to London.) Was it being played in the lorry? (If you like) . . . No wonder the men in Covent Garden went on strike . . . What union did they belong to? (I didn't know and didn't care.) Nice little baskets they used for mushrooms . . . They drank tea did they? (Of course.) What about beer? (The pubs opened specially at about five in the morning: I hadn't used them: too 'obvious'.) Who was that gaunt-faced fellow looking into the camera? ('Johnny Ray' — a busker.) What was a busker? (A street musician.) I guess now that some of these enquiries were genuine; at the time I could only feel my 'poetic' impressionism shrivelling into prose under the barrage. As the night people in Albert's Cafe drifted off into their own thoughts, or into sleep, and the camera tracked along the rows of tulips standing like a motionless crowd on the shelves of the silent flower market, Ford let up for a moment. The accordion music was gentle; the camera moved dreamily over flowers and tilted up into the darkness. A moment of dream. Ford smashed in with a knockout blow: *'When do the fish come in?'*

I controlled myself mightily and submitted. All through the moonlit shots that followed, of silhouetted roofs and empty, echoing streets, I obliged myself to jabber on like a travel courier. London had three main markets — one for meat, one for fish, one for fruit, flowers and vegetables. Smithfield, Billingsgate and Covent Garden. This was Covent Garden. There was no fish. Ford listened impassively.

The market came to early morning life. 'All wholesale goods, eh?'. . . 'God, what types' . . . Amongst them I had picked out bustling Alice, last of the women porters, sharp-nosed and no nonsense. 'I like Alice . . .' said Ford. I ended the film with a montage of characters and faces, working and talking, most of them laughing, Alice among them. For the last image I chose one of the youngest porters, smiling straight into camera, the shot held long. *(Expendable? Clementine?)* 'You ought to have finished with Alice . . .' said Ford. I said nothing.

Ivan the Terrible came on and Ford was quiet for a bit; I couldn't be sure what he was making of it. Then, 'Eisenstein was a cameraman, wasn't he? . . . a pure cameraman.' It sounded like criticism rather than praise. 'Not a dramatic director, you mean?' I hazarded. 'No use with people,' Ford went on. 'Look at the way they move. Like puppets.' I suggested that it was like ballet: he went along with this. (I forebore to mention *The Fugitive*.) I didn't really feel he enjoyed the film too much. But he watched it through to the end, and admired a lot of the camerawork.

I commented no further. I realised that he could accept facts, but not opinions.

When the projection ended, we went into the bar. Ford didn't drink anything. 'I don't drink when I'm working.' He posed obligingly for Chief with his 16 mm. camera; joked with Fred behind the bar ('We've just seen you in the picture'); and wrote graciously in the visitors' book — sitting down to it, his good eye close to the paper. Then he and Killanin departed, to see if Freddie Young had managed to get any good shots of the Horse Guards.

139

When the shooting of *Gideon's Day* was over, before Ford left for California, Alex Jacobs and a group of devotees threw a dinner party for him. I stayed away; I had had enough. Ford didn't drink much, my friend Derek York told me later, but just a couple of glasses had their effect.

'But there was one thing he said,' Derek remarked, 'I found rather touching. He said, "You put things into a picture — little things — and generally nobody notices. But you people notice a lot of the things I've tried to do. It's very heart-warming."'

'Hmm . . .' I said.

Opening of the National Film Theatre, London (1957). Ford with Vittorio de Sica and René Clair.

P.S. Ford's viewing of *Every Day Except Christmas* at the National Film Theatre was the nearest he came to contact with our Free Cinema movement of those days. But it seems to have given rise to a choice item of Fordian mythology. The Filmography in Peter Bogdanovich's monograph lists the following entry for 1958:

So Alone (Free Cinema — British Film Institute). Director: John Ford. Photographers: Winton Hoch, Walter Lassally. Music: Malcolm Arnold. Filmed in London, winter 1957. 8 minutes. Released: July. With John Qualen, James Hayter (two minstrels).
The relationship between (and incidents in the life of) two men as they wander through Wapping on a cold, winter day.

This film, which never existed, seems to be a leg-pull in the best Fordian tradition. Its description clearly derives from *Together,* the 50-minute picture by Lorenza Mazzetti which featured in the first Free Cinema programme in 1956. In this, two young artists, Michael Andrews and Eduardo Paolozzi, played deaf-mute friends in London's dockland; I supervised the editing and completion of the film, and Walter Lassally provided some additional photography. The conjunction of Walter with Winton Hoch (on an 8-minute film!) is as weird as the teaming of John Qualen, regular member of the Ford stock company, with James Hayter, one of the British actors in *Gideon's Day*. This notion of *So Alone* as Ford's contribution to Free Cinema is delightfully absurd — perhaps there was even a touch of friendliness in the joke.

Meeting at Burbank

1963

IN September 1963 I found myself in Hollywood. *This Sporting Life*, my first feature film, had been shown earlier in the year, and particularly well received in America: I began to experience for the first time the heady, absurd world of telegrams and agents. In August, at the Montreal Festival, I was called by Rachel Roberts in California: she was under intense pressure, it seemed, from a venerable old producer who was anxious to have her and Richard Harris appear under my direction, in what sounded like a remake of *This Sporting Life*, set on the San Francisco waterfront. The old producer was Merian C. Cooper, co-author of the first film I had ever seen (the animal classic, *Chang*) as well as of *King Kong*; more recently he had been John Ford's partner in Argosy Productions. Cooper called me himself, urging that we should meet (he had another project, about the pursuit of a man-eating tiger). It was irresistible. Rachel, then married to Rex Harrison, was in Hollywood for the shooting of *My Fair Lady*. I could combine an excursion into fantasy with a visit to friends. I flew out.

(I never met General Cooper — as I discovered he was known. By the time I arrived on the Coast, he was in the Far East, on some reconnaissance. He summoned me by telegram to a meeting in Bangkok. I nearly went — until I discovered that cholera and typhus injections were compulsory, and would take another six days to get. The joke was becoming too elaborate. I decided to stay a week with my friends and then return to Britain.)

On my second day in Hollywood, we drove out to the studio to visit the set of *My Fair Lady*. It was impossible not to be excited. It was ten years since the Era had ended: television had finished it. Yet Hollywood remained — as it always will — a haunted place, with names that echo with romance. We were driving from Beverly Hills to Burbank, to Warner Brothers. Jack Warner was still in command there. Spaces in the car park still carried legendary names. B. Davis. George Cukor. John Ford.

I had heard that Ford was preparing an Indian story, but had not expected him to be there, at Warner Brothers. In recent years my devotion had flagged. So much of his work (pictures like *The Rising of the Moon* and *The Horse Soldiers*) seemed to have lost real warmth and impulse: I no longer saw his new films as a matter of course. In 1960 *Sergeant Rutledge* had stood out as an exception, and I had written to thank him for it. But his two most recent films I hadn't even seen. Probably I still smarted a bit from our last meetings. All the same, it would be ridiculous not to pay my respects if he was in the studio. I got Cukor's production office to check. The answer came back: yes, Mr. Ford was in today, and would be pleased to receive me and Miss Roberts. After lunch we went across.

We were greeted warmly by Meta Stern, Ford's secretary for many years: a cheery, unsmart, late-middle-aged lady, homely in the English sense, who remembered me from letters. She showed us into Ford's office. He was sitting behind dark glasses at a functional desk, in a rather bare, functional room. He got up slowly, excusing himself. It cost him pain to move: he had fallen downstairs a few weeks ago, he said, with his dog in his arms, and broken six ribs. He seemed less bulky than when I'd

The Rising of the
Moon. *Back in Ireland,
on location for one
of the three episodes,*
The Majesty of the
Law *(1957), with Jack
MacGowran.*

seen him last, his face very white, the sandy tones almost vanished now from his thinning hair.

He knew I'd made a film. He hadn't seen it, but he knew it was about a footballer. 'You're a capitalist now, you'll have to stop calling yourself a socialist.' I wasn't going to get rich on it, I said — but he waved that aside. His impatience and wilfulness in conversation hadn't changed. And he was deafer.

I introduced him to Rachel, who reminded him that they'd met before: he had been at the first night of *O My Papa!*, the first play she'd done in London. He remembered, and reminded her that the Gallery had booed. 'I don't know why they booed, it was a good show. That boy O'Toole was in it, wasn't he? You were good — you've got a fine pair of legs.' (Delighted reaction from Rachel.) 'You can sing too.'

He was starting his picture in a few weeks, a big picture, a new kind of Western for him. 'It's a true story: we're going to do it like a documentary . . . This is the West from the Indian point of view. I've killed more Indians in my career than any other director, so I felt it was only right now I should tell *their* story . . .' He told us the title, *Cheyenne Autumn*, and asked us what we thought of it. 'It's a good title isn't it? I've got an egghead producer — who thinks he's the producer — who wants to change it. He wants to call it *The Last March* or *The Long March* or something vapid like that. I'll get him in here before you go — you can tell him what an idiot he is.'

In London I had met the two Americans who owned *Young Cassidy*, a script based on Sean O'Casey's autobiography, and were going to produce it in Ireland. (In fact they had wanted Richard Harris to play the lead and had suggested I might direct it.

But they had seemed overbearing and possessive, and the idea had not jelled. I kept quiet about this.) I knew that Ford's name had been linked with the project. 'I might do that,' he said, 'I don't know yet. There are two egghead producers on it, who've never made a movie before and think they know everything . . . It's a beautiful script.' He was right about Robert Graff and Robert Emmett Gina: their arrogance and lack of sensitivity were probably the chief reasons why he was so unhappy on *Young Cassidy* and failed to complete it. 'But I won't shoot it in Dublin. It's impossible to shoot in Dublin . . .' I dared to tell him that friends of mine had recently had an excellent experience shooting a film in Dublin (*The Girl With Green Eyes*), but Ford would have none of it. 'The Dubliners aren't Irish. They're scum. We might go out to Limerick or Galway and take a street and shoot it there . . . I wouldn't get any money for it, but I'd like to do it.'

He reverted to *Cheyenne Autumn* and his producer's idea that they should change the title. 'I'll get him in. You tell him: he'll listen to you.' Bernard Smith came into the office, urbane and well-mannered. These qualities clearly brought out the worst in Ford. He introduced me as the editor of *Sight and Sound*. 'He's a producer,' he said, nodding in Smith's direction. 'Some kind of intellectual . . . he takes notice of all those egghead magazines . . . Now,' he went on, 'tell him what you think of the title.' I did my best. 'I think it's a fine title. It's got a great ring to it.' 'They're not going to find it incomprehensible in Europe, are they?' 'I don't think so; they know all about the Red Indians there . . .' Ford switched to Rachel Roberts. 'What do you think, Rachel?' Rachel, eternal Welsh, shifted uneasily and temporised. After all Bernard Smith was a producer. 'You're chickening out,' said Ford. 'That's not how you were talking before he came in.' Rachel shied nervously. 'Oh, it's a wonderful title! I love it!' Bernard Smith smiled politely. I doubted that the title would be changed.

We left. Ford murmured something about hoping we'd meet again, but I didn't think it was likely. (We didn't.) A couple of days later I dropped into his office to pick up a signed copy of the novel of *Cheyenne Autumn*, which Ford has inscribed for Rachel. He wasn't there. I asked Meta Stern if she thought Ford would sign a still for me. She produced a file, and I chose one from *She Wore a Yellow Ribbon*, of

The Rising of the Moon. *On location for the second story.* A Minute's Wait.

Indians attacking in full cry across a Monument Valley landscape. Rex Harrison brought it back from the studio, inscribed: *'To Lindsay. Here are the "Red Indians!" With sincere thanks and gratitude for your friendship thru' the years. Jack — John Ford.'*

Eight years later, out of the blue, I received another inscribed picture. I had not seen Ford again, nor heard from him, since our meeting at Burbank. I had written to him now and again — though not, alas, after seeing *Cheyenne Autumn* (to be honest, I have never managed to sit through all of it) nor after *Seven Women*. But I sent him my appreciation of *The Man Who Shot Liberty Valance,* and told him of seasons of his pictures on British television, and sent greetings at Christmas. These letters were never answered; nor did I expect them to be. But I thought he might be pleased to get them.

In 1971 we presented our Royal Court production of David Storey's *Home* at the Morosco Theatre in New York. Our stage manager was Bob Borod, aficionado of theatre and film. Eric Harrison, emigré from the English North and veteran of *Soldiers in Skirts,* was Ralph Richardson's dresser. I met them in London again a year later, and they gave me my picture. They told me its story.

After *Home,* Bob and Eric had gone on the national tour of *Coco,* with Katherine Hepburn. I shuddered slightly at this name — though not through anything but guilt. Some time before I had been sent a book by this great artist, who wanted to play in a film of it. It took me at least nine months to acknowledge it. (Guilt, of course, is cumulative in these situations.) At last I had written while on holiday in St. Lucia (feeling obscurely that a remote address somehow palliated the sin) regretting that the subject had not rung my bell . . . I knew I had behaved badly, chiefly through shyness.

In Los Angeles Miss Hepburn had invited Bob and Eric out to have tea with her old friend John Ford. They had only worked together once, on the unfortunate *Mary of Scotland,* but they had formed a loving, warring respect for each other. And later Ford had done *The Last Hurrah* with Spencer Tracy. Conversation had ranged wide at the tea party, when somehow my name fell into the conversation. 'You worked with him?' said Ford, 'I've known him for years.'

Miss Hepburn growled. 'That sonofabitch,' (or something like) 'I sent him a book I wanted to do and it took him a year to answer, from some godammed island in the Caribbean.'

'What did he say?', asked Ford.

'He didn't want to do it.'

'He's got too much sense,' said Ford.

When the party broke up, Ford went off and returned with a large envelope, which he gave to Bob and Eric. They had said they were planning a holiday in London when the tour ended.

'If you see Lindsay Anderson in London, give him this. You can tell him it's from an old friend.'

The envelope contained a mounted picture of Ford, pipe in hand, stars and stripes on his combat jacket sleeve, naval insignia on collar and cap. The familiar caustic look from behind smoked glasses. On the mount he had written:

'To my colleague. Lindsay Anderson. With best regards from his friend of many years, Jack. John Ford.'

I wrote and thanked him, from the heart. I didn't get an answer, of course, not even from some goddammed island in the Pacific.

To my colleague. Smday Anderson
with best regards from his friend of
many years
        Jack.
                Johnford

Sergeant Rutledge. *Ford's cherished myth of the Cavalry, with its themes of duty and service, is complicated by new issues of racialism and intolerance. (Jeffrey Hunter, Woody Strode).*

The Film Maker

4. The Last Decade

It was with a certain relief that I learned, twenty-five years ago, that funds had run out and the British Film Institute was not going ahead with its Great Director series. So I was not going to have to round off my account of Ford's career with a dispiriting anti-climax.

That certainly would have been the effect of a coda devoted to the period immediately following *The Sun Shines Bright*. In 1953 Ford made *Mogambo* for M-G-M, an excursion undertaken for enjoyment and escape, neither ambitious in conception nor notable in the result. In the same year he paid friendly visits to John Wayne's production of *Hondo*, directed by John Farrow, to which he contributed a few shots. 1954 seems to have been a year out. Then in 1955 came *The Long Gray Line* for Columbia, a sentimental-military chronicle with some characteristic passages, followed by *Mister Roberts* for Warners, a version of the enormously successful Broadway play, in which Henry Fonda had starred. This started propitiously, reuniting Ford with Fonda; but the outcome was sad. Fonda knew and understood the material intimately and he made clear his disappointment with Ford's rough handling of it: there was a violent dispute, and the last scenes in the picture were directed by Mervyn Leroy. The end of 1955 saw Ford in the television mill, with two half-hour films for TV Playhouse programmes. *The Bamboo Cross* featured Jane Wyman and Betty Lynn as Catholic nuns in China; and *Rookie of the Year* brought Ford together with Ward Bond, Vera Miles and Pat Wayne with John Wayne looking in as 'Mike, a reporter'. He was back where he had started forty years before, in the mainstream of popular entertainment, only that mainstream now was more like a treadmill. Television had arrived and innocence had been lost.

It would not have made a happy rounding-off. It is not much happier to look back on today; but at least we can now see the waste of those years in perspective, as part of history, finally insignificant in comparison with the achievements which had gone before. I would not wish to imply that in the last ten years of his working life — there were thirteen more feature films still to come — Ford produced nothing of value. He made at least two fine, characteristic pictures, and a third of which many critics do not hesitate to use the word 'masterpiece'. Nor was it a question, certainly not *just* a question, of diminished creative power. It was a question of history. In the early fifties, even earlier, the Hollywood in which John Ford, film maker and poet, had been formed and matured, underwent cataclysmic changes. The world had changed, too: how could the myths on which the American cinema was founded and from which it had drawn its strength, survive unscathed? History, which had always seemed to be on his side, turned against John Ford. In his seventieth decade, and his fiftieth as a Hollywood film maker, he ran out of luck.

He was not a career man, of course — as he never ceased to assert. This did not mean that his profession meant nothing to him. 'I've always enjoyed making pictures — it's been my whole life,' he told Peter Bogdanovich. He meant simply that he was not possessed by the urge to excel, to build a great reputation for himself. (Which did not mean that he had no pride in his reputation.) He was happiest as a professional. His object was not to win awards, but first and foremost to work, because he liked it.

Not to be a 'career man' may seem to imply an attractive lack of pretension. In Ford's case there was more pride than modesty behind the stance. Justified pride, certainly, and also confidence. It was not a matter simply of pride in his talent, which was self-evident and had no need to make claims, but of confidence that there would always be a use for that talent. This kind of confidence, which is one of the strongest supports an artist can have, amounts really to a confidence in history — the belief that not only is your talent a valuable one, but that it will always be valued. There will always be a use for it. This involves a special kind of luck.

For the first thirty-five years of his career, Ford had this kind of luck: the luck of being born in the right place and at the right time. He was born in

Old comrades: Ward Bond (as John Dodge), John Wayne (playing Spig Wead) and Ford, on the set of Wings of Eagles.

America, the country in the world whose democratic, economic and technological thrust most suited it to the development of the democratic, technological and expensive art of cinema. He arrived in Hollywood (by luck again, since it was his brother's success as an actor and a director that took him there) just when the foundations had been laid. Men with names like Goldfish and Loew, Mayer, Zukor and Laemmle were building the business: Griffith, almost single-handed, had provided the film with its grammar and also with its dignity. The vigorous, expanding business-art was just entering its youthful prime, providing the open, optimistic, largely naive American public, stimulated by capitalism and not yet brainwashed and vulgarised by it, with the entertainment and refreshment it demanded. The young John Ford's talent was trained in the unselfconscious golden age of the silent cinema: the golden age of the image. And it reached maturity through the years of Hollywood's arrogant and confident supremacy.

In the 1950s this supremacy was challenged — and defeated. Hollywood's domination of the U.S. entertainment market had lasted all through the thirties and forties, or up to the end of the Second World War at least. What else was there for the mass audience, in search of entertainment and escape, to spend its money on? At the end of the thirties seventy-five million Americans were going to the movies every week: by 1946 there were a hundred million of them, two-thirds of the entire nation. Then came television. In two years there were fifteen million fewer moviegoers a week. By 1957 forty-five million more had deserted, to stay at home and watch the box. Gable was right; it was the end of an era.

As the catastrophic decline got under way, the Hollywood studio system received another blow. In 1948, the United States Supreme Court ruled that for the studios to own large chains of theatres (which gave their product a guaranteed sale) constituted an infringement of the anti-trust laws. The major production-and-distribution companies were ordered to sell their theatres. In December, 1949, Paramount lost its chain, followed by RKO in 1950, M-G-M and Twentieth-Century Fox in 1952. The old order was changing.

It was in this climate of anxiety and speculation that Ford determined to go independent. But the changes in Hollywood were not simply economic: inevitably, they reflected changes of taste and belief in the world at large. It was hardly to be expected that American audiences — to say nothing of audiences the world over — would come out of the

Latter-day heroes: James Stewart and Richard Widmark in Two Rode Together.

war years with the same entertainment expectation and demands they had at the start. Certain values, certain ideals had lost their authority. Progressives who had applauded the passionate humanism of *The Grapes of Wrath*, found *They Were Expendable*, with its equally staunch and deeply-felt celebration of the warrior's creed, irrelevant, even repugnant. Patriotism had become 'flag waving'. Issues of racism and 'tolerance' began to be the stuff of popular entertainment. Ford may have loathed racism, but such stuff could not be the stuff of his art: he was not a propagandist. Instead, his nostalgic sense of hierarchy and traditionalism (the Black chorus of *The Sun Shines Bright*) could not but affront liberals and Blacks in the revolt against the patronage and the stereotyping of the past.* Films like *Home of the Brave, Lost Boundaries, Gentleman's Agreement,* breathed the spirit of the times: it was inevitable, and symbolic too, that the old-time sentimentalism which Ford brought to his handling of *Pinky* should be replaced by the specious liberalism of Kazan. Inevitable, and also humiliat-

* The intellectuals have not yet forgiven Ford. For instance a review of McBride and Wilmington's *John Ford* in *Film Quarterly* congratulates the authors on the 'aplomb' with which they handle 'Ford's abominable favourite *The Sun Shines Bright*'. (University of California, Berkeley, September 1976.)

ing. Ford was no stranger to conflict with producers and studio bosses; but his autocratic self-indulgence had been in defiance of convention, in defence of liberty. And he had generally won his battles. He was not accustomed to rejection.

Hollywood's troubles in the fifties were not simply economic. Just as traumatic, in a different area, was the hysterical reaction against the pro-Russian policies of the later war years (undertaken, of course, with official encouragement), the intimidation of the studios by the House Committee on Un-American Activities, and the McCarthyite persecution of Communists, ex-Communists, and simple, benevolent 'liberals'. The American cinema was split apart. Ten noted film makers went to prison for refusing either to confirm or deny that they were or had been Communists. Others were driven into exile. Still others were black-listed and denied the right to work.

These disputes hardly touched Ford directly. He might claim on occasion to be a socialist, but his essential conservatism, and his patriotism, were unquestionable. His friends John Wayne and Ward Bond were among the most notoriously aggressive defenders of the flag. His record of service was unsurpassed. But a man of Ford's sensitivity and national pride could not exist unaware of this kind of atmosphere, or unaffected by it. Indeed we know, from his action on one famous occasion, that he did not.

The occasion was a meeting of the Directors' Guild at the Beverly Hills Hotel in October 1950, the result of a petition signed by twenty-five rebellious directors to protest against and if possible to frustrate the resolution of Cecil B. de Mille to recall (i.e. have dismissed) the 'liberal' Joe Mankiewicz from his position as president of the Guild. The best description of this meeting is by Robert Parrish in his book *Growing Up in Hollywood.**

The signatories to the petition included some of the biggest, most respected names in Hollywood: Wyler, Wilder, Huston, Zinnemann. More attended: Milestone, Kazan, Stevens, Capra, Lang ... Ford was there with his pipe and his handkerchief. Mankiewicz defended himself for an hour; a succession of liberals talked, reproachfully, defensively; George Stevens offered his resignation (refused), spoke brilliantly and called up de Mille to retract, de Mille refused. Stevens sat down. At last, when it looked like stalemate, Ford made his play. Robert Parrish tells it:

'After the applause for Stevens stopped, there was silence for a moment, and Ford raised his hand. A court stenographer was there, and everyone had to identify himself for the record. Ford stood up and faced the stenographer.

'"My name's John Ford," he said. "I make Westerns." He paused for a moment to let this bit of news sink in. "I don't think there is anyone in this room who knows more about what the American public wants than Cecil B. de Mille — and he certainly knows how to give it to them. In that respect I admire him." Then he looked right at de Mille, who was across the room from him. "But I don't like you, C.B.," he said. "I don't like what you stand for and I don't like what you've been saying here tonight. Joe has been vilified, and I think he needs an apology." He stared at de Mille while the membership waited in silence. De Mille stared straight ahead and made no move. After thirty seconds, Ford finally said, "Then I believe there is only one alternative, and I hereby so move; that Mr. de Mille and the entire board of directors resign and that we give Joe a vote of confidence — and then let's all go home and get some sleep. We've got some pictures to make tomorrow."

'Walter Lang seconded the motion. Ford sat down and lit his pipe. The membership voted in favour of Ford's motion. De Mille and the board resigned and we gave Mankiewicz a unanimous vote of confidence, with four abstentions.'

I quote this incident in detail because it carries a significance beyond the immediate. Ford succeeded where the liberals failed, because he had a better sense of timing, a better sense of drama, and more courage. George Stevens offered his resignation, and, in the face of de Mille's intransigence, could only sit down. Ford challenged de Mille and moved his resignation. Amazingly (and illuminatingly) no one else had thought to, or dared to, do as much. And so he won.

But if Ford led the liberals, he did not make one with them. His friends remained his friends; and politically he did not make one with them either. He remained isolated, an anarchic traditionalist in an increasingly conformist climate. And of course, though that particular battle was won, the whole campaign was not. The blacklist lengthened and was used to deprive good artists and good people of work. Joseph Losey, one of the signatories of the Guild's petition, was forced into exile and became a European director. Huston crossed the Atlantic; so did Nicholas Ray. Some people died.

2

In the ten years from *Mr. Roberts* to the end of his career, Ford completed twelve more pictures, as well as a segment of the Cinerama *How The West Was Won,* a documentary on Korea in 1959, and a couple of films-for-television. John Wayne made sneak appearances in both the television shows (one of which featured his son Pat), and starred in six of the full-length films. After the debacle of *Mr. Roberts,* Ford and Fonda never worked together again.

Nor did Ford ever again work for his old studio, Twentieth Century-Fox. Fundamental changes took place there too. In 1956, after twenty years in charge of production, Darryl Zanuck gave up his job and moved to Europe, where he embarked on a series of independent, generally mediocre productions. His parting words emphasised another aspect of Hollywood's transformation:* 'Hollywood drove me out ... Actors have taken over Hollywood completely, together with their agents. They want approval of scripts, stars, still pictures. The producer hasn't a chance to exercise authority.'

Here was another gap for Ford. He had always been happy to benefit from Zanuck's picture-making sense and concern, as well as from the continuity of collaboration and the fine craftsmanship of the Fox studio tradition. Now he had to go

* Published by Bodley Head, London, and Harcourt Brace, New York, 1976, a unique, indispensable book for Fordians especially.

* Quoted in *Zanuck: Hollywood's Last Tycoon* by Leo Guild (Holloway House, New York, 1970).

Sergeant Rutledge. *The Buffalo soldiers under fire (Woody Strode and Constance Towers in foreground). This was Ford's last fine foray in Monument Valley.*

from studio to studio, according to the ownership of his subjects or the possibilities of finance; there were two pictures for M-G-M, three for Warners, two for Paramount and three for Columbia. Two of the least happy ventures of these years were shot in Europe: *The Rising of the Moon* in Ireland and *Gideon's Day* in London, England.

The quality of Ford's work in this last period may be described as consistently uneven. There is a continued recurrence of themes — the family, duty, stubborn individualism, suspicion of the present, romantic nostalgia for a cleaner, simpler past. From time to time there was a valiant attempt to come to terms with the changed values of post-war America and the changing demands of commercial cinema. Sometimes it seemed as though these attempts might give a new stimulus to the work, as with the collision of black pride and white prejudice within the military tradition in *Sergeant Rutledge,* or the attempt to pay the debt of honour and atone for the arrogance of the past in *Cheyenne Autumn.* But the sources of inspiration cannot easily (or voluntarily)

be transformed; and certainly Ford could never become a 'liberal' in order to accommodate himself to the fashion of the time. It is easy to sense his regret or his resentment at the demand. And often the result was an unhappy roughness, of tone or of style, even sometimes a coarseness that only made glow more strongly, in retrospect, the lyricism of the past.

The past is recalled continually in these films. Only four-and-a-bit, in fact, can be said to have any connection with the present, and tenuous at that. *Donovan's Reef* is an escapist romp (with some more serious allusions) set on a remote Pacific island; and two of the three stories in *The Rising of the Moon* are Irish yarns, one farcical and one ironically suggestive. (The third and most substantial part is another backward look at the Dublin of the Troubles.) The picturesque London of *Gideon's Day* is closer to the Never-Never Land of comedy-thriller mythology than to 1959 Britain. And Ford's last two 'contemporary' subjects have little sympathy with the present: *The Wings of* 151

Eagles is a comradely obituary, told mostly in flashback, of his old friend Frank Wead, flyer and writer, who had scripted *Airmail* for him in 1932 and *They Were Expendable* twelve years later; and *The Last Hurrah* chronicles the last mayoral campaign of an old-style New England politician, whose final struggle against the specious men of the future (unlike that of Billy Priest, when the old world still had a little time to run) ends in defeat and, a short while later, death.

The heroine of *Seven Women* dies too, self-sacrificed with the bandit villain who has demanded her as his price for releasing a party of women missionary prisoners — a curious, inappropriate subject for Ford's last film, released in 1966 and set in China thirty years before. With this exception, every film he made after his return from Korea in 1958 reached back into American history, from the Civil War of *The Horse Soldiers* and *How The West Was Won* to the pioneer West of *The Searchers*, *Two Rode Together* and *Sergeant Rutledge*, the Indian oppression of *Cheyenne Autumn* and the ironic triumph of 'civilisation' over frontier anarchy in *The Man Who Shot Liberty Valance*. These films form a group, but not a confident, close-knit one like the cavalry pictures of the early fifties. Choice of subject no longer has the personal stamp, the heaven-sent certainty which characterises (even when they lurch or stumble) *Fort Apache, Rio Grande* and *She Wore A Yellow Ribbon*. New themes and issues intrude, issues of colour, racial injustice, shadows of the future.

Of all these films, the most successful was *The Searchers*, released in 1956 after the pot-boiling *Mogambo* and the indulgent military sentimentalisms of *The Long Gray Line*. A spacious Western, magnificently exploiting the familiar landscapes of Monument Valley, starring John Wayne and featuring many of the old stock company faces, this had a reassuring appeal which won it immediate popular success. Darker themes lurked beneath the spectacular surface, but these were scarcely remarked; at any rate the film does not seem to have attracted much 'serious' attention at the time. It is only in recent years that the auteurists and semiologists have descended to claim for *The Searchers*, in the perspective of Ford's whole career, the status of masterpiece. The encomia are lavish, and remarkably consistent.

'Perhaps Ford's most perfect philosophical statement.'[*] 'His greatest tone poem.' [†] *'The*

Searchers has that clear yet intangible quality which characterises an artist's masterpiece . . .'[‡]

The film has become, in fact, the object of a cult, particularly among those latter-day critics of Ford who see in the work of his last ten years no decline or loss of vigour, but rather a matured vision, a deepened understanding of history and of life. Unhappily, this is not a view which can be supported by the evidence on the screen.

3

Writing about *The Searchers* when it first appeared, my own assessment was far less favourable: and so it has remained. Disagreements between critics are often tiresome, particularly when they seem principally to represent (as is so often the case) a clash of journalistic *amours propres*. Yet differences of evaluation, of interpretation can be illuminating. And where dissent is so strong, and acceptance so unqualified, an unfavourable judgement has to be reconsidered. There is always the risk that when one has grown to know and love an artist's work, one may find an unforeseen development or a radical departure unacceptable. Is this the case — I have asked myself — with *The Searchers*? After seeing the film again, more than once, and examining it on the editing table, I have to say not. *The Searchers* is an impressive work, the work of a great director; but it is not among John Ford's masterpieces.

Moving always grandly through the deserts and towering outcrops of Monument Valley, *The Searchers* is, no doubt about it, an exceptionally handsome film. From the start, the set-ups are emphatically composed, with strong, monumental grouping and movement within the frame. The opening sets the style. After the titles, which are accompanied by a rhetorical-romantic Stan Jones ballad ('What makes a man to wander, what makes a man to roam? . . .'), the screen goes black. A door opens out of the darkness, on to a sunlit desert. A woman walks from behind camera, to stand for a moment, silhouetted against the bright landscape. She moves forward on to a porch, the camera tracking with her to lose the black surround, into the open air. Cut round: the woman, in mid-closeup, raises her left hand against her forehead, shielding her eyes from the sun. Cut round: a man approaches on horseback, framed between huge outcrops of red rock in the distance. Cut again to the reverse: a man

---

* John Baxter: *The Cinema of John Ford*. p. 144.
† Andrew Sarris: *The John Ford Movie Mystery*. p. 175.
‡ Joseph McBride and Andrew Wilmington: *John Ford*. p.147.

The Searchers. *Left: Olive Carey, John Qualen. Below: Ethan and Martin return to the Jorgensens' farm.*

steps down from the porch, crosses behind the woman and comes forward of her into closeup. Wordlessly they gaze out at the rider. A shot down the porch groups a little girl with a dog at her heels and an older girl, her full skirt blowing in the wind. A young boy, carrying wood, crosses foreground to stand with the others, looking out. The rider approaches, dismounts, walks forward: a black, broad-brimmed hat shadows his eyes ominously. The woman comes to greet him. A long shot shows the homestead, the family group, the woman embracing the traveller. He is led into the house. Ford's opening sequences are usually composed with firmness and clarity, stating the main theme early, but without loss of spontaneity. Here the effect is more studied than defined. The balance tips from style into formality.

The interior scenes which follow introduce the characters and suggest their relationships. The rider is Ethan Edwards, arriving at his brother's home after a long absence fighting in the Civil War and straying mysteriously in the years since (an initial title has told us that the year is 1868 and the place Texas.) Aaron Edwards is less welcoming to his brother than his wife Martha. Living with the Edwards and their three children is their adopted son Martin Pawley, a boy of eighteen or so, one-eighth (he claims) Cherokee. Ethan's prejudice is clear from his harsh, insulting way with the boy — compared with the fondness and generosity he shows to his nephew and nieces. We sense bitterness, and isolation. As the evening draws to an end, Ethan walks out on to the porch and sits alone on the step, with only a dog for company. Looking back into the house, he sees Aaron and Martha go into their bedroom together and close the door. In this story, from the start, we are far from the deep, idyllic family feeling that has been Ford's most consistent theme.

The development of The Searchers is precipitated by tragedy. The little community of homesteaders is disturbed by reports of Comanche marauders. Led by the Reverend Clayton, preacher and ranger, a posse of farmers rides out in pursuit. The posse is tricked: the Indians are not out to rustle cattle but to destroy the homesteads. Ethan and Martin return to find the Pawleys' farm a burned-out ruin: Martha has been raped and slaughtered with her husband and her son. Lucy and Debby, the two girls, are missing, abducted by the raiders. After a desert funeral service, the posse is reassembled, with Ethan grimly set on vengeance, to chase after the Comanches. There is a skirmish; the Indians beat a retreat; the posse turns back. Only Ethan goes on, accompanied

(to his reluctance) by Martin, and by young Brad, Lucy's beau. Ethan finds Lucy's violated body in a desert grave: and when the trio catch up with the raiding party, they see one of the Indians dancing grotesquely round the camp fire in Lucy's dress. Brad runs amok and is shot down. Ethan and Martin ride on in search of Debby.

The Searchers is the story of a quest, but a different quest entirely from the aspiring journeys of The Grapes of Wrath or Wagonmaster. And its hero is very differently natured from the man of good will who for so long occupied the centre of Ford's poetic world, from Dr. Samuel Mudd and young Abraham Lincoln to Wyatt Earp, Nathan Brittles and little Billy Priest. From his first appearance, Ethan Edwards is presented as a dark, ambiguous character; a man condemned to exclusion; loving to those he loves, but dangerous to all others; mean in his prejudice, with a grim dedication to revenge that suggests a festering bitterness against life itself. How soon does his determination to rescue his little niece from the Comanches become a secret determination that she must die? We do not know. Martin Pawley realises only gradually that to Ethan the object of their quest is not rescue but death. Martin, in fact, who unquestioningly risks his own happiness to continue the search, could be a hero, if he were presented with more depth and care, in the classic Ford tradition. But in terms of dramatic emphasis, Martin is never given equality with Ethan: the hero of The Searchers is an outsider, and although in the end his heart is melted and his fatal resolve abandoned, an outsider he remains. The rescue is made. Debby finds a new family and Martin is united with his girl. But Ethan walks away, back into the desert from which he came, as the camera pulls back through the doorway of the homestead and the door swings shut, in a reverse repetition of the opening shot of the film. It is a memorable end, yet not a poetically satisfactory one: the metaphor is forced. The door swings to, and rounds the story off with perfect symmetry. But of course no one in the drama closes it — why should anyone want to exclude Ethan? —it has to be the hand of an unseen assistant, standing in for the author, that motivates the symbol. The idea is seductive but it lacks that sense of the organic, the 'natural' which characterises Ford at his best. And the gesture, left hand grasping right arm, with which John Wayne stands for a moment evoking the memory of Harry Carey, is revealing too, taking us outside the work in a different way. It is a touching

The Searchers: *opening sequence.*

The Searchers. *The Edwards' burial.*

gesture, and the homage is a merited one. But it tells us more about Wayne and Ford and Carey than it does about Ethan Edwards.

Writing about *The Searchers* when it first appeared, I described Ethan Edwards as a 'neurotic'. Perhaps the term is not clinically justified: but it seems to describe reasonably enough the bitter, obsessive, secret nature of the man. 'Now what', I asked, 'is a director like Ford to do with a hero like this?' The question could well give the impression of an *a priori* dismissal of the film, not on grounds of quality but of intention. This was not what I meant. In fact my question, and its implied answer, was rather an attempt to find a reason for the film's ultimate inadequacy — for the fact that in the end it impresses rather than satisfies.

The Searchers sets out to be, and needs to be, much more than a spectacular Western with a happy rescue at the end. A more sombre, more complicated theme is crystallised in the character of Ethan, whose craving for vengeance motivates the search and whose bitterness at last surrenders to compassion. 'A loner', Ford described him to Peter Bogdanovich, but the term is not really adequate. A more immediate, personal motive for Ethan's profound sense of exclusion is provided by the clear indication of his love for his brother's wife, and hers for him. Others are aware of this, but no-one speaks;

nor do we know how much importance to give it. It is too much — or not enough. The character is insinuated, sketched rather than firmly drawn. Perhaps this is one reason for the inadequacy of the film's central performance — for which, of course, the director was as much to blame as the actor.

John Wayne was for long an underestimated actor; and no one seems to have underestimated his ability more doggedly than Ford. (As everyone knows, Ford was Wayne's great patron and friend. But sometimes this kind of special relationship can limit a director's understanding of an actor's potential. Howard Hawks — also a good friend of Ford — reported that, when he saw *Red River,* Ford commented: 'I never knew that big fellow can act.') Yet certainly Wayne's performance in *She Wore a Yellow Ribbon,* which was made the year after *Red River,* is a memorable characterisation, touching in its gruff sensitivity and humour, remarkable for the actor's ability to project himself forward a good ten years into a personality something like, yet not really like, his own. Wayne's Nathan Brittles is a warmly human creation, all of a piece. His Ethan Edwards is uneven, a character not organically conceived, its tone and emphasis (like that of the film itself) faltering and varying from sequence to sequence.

An instance. Early in the story the posse, under

Clayton's command, flees from the Comanche raiding party, superior in numbers, and takes defensive position on the far bank of a river. Their withering fire drives the Indians back across the water. During the attack Ethan is in confident, relaxed control — the familiar Wayne man of action. Clayton, alongside him, runs out of ammunition, curses. Ethan notices, throws him his revolver, joking caustically: 'Watch it, it's loaded'. Hot-tempered, Clayton grabs off his hat and sends it spinning back across. A moment of familiar, man-to-man humour. Moments later, as the Indians retreat to the river's far bank, Ethan continues savagely firing. Clayton grabs his gun to stop him: 'Leave them to carry out their hurt and dead.' Ethan shows fury and snarls: 'Well Reverend, that tears it. From now on you stay out of this.' The moment is crude, overstressed, 'planted'. We can see, only too plainly, the character and narrative point that is being made; but the stiffness and reserve, through which Ethan's violence should break like a sinister revelation, is never really there.

This pattern is repeated many times in the performance. Where grimness needs to be demonstrated, Wayne looks grim and snarls. Several times Ford stresses the sinister aspect of the character with a portrait close-shot of almost expressionist emphasis: there is one at Ethan's arrival in the first sequence, his eyes darkly shadowed by the brim of his black hat. And another, similarly threatening, when he and Martin find themselves confronted for the first time by a party of abducted white children who have been living with the Indians. Undeniably these closeups are strong; but their effect is spasmodic. They startle, in a way uncharacteristic of Ford (like the sudden zoom-in to Lucy's scream as she realises the threat of Indian attack). They cannot compensate for a performance that gives no sense of having been consistently thought through, and which relapses too often into the rough, easy-going geniality which represents the director's as well as the actor's most comfortable, most natural style.

Almost all the acting in *The Searchers* is uneven in this way. Only some of the supporting character actors play with that direct, effortless reality which is the hallmark of Ford's work at its best (Ward Bond, of course, Olive Carey, John Qualen). Jeffrey Hunter's Martin, sturdy and sensitive enough in other respects, suffers from the same superficiality

The Searchers. *Top: John Wayne as Ethan. Centre: The Rev. Clayton senses Ethan's feelings for Martha. Ward Bond, Wayne, Dorothy Jordan. Bottom: Ethan excluded.*

The Searchers. *Top: The sheriff's posse is tracked by Indians. Centre: Impassive witnesses. Left: Ethan and Martin pursue the search alone (Jeffrey Hunter, John Wayne).*

as Wayne's Ethan. A number of incidents seem intended to show the struggle within the boy, aware and not ashamed of his Indian blood, passionately loyal to his white family and his lost adoptive sister, loving and naive: but the handling is often impatient, even crude. The episode in which Martin finds himself shadowed by an Indian 'wife', docile but obstinately clinging, and sends her rolling down the hill with a maddened kick, surely needs to suggest these conflicting impulses. Its humour can only be painful. But Ford stages the scene almost farcically, with the subtlety of one of his bar-room brawls, provoking a horse-laugh from Wayne in which the audience inevitably joins. There is stridency too, rather than humour, in the scenes between Martin and Laurie Jorgensen. Vera Miles plays these with a tomboy aggressiveness which avoids sentimentality only at the expense of charm. Ken Curtis presents Laurie's other suitor as an absurd booby with a parodic Texan accent; Hank Worden's Moss Harper, the fool wise in his madness, is amateurish; and one can almost hear the bark of a hectoring director as Harry Carey Jnr. shouts his way through the role of Brad Jorgensen.

All this is not to criticise the actors. This kind of overemphasis is the result of direction that lacks artistic firmness, overall consistency. The style of *The Searchers* varies continually between the poetic and the farcical, the grand and the mundane, the convinced and the perfunctory. I should make it clear that it is not the tragi-comic manner as such that I am calling in question, or that I find 'incomprehensible'.* Ford at his best is never a neo-Classic. Films like *The Informer* and *The Fugitive* — even *Stagecoach* — pay a certain respect to the unities of mood and theme: but his most personal, characteristic style is always open, epic, Shakespearian. From *Judge Priest* to *The Sun Shines Bright* we find scenes of humour and pathos, suffering and laughter juxtaposed, sometimes violently, with absolute assurance and success. *The Searchers* lacks this kind of wholeness, this command of modulation — the Ethan who jovially bustles Mrs. Jorgensen back into the house as her

* 'Odd as his incomprehension may seem today ... it is this grotesquerie, and the anarchic humour which accompanies it, which Anderson found incomprehensible.' McBride and Wilmington, pp. 148, 150.

The Searchers. *Rescued by Martin, Debbie finds herself chased by Ethan: she flees in panic.*

daughter's suitors prepare to do battle ('No bitin' or gougin'') is not the same Ethan we have seen implacable to rescue Debby from her shame by death. The sequences do not complement each other; they jar harshly. So does the comic 'business', inserted with a heavy hand into the film's climax, of the greenhorn cavalry officer (Pat Wayne) whose numbskull devotion to the drill manual imperils the rescue. Such episodes as the juxtaposition of Debby's rescue — Ethan at last clasping her in a compassionate embrace — with the extraction of a bullet from the Reverend Clayton's backside, represent to McBride and Wilmington 'abruptly shifting moods and moral emphases . . . determined by the imbalances in the relationships between Ethan and the other pioneers'. By less pretentious judgement, they are simply blemishes. Or perhaps, more fundamentally, they betray Ford's lack of deep response, commitment to the whole idea of this story. Certainly a lack of real belief in its resolution. Undeniably *The Searchers* is powerfully shot. Image by image it proceeds with the sure, unhasting authority of a master. But the style is more pictorial than poetic — always a sign that the feeling is not deep. And the telling of the tale lacks grasp. Ethan and Martin spend years on their obsessive search;

but this is stated rather than conveyed, the time clumsily telescoped by the device of a letter from Martin which Laurie reads out to her family. Partisans of the film have excused this faulty structure with ingenious special pleadings: 'The lengthy, circuitous trek of Ethan Edwards and Martin Pawley does not appear to last more than a few weeks . . . The significance of this is that time has a different meaning for Ethan and Martin, who live a nomadic existence, and for the Jorgensens, who live a fixed life on the land.'* This is tortuous and unconvincing. More likely explanations are an unsolved problem of script construction; the difficulty or undesirability of ageing the characters; and, above all, Ford's impatience with narrative.

I am not suggesting that there are no themes present in *The Searchers*. There are: but there is not *a* theme. It is in this that it can be called un-Fordian, and this is why it can be called poetically unsatisfactory. Its appeal to the critical intellectuals of the sixties and seventies, to younger film makers in revolt against the discredited idealism of their fathers, is not surprising. Where they are unable to

---

* Philippe Handiquet: *John Ford*. Quoted by McBride and Wilmington, p.155.

identify with the honourable, straightforward heroes of duty who expressed Ford's vision in the past, they can claim neo-romantic kinship with the 'alienated' Ethan Edwards, and fasten sympathetically on indications of disillusion in the story or dark, mythic complexities in its development. No doubt there is some significance in the fact that Scar is finally scalped by Ethan: but whether this justifies allusion to 'mirror-images' and White Man's guilt is another matter altogether. The Cavalry in *The Searchers* plays a cruel, destructive role: but this cannot be taken as proving that Ford had lost his admiration for the 'dog-faced soldiers, the fifty-cents-a-day professionals, riding the outposts of a nation...' (In fact *Sergeant Rutledge* is there, made four years later, to show that he had not.) And Ethan's exclusion from the idyll of family certainly tells us something about Ford himself, hinting at a sense of isolation, an unappeased longing that gnawed at his innermost heart: but the idyll itself is not thereby shadowed or discredited. Indeed, its intensity and its persistence are explained. There is a lot of John Ford in *The Searchers*, a lot of his splendid craft and his ambiguous, divided personality; but the sense of harmony, of resolution and of faith which gives his work at its best a special grace is not there.

The sequence which crystallises most sharply the limitations of the film is its climax. The final confrontation between Scar and the searchers is achieved only by coincidence: into Laurie's 'wedding' party breaks a young Cavalry officer with news that the Comanche chief has been reported in the vicinity. It is a weak development, and the action that follows is acceptable only on conventional genre terms. Martin ventures ahead into the Indian camp — finds and awakens Debby (now metamorphosed into Natalie Wood) in Scar's tepee — persuades her instantly to escape with him ('I've come to take you away. I'm going to get you out of here, Debby.' 'Yes, Marty . . . Yes, Marty . . .') And if the dénouement 'works,' it is by sheer, canny melodramatic skill. Ethan chases after Debby, rides her down, grabs her with every appearance of ferocity. Martin shouts desperately, sure he is going to kill her; and of course Ford means us to feel the same. But Ethan lifts the terrified girl high in the air, clasps her to him, speaks gently (the camera shooting tactfully off his face, over his shoulder): 'Let's go home, Debby.' Whatever subtleties of emotion and significance may be read into the idea of those last scenes, they are certainly not expressed in their shooting.

4

However *The Searchers* may finally be judged, one thing is certain: it is a watershed film in Ford's career, and the last. If, as some critics have claimed, it is a masterpiece, then there were no more to follow. And if it is less than that, a triumph of story-telling technique, hard-worked rather than spontaneous, disenchanted if not soulless, then it still represents the last time he was able to maintain such firmness of grasp, such consistent mastery of handling. From now on the work was rougher, less careful, more evidently a labour.

This is not to say that the films which followed necessarily lacked significance of theme, or personal accent. Now more than ever, anything he touched bore the imprint of his personality, individual and unmistakable; but it was a personality at odds with history, and past its creative prime. *The Wings of Eagles,* which he directed the next year, was a tribute to an old friend and comrade, Frank (Spig) Wead, who had written *Airmail* for him in 1932 and *They Were Expendable* in 1945. The idea of the picture came from M-G-M, in response to requests from the Navy for a film that would promote the idea of Naval aviation; but in theme as well as in its principal character the story related intimately to Ford's own experience. 'Spig' Wead was his friend; and there is an authoritative Ford impersonation in it — Ward Bond, with pipe and old, wide-brimmed hat and a picture of Harry Carey in his office, giving rough-tongued instructions to his prentice-writer: 'What do I write about?' 'People — Navy people . . . I want it from a pen dipped in salt water, not dry martinis.'

Undoubtedly the portrait of Wead, the rebel whose devotion to flying and dedication to the service (to say nothing of his fondness for brawls and booze-ups) drove him to neglect his family and ruin his marriage, had features that recalled Ford's own temperament and experience. *The Wings of Eagles* has a loving, unsuccessful relationship between John Wayne and Maureen O'Hara, moments of egoism, selfishness and courage — particularly in Wead's unyielding fight against paralysis — that give a lot of it distinctive dignity. Too much of the drama, though, is simplified and sentimentalised in an old-fashioned way, and too much of the writing is familiar Hollywood reach-me-down stuff: 'All I know,' Wead's wife is made to say, 'is I'm in the arms of a fellow named Spig that I'm nuts about.' Wayne, for all the strength and conviction of his presence, was not the actor to give more than conventional life to a character as

The Wings of Eagles. *The crippled Spig Wead says goodbye to the Navy. (Louis Jean Heydt, left; John Wayne as Wead.)*

complex as Wead, and the role of his wife was not one to which Maureen O'Hara was able to bring much more than her accustomed spirit and beauty. Most uncomfortable of all are the scenes of Army-Navy rivalry, charmlessly rowdy and full of liquored-up horseplay, Ford's heavy laughter at its least infectious.

There is a lot — too much — of this kind of humour in *The Wings of Eagles*, as indeed there tended to be in all Ford's late work. But the pervasive mood of the film is regretful: Wead's story of effort and dedication ends as he is swung away from his aircraft carrier in mid-ocean, enfeebled now after a heart attack, with only death to look forward to as bitter-sweet visions of the past flash through his memory.

There is a similar sense of rueful recollection, of a long life of achievement drawing to a reluctant close, in Ford's next picture *The Last Hurrah*, adapted by his familiar collaborator Frank Nugent from Edwin O'Connor's best-selling novel. Here the story goes further, to the moment of death and past it. Frank Skeffington, wily politician and longtime Mayor of a Bostonian city, has at last been defeated in the electoral battle: the torchlight procession and the bands are no longer for him: he makes his solitary way home, and there his heart gives out. His cronies, companions and faithful adjutants in a lifetime of canny politicking, gather round his bed for a last, sad meeting; his Eminence the Cardinal pays Frank a last visit; and his scapegrace son breaks down in

The Last Hurrah. *Mayor Frank Skeffington, the old-style politico, has lost his last campaign: he says goodbye to his cronies. (Behind: Ed Brophy. Front, left to right: Ricardo Cortez, James Gleason, Spencer Tracy, Pat O'Brien).*

repentant tears. Only Spencer Tracy's warmly stoic humour, and his constitutional inability to sentimentalise, makes bearable what must be one of the most stubbornly prolonged death scenes ever filmed.

Skeffington, like Wead, is a character with whom Ford must have felt a certain melancholy identification; and this gives *The Last Hurrah,* even at its least satisfactory, a resonance well beyond that of routine picture-making. A faithful but unortho-dox Catholic, wily and unscrupulous in the service of what he has always considered to be right (usually identified with his own self-interest), loved by his friends for his generosity, resented by his enemies for his lack of scruple — Frank Skeffington is at last the lonely victim of time. His tactics, for all their cunning, are as old fashioned as his ideals, and they prove in the end no match for his opponents' more modern methods, which include the selling of their dummy candidate to the voters by television. Significantly, it is here the film is weakest. Skeffington's rival as presented by Charles Fitz-simmons (brother to Maureen O'Hara, recruited into the Ford stock company on *The Quiet Man*) is a

grimacing booby; and his TV election broadcast from the bosom of his family ('Naval man, scholar') is farcical with an exaggerated absurdity that robs the whole situation of conviction. Clearly Ford is as little at ease with the modern world, and as contemptuous of it as Skeffington. But his caricature of it is too gross and too inaccurate for his dismissal to carry authority.

In its casting as well as its theme, there is a testamentary feel about *The Last Hurrah.* It is full of familiar Fordian faces (Donald Crisp and Jane Darwell, John Carradine, Anna Lee and O. Z. Whitehead), as well as a host of veterans of the Hollywood tradition — Pat O'Brien, Basil Rath-bone, Frank McHugh, Edmund Lowe, James Gleason, Ricardo Cortez ... Yet the charm generally refuses to work. Perhaps Charles Lawton's handsome photography is too sombre. Certainly much of the handling is stiff, even laborious. And the comic sequences are painfully overemphatic. These had become characteristics of Ford's work.

They are the characteristics, unhappily, of the project for which Ford turned his back on Hollywood and returned to Ireland after *The*

Searchers. Some years before, about the time of *The Quiet Man,* he had joined his friend Lord Killanin and his 'cousin' Brian Desmond Hurst in founding a company, Four Provinces Films, the aim of which was to animate the production of films in Ireland. In 1955 Ford undertook a three-episode picture for Four Provinces, made up of three native subjects — a short story by Frank O'Connor and two one-act plays by Michael McHugh and Lady Gregory. It was not a pretentious undertaking but it was a sympathetic one, which might have achieved modest commercial success for all its lack of star names. There is no shortage of good actors in Ireland, and the subjects were well chosen, well balanced, with strong emphasis on Celtic qualities of spirit, illogicality and anarchic independence.

Ford claimed afterwards that he made *The Rising of the Moon* 'for fun' and that he had enjoyed the experience. Maybe so, but that was hardly the object of the venture. The truth is that the picture failed — artistically as well as commercially — because not enough of the right kind of care or concentration went into it, and the mood was more self-indulgent than fond. (There are parallels here with *The Fugitive.*) The feeling is clumsy from the start, with Tyrone Power, who had also been recruited as a member of the Four Provinces board, addressing the audience stiffly from a Dublin doorstep and assuring them that they are going to see a story 'about nothing — or perhaps about everything'.

A similar self-consciousness runs through the episodes that follow. The O'Connor story, *The Majesty of the Law,* is a whimsical comedy of pride, in which old Dan, last survivor of a noble line, now solitary in his crumbling ancestral tower, must be arrested for assaulting a seller of bad poteen — and embarrasses the sympathetic magistrate by refusing to allow his fine to be paid and insisting on going to gaol. This indulgent celebration of the 'old ways' suffers from a general heaviness of touch, some rather disappointing location photography, and a lot of hearty overplaying in long, laxly shot sequences of dialogue.

A Minute's Wait is even more strenuously overplayed — no one can say that Irish actors, given their heads, don't take them — as the Dublin train's

The Rising of the Moon: '1921'. Donal Donnelly as Sean Curran, patriot on the run from the British, done up as a ballad-mongering tinker.

brief halt at a little country station is extended into an hour of celebration and general chaos, first to await a consignment of lobsters for the Bishop's Jubilee dinner, then by various farcical twists and a strong reluctance to let the natural rhythm of life be disrupted by anything as impersonal as a railway timetable. Again the touch on those picturesque goings-on is anything but light: Ford enjoyed his usual hit at the Anglo-Irish, though, with Michael Trubshawe and Anita Bolster as a crassly Blimpish couple who survey the high jinks with uncomprehending disapproval — 'Charles, is it another of their rebellions?'.

The third episode, which gives its name to the film, is the most substantial. Derived from Lady Gregory's touching little dramatic anecdote, in which a fugitive patriot is recognised by a sympathetic policeman and allowed to escape, *The Rising of the Moon* is described by McBride and Wilmington as 'virtually a remake of *The Informer*'. This it is not. *The Informer* is a drama of betrayal, the portrait of a brutish primitive who betrays his comrade to the British, is paid his twenty pieces of silver, and perishes, repentant on the altar steps, at the hands of the I.R.A. *The Rising of the Moon*, a comic-dramatic escape story, is alike only in its period (updated to the twenties from the pre-First World War setting of the original), and in a certain stylistic self-consciousness (most of it is shot, in low-key black and white, with a tilted camera, perhaps influenced by its cameraman Robert Krasker, who had used a similar technique in *The Third Man*). Still an anecdote, though an expanded one, the mood varies, not altogether convincingly, between melodrama, comedy and suspense. The hated Black and Tans patrol the streets of occupied Dublin, while in the castle the young captain cries out against his duty: 'Four years of war and I end up a hangman. How much longer are they going to keep

Gideon's Day. *Jack Hawkins.*

us here?' The patriot escapes from his cell disguised as a nun and is fitted out as a stagey-looking tinker backstage at the Abbey Theatre. He escapes to freedom from the dockside, where Lady Gregory's policeman has been supplied with a nosey wife — 'I see you're having a spot of Blarney with the old Judy,' a patrolling Britisher calls out. It is all simple, nostalgic stuff, not very persuasive. For all its authority of style, the film is closer to charade than to drama. Ford remains an outsider in this country: the myths he is trying to perpetuate, to prove himself a part of, are not really his.

So, and sadly, ended Ford's artistic romance with Ireland. He did return, ten years later, to undertake a version of the early chapters of Sean O'Casey's autobiography, but it was a fated venture. *Young Cassidy* was maimed from the start by the casting of the burly Australian Rod Taylor in the name part (rather as if the young Robert Preston had been assigned to Ford for Lincoln), and Ford found himself, not surprisingly, continually at odds with his young American producers, who regarded the project as their own. He no longer had the strength or the conviction to dominate the enterprise, spent most of the preparation time in his hotel bedroom, fell or made himself ill, and finally quit the picture after only a few days work.

One other project, some years before this catastrophe, brought him across the Atlantic. After *The Last Hurrah,* Ford came to London where, again with his friend Killanin as 'producer', he directed a most unlikely subject — a Scotland Yard thriller by John Creasey called *Gideon's Day.** For connoisseurs of Ford's work this is a fascinating curio, almost a throwback to the time thirty years or so before, when he would undertake any piece of programme material that Fox put him down for. Completely without pretensions of any kind, *Gideon's Day* came out as an engaging entertainment, an almost absurdist pastiche of its middle-class English genre, theoretically contemporary but in fact more reminiscent of the thirties in its crooked stereotypes and its clean-limbed social attitudes. Unfortunately, Ford's tongue-in-cheek approach was rather sophisticated for popular audiences — and quite beyond the intelligentsia — and in America the hour-and-a-half original was cut to fifty-five minutes and sent out as the lower half of a double bill. And although the film was shot in colour, the American release prints were printed in black and white, on the principle, presumably, of not throwing good money after bad.

---

* In America released as *Gideon of Scotland Yard.*

John Ford's yacht, the Araner, *being used on location for* Donovan's Reef.

5

Failures like these — and nothing he had done since *The Searchers* could be called a success, either artistically or commercially — were dismissed by Ford with his usual shrug. He talked of *Gideon's Day* as a mere diversion. All the same, its fate was ignominious. Ford had always prided himself on being a mainstream director, confident that when he had no subject of his own choice or imagining, he could turn his hand to an unassuming piece in a popular genre and come up with a crowd pleaser. Now he was plainly losing touch with the crowd, which was becoming less predictable as it diminished, and harder to please.

Paradoxically, as Ford's work decreased in vigour, it seemed to become more whimsically, even wilfully personal; and this meant that it became less appealing to the general public. By the end of the fifties, popular audiences were a great deal more sophisticated than they had been even ten years before; and television had established itself as the chief provider of routine entertainment. With films like *Compulsion* and *Anatomy of a Murder* (both released in 1959), Hollywood was popularising themes which would formerly have been restricted to art houses. *The Defiant Ones,* in the same year, was not even particularly daring in manacling together a black and a white hero; and *Some Like It Hot* created witty amusement out of transvestism. It was not to be expected that Ford could or would sympathise with any such transformation of values. Whether as an entertainer or as an artist, there seemed only one tradition still open to him, still largely inviolate, and it was the one which he had made particularly his own — the Western. So, in 1959, he returned to the genre with *The Horse Soldiers,* and during the seven years of work that still remained to him, the directing of Westerns remained his chief occupation. He made four more, as well as one of the three parts of the spectacular Cinerama *How The West Was Won* and an episode on the *Wagon Train* TV series (which starred Ward Bond and was derived from his own *Wagonmaster*). 165

Donovan's Reef: 'A long way from Innisfree...'

Of his two remaining pictures outside the genre, neither was exactly contemporary; nor was either really successful. (Both, though, have their apologists.) They may as well be discussed here, for neither is the kind of film with which one would want to bring to a close the account of a great career.

Donovan's Reef, released in 1963, is an escapist romance, set congenially (for Ford and the *Araner*) on an island in the South Seas. Based on a story which the novelist James Michener had himself adapted from an original by Edmund Belorin (author of a number of Bob Hope scenarios) it was scripted for Ford by Frank Nugent and a Hollywood treadmill writer, James Edward Grant who had worked on a number of John Wayne vehicles from *Sands of Iwo Jima* to *Hondo,* including the crude anti-Red *Big Jim McLean.* Boisterous in its comedy and carelessly idiosyncratic in style *Donovan's Reef* has affinities both with *The Quiet Man* and *What Price Glory.* The bickering Flagg and Quirt here are John Wayne and Lee Marvin, as 'Guns' Donovan and 'Boats' Gilhooley, ex-Naval comrades who meet again every year to enjoy a ritual fight. Donovan has settled down on the little island of Haleakaloa, where a third comrade from the service has charge of the local hospital. Dr. Dedham, played by Jack Warden, has three children by a native mistress (safely dead) and a high-mettled daughter whom he has left behind in America to be brought up by his divorced wife. This daughter, Amelia (Elizabeth Allen), has become head of the family shipping business in the absence of her father: she comes to Haleakaloa to meet him again and find out if he is a fit person to receive the inheritance. The clash and the attraction between the confident Amelia and the gritty, chauvinistic Donovan (who has 'adopted' Dedham's children so that Amelia shall not discover his profligacy) provide the mainspring of the story, as well as some of the shrew-taming tensions of *The*

166

Quiet Man.

It is an elaborate, far-fetched plot, though perhaps hardly more fantastical than *The Tempest* or *The Winter's Tale,* whose themes of conflict and eventual harmony, all in a remote, idyllic setting, it to some extent echoes. There is indeed a kind of late-Shakespearian expansiveness about *Donovan's Reef,* a fairy tale humour and eccentricity that is refreshing in a cinema from which the easy-going and the poetic seem to have been mostly squeezed out. Only Ford could have conceived, in Hollywood of the 1960s, the sequence in which the children of Haleakaloa perform a naively charming Christmas play, in which Marcel Dalio is reduced to tears, Caesar Romero reads the story of the Nativity, and Dorothy Lamour sings "Holy Night": and only Ford would have known how to puncture the sentimentalism with a storm, a leaking roof and a sudden sprouting of umbrellas among the rapt audience. There are moments of emotion that are felt and 'played through' with a truthfulness that is touching — father and daughter meet again after many years of separation, some real understanding and mutual sympathy begins to grow between Donovan and Amelia in spite of the defensiveness and aggressivity of them both. The successful passages, though, are only intermittent: as a whole, the film quite fails to cohere. Taste and style are erratic. Essentially what is missing is any poetic consistency to bind melodrama to sentiment, lyricism to farce in the way Ford once so effortlessly could. This is most painfully evident in the scenes between Wayne and Elizabeth Allen. The moment Amelia steps out of the longboat on her arrival at Haleakaloa, Donovan roars with laughter to see her soaked by the breakers and pulls her roughly after him through the water as he strides to the beach — much as Sean Thornton marches Mary Kate Danaher across the fields at the climax of *The Quiet Man.* Only here there is no reason for his boorishness, and no generosity in the humour. *Donovan's Reef,* indeed, is full of this kind of misogynistic fun: women are constantly falling on their backsides; Dorothy Lamour is thrown into a pond; and for a happy finale Elizabeth Allen gets a spanking and Wayne lays down the marriage terms: 'From now on I wear the pants'. There is hardly more appeal in the Gilhooley-Donovan punch-ups, less genial than uncouth. Certainly the fight fails to live up to Gilhooley's epic claim: 'The tradition, the legend, the crowd'. Rowdy it is; poetic it is not. Haleakaloa is a long way, and a sad way from Innisfree.

Two years later, after the intervening experience of *Cheyenne Autumn,* the most ambitious and the most taxing of his late Westerns, and the *Young Cassidy* debacle in Dublin, Ford arrived at the last film of his career. It could hardly have been in more complete contrast to *Donovan's Reef* — except that it was equally remote from contemporary fashions and concerns. It was called *Seven Women,* and it was the work of two English scenarists, Janet Green and John McCormick, who had together written a number of British pictures, the most notable of which were conventionally 'relevant' thrillers like *Sapphire* (racial problems) and *Victim* (homo-

sexuality half-way out of the closet); their screenplay was adapted from *Chinese Finale* by Norah Lofts, an English novel about a beleaguered Christian mission in revolution-torn China of the 1930s. A heavily dialogued, peculiarly feminine-orientated piece, it was the choice of Bernard Smith, now Ford's producing associate: Ford himself kept planning script conferences but never managed to meet the writers.

Seven Women was shot almost completely on studio sets, with a tense concentration on plot that left no room for relaxation or the grace-notes of humour. Its style of significant melodrama harks back, indeed, to Ford's collaboration with Dudley Nichols. Here again is the little community trapped in a perilous situation, in a story designed to illuminate moral or philosophical issues — in this case chiefly the conflict between the sterile and anti-human religiosity of organised religion, and the generous, disrespectful humanism of the woman doctor thrown by crisis into the threatened Mission. Ford was never one to sympathise much with cloistered virtue, and it is easy to see the elements in this situation that appealed to his anarchic, morally responsible imagination: Ann Bancroft's Dr Cartwright has some of the qualities of Claire

Seven Women. Iconoclastic Dr. Cartwright shocks the missionaries with her unorthodoxies. Left to right: Sue Lyon, Mildred Dunnock, Anne Bancroft, Margaret Leighton, Hans William Lee, Eddie Albert, Betty Field.

Trevor's Dallas in *Stagecoach* (though with a great deal more aggression), fighting back against the self-righteous puritanism of the Law and Order League. The drama is extended, and brought to a violent climax when the Mission is invaded by a brutal, massively physical bandit chief (Mike Mazurki as Tunga Khan), who demands the doctor's body as the price of the missionaries' release. Dr Cartwright accepts the sacrifice, and kills Tunga Khan and herself in a final ironic gesture of revenge.

It is heady stuff, the old-fashioned melodramatics of the plot given a somewhat specious gloss by the introduction of psychological, not to say Freudian themes. The obsessive, inflexible Mission head, Miss Agatha Andrews, is a suppressed Lesbian, obsessed by Emma, the youngest member of her group, an innocently voluptuous blonde. Dr Cartwright, on whom there are no flies, is determined to wrest Emma from her perverting influence: defeated and exposed, both emotionally and ideologically, Miss Andrews retreats into glazed insanity. The other missionaries (there is only one man, a weak and self-regarding husband) combine innocence and foolishness in varying degrees. To add the spice of action, there is a titanic wrestling match in which the Khan (a symbol, as presented by Mazurki, of maleness at its most brutish) snaps the neck of the adjutant (Woody Strode) who has dared challenge his supremacy. Ford tackled it all head-on, without apology or pretension, and one can only admire the force and commitment of the shooting; but not all his skill in camera placement, nor all his artful manipulation of imagery could disguise the artificiality of the conception, or the banality of the characters. Bernard Smith apparently chose the cast, and with the exception of Sue Lyon (the *Lolita* nymphette, both over-and under-equipped for the role of Emma) he chose well. But the kind of nuanced playing that might have disguised or transformed the clichés of the script is not forthcoming. Ford has directed his actresses with a forthrightness that cements them firmly into stereotypes. Anne Bancroft, swaggering manfully through the role of Dr Cartwright, is smug rather than appealing in her non-conformity; and Margaret Leighton, always stronger in the theatre than on film, plays Miss Andrews with a neurotic flourish more bizarre than believable, like an evangelical Mrs. Danvers.

It is only fair to add that *Seven Women* has its enthusiasts. McBride and Wilmington analyse the plot in detail and come to the conclusion that the film contains Ford's 'bleakest vision of destruction' and 'ultimately affirms...the necessity of indivi-

dual integrity in the face of nihilism'. Andrew Sarris goes further, judges it 'a genuinely great film' and discovers in it 'a pure Classicism of expression in which an economy of means yields a profusion of effects'. 'The beauties of *Seven Women*,' says he, 'are for the ages.' They were not, alas, for the audiences of its time. One of the most revealing, and one of the saddest, stories in Dan Ford's book is of Ford on his yacht in Hawaii, in retreat after the shooting of the film. 'He was lathering on about *Seven Women*, saying that it had been a mistake to make it and that it would probably finish him. I had never seen him so depressed.' He was right. He never managed to get another project off the ground: it was really only the Westerns he had been making during these last ten years since *The Searchers* that preserved the stature of his professional reputation.

6

If any territory was safe for Ford now, it was surely the West. Its myths were still attractive to the general audience, and largely unquestioned by critics. It was agreeable to get away from a changed Hollywood to spend time on location among friends of many years — actors, technicians and horse-handlers — by whom he was understood, or at least accepted with proper respect. And had he not always been fired, from his earliest film making days, by the Western theme, by its vigorous faiths and ideals, its basic conflicts and villainies, uncomplicated by the sophistications of psychology, and by the ultimate, historically undeniable victory? *'Wherever they went, and whatever they fought for, that place became the United States.'*

But even the mythic West of Hollywood could not remain unaffected by history — any more than Ford himself could be unaffected by the passage of time. It was not so easy now to justify, or to feel justified by the simple fact of conquest. For all the apparent militarism of their themes, his Westerns of the early fifties, lyric in feeling and pacific in intent, looked forward to a Republic of harmony and achievement. It was a dream that had faded. It was no longer possible to believe in the possibility of progress in the old, simple way, or to be sure that visions of the traditional ideal would any longer be either accepted or even understood. Like Wordsworth, Ford must surely have mourned the disappearance of 'the homely beauty of the good old cause'. Also, he was into his sixties. The lyric gift rarely survives so long. In 1966 Peter Bogdanovich questioned him about the apparent sadness of his later view of the West. 'Maybe I'm getting older,' said Ford.

On location for The Horse Soldiers. *Ford to Bogdanovich:*
'I've always enjoyed making pictures...I like the people
I'm around, the actors, the actresses, the grips, the
electricians...I like to be on the set and, regardless of
what the story is, I like to work in pictures.' Ford with
Wayne — in conference with Holden, Constance Towers,
Wayne — yarning with Hoot Gibson.

Age, doubtless, was one of the factors that weighed down *The Horse Soldiers,* with which, in 1959, Ford began his last period of Western film making. Even more of a handicap was the fact that the picture was essentially a commercial concoction. Scripted by Martin Rackin, a Hollywood writer with a long string of routine credits (from *Air Raid Wardens* and *Fighting Father Dunne* to *Long John Silver*) and John Lee Mahin (*Mogambo*), it was based on a Civil War novel which told the story of a Union Cavalry detachment ordered to make a destructive foray into Confederate territory. Rackin managed to get John Wayne for the Cavalry commander, Col. Marlow, a wartime soldier; and for Major Kendall, the resentful doctor forced to accompany Marlow on the mission, the noticeably unFordian William Holden, as out of period in his haircut as in his acting style. Ford completed the 'bankable' package, and a Southern aristo, Hannah Hunter (Constance Towers) was thrown in to provide traditional antagonism and to fall in love with the Colonel. *The Horse Soldiers* has all the values of a major production: spectacular action, some handsome images of the skyline variety, and a rousing music track, somewhat over-orchestrated. But none of these compensate for the lack of a real subject. The bickerings of the main characters are wearisome — the grouchy rivalry between Marlow and Kendall is all too plainly the device of a screenwriter working hard to fabricate a 'situation'. (A cliché that Ford himself had side-stepped in *They Were Expendable*, in which Brickley dismisses Ryan's recurrent explosions of resentment with the benign amusement they deserve.) There is not much more truth in the dislike and attraction felt by Hannah for Marlow — a pale echo of the conflicting allegiances at the heart of *Rio Grande*. And with no real interest in the troop's mission, there is nothing to give the film dynamic. One is not surprised to learn that Ford was dispirited about the enterprise.[*] As John Lee Mahin told Dan Ford: 'I don't think Jack ever liked *The Horse Soldiers*. He never really got into the script ... One day we were sitting aboard the *Araner*, and he said to me, "You know where we ought to make this picture?" "No," I said, "Where?" "In Lourdes. It's going to take a miracle to pull it off".'

There was no miracle, at least not artistically. *The Horse Soldiers* only makes it clear how Ford, like any artist, needed to believe in his material if he was to bring it to life. Even the acting is never more than serviceable. Late in the picture there is a long

[*] Dan Ford, *Pappy*, p. 280.

169

dialogue, a single, sustained two-shot, in which Wayne has to 'explain' to Constance Towers the reason for his hatred of doctors (his wife died at the hands of a clumsy surgeon): the heavy, unmodulated playing, the functional staging, convey almost explicitly the director's contempt for the scene. Even the one truly original, potentially poetic sequence, in which the child-cadets of a Confederate Military Academy march out with gallant folly to attack the Union cavalry, achieves little more than the impact of record. It must have seemed a sad confirmation of failure when, towards the end of the schedule, one of Ford's veteran stunt-men and old friend was killed while performing a reasonably simple fall. The picture should have ended with the Cavalry returning to their lines, flags flying and drums beating: Ford finished with Wayne's farewell to Holden (who has opted to face prison with his wounded) and the obligatory promise to return to Constance Towers when the war is over. He never shot the finale.

If Ford could not generate any enthusiasm for *The Horse Soldiers,* he seems to have positively disliked *Two Rode Together,* which he made in 1961. He told Peter Bogdanovich that he had only undertaken it as a favour to Harry Cohn, the head of Columbia. 'I said "Good God, this is a lousy script." He said "I know it is, but we're pledged for it". . . I said "O.K., I'll do the damn thing." And I didn't enjoy it.' Dan Ford makes it clear that there were other inducements: a substantial fee, a healthy percentage, two good and congenial leading actors — and perhaps most attractive of all, the prospect of work after a nine-month spell without a movie to make or a project to nurture. He never liked the story. Even while he was preparing the script he was calling it 'The worst piece of crap I've done in twenty years'; and when it was finished he made out to a French journalist that he had already forgotten the title. 'Great actors, but the story is rubbish.'

Ford's particular dislike of *Two Rode Together* is all the more interesting when we compare it with *The Searchers.* (The titles could have been interchangeable.) Again the theme is the rescue of white children stolen years before by Indians, and again the adventure is darkened by the implication that the girls will have grown to maturity and been bedded by their Comanche captors: there is the further certainty that, their sexual fates apart, the prisoners will have by now adopted Indian ways and faiths. It is a dark story, raising modern themes of racial prejudice, unromantic in its vision of the West: Ford accepted the assignment on the understanding that he would rework the script with Frank Nugent, add some humour, and find a way of ending it happily. The material, however, proved resistant. Whereas *The Searchers* had at least a deeply committed character at its centre, a powerfully feeling man even at his most ambiguous, *Two Rode Together* is centred on a cynical and opportunist Sheriff (a not too happy role for James Stewart), who is motivated only by the $500 reward he can claim for every captive rescued. To wrench this character out of his greed into compassion and to engineer his eventual marriage to one of his captives and their departure to a better life in California was the task that Ford and Nugent set themselves. It is not surprising that they failed to manage it convincingly. There was the further problem that McCabe's companion on the search, a cavalry lieutenant played by Richard Widmark, was never motivated by anything more dynamic than decency. There are some strong dramatic incidents in *Two Rode Together,* particularly the lynching of a rescued boy who has gone berserk and murdered the woman who hysterically claimed him as her son; but for all Ford's ease with the Western atmosphere, the handling is stiff, and his determination to temper the grimness with humour results only in a succession of gags in his most heavy-handed style. Essentially *Two Rode Together* needed to be a bitter, even a tragic tale — not at all suited to the kind of cinema in which Ford had spent a lifetime. His attempts to turn it into something nearer his own heart were bound to fail, as he knew they would, and as they did.

At least, with pictures like this, Ford was able to maintain his position as a top Hollywood director, not merely dependent on the glories of past reputation. But it was becoming harder: and harder still to infuse the work with any real creative energy. His part in the giant Cinerama epic, *How The West Was Won* was modest — one episode of six — and despite some evocative images in his familiar style, not a great deal more memorable than the straightforwardly professional contributions of Henry Hathaway and George Marshall. Not that the material of it was thin. It tells the story of Zeb Rawlings, a naive country boy who is seduced from his family to join the Northern army, witnesses the horror of war, makes friends with a Southern deserter, is forced to kill his new friend when he attempts to assassinate General Grant, and returns

The Horse Soldiers. *Left top: The romantic folly of the charge by cadets from the Military Academy. Left: Behind the confederate lines (John Wayne).*

home to find his mother and father dead and buried. Finally he sets off for a new life in the West. There is material here for a whole film, or two: Ford compresses it, or is obliged to compress it into not much more than a reel — ten minutes. He disliked intensely the clumsy triple-screen Cinerama system in which he had to work: 'Worse than Cinema-Scope . . . the audience moves instead of the camera. You have to hold on to your chair.'* He shot very simply, as if to counter the 'spectacle' of the overblown image, and managed to include a number of characteristic touches — the perplexed mother talking to her dead family in the graveyard, a drunken doctor desperately operating on the wounded, the weary commanders (John Wayne as Sherman, Henry Morgan as Grant) revealing their fallible humanity, the callow boy initiated into manhood by the witness of suffering. But the Cinerama format continuously obtrudes and intimacy and spontaneity are lost. Emotion is distanced. The poetic flame burns low.

In *Cheyenne Autumn* it flickers to extinction. Shot in 1963 and released, after many agonising weeks in the cutting room, in 1964, this was to be Ford's last Western, and one of his most ambitious. It was based on a novel by Mari Sandoz by which he had been intrigued five years before and which, as Dan Ford points out, directly reversed (or complemented) the viewpoint and the ethos of the James Warner Bellah Cavalry stories.

'Far from romanticising the expansion of the American empire, *Cheyenne Autumn* told of the victims of that expansion, the American Indians.' It was the story of the Northern Cheyenne tribe, wearied by the duplicity and the broken promises of the United States Government, who in 1878 defiantly quit their barren reservation to trek back to their ancestral lands in the Dakotas. Ford had, it seems, worked on a treatment of the book with Dudley Nichols when it first appeared in 1957, but had been unable to generate interest in it. Now Bernard Smith (who had produced *How The West Was Won*) persuaded Jack Warner to back the project with a budget of over four million dollars. For a director coming up to his seventies, the sheerly physical challenge was formidable.

The artistic challenge was perhaps greater. *Cheyenne Autumn* was not just a departure in terms of theme; it also presented severe problems of dramatisation and performance. Ford's Indians had never lacked dignity, but he had never attempted familiarity either: he had always respected the

privateness of their world, and its integrity. When they appear, on a rocky eminence, looking down on the White intruders, they are in their territory, as little to be questioned as the desert or the hills; when Captain Brittles and Sergeant Tyree meet Pony That Walks in *She Wore a Yellow Ribbon*, we ride into the camp with them, and we witness the meeting as guests, knowing that we really are meeting Chief Big Tree and that he is not demeaning himself by pretending seriously to be anyone else. (It is significant that when drama was the object, as in *The Searchers* or *Two Rode Together*, Ford cast a white American actor, Henry Brandon.) But the heroes of *Cheyenne Autumn* are the Cheyenne. As Patrick Ford wrote in the production notes he prepared with his father: 'The basic premise . . . is to dramatise the Indian side of the conflict. The Cheyenne are not to be presented as heavies, nor are they to be ignorant misguided savages . . . Their motives must be expressed early in the picture.' At the same time, though: 'My father and I are agreed that the Cheyenne should not speak English in the picture. They should serve, in his words, as a "Greek Chorus".' There is a contradiction here that probably no screenwriter could have overcome. If the motives of the Cheyenne were to be expressed, how could they not speak English? And if they were to be treated as a Greek Chorus, they would almost inevitably be reduced to dignified abstractions, passive monuments to injustice. The White characters invented to carry the narrative were equally condemned to impotence: Richard Widmark, as a Cavalry officer reluctantly obeying orders to hunt down the escaping Indians, and Carroll Baker as a sympathetic Quaker schoolmistress, could not overcome the limitations inherent in their roles. Only Edward G. Robinson, playing the historical character of Carl Schurz, a Secretary of the Interior struggling with conscience against ruthless military opportunism, managed to bring a true sense of epic to the film. Otherwise the tragedy was weakened by contrivance.

And of course the Cheyenne, whose fatal dissensions were a mainspring of the plot, had to speak English. Ford cast them with American and Mexican actors: Victor Jory, Ricardo Montalban, Sal Mineo and the still-beautiful Dolores Del Rio. The result was unconvincing, as it had to be. Ford did not get on with Montalban or Mineo — neither of them actors he would normally have cast — probably because he knew he would never be happy with the best they could do. He struggled, often through a statuesque simplicity of composition, to give his Indians dignity; but it is the kind of dignity, applied

* Bogdanovich, p. 204.

Cheyenne Autumn.
*Dolores Del Rio, Sal
Mineo.*

rather than organic, that runs through a similarly theoretical work like *The Fugitive*. (Only here the photographic style is less consistent.) And a final, but crucial dramatic error was made by the insertion, for obvious crowd-pleasing motives, of a 'comedy' sequence in the middle of the story, with James Stewart as a demystified Wyatt Earp dispensing farcical justice in a music-hall version (all-shooting, all-gambling) of Dodge City. Audiences who could respond to the central theme of the film could only resent this hefty leg-pull: and audiences who relished the joke were likely to be bored by the extended sufferings of the Cheyenne. The studio compounded the error by clumsily inserting an interval in the middle of this sequence — and when that failed to work, cut the second half of it altogether.

There is heroism in *Cheyenne Autumn;* but it is heroism in the attempt rather than the achievement. Heroism in defeat is, of course, the subject, but here the defeat is a creative one. To make a personal admission: I have seen *Cheyenne Autumn* twice, and neither time have I been able to sit it through to the very end. It is too painful. There is a leaden, effortful determination about the film: characteristic Fordian ideas are executed mechanically, without freshness of feeling: it comes as no surprise to read of his disenchantment and depression during shooting, and his flagging energy. Dan Ford tells sadly how George O'Brien, who had worked so often for Ford since the great days of *The Iron Horse* forty years before, and was now playing a small featured role in *Cheyenne Autumn*, came to his room, to which he had retreated in exhausted depression on the Monument Valley location. O'Brien talked and joked about the past with his old friend and tried to cheer him up. 'But it was no use. Every time he mentioned *Cheyenne Autumn* John grew sullen and withdrawn and simply said, "It's just no fun any more".'

173

7

Bellagio Drive runs north off Sunset Boulevard, up through the luxuriant hillside estates of Bel Air, west of Beverly Hills, where elaborate, multi-styled mansions, glimpsed up driveways or behind screens of foliage, evoke the Hollywood aristocracy of yore who mainly built and occupied them. Driving up there one September afternoon in 1978, I was glad to think that at least one veteran had preserved his fortune, even if he was now neither heeded nor known by Hollywood's new ruling class, a fashionable selection of which I had just left behind at the restaurant Ma Maison, talking deals or just being seen, while their attendant Rolls-Royces and Mercedes glittered and grew hot in the sunshine. I was in search of Willis Goldbeck, sometime writer, director and producer, whose name figures on the credits of the two films directed by Ford in these last ten years of his career which stand out from the rest with their revived (even if uneven) sense of creativity, their unmistakable, personal warmth: *Sergeant Rutledge* and *The Man Who Shot Liberty Valance.*

I had been given Mr Goldbeck's address on Bellagio Road by my friend Kevin Brownlow, who had tracked him down while searching for movie pioneers to interview for his television series on the great days of the American silent cinema. I was ignorant. At that time I did not know that long before he worked with John Ford, Willis Goldbeck had directed the last two pictures both in the Dr Kildare and the Hardy Family series (he had worked on most of the Kildare scripts); that his name is listed among the writers of Tod Browning's *Freaks*; that he had co-authored *Wild Orchids*, one of Garbo's late silent films; and that he had written two of Rex Ingram's most famous pictures, *The Garden of Allah* and *Mare Nostrum*. And now he was living in Bel Air.

Or was he? The road turned and twisted through the fabled estates, crested the hill — and we found ourselves descending the slope on the further side, The properties became less splendid. Bellagio Road stretched on across the Freeway. Bel Air was left behind as the houses became recognisably of the kind inhabited by people rather than celebrities. At last we arrived at the number: an unpretentious apartment block of recent date, two-storeyed and plain behind its smooth strip of lawn. The first ground-floor apartment you came to had Mr. Goldbeck's name beside the door. I walked on, to a back courtyard, where I relieved myself among the dustbins. When I came back, Mr Goldbeck's door

was ajar. I sensed that my arrival had been observed, and that now I was awaited. I pressed the bell.

Mr Goldbeck was neat and handsome, grey-haired and rather severe. He wore a blazer (or he gave that impression) and what I thought might be an R.A.F. tie. He looked at me suspiciously. I tried to explain, as succinctly as I could, who I was and what had brought me there. The idea did not seem to please him. Yet he did not seem — not quite — to want to send me away either. For a moment the issue hung in doubt. Then he invited me in.

The apartment was modest. Mr Goldbeck evidently lived alone. It was well-ordered (like him) with homely, functional furniture, papers and a lot of books. Mr. Goldbeck protested, with an edge of irritation that never made him seem unmannerly, that he had talked lengthily to Kevin Brownlow, and surely that was enough. Also he was thinking of writing his memoirs himself, and he didn't want to give all his material away for other people's books. However, I still felt that he didn't exactly want me to leave. And when I began to ask him about Ford and *Sergeant Rutledge,* he was, though not loquacious, prepared to talk.

He had the written the original story in the early sixties, when Hollywood had assimilated the idea of the Black 'problem' picture: the idea came to him of combining the racial theme with the Western. History provided a context. In 1866, the year after the Civil War had freed the slaves, two black troops, the Ninth and the Tenth, were organised in the U.S. Cavalry. Officered by whites, these units offered equality of status to the black soldiers, although traditions of prejudice and suspicion still persisted. No white troops had a higher reputation for *ésprit de corps* than the Buffalo Soldiers — as the Indians called them, on account of the buffalo coats and caps they wore against the cold. Willis Goldbeck had the idea of using one of these detachments as a setting for a drama of violence and prejudice: a negro sergeant of the Ninth Cavalry is suspected, on circumstantially incriminating evidence, of raping his Colonel's daughter and murdering her and her father. The appearance of guilt is strengthened by the sergeant's desertion after the crime: later he explains his flight on the grounds that, with appearances against him, he would stand no chance of a fair trial in a white court. He is pursued and captured, and returns to face the accusation.

As Willis Goldbeck first conceived it, the story was to end there, unresolved. The audience would be left with a question — not simply who had committed the crime, but was justice possible in a climate of prejudice? Even in the liberal sixties, this was not

Sergeant Rutledge. *The courtroom — centre of the drama. Mary Beecher resists the prejudiced innuendoes of the prosecutor (Constance Towers, Carleton Young).*

likely to be an easy subject to finance. But, Goldbeck reasoned, if John Ford could be interested, a studio would probably go with the project. How could Ford be interested? Now he thought of James Warner Bellah. There had been something of a rift between Bellah and Ford since the great days of the Cavalry 'trilogy' ten years before. In *Fort Apache, She Wore a Yellow Ribbon* and *Rio Grande*, Ford might be thought to have done Bellah pretty proud: but 'the American Kipling' (in Dan Ford's excellent phrase) did not like his stories or his scripts being messed around with. And by 'messing' he meant the kind of liberties Ford insisted on taking with a script once he got a picture in front of the camera. However, Willis Goldbeck managed to get Bellah interested in his story, and willing to consider the idea of renewing the collaboration. The two writers prepared a treatment and sent it off to Ford. A telegram came back from Hawaii, where he was taking a holiday on his boat, announcing his interest, and Goldbeck and Bellah flew out. Bellah and Ford were reunited and ,went off on a monumental spree to celebrate. Then the three of them started work on the script.

Ford's influence on the development of *Sergeant Rutledge* (as the film became) seems to have been strong. Willis Goldbeck's original idea, by his account, stopped short at the Sergeant's trial; but to leave the outcome suggestively doubtful in this way would have been quite out of style for Ford. In the film, the courtroom becomes the principal set, with a crucial role being played by Tom Cantrell, a young Cavalry lieutenant who is also Rutledge's officer, friend and defender. All this is very reminiscent of *Young Mr Lincoln*, with Abe's dogged defence, against all the odds of appearance and prejudice, of Mrs Clay's sons and his final unmasking of J. Palmer Cass. Here, however, the trial is not just the culmination but also the spine of the film, from which we are carried back into the story, episode by episode, as the witnesses give their evidence. The real climax is Rutledge's own impassioned affirmation of dignity and loyalty, which is followed by the revelation of the real rapist by an ingenious (though not very convincing) feat of detection by Cantrell.

The tone of *Sergeant Rutledge* is far from the springtime simplicity of *Young Mr Lincoln*, with its confident idealism and its open purity of feeling. Here the emotions are complex, more subterranean; passion is suppressed or perverted, decency and loyalty are threatened by violence and fear. A lot of the film takes place at night, from the tense melodrama of the opening flashback, narrated by 175

Constance Towers as Mary Beecher, returning to her father's ranch after twelve years in the East. The railroad stop is dark and deserted: her father is not there to meet her. The train must go on its way, and she finds herself alone in the night, until the powerful, huge figure of the negro sergeant materialises out of the darkness, first as a threat, then as her protection against the marauding Indians who have killed her father. This is how we first see Rutledge, himself on the run, suspected of rape and murder. Ford directs these scenes with strongly suggestive melodramatic power. The transitions from the courtroom are effected not by straight cuts, nor by more conventional dissolves, but by formal artifice, an expressionist shift of lighting from the common daylight of the trial into dramatic silhouette, a threatening chiaroscuro that is almost like a descent into the subconscious.

These, inevitably, are the aspects of the film which occupy most contemporary critics. For instance, Ms J. A. Place: 'As might be expected in Ford's only film about a black negro, the underlying theme is racism.'* But *Sergeant Rutledge* has more than one hero, and it has another theme, equally central and finally more significant. This is the old theme, dear to Ford's heart although no longer fashionable, of dignity and service, identified, as so often in the past, by the tradition of the U.S. Cavalry. Both the film's heroes express this theme; for the

first time in Ford's work one of those is black, Sergeant Rutledge himself.

Rutledge, in the towering person of Woody Strode, is less a naturalistic (or a psychological) presentation of the character, than a poetic, even a mythic one. Shot in low-angle silhouette, monumental against the night sky on a desert hillside, he is identified by image and by song with the legendary Captain Buffalo, incarnation of all that is strongest and finest in the tradition of the black soldier. More usually an up-tempo march, the song is taken slowly, elegiacally:

> Said the Private to the Sergeant,
> 'Tell me Sergeant if you can
> Did you ever see a mountain
> Come a-walking like a man?'
> Said the Sergeant to the Private,
> 'You're a rookie ain't you though —
> Or else you'd be a-recognising
> Captain Buffalo.'

Right up to *The Sun Shines Bright,* Ford (who was never, ever a 'racist') had remained faithful to the comic or sentimental stereotypes of the young American cinema. These were affectionate and innocent, never cheap and never without their own dignity or pathos; but the characters were always marginal, and latterly too close for comfort to the kindly spirit of Uncle Tom. *Sergeant Rutledge* gave him a chance to show a black man with dignity and importance, as he never had before.

There is, of course, nothing modern or radical about this film: Ford was responding to an old inspiration, not discovering a new one. Nor was there anything of the radical about either Goldbeck or Bellah. Rutledge is an agonised not an angry man, finding his dignity and his manliness in the service — 'The Ninth Cavalry was my home. My real freedom. And my self-respect' — and Ford was able to present him with all the still-strong romanticism of his own reverence for tradition. The film's other hero, Tom Cantrell, is also a man of duty, courageous and committed. Jeffery Hunter does not have the stature or the resonance of a Fonda or a Wayne, but his directness, his boyish decency and the forceful honesty of his playing make him a not unworthy Ford hero. Cantrell's allegiance to the soldier's code of discipline is as central to the film as its issues of prejudice and justice; and Mary Beecher, crisply and unsentimentally presented by Constance Towers,

* J. A. Place. *The Western Films of John Ford,* 1974.

learns to recognise its worth and to accept its rightness. If Ford saw the possibility of profitable innovation in Willis Goldbeck's idea, he must also have sensed the opportunity it offered to return to and reanimate these favourite old themes.

The spirit was there; but the grasp was less sure than it had been ten years before, as James Warner Bellah noted even while they were working on the script: 'It was pretty obvious from the start that some of the old fire was missing in Jack. He had always been a real tyrant in story sessions, needling and picking away at you. It was his way of making you reach in and give your best. But on *Rutledge* he was awfully mild.'* Dan Ford notes too how some of the shooting was perfunctory, with Ford working 'quickly and impersonally, cutting corners where he could', and cites as an example the early scene between Cantrell and Mary Beecher in the train carrying her home — where the moving wagon remains as firm and static as a house, because Ford had not troubled to get it mounted on rockers. This kind of carelessness runs through much of the film, and spoils some of it. Much of the humour that was introduced to lighten the courtroom scene (and Mr Goldbeck frowned as he recalled it) was heavy-handed and out of key, with Billie Burke and Mae Marsh twittering self-righteously as they await the thrill of scandal, and Willis Bouchey as the presiding Colonel, impatient for a drink or a hand of poker. A good deal of the acting lacks (to put it politely) *finesse:* Carleton Young as the prosecuting officer has not the distinction of personality which alone could make acceptable the harsh clichés of prejudice of which his role consists; and as so often in these late works, the inexperienced youngsters suffer either from impatient, overinsistent direction, or from a complete lack of it. As always, though, good actors act well. In particular there is a beautiful performance by Juano Hernandez as a veteran black sergeant who lies about his age to stay in the service — here is Fordian sympathy at its most touching.

In any case, a film like *Sergeant Rutledge* is to be judged, and valued, not by its weaknesses but by its strengths. Of course we regret the haste of it, the slapdash staging, the perfunctory winding-up: the Buffalo Soldiers march grinning down a colonnade, with an eyes-left for Tom and Mary as they stand reconciled in a routine clinch — then out to Monument Valley for the traditional ride past. This is token stuff: we can feel the director's impatience to 'wrap'. Elsewhere though, just as surely, we can feel Ford's talent kindling to his theme, as it had not

* Dan Ford: *Pappy,* p. 284.

for a long time; the scenes come alive with warmth and tension and the vibrancy of convictions deeply held. The exteriors were shot rapidly (eighty per cent of the schedule, Dan Ford tells us, was in the studio), but these in particular have a splendid, breathtaking vigour — the effortless, unanalysable magic of an old Master. Ford was to shoot again in Monument Valley, but never again with this intense and heartwarming lyrical charge. It was his final salute, and a stirring one, to the good old cause.

Sergeant Rutledge did not achieve the success that everyone — Goldbeck and Ford and Warner Brothers — had anticipated. Nor was this really surprising. Ford could not turn himself into a fashionable, contemporary director simply by taking on a fashionable, contemporary theme. His romanticism was too ingrained, and it was too late for his traditional, simplistic approach to character and popular entertainment to be changed. At a time, too, when technique was becoming more showy and more sophisticated, his impatient (not to say slapdash) approach to shooting was making his films seem dated. It took him time, now, to find work; and longer still to find a subject to which he could respond personally. He spent time 'helping John Wayne with his huge and risky *Alamo;* he directed Ward Bond in an episode of *Wagon Train*; he made a film for Columbia which echoed the theme of *The Searchers* and which he did not like. Then he found *The Man Who Shot Liberty Valance.*

This was a story by Dorothy Johnson which Ford himself picked, and for the script of which he renewed the collaboration with Willis Goldbeck and James Warner Bellah. All that it has in common with *Sergeant Rutledge* is that it is a Western (not a Cavalry) story, and that it is constructed in flashback. There was a good leading part for John Wayne, who had just signed a contract with Paramount, so Ford took the project there, with James Stewart and Lee Marvin as co-stars. Even so, and with Ford taking responsibility for half the budget, the studio did not jump at the idea: it took five months of consideration before they gave the go-ahead. It must have been a frustrating, even an ignominious business. *The Man Who Shot Liberty Valance* is a fine, suggestive story, strongly cast and laced with humour. All the same, one can understand the studio's hesitation. This was a picture that had to start with one of its stars (James Stewart) aged beyond his years, and then go back into the past in which he has to play some thirty years younger, with youthful makeup and hairpiece. In the framing 'present', John Wayne is dead, represented only by a plain wooden coffin. For all

the humour in the story, its keynote is wry, ambiguous, ironic. The hero does not win. The winner is not heroic.

From the start, there is a pervasive, underlying sadness in this film. A train approaches us through a blossoming desert: there is no date, but the design of the engine speaks of the old West, perhaps at the turn of the century. It is not a spectacular opening: this is not the rugged West of legend, but a landscape that has been tamed, on its way to civilisation. An old man, bulky and ungainly, waits nervously, emotionally, his hat twisting in his hands. The train draws in to Shinbone Station, and two well-dressed figures descend, a husband and wife, darkly clad, also elderly. They greet the old man, Link Appleyard, like old friends: the woman particularly is full of emotion, near to tears. The meeting is suffused with a sense of the past, of experiences shared between those three people that they have no need to speak of. Or perhaps they could not trust themselves to. The man seems less sensitive. A young reporter, who has not recognised him (whatever events drew these three together in this place happened a long time ago), learns from the station master that this is Rance Stoddard, U.S. Senator, and his wife. The reporter asks for an interview and Stoddard, who has a politician's loud voice and self-satisfaction, readily agrees. So Appleyard drives Hallie Stoddard out into the desert, where they halt to look at a broken down, burned-out shack. 'He never did finish that room', murmurs Appleyard. 'Still, you know all about that.' Cacti are flowering in the ruins of the house. Link walks over to pick one, and Hallie's hands move towards the box she has set on the seat beside her. There is a fullness of emotion in all this, but there is nothing sentimental about the scene. The tone is reserved, almost terse. Hallie is accompanied by music; it may be recognised as Ann Rutledge's tender theme from *Young Mr Lincoln*. This, variously arranged, provides the film with almost its only music.

While Hallie and Link Appleyard share unspoken memories, Stoddard is talking with the editor and a couple of reporters at the Shinbone *Star*. They ask the question we are asking too: why is he here? 'I'm here for a funeral.' 'Funeral — who's dead?' Tom Doniphon? No one has heard of him. At this point Hallie and Link return, and Stoddard goes with them to the all-purpose store that serves as a funeral parlour. Here, where the poor man's coffin (the

The Man Who Shot Liberty Valance. Top: James Stewart, John Wayne. Below: Woody Strode.

The Man Who Shot Liberty Valance. *Hallie and Link visit Tom Doniphon's ruined home and pick a cactus flower. Tom's pauper's coffin, visited by Hallie and Rance. Link carries the box with Hallie's flower.*

funeral is at the public expense) stands in a little back room, they meet Pompey, an old negro, another familiar from the past. The undertaker nervously holds open the coffin lid. Stoddard looks in, without evident emotion, then speaks sharply: 'Where are his boots? Where is his gun belt?' He hadn't worn his gun belt for a long time, Pompey says. And the undertaker explains that he won't be paid much for the funeral; and they were a good pair of boots...'Put his boots on,' demands Stoddard. The scene is interrupted by the men from the *Star,* who demand, on behalf of the public, the reason for the Senator's visit to their town. Stoddard is hesitant; Hallie, with a little nod, signals him to tell them what they want. So he motions the newspapermen out into the store that adjoins the little lying-in room, and there, amid the junk and discarded furniture, where an abandoned stagecoach stands dusty in the middle of the floor, he gives them his story.

Perhaps it was this set that Wingate Smith, Ford's faithful assistant, complained of, saying that it didn't look 'lived in'. 'John said curtly, "If they notice it, then we'll give 'em their nickle back".'* Certainly the decors here, and through much of the film, lack detail and atmosphere: they serve their purpose, but barely, as if cheaply or hastily made ready. Dan Ford mentions how many of the people who worked on *Liberty Valance* remarked Ford's 'lack of energy', his 'complete disregard for background effects, for extras, for smoke and commotion'. Partly, no doubt, this was yet another instance of Ford's growing impatience with the business of shooting: it was no longer 'fun'. He resented the demands of narrative, of crowd-pleasing spectacle, the trappings of 'art'. And in places the work suffered. The lighting of this picture is at times only serviceable, inexpressive even when the image is an important one: a shot of the cactus rose which Tom has brought for Hallie, and which Pompey has planted for her, looks like something shot in a hurry, in the last ten minutes of a long day; and the hold-up of the stage which introduces Liberty Valance has the cramped artificiality of a scene in a 'B' picture. And yet, whether by design or by accident, this lack of visual refinement has an artistic result which is not just negative. The lines of the story emerge clearly,

* Dan Ford, *Pappy.* p. 292.

sparely, with no decorative distraction. Ford is an entertainer, certainly; but he is not making this film simply to divert us. He has something to tell us. The approach and the style seem to have something in common with a writer who worked in quite a different tradition. Yet perhaps Ford and Brecht — here at least — were not as dissimilar as one might think. Both felt themselves to be in possession of truths — useful truths which they needed to communicate. Brecht called his plays Parables for Theatre. *The Man Who Shot Liberty Valance* is a parable for cinema.

It is also a poem: the film develops with the simplicity and concreteness of a ballad, the objectivity and the historic sense of an epic. And it is very much a story. Rance Stoddard, the young, naive idealistic lawyer is on his way out West (so the flashback starts): the stage in which he is travelling is held up and robbed by the brutal and violent Liberty Valance, terror of the locality. Beaten to the ground by Valance, impotently protesting, his law books torn and scattered, Stoddard is rescued and brought into town by Tom Doniphon, the only man in Shinbone with the strength and the courage to stand up to Liberty Valance. Tom deposits Rance with his friends the Ericsons, who run 'Peter's Restaurant', and whose pretty, spirited daughter Hallie he means, one day, to marry.

It is the contrast, the conflict and the relationship between these two, Tom and Rance, the man of the past and the man of the future, the man of action and the man of ideas, that form the substance of the parable. At first the advantage is all with Tom: it is he who rescues Rance, generously arranges for him to be looked after, instructs him in common sense and protects him from the ruthless violence of Liberty Valance. Rance in these early sequences is self-righteous and rather silly, priggish in his refusal to understand the realities of the situation. He acts as a waiter in the restaurant to pay for his keep, and wears an apron. (Tom's amusement at him is kindly, though, and shows a certain respect: he calls him 'Pilgrim'.) Then he begins to acquire dignity. Tom leaves town for three weeks on the range, and Rance starts to put his principles into practice. He goes better than his promise to teach Hallie to read: he starts a school, for any of the townsfolk who wish to come, and he teaches not only reading and writing but the principles of good government. He leaves the restaurant kitchen, puts up his lawyer's sign and gets himself a job assisting Dutton Peabody, the owner-editor of the Shinbone *Star,* a man of intelligence, rhetorical command and a powerful thirst for liquor. Rance — and Peabody —

understand the challenge that history is presenting to the citizens of Shinbone: to save themselves from the rapacity of the cattlemen, they must abandon the anarchy of independence and opt for Statehood. But Liberty Valance is the strong arm of the cattlemen: without Tom's gun and the faithful Pompey to cover him, democracy would not stand much chance. The townsfolk know it, and they roar approval when Rance proposes Tom as their candidate for the State legislature. Tom will not accept and he proposes

The Man Who Shot Liberty Valance. *'Print the legend.'*

Rance; and it is Rance who is elected, famous now as the man who shot Liberty Valance. But it was Tom who did the shooting, and who lost Hallie by it; and Rance knows, because Tom tells him . . .

So warm is its sense of the past, so strong its underlying sentiment of regret, that it is tempting to think of *The Man Who Shot Liberty Valance* as an elegy for the heroic simplicities of the pioneering West. Tom Doniphon — especially in the person of   181

The Man Who Shot Liberty Valance. *Alone in the deserted schoolroom, Hallie looks sadly at the bell for which there is now no need. A characteristic moment of solitary feeling.*

John Wayne — is almost the Western legend incarnate: honourable and laconic, generous and skilled, wise to the ways of his world. *Equitare, arcum tendere, veritatem dicere* — to ride, shoot straight and tell the truth — the ancient law of nobility. There is an overpowering nostalgic warmth about this man and his world: the homely companionship of Peter's Restaurant, the saloon, the jail where only the Sheriff sleeps. Andy Devine, John Qualen, Woody Strode. The ham actor's rhetoric of Edmund O'Brien as Peabody, and John Carradine as a bogus 'gentleman' pleading the cattlemen's cause. Even Liberty Valance and his two acolytes are part of the myth. And the cactus rose that flowers in the desert. At first Rance Stoddard and his ideals seem callow and theoretical by comparison. (Although James Stewart acts excellently, without any embroidery of mannerism, he is at the extra disadvantage for most of the picture of playing a character some thirty years younger than himself — a greater handicap for Stewart playing the immature Rance than for Wayne playing the ageless Tom Doniphon.)

But Ford gives Stoddard and his aspirations their due — aspirations which have so often been voiced in his films. 'Some day', says Wyatt Earp to his young brother in his grave ... 'Some day this country is going to be a fine, good place to be,' says Mrs. Jorgensen in *The Searchers* ... 'Maybe not now,' says Tom Cantrell, 'but ... as Rutledge says ... "Some day" ...' Rance is a teacher, showing and leading the way to that future, and his schoolroom is a place of pride and belief. Nor is he without courage. Of course, he is, or he becomes, a politician too: that is a handicap he can never quite overcome. There is no doubt where Ford's sympathies lie — a man is entitled to his feelings — but his judgement is another thing. And in the end both feelings and judgements must yield to the inevitability of history. Hence this picture's endless paradox: for we know that the future cannot be more simple than the past, and probably not much better, just different. One is reminded of the words with which another great artist concluded a story — and with which Max Ophuls concluded his Maupassant film, *Le Plaisir*. *'Ce n'est pas gai, le bonheur.'* It can take a lifetime to learn that.

So, all through the story, the ironies and ambiguities multiply. The young lawyer who believes in the rule of law can only survive by the strong arm of the man of action: the generosity of the man of action costs him his hope of happiness. The idealist wins acceptance for his peaceful creed because he is believed to have killed a man: the man who really fired the shot receives no honour for it. Tom Doniphon 'kills the thing he loves' when he saves Rance Stoddard's life: and Rance is thereby condemned to a life of acclamation that is based on a lie. (Even Hallie's successful marriage is built on the same deception: when, one wonders, did she learn the truth?) Only a great poet — as Ford was to the end — could have filled an anecdote so neatly ironic with such regret, such humour, such reverberation of emotion. In *The Man Who Shot Liberty Valance* the realist and the romantic come together. The desert, yes, has become a garden; newspapers are published, children grow up safe; 'some day' has become a reality. And the price has been paid. Tom Doniphon lies forgotten in his plain wooden box, with only Pompey to mourn for him; and a certain gallantry has gone with him.

'Print the legend,' says the editor of the Shinbone *Star*. It is both a cynical and a poetic statement: in any event, a summing-up. The train that puffs busily away from camera at the end of *The Man Who Shot Liberty Valance,* carrying Rance and Hallie back to Washington, carries us back too in memory, to other departures with which Ford has ended earlier stories. Only now there are no figures left standing on the hillside or on the beach; no tasks waiting to be fulfilled. The line of departure is no longer straight and purposeful, but gently curving into the round of experience, hinting return, the sense of completeness. If to the grand design of John Ford's career *The Sun Shines Bright* was the finale, *The Man Who Shot Liberty Valance* is its coda, somewhat casual, certainly ironic, rich with experience, entirely worthy of the poet's lifetime which it brings to a stoic and accepting close.

The final images of Liberty Valance *have a powerful sobriety perfectly expressive of the regretful, poetic ironies of the work. The cactus flower on the wooden coffin; husband and wife, together but separate, for ever in debt to a dead man: 'Who put the cactus flower on Tom's coffin?' 'I did.' And the Western landscape, tamed and fertile, emblematic of achievement, but no longer free.*

183

Tea-time on The Man Who Shot Liberty Valance. *The tea served English-style, the Jacobs' biscuits, the hierarchic formality of the occasion — all evoke the essence of the Ford style. Left to right: Vera Miles, James Stewart, Andy Devine, Woody Strode, Lee Marvin, Jeanette Nolan, Edmund O'Brien, Lee Van Cleef, Strother Martin, Shug Fisher, John Wayne. And with their backs to us, Admiral Ford and his faithful amanuensis, Meta Sterne.*

Last Meeting:
Palm Desert

1973

In the summer of 1973 I was in Los Angeles for a few days in the middle of a publicity tour talking to journalists, disc jockeys, and Dial-a-Dollar show presenters about my film *O Lucky Man!* The Warner Bros. publicity department (who clearly had no very precise idea what to do with me) asked me if there was anything I particularly wanted to do in Hollywood. When I said I would like to call on John Ford, I sensed a certain unease: he was not in Los Angeles any more, he was a very sick man. People must have looked like this, I couldn't help reflecting, in the forties if anyone was tactless enough to mention the name of D. W. Griffith. I said I knew Ford wasn't well, and I knew he had moved out to Palm Desert: but I wanted to call him. His telephone number was produced. To my surprise, it was the correct one.

My friend Marion Billings, who was shepherding me on my tour, put the call through from my room at the Beverly Hills Hotel. We both felt rather strange about it. I remember how she went pale and tottered slightly when she found she was talking to John Ford. I took the phone. His voice was vigorous and welcoming, as though we had met a month or two ago. 'Hello — Lindsay! What are you doing in L.A.?' I explained, and said I'd like to come and see him, if that was possible. 'Yeah . . . Come on out — it'll be good to see you.' I told him I was only in town over the weekend.

'I've got my lawyer coming out tomorrow — I've got some business to talk over with him. Can you make it Sunday? Anytime: come out in the afternoon. You've got the address?'

It was difficult to believe he was dying of cancer.

I drove out on Sunday afternoon in the large limousine provided by the studio. Palm Desert is well into the San Fernando Valley, beyond Palm Springs, where the landscape is flat and featureless and the air very dry. It didn't seem much of a township. Just a spatter of houses, and the usual restaurants and drive-ins lining the highway. We stopped at a garage and asked the way to Old Prospector Trail. That was where Ford had come to make his last home.

We drove down a dusty road and stopped outside a sizeable bungalow, shuttered against the sun. I got out of the air-conditioned limousine into intense heat. At the gate I turned back, realising I had left my shoes in the car. I slipped them on and suggested to the driver he come back in an hour. I rang the bell at the front door. There was no immediate answer. My black limousine sat waiting to make sure I was taken in. No sound, no breath of air broke the intense heat of the desert afternoon. Then there was the sound of unlocking, and the door opened a little way, cautiously. I made out a middle-aged lady, standing in some kind of shift or housedress, barefoot. I explained that I'd come to see Mr. Ford, at his invitation. The lady hesitated, then asked me to wait. She closed the door again. The silence reasserted itself. I signalled to my driver and the limousine glided away. A minute or so and the door opened again, and I was asked in.

The bungalow was cool, air-conditioned and shaded. We went through a small hall into a spacious living-room. Barbara Ford, who had greeted me, introduced herself as Ford's daughter and asked me who I was. Her father had mentioned that a friend would be coming to see him, but had given her no details. I realised that my name meant nothing to her, but she was very friendly. There were two other ladies in the room, one middle-aged and one old. The old lady, delicately handsome, moved laboriously, using one of those tubular framed devices which enable the arthritic to walk. Barbara introduced me to her mother, Mary Ford. I was acknowledged graciously, then Mrs. Ford made her way to her room. Barbara left me to go and see if her father was ready to receive me.

I made small talk with the other lady, who seemed to be some kind of cousin. As we talked, I glanced round the large, homely, well-ordered room. The furniture was comfortable, substantial. It was a room full of the past: pictures, photographs, groups and signed portraits. The odd framed document: naval appointments, citations. There was an Admiral's sword on the wall. Oscars and other awards. Tradition, pride in achievement was all around me. I found myself consciously resisting the temptation to examine, to list, to think 'I will write about this'. Barbara Ford padded back in her slippers and told me that her father was ready to see me. 'Excuse me,' she said, 'but could you tell me your name again . . . Daddy only said he had an old friend from England coming.' I told her. 'Are you a film maker?' I said, sometimes. 'Daddy didn't tell me anything about you, but he was determined to look smart.' We were on our way out of the drawing room, down a passage to a room at the back of the house, when she stopped.

'It's the big one, you know,' she said, and I knew she meant cancer. 'It's only a matter of time. He's had the last rites: and last week we thought he'd gone. He had a giant haemorrhage and they rushed him to hospital in the middle of the night, but he fought his way out of it. He insisted on coming home.' 'Who is that lady I was talking to?' 'She's my cousin,' Barbara told me. 'She's come to help. We have a nurse too, who comes in part time.' She talked familiarly: I felt no constraint.

'What shall I call him?' I asked. 'What does he like to be called?' Like Robert Parrish, only, of course, Bob had served under him, I had always found it impossible to address Ford as anything but 'Mr. Ford' or 'Sir'. Barbara seemed surprised. 'Who, Daddy? Call him Jack. That's what he likes to be called.'

We went down the passage and into a light, quite small room, mostly occupied by a bed. Ford lay there, propped up on pillows, smoking a cigar and drinking brandy. Revolver shots rang out from a portable TV set by his bed. Figures on the screen were chasing each other up and down a ship's gangway. 'Hello, Lindsay,' he said warmly. 'Hello, Jack — it's good to see you.'

He looked gaunt and old. It was easy to see how disease had eaten into him. But the pugnacious, commanding spirit was still strong. It only took a moment to get used to his appearance, and then he looked much the same. It was easy to forget that he was fatally ill. I glanced at the TV screen: a bulky figure came clattering down a stairway, firing back at the deck above.

'Is that Victor McLaglen?' 'No, Tommy Mitchell.' Ford leaned across and switched off the set. 'Some rubbish.' Ford asked me what I was doing in L.A., and I gave him a copy of the book we'd produced of the *O Lucky Man!* script. It would mean nothing to him, I knew, but I thought he might appreciate the gesture. He looked at it a moment and put it on the table beside his bed.

187

'I missed that last one of yours,' he said. 'But I enjoyed that football picture you did.'

'Did you see it?' I said, surprised.

'Of course I did', he said. 'Good picture.'

I couldn't help wondering if he'd really seen *This Sporting Life*. I couldn't think of any good reason why he should have. Not that it mattered. I asked him if he'd been working on any projects, knowing there had been several in the last few years.

'Oh I had a couple of scripts,' he said, 'but I'm beyond that now. This has put a stop to all that. Haven't got the strength for it.'

He didn't say it bitterly. It was almost as though it was a truth he had long avoided and now was glad to face.

We chatted in a relaxed way. The send-up tone had gone. No need for that now. We had no great store of common experience, and not much old acquaintance: but I knew that in a strange way the fact of my visit mattered to him, and I was glad. We talked a bit about picture-making now and in the old days. He talked contemptuously as ever about producers. I asked him if there was anyone he liked working with.

'Oh, Zanuck. He knew the business. When I'd finished a picture I could go off to Catalina on my boat and fish. Didn't have to hang around. I could leave the editing to him. None of the others knew anything.'

I congratulated him on his award from the American Film Institute. The ceremony had been made a few months back; the presentation had been made by Richard Nixon, and Jane Fonda had protested outside against his presence. 'Did they do it well?' I asked. 'Oh, it was fine,' he said. 'A great occasion. The President made a speech. Of course he didn't know much about it, but he did it very well. I was very touched.'

People had been to see him. 'Hawks has been over a couple of times. He was here last week. And Hank Fonda — he's a nice man, Hank.' Maureen O'Hara was on an island somewhere in the Pacific. He reserved his familiar caustic tone for John Wayne. 'Duke's up in Seattle shooting some rubbish. Playing a goddam policeman . . .'

After twenty minutes or so, Barbara came back. 'Well, Jack, 'it was a piece of great luck that brought me out to California now. I'm glad I could see you.' His hand lay on the bedcover, freckled with age. I held it for a moment, then kissed it goodbye. 'Thanks for coming,' said Ford, 'It's a long drive out. It was good of you to come.'

I turned at the door. 'Anything I can do for you in England?' 'Oh, give Brian Hurst a call. Tell him you saw me.' 'Is there anything you want?' 'Only your friendship.' 'You have that.'

I left him with his brandy glass and cigar stub. I called Barbara a couple of times during my American tour. And from Washington I sent him a postcard of Lincoln with his son Thad. Six weeks later, back in London, I switched on the radio one morning and heard that he was dead.

188

End of voyage:
The Long Voyage Home.

Ford and friends: The Rising of the Moon.

The Film Maker

5. Ford and His Critics: Auteur or Poet?

A strange thing happened to John Ford's reputation in the last years of his career — years when, it might be said, his creative energies were diminishing and his grasp of public taste had become less sure. Professionally his standing weakened: critically his position began to grow more strong. This was not the result of a rediscovery of his early work; nor of a more appreciative assessment of his achievements at his prime. It reflected rather a shift in critical fashion which had the surprising — not to say perverse — effect of awarding more praise to the productions of decline than of maturity. In other words, Ford, who had always been an artist, though not always recognised as one and not always acting as one, was discovered to be an *auteur*.

Critically his case had always been a special one. From the start, his work was singled out in the trade press and in the fan magazines for its outstanding technical and pictorial qualities as well as for the strength of its popular appeal. The excellent filmography in Peter Bogdanovich's monograph quotes typical comments by contemporary reviewers. From the *Motion Picture World* review of *Bucking Broadway* in 1917: 'Jack Ford again demonstrates his happy faculty for getting all outdoors onto the screen.' 'Few directors put such sustained punch in their scenes as does this Mr Ford', (*Motion Picture News* on *Hell Bent* in 1918). And in 1919 *Photoplay* singled out *The Outcasts Of Poker Flat* for its 'marvellous river location and absolutely incomparable photography'. But of course these were not works of sophistication. By comparison with directors like Ingram, Stroheim or Chaplin, Murnau or Lubitch, Ford seemed an artisan, or an entertainer, rather than an 'artist'. The homely virtues of films like *Kentucky Pride* and *Riley The Cop* were not of the kind to attract serious attention; and even epic works like *The Iron Horse* and *Three Bad Men* were apt to be regarded as emanations of popular tradition rather than as original creative achievements. No doubt it was his awareness of this, rather than any real lack of ambition, that caused Ford to reject so insistently the title of 'career man', preferring instead the unpretentious status of 'journeyman' or 'traffic cop'. It may also have been the caution of one who knew himself to be a late developer. Ford had been a director for twenty years before his work achieved a personal, unique quality of statement.

By the time sound came in he occupied an oddly indeterminate position: much more than a routine talent, yet something less than an artist. His professional reputation was unassailable. He was already a veteran, a second-generation film maker, old enough in the business to have sat at Griffith's knee, experienced and confident in almost any genre, and with a healthy reputation for success. The movie business loved him. 'Strike Up the Band!', shouted *The Hollywood Reporter* lyrically, reviewing *Airmail* in 1932, 'Oil up the cash register!... Here, boys and girls is a honey, a wow, a smash and seven kinds of a knockout ... Here, exhibs, is something you should strain a suspender button to get your mitts on. Anybody who can't make dough with this should retire.' And the praise of Ford's direction was specific. 'John Ford's direction never falters for an instant. There isn't a foot of static in the whole production. Every shot shows carefully figured composition, and the movement is continuous ... The lighting and effects have been handled with consummate skill.' Two years before, *The Film Spectator* had commented on *Men Without Women* with similar enthusiasm, and with a very accurate summary of Ford's individual personality as a director. 'Because John Ford is a great motion picture director, because he has an inborn sense of dramatic values, because there is a strong human streak in him, because at heart he is a sentimentalist with a tender, poetic and whimsical outlook on life, *Men Without Women* is a truly great motion picture.'

This kind of acclaim was fine for Ford's credit in the industry: but it was not the stuff of which artistic reputations are made. It was only as the thirties drew on, with such maverick successes as *The Lost Patrol* and *The Informer*, that more serious

The Prince of Avenue 'A' (1920). Ford and 'Gentleman' Jim Corbett.

Steamboat Round the Bend (1935). Will Rogers, Ann Shirley, John Ford.

recognition came. It was his collaboration with Dudley Nichols that brought Ford distinction, and the poetic, symbolic ambitions ('the artistic lie') of the films they made together. At last it seemed possible to identify the protean director with a theme: the group isolated by circumstances, the microcosm of human society, put at risk, confronted by destiny. Stagecoach could be made to conform to the pattern; and so could The Long Voyage Home. For the first time, indeed for the only time in his career, Ford was pleased to admit to artistic ambition and prepared to accept the title of professional rebel. To a journalist interviewing him for the left-wing New Theatre in 1936, he complained of the frustrating restrictions imposed on film artists by the studios: 'Got to fight it every time . . . Never any point where you can really say you have full freedom for your own ideas to go ahead with . . . They've got to turn over picture making into the hands that know it. Combination of author and director to run the works: that's the ideal. Like Dudley Nichols and me . . .' It was the nearest he ever got to talking like a career man.*

*Twenty years later, talking in Paris to Jean Mitry, Ford even went so far as to propound an aesthetic. '. . . I would think that it is for me a means of confronting individuals. The moment of tragedy allows them to define themselves, to take stock of who they are, to shake off their indifferences, inertia, conventions, their "ordinariness" . . .' (Cahiers du Cinéma, March 1955). Could this be a remnant of Dudley Nichols' theorizing, dusted down for the occasion?

But Ford's gift for self-preservation soon reasserted itself: he was not going to allow himself to be labelled a maverick for long. As the forties began, and his more conformist career at Fox soared precipitately into triumph, he retreated again behind the defences of professionalism; however disrespectful his behaviour, however wilful his style, he now stood for orthodoxy at its best. There would be no more talk of principled refusal of Oscars. (In 1936, as a result of conflict between the Guilds and the Academy, both he and Nichols announced that they would refuse their Oscars for The Informer: Nichols maintained his resolution, Ford did not.) In September 1941, when he left Hollywood for the Navy after completing How Green Was My Valley, John Ford was indisputably the leading director of the American cinema, on every level. There were some liberals and intellectuals who could never quite forgive a film like The Grapes Of Wrath for not being a realist documentary, but their reservations were more than compensated by the praise that rang round the whole of the 'free' (non-Germanic) world. In Russia Mark Donskoi, the director of the Maxim Gorki trilogy, declared: 'Quite simply, I was stunned by The Grapes Of Wrath . . . Everything about Ford is original, profound and new, unmatchable by any other American film maker.' And Sergei Eisenstein gave his palm to Young Mr. Lincoln, which he loved for the 'astonishing harmony of all its component

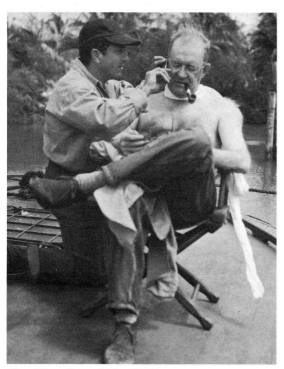

They Were Expendable *(1945).*

Sergeant Rutledge *(1960). Billie Burke, John Ford.*

parts ... a really amazing harmony', sensing that the source of the magic was 'the womb of popular and national spirit, from which spring its unity, its artistry, its genuine beauty'. He added, with the greatest generosity one director can show another, 'If some Good Fairy were to ask me: "Is there any American film you'd like me to make you the author of, by a wave of my magic wand?", I would not hesitate to accept. It would be *Young Mr Lincoln*, directed by John Ford.'

It was Ford's impassioned humanism that won him his golden reputation; his celebration of Lincoln, the righteous saviour of his people; the warmth and strength of his apparently populist conviction; his sympathy with the humble, the rejected, the dispossessed. His spirit was not revolutionary: it was radical, reformist. As his style, rich, simple and eloquent, represented American classicism at its best. Inevitably, the war changed things. It did not change Ford; but it changed the world and its ideas. Certain traditions were, it seemed, destroyed for ever. The notion of justly ordered society, of benevolent hierarchy, shrivelled before a universal — however shallow — acceptance of the egalitarian ideal: in the name of liberation, a devotion to duty became suspect; and affirmative humanism became equated with conformism and sentimentality. Films like *Sciuscia, Paisan, The Bicycle Thieves* could be accepted because they ended tragically: *They Were Expend-*

able, which would not accept defeat and ended with "The Battle Hymn of the Republic" could not. Rapidly Ford became old-fashioned. When other American directors were pushing forward into European-influenced realism (*The Best Years Of Our Lives, Crossfire, Boomerang, The House On 92nd Street*), he was following *My Darling Clementine* with *The Fugitive,* and *The Fugitive* with *Fort Apache.*

By the late forties and early fifties, admiration of John Ford seemed eccentric: even Westerns were out of favour, unless (like *High Noon*) they could be justified in terms of progressive parable. In France, the approved birthplace of cultural fashion, there even began a movement of specific denigration. I have quoted earlier the absurd comparison by the film historian Georges Sadoul of Ford with Julien Duvivier — a polished and sometimes sensitive director, but with no very marked personality or point of view. A coat-trailing article in the progressive film weekly *L'Ecran Français* by the director-critic Roger Leenhardt propounded the aesthetic of 'objectivity' under the heading of *'A Bas Ford! Vive Wyler!',* the kind of 'intelligent' idiocy of which French intellectuals are uniquely capable. (Leenhardt was influenced by the far-fetched lucubrations of André Bazin, doyen of Parisian film theorists, who commended the modern 'democratic' style of Wyler, based on deep-focus composition, and condemned the classic 'authoritarian' style of

Ford, based on unambiguous composition and on cutting.) A few years later, the young François Truffaut, reviewing *The Long Gray Line* in *Les Lettres Françaises* stigmatised Ford's 'inexpressive' (*nulle*) technique, described him as a Saint-Exupery of the nursery, and compared him unfavourably with Raoul Walsh. Commitment, in other words, was out: the *auteur* theory was being born.

A note on this 'theory' is necessary here, because although the term has been common among critics for over twenty years, it has remained recondite rather than popular, allusive in a superior way rather than helpful or enlightening. It is a French term because it was coined in Paris where, in the fifties, it became the fashion to refer to certain film directors as 'authors' (*auteurs*). The significance of the term was not literary: it did not suggest that these directors had actually written their films. It implied rather, or was concerned to reveal, a consistency of personality, of approach or of theme in the work of directors who had hitherto been undervalued or under-remarked, dismissed simply as artisans — 'craftsmen' if you liked their films and 'hacks' if you did not. The theory was consciously propounded and energetically argued by a group of young critics associated with a monthly magazine called *Cahiers du Cinema*, many if not most of whom wished to overturn the established tradition of French cinema and become film makers themselves. The campaign was launched in an article by Francois Truffaut published in the *Cahiers* of January 1954, a year or two before he himself started directing: it was titled *'La Politique des Auteurs'*.

As so often with European intellectuals, these young French critics were fascinated by America. Their first achievement was the celebration of directors as varied, and as variously deserving of attention, as Hitchcock, Preminger, Hawks, Bud Boetticher, Raoul Walsh ... Sometimes, like most theorists, the auteurists became silly: King Vidor was an *auteur*, therefore *Solomon and Sheba* was a masterpiece. At its least silly, the tendency was a healthy one; but there was nothing essentially original about it. English-speaking critics who took up the cry tended (and still tend) to write as though it had been newly discovered that a director's personality might be evident in his handling of material for which he was not wholly responsible. Of course this was not a new discovery. But certain

The epic style of The Iron Horse *comprehends the sweeping panorama as well as the intimate glimpse, affectionate and humorous, always human in focus.*

personalities were freshly revealed by these critics, certain continuities of values and ideas which had been previously obscured by the 'commercial' nature of their work and by the snobbishness of a literary tradition of film criticism. (Hitchcock and Hawks were the most obvious of these.) Unfortunately the detection of such continuities rapidly became the auteurists' chief objective; and the mere indentification of recurrent theories or obsessions became of more importance than their interpretation or an assessment of the value of the works in which they figured. An *auteur* was recognised by the consistency of personality in his films, not by their excellence. 'Value judgements', to use the cant phrase, were out.

It might be thought that Ford, whose personality was strong and whose values were distinct, would be a natural candidate for celebration. For two main reasons, he was not. Firstly, the *auteur* theory was iconoclastic. The writers of *Cahiers*, many if not most of whom were themselves anxious to direct, were intent on demolishing the classic cinema of 'quality', and above all the cinema of 'literary' repute which had resulted from such alliances of director and writer as Marcel Carné, with Jacques Prèvert (*Le Jour se Lève, Les Enfants du Paradis*), or Claude Autant-Lara with Aurenche and Bost (*Douce, Le Diable au Corps*). A similar aggressive disrespect was practised, with less excuse, by English-speaking disciples of the theory, who were not themselves trying to break into film making, but were anxious to establish reputations as vitally original critics. In this perspective, Ford was a pillar of the establishment, universally recognised. There was nothing to be gained by acclaiming an *auteur* whom the world had shown no sign of underestimating.

The second reason for Ford's dismissal from the essentially moral basis of his artistic nature. Philosophic fashion in the existential post-war world dictated moral neutrality if not despair. 'Le Cinéma de Papa' was written off as (amongst other things) essentially pietistic. An artist who had always, with absolute clarity and commitment, taken sides with goodness was infinitely less 'interesting' than an artist ambiguous in his responses, with obsessions only to be apprehended by the discerning eye of the auteurist critic. As I have noted, citing Bazin, it even became obligatory to disapprove the strong, unmistakably composed image — on the grounds that strong composition 'dictated' to the audience, instead of leaving it free to

Rio Grande. *Return from battle: Maureen O'Hara, Claude Jarman Jnr., John Wayne.*

look where and to think what it wished. (Such strictures did not apply, of course, to favoured artists like Hitchcock and Welles. But once a director had been identified as an auteur, he could by definition do nothing wrong.) For the intellectuals of the mid-fifties, Ford's style and everything that it expressed, as well as the respect in which he was universally held, barred him from the company of the chosen.

2

Discovery was important for the new critics. Writing about films had become a specialised, inbred, highly competitive business: it was necessary to make one's mark, to show oneself more perceptive and more authoritative than the established practitioners, 'knowing better' than one's peers. Classic Ford, we have seen, could make no appeal to the auteurist generation. But as his position became lonelier, his personal accent more marked and less respectable, he grew ripe for discovery. Andrew Sarris, the first American critic to adopt auteurism as a creed, describes the process with a certain complacency — having explained first how the British 'New Cahierist critics of *Oxford Opinion* and *Movie* . . . rebelled by declaring a preference for Sam Fuller over John Ford'.

> '. . . in the early sixties a two-man cabal of New York auteurists (the late Eugene Archer and myself) confounded the *Cahiers* line by placing John Ford on the same exalted level as Howard Hawks and Alfred Hitchcock. *Cahiers* itself finally re-evaluated Ford's stock in the mid-sixties. But by then it was not nearly enough to say whether or not you liked Ford: you had to specify the key films and the richest period. Old Guard: *The Informer* and *The Grapes Of Wrath* (1935-1940); Commitment School: *She Wore A Yellow Ribbon* and *Wagonmaster* (1949-1952); Auteurist School: *The Searchers* and *The Man Who Shot Liberty Valance* (1956-1966).'

The Ford who achieved critical recognition in this way was very different — had to be very different — from the Ford who had been loved by Eisenstein, had been awarded more Oscars than any other Hollywood director, and had maintained with grand obstinacy and dogged consistency his belief in human values and the values of the American tradition. Not only had those beliefs been staled by cheap rhetoric ('It is difficult to speak of such values today without sounding platitudinous': McBride and Wilmington, p. 201): they were too simple and too widely recognised. Something more sophisticated was called for. Thus: 'It is only when

Ford became old that he became fully liberated from the constrictions of his calling. And it is only when he became completely unfashionable that he became completely himself. These are propositions that remain to be argued.' (Andrew Sarris: *The John Ford Movie Mystery,* p.15). The propositions never were argued: there were merely asserted. But their assertion has involved the depreciation of much of Ford's finest work (because it had been widely appreciated and was therefore 'fashionable'), the overpraise of many of his lesser productions (because their freedom from 'constrictions' made them more personal) and the outpouring of more nonsense, of a more specially pretentious kind, than has been accorded probably to any other great artist of the cinema. 'The ultimate argument for Ford rests on the ability of an unexpectedly supple talent to transcend flaws in areas of the cinema which failed to excite and involve him' (Sarris). 'In essence Ford's subject is history, but history seen in the oblique and deceptive illumination of hind-sight and self-interest' (John Baxter: The Cinema of John Ford). McBride and Wilmington find that *The Searchers* is 'a crystallisation of all the fears, obsessions and contradiction which had been boiling up under the surface of Ford's work since his return from World War II' (a 'boiling-up' singularly *un*evident in films from *My Darling Clementine* to *The Sun Shines Bright*). Likewise Ethan Edwards is 'a volatile synthesis of all the paradoxes which Ford had been finding in his Western hero since *Stagecoach,* and 'it is chillingly clear that Ethan's craziness is only quantitatively different from that of civilisation in general.'

All these critics, although roughly similar in their approach, do not of course agree all the time. Andrew Sarris calls *Wagonmaster* 'a film with a rollicking ballad gusto' in which 'there are no moral shadings', while McBride and Wilmington find it 'a deeply ambiguous, almost perverse moral fable'. McBride and Wilmington praise the landscape beauty of *The Quiet Man,* though with shaky visual recall ('. . . filmed in colour through a veil of diffusing mist, rural Ireland has, as Manny Farber put it 'the sunless, remembered look of a surrealist painting'), while John Baxter inexplicably and with startling inaccuracy maintains that 'in all Ford's films his response to the Irish landscape . . . is disinterest; except for some brief and attractive shots at the beginning of *The Quiet Man* it is hardly seen, Ford preferring to concentrate his conflicts indoors.' Baxter exalts *The Fugitive* for its 'insight into the nature of belief and the higher motivations of spirituality', while even Andrew Sarris finds

Wagonmaster: 'A hundred years have come and gone
since eighteen forty-nine...' Stan Jones' ballad sets in
perspective one of Ford's most purely lyrical sequences,
imaging his sense of the courage and frailty of men and
women. Such intimations of mortality are at the heart of
Ford's poetic vision.

Ford's treatment 'pious rather than religious' with Fonda 'trudging through the film in a state of somnolent sanctimoniousness'. For all these divergencies, however, the auteurist critics share an approach that may be described as conceptual rather than intuitive: they intellectualise their responses instead of experiencing them. The result can only be to misinterpret, to falsify.

'All Ford's Westerns', writes J. A. Place in her *Western Films of John Ford,* 'are a ritual affirmation of the society they represent and grow from. The maturation process is one of disillusionment with the society while retaining the rituals as existential values within themselves.' This is 'academic' criticism at its least helpful (Dr Place received her Ph.D. at U.C.L.A. and teaches film theory and criticism at the University of California, Santa Cruz.) That Ford's films in the last ten years of his career expressed a less hopeful sense of progress, a less vibrant sense of romance is plainly true: but to make this the foundation of a theory of disillusion, alienation and nihilism (*Cheyenne Autumn* is a 'nihilist statement', *Seven Women* is 'black and nihilistic') is to misunderstand the work and misrepresent the man. *Cheyenne Autumn* was the attempted payment — too late, alas — of a debt: it was not nihilistic, nor was it evidence of Ford's 'declining opinion of the value of Western civilisation'. *Sergeant Rutledge* was not 'a brief respite from the growing disillusionment with values he previously held most dear'; it was an opportunity for him once again to state those values, with all the vigour at his command. Travis' self-sufficiency in *Wagonmaster* is not an anticipation of 'Ford's later hero who is alienated from the social unit'. And no one who feels at all with Ford can talk about the 'hopelessness' of *They Were Expendable,* its 'despair' or its 'transcendent failure of meaning'.

The essential absurdity of this kind of critical method is clearest in Dr Place's essay on *She Wore A Yellow Ribbon,* which the exigencies of theory demand should become 'one of Ford's earliest really dark films', with Nathan Brittles 'the most alienated individual in the film', rituals (a favourite word) 'meaningful in existential terms', and a Sergeant Tyree 'cut off from every form of meaningful social contact except what ritual and formalized relationships will provide'. We can only pity the critic whose heart cannot leap at the bugle's call, whose spirit cannot be stirred by Corporal Quayne's fiery report for the Paradise River patrol, and who can see nothing in Captain Brittles' habit of talking with his dead, beloved wife except a man 'giving up the living present and future for the dead but more meaningful past'.

The determination to force these films into a framework, psychological, philosophic or aesthetic, into which they do not naturally fit has a double effect of distortion: the distortion that comes from trying to provide insights into conceptions which are not really there at all, and the distortion that comes from a resulting insensitivity to the beauty, expressiveness and humour which really is there. Take, for instance, Peter Wollen's theory (he is presumably not an 'auteurist' at all, but a 'semiologist') of the 'master antinomy' in Ford's films between the wilderness and the garden, and his application of this to the scene in *My Darling Clementine* after Wyatt Earp has been to the barber, 'where the scent of honeysuckle is twice remarked on: an artificial perfume, cultural rather than natural'. (Why honeysuckle should be considered more 'artificial' than any other flower, and why its scent is less 'natural' is not clear.) Wollen continues:

'The moment marks the turning-point in Wyatt Earp's transition from wandering cowboy, nomadic savage, bent on personal revenge, unmarried, to married man, settled, civilised, the sheriff who administers the law.'

This may sound convincingly schematic, until we pause to consider that Wyatt Earp at the start of *My Darling Clementine* is *not* 'a wandering cowboy' — he and his brothers are driving their cattle West for settlement — and *not* therefore 'nomadic', certainly not 'savage' nor 'bent on personal revenge' — he arrives in Tombstone with the reputation of a famous lawman, feared and respected: he becomes town marshal in order to avenge his brother's death, and his determination lasts to the end of the story. He is unmarried, but so he remains at the fade-out, when he is *not* settled, no more 'civilised' (and no less) than he was at the start of the fable, and no longer sheriff. The theory, in other words, does not fit the facts. Worse, it leaves no room for humour or character, for sentiment or for moral imagination: and these are the stuff of Ford's poetry.

Inevitably those theoretical preoccupations, if they are allowed to dominate our consciousness, will falsify the experience of actually watching the films and act as a barrier to their emotion and their charm. A lack of sensitivity to performance — and how can one imagine Ford's films without their

My Darling Clementine. *Another confrontation of evil and good, rapacity and humane strength. Fonda once again — for the last time — as the Fordian hero, natural, modest, unrhetorical, rooted in integrity.*

They Were Expendable. *The men of the Squadron see the Commander-in-Chief arrive and take position on the bridge of their Captain's boat. A Homeric evocation — too martial for most liberals — with the Battle Hymn of the Republic under-scoring its heroic flourish.*

characteristic players and acting style? — is particularly revealing. Andrew Sarris imagines that casting 'was never his strongest point. The same old faces kept popping up...' McBride and Wilmington find that Anna Lee in *Fort Apache*, Mildred Natwick in *Three Godfathers* are 'as memorable as any of Ford's male characters from the period', and that Margaret Leighton's performance in *Seven Women* is 'one of the finest in all of Ford's work'. Dr Place is too distanced by intellectuality to be able to receive much more from Henry Fonda's acting than a quality she calls 'withdrawn, rigid'. Thus in *The Grapes Of Wrath* she finds 'Ford keeps him lacking in personality'; in *Fort Apache* he is 'empty, lacking in personality'; and in *Drums Along The Mohawk* 'his awkwardness and stiffness serve as a self-contained foil to enhance the humanity of the character he is playing' (an ingenious feat, at least). In *My Darling Clementine* 'this wooden quality is used in a similar way'. We are forced to ask ourselves: if she can describe Henry Fonda's acting as 'wooden', what satisfactory epithet can we find for Dr J. A. Place's own performance as a critic?

Acting is only one creative element in a dramatic film. One might expect critics who have set themselves so firmly against old-style 'literary' values to be more receptive to the expressiveness of performance — as well as to other significant elements such as editing (or rhythm), camera-style, music and design. One might also expect accuracy of observation, beyond a close examination of the script. But the substitution of aesthetic theory for 'literature' in the forefront of the critic's concern proves just as much an obstacle to understanding: and the imprecision extends to what these films are actually like to experience, actually (as opposed to theoretically or thematically) *are*. The swing of critical fashion has, in fact, resulted in a distortion of the director's role just as severe as anything in the past. Now he has to be overmuch the 'author'. Dr Place can write pages on *The Long Voyage Home* without discussing or assessing the contributions of Eugene O'Neill or Dudley Nichols. She analyses *How Green Was My Valley* exhaustively and exclusively as the work of its director, as if there were no novel behind it, no producer, no screenwriter and no cameraman, no actors to personify and interpret the characters more or less well. 'In *How Green Was My Valley* . . . Ford must construct his own distancing devices to protect against too directly confronting the Freudian implications (the death of the father which frees the son and finally allows him a place in the usual world

of the film) . . . Thus the flashback structure and voice over are devices which maintain a specific point of view and function as distancing devices in a form which does not automatically provide them.' And so on . . .

It is tempting, and it would be possible, to continue such quotation, following absurdity with inaccuracy, almost endlessly. (As for instance, choosing at random, Andrew Sarris' 'justification of Ford's classical editing' — that it 'expresses as economically as possible the personal and social aspects of his characters.' Or his comment on the camera style of *They Were Expendable:* 'Ford's camera . . . stands back at an epic distance, for which he pays a price in the imprecision of his psychological delineation.' Or Dr Place's description of the end of *My Darling Clementine:* 'Looking forward to *The Searchers*, Wyatt's inner solitude cannot be healed by the town, and in leaving he legitimizes the myth through his sacrifice.' Or the opening sequences of *The Searchers* as fantasised by McBride and Wilmington: 'Ethan rides slowly, silently, inexorably . . . Ford cutting again and again from him to the waiting family; the intercutting gives a feeling of magnetic attraction', (where in fact the film cuts to and back once only). But the point has been sufficiently made. This is a critical approach that tells us more about the critics, their personalities and their pretensions, than it does about the films.

What does it tell us? And are they worth refuting? I think so. If these critics remained confined within their specialised or academic goldfish bowls, they would do no great harm. The films, after all, are there, unaffected. But the infection spreads, if only because of the lack of conviction and authority in the central critical tradition: the lunatic fringe becomes the voice of received opinion. 'Film Studies' generate teachers as well as students: academicism proliferates and its baleful influence widens. When the National Film Theatre in London presented a Ford season in 1972, its members were informed (in programme notes signed by John Baxter and John Gillett) that the 'drop-outs' (?) in *Stagecoach* 'fleeing from an Indian band are the West in microcosm, as Ford uses them to express his sadness at the decline of frontier values in the face of urban invasion'; that *The Man Who Shot Liberty Valance* is essentially a reappraisal of *Stagecoach* and shows the morality of the West 'finally destroyed by democracy, with literacy as its most insidious weapon'. What chance has an audience, its head stuffed full of such misconceptions, of understanding, let alone enjoying the

201

films? The thing spreads. Readers of *The Times,* in a piece commemorating the same season (this time signed by Baxter alone) were told that they will find in *The Quiet Man* 'a hard look at Irish rural hypocricy', and at the heart of *My Darling Clementine* 'a touching homosexual love story'.

If we can fight our way through the jargon, through the posturings and rationalisations, what do we find? We find that we have been fighting our way past defences, through smoke screens. Ford's art at its best, the simplicity and the subtlety of it, the lack of ambiguity in its commitment, is too direct, too unmistakeable, too morally and emotionally challenging, for intellectual fashion in our declining West in this latter half of the twentieth century. Nor is this just a malaise of the last twenty-five years. It is a hundred and thirty years since Matthew Arnold mourned the death of Wordsworth with the cry: 'But who, ah! who, will make us feel?'

It is a cry we can echo. With all the brilliance, the intelligence and sophistication that goes into film making today, with all the multiplicity of elaborate and costly techniques, there is still this lack of feeling, of emotional exposure and commitment. Which is one reason why, again and again, we return in our dissatisfaction (not just with nostalgia) to the great films of the past in which we can still feel 'the freshness of the early world', and from which we can still receive refreshment. So it is with the films of Ford. And the reason why we may find so many of his critics, however highly they rate him, damaging as well as wrong-headed is because they obscure his feeling, apologising for it or rationalising it out of existence. They are not too wise for his simplicity, merely too clever.

3

To trace and analyse a continuity of theme or obsession in a film director's work can be an intriguing exercise; but it does not prove that director to be an artist, or his films to be worth writing about. To abstract films from the notion of value, whether artistic or moral, and to write about them not in relation to life, but in relation to concepts and themes, to abstracted philosophical, psychoanalytical or sociological theory, or to each other ('Movies are about Movies'), can certainly make the critic's task a great deal easier. Taking refuge in intellectualism, he does not have to expose himself (or herself) to judgement by the quality of his own experience of life, or by his capacity to evaluate and interpret it. 'Value judgements' are not

irrelevant to criticism, they are the very heart of it; but they do expose the critic to the same risks as are run by the artist every time he ventures on the creative act.

Critics, particularly 'academic' critics, prefer not to run these risks — and being often weak in emotional response, who can blame them? A proliferation of socio-aesthetic jargon can provide a fine smokescreen for the concealment of emptiness, shallowness or absurdity: 'Bullshit Baffles Brains', as the old army saying goes. A quotation from a recent (August 1980) programme of the National Film Theatre will serve to illustrate the way in which reputable institutions now habitually give credit to nonsense: the director here does not happen to be Ford, but he very well could be. Three films by Hitchcock — *Psycho, The Birds* and *Marnie* — are being presented by Mr Donald Spoto, the 'world-famous expert'. 'The trilogy', writes Mr Spoto, 'is Hitchcock's ultimate meditation on a collective moral flaw in the universe, and on the nature and quality of our perceptions through and beyond film art.' Inspired by *The Birds* ('the most demanding film in the Hitchcock catalogue'), Mr Spoto flies even higher: 'The sudden rush of wings expresses and makes explicit jealousy, anger and sexual and family tensions . . . Structured around an alternating series of conversations about being abandoned and the violent, inexplicable bird attacks that represent and actualise that terror, the film is a darkly lyrical puzzle-poem about human need, and nature of the universe, and the possibility of salvation.' *Mutatis mutandis* such terms might well be applied — perhaps already have been — to a grouping of *The Searchers, Donovan's Reef* and *Seven Women.* But such an approach is going to be of no help at all in understanding or appreciating John Ford.

The best way to approach the films of Ford is the way he himself approached the business of making them, empirically, practising his trade. He was a creator, a poet in the original Greek sense of the word — 'one who makes, a maker . . . the creator of a poem'. From the start, and all his life, he was a teller of tales. And like Homer with his 'blooming lyre', his tales were traditional, told for an audience who wanted only to be entertained, were not looking for originality or enlightenment, were happy to hear old tales well told.

When 'Omer smote 'is bloomin' lyre,
He'd 'eard men sing by land and sea;
And what 'e thought 'e might require,
'E went and took —'the same as me!

The Searchers. *Martin shields Debbie from Ethan's fanatic gun, the conflict resolved by an Indian arrow. Authority of style gives persuasion to the meldodrama, but cannot make more credible Ethan's final 'change of heart'.*

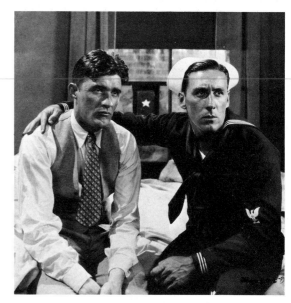

At the heart of Ford's ideal world: the family and its sustaining relationships. Top left: The mother as provider and source of strength (Jane Darwell in The Grapes of Wrath); top right: mother-love, never-failing, all forgiving (James Hall, Margaret Mann in Four Sons); centre: the family trinity (Richard Cromwell, Arleen Whelan in Young Mr. Lincoln); left: father and sons (Donald Crisp, left, Roddy McDowell, Anna Lee in How Green Was My Valley; above: brothers (Phillip Ford, George O'Brien in The Blue Eagle).

Ford could take from Griffith or from Murnau, from O'Neill, Irvin S. Cobb or James Warner Bellah: he took what he required for his business, which was to entertain. He entertained, of course, in a very distinctive, entirely individual way. His personality was strong; his accent was always his own. But if we are to understand his work, to recognise what is truly his about it, we need to understand also the tradition which produced it, to know which tales were truly his own, and which were derivations when inspiration was running short, or works *sur commande*. Shakespeare was obliged to hack out *The Merry Wives of Windsor* because the Queen wanted to see the Fat Man again; and Ford had to direct *Two Rode Together* because Harry Cohn had contracted Columbia to make it. (And maybe because he had nothing of his own going at the time.) The fact that he was a great and universally respected director did not free him from the constrictions and pressures of the industry in which he worked.

And in which he was pleased to work. We run up against ambiguity very fast when we talk about Ford. There were times when he chafed against the restrictions of the film industry, most notably in the mid-thirties when the influence of Dudley Nichols threatened to turn him for a short while into an artistic rebel: 'They've got to turn over picture-making into the hands that know it . . .' But his period of dissidence did not last very long. Fifteen years later he was saying, with his habitual gruff ingratitude: 'Oh — so Nichols wrote *The Informer* did he?' Ford always preferred — no doubt wisely, to rebel from within the organisation.

An aspect of his Irishness? The better one knows Ford, the more powerful seems the influence of his Irish background, his Irish consciousness. Not just for the pull of rebelliousness, consanguinity and strong drink — forceful though that was. But also for the complementary lyricism of the Celtic temperament, the sweetness of it and its underlying melancholy, the consciousness of time and transience, of partings that must sever the closest bonds of family and friendship, of men who march away, loved ones who disappear into distance, the eternal longing of the dispossessed. It is this apprehension of impermanence, this sense of man's ultimate isolation that make so dear and so joyous the bulwarks we erect against the assault of mortality; bulwarks of comradeship, family, love.

In nothing was Ford more Irish than in his vision of family: the men who work, the women who tend them, spirited and devoted, the mother who gives care and inexhaustible love, to whom her sons will always be boys. The vision is an ideal one, of course, and not without its risk of sentimentality. But the inspiration is authentic, buried deep no doubt in the artist's own childhood, in some experience of community early on, lost and longed for, which he could never recreate in his own family life, for which he could only substitute the comradeship, largely male, or work and the fellowship of friends.

Ford's units are organised in service style, benevolently hierarchic; and his 'stock company' of actors who appeared again and again in his pictures, were a family. A patriarchal family, stern rather than indulgent. Ford's will and his whim were of iron; and there was a demanding deviousness about him which would not be crossed and could not always be trusted. It is not to be wondered at that certain independent spirits refused to accept his patronage and the bullying that went with it. There is a dark side to the Celtic temperament, and the legends that grew up around John Ford were as likely to feature cruel or tyrannical behaviour, the cunning of the peasant, as they were to embody generosity or consideration.

The peasant strain is important for an understanding of the man, and it explains a lot of the tension in him and his work. Willis Goldbeck called Ford 'a son of the soil' and contrasted him with another Irishman, Rex Ingram. Ford never was a gentleman, even if half of him wanted to be. (Perhaps it was less than half; but it was a strong impulse none the less.) He was bourgeois neither in dress nor in manner; and he was always ready to deride the established and the self-satisfied. Hence another dichotomy in this divided man, 'the son of an Irish saloon keeper in Maine', who despised careerism but kept his Oscars on proud display together with his Admiral's sword. Was that Admiral's uniform ever really more than a fancy-dress? There is something profoundly comic — and revealing — about Captain John Ford U.S.N.R., as he was then, directing a heroic film dedicated to the ideal of discipline and service, unable to resist a malicious jibe against his actor and disciple John Wayne, wounding his friend and throwing his unit into disruption. The tension between anarchy and tradition was always strong in Ford; he was a leader rather than an officer, always a rogue. And rogues, of course, can do a lot of damage, to themselves as well as to others.

He was capable of sentimentalism, but he was not soft; he was a disciplinarian, and he could be shockingly undisciplined; he demanded more loyalty than he was prepared to give. With all his vices and ambiguities, though, he carried an ideal (in 205

'...Music of humanity.' Ford's humanistic faith, like Wordsworth's, was never without a certain sadness, hard to define or to explain except poetically. There is a pathos underlying human experience which all the love and hope in the world, all the laughter and all the joy can never wholly assuage.

Amiel's words) 'hidden within him'; and it was this ideal that inspired his poetry. He told tales. He did not make films 'about' things, about conceptions of History, or revaluations of the Western Myth. *They Were Expendable* is not 'about' war; and when John Wayne puts his arm about Donna Reed he is not 'embracing the symbol of his lost world' (*pace* Mr John Baxter). *The Grapes of Wrath, Tobacco Road* are not 'about' social problems. Experience, not abstract ideas, is the stuff of the work.

And yet, the hidden ideal is there. An ideal implies a morality: Ford's poetic gift was essentially a moral one, not abstracted from the business of living or standing aside from it, but wholly involved in it. In this way (and in this way only) he was a 'committed' artist. His films give the lie to the commonly received notion that evil is so much more 'interesting' or attractive than goodness. Ford's villains are bad, unpleasant, not in the least seductive (perhaps with the exception of Lee Marvin's charismatic Liberty Valance); his heroes are charming, humorous, warm-blooded. Generosity, fidelity, truthfulness: these are not just respectable, they are loveable, life-enhancing.

Ford's tales at their best always mean more than they seem to: they transcend narrative. They have a soul, and this is why we call them 'poetic'. He was born, it seems, with this gift of telling stories clearly, understandably, so that they could appeal to the simplest, least thinking in his audience; and simultaneously he could transform them into poems, for those who have eyes to see and ears to hear. The magic is in the style, which with its undeviating simplicity and directness expresses the real content, as opposed to the mere circumstances, of the story. It is a powerful style, not an assertive one. For all the strength of personality behind it, it never proclaims itself. Ford's aim — though he would never have used the term — was always *empathetic*. Nothing should come between the audience and the experience; and what is to be experienced is not 'the movie' but a story, a situation, a character, a sharing of feeling. Harry Carey remarks how Ford shunned the close-shot. This is true as far as the merely functional close-shot, the hall-mark today of reach-me-down television shooting, is concerned: but the expressive close-shot, intensely revealing, often tender, always

dignified, is one of the glories of his style. Close or far away, it is the people who inspire the film. There are very few shots in Ford's pictures whose composition is not determined by a human presence.

Ford's camera rarely moves. If it does it is to go with a character, for ease, and in a way that no audience will remark. Sometimes, though rarely, the camera may pan for a sudden revelation, but only when the movement can be justified by the dynamic of the narrative (those abrupt movements forward into close-up in *The Searchers* curiously lack his inevitability: there is something 'applied' about them, unFordian). The style is one of statement, not of suggestion. Composition, texture of lighting can vary according to whether the film is being lit by this cameraman or that: *They Were Expendable* would have looked, and therefore felt different if it had been photographed by Gregg Toland instead of Joe August; yet the essential personality of the film, we can be sure, would have been the same. Only when inspiration was thin or self-conscious, when Ford allowed himself to 'play the poet', did his style become mannered or conspicuous in virtuosity. (And conversely, when the images do display themselves in this way, it is a sign that there is something forced about the feeling.) Above all, the appeal is never academic or theoretical: we have seen how the effort to assimilate Ford into the ranks of auteurism results inevitably in distortion and the imposition on his work of historical or philosophic pretensions which he would have rejected with scorn. Nor is this so-accessible work more easily accessible to the sophisticates of fashion. The *New Yorker* magazine in 1946 could only see *They Were Expendable* as 'a well-told adventure story for juveniles': in 1980 it still finds *The Grapes of Wrath* 207 'grossly sentimental . . . all wrong . . . full of the "they-can't-keep-us-down-we're-the-people" sort of thing'. Truly was it said: 'Except ye become as little children . . .'

The lyric gift rarely survives for a long lifetime: energy wanes and experiences blunts aspiration. Ford said it himself when Peter Bogdanovich asked him why his picture of the West had become 'increasingly sad'. 'Maybe I'm getting older,' he answered. What more is there to say? Age accounted for the slackening of grasp, the faltering of poetic thrust; and it arrived, as it so often does, with a change in the climate of culture, with altered expectations from his audience and different demands from the industry of which he had been a part so long. But only by wrenching Ford's later work out of its human and historical context can it be made to conform to a pattern of 'alienation', of blackness or despair. There were conflicting impulses at work in him, we know, dark strains of violence and even self-destruction. Sometimes these showed. But he used his work to resolve, not to indulge them; they never became the substance of his art. Weariness of spirit as well as body drove him to his bed when he was shooting *Cheyenne Autumn*; but he did not make his film about it. No director stuck to his guns longer or more obstinately than John Ford.

To say that an artist sticks to his guns may mean a number of different things. It may mean insistence on a personal, original style, incomprehensible to his contemporaries. It may mean commitment to views repugnant to his fellow men. It may mean rejection of authority at a time of conformism, or loyalty to tradition in a time of revolution. For John Ford it meant above all the preservation of an unyielding integrity of personality, both as an artist and as a man. His ideas and emotions matured; and changing circumstances provoked him to changing reactions. But his essential character did not change; nor did his feelings, his values or his conviction.

Poet of faith in an age of unbelief, he saw the world going in a way he could neither approve nor wholly understand, and this made him sad. But the John Ford — Sean O'Fearna, Sean Feeney — who at the end of his life was proud to accept honour from his country's President, rising to his feet from what was virtually his deathbed, was not a man or an artist who ever surrendered himself to bitterness or disillusion. He had a great heart, and so he was able and still is able to 'make us feel', to 'loose our hearts with tears'.

> Smiles woke from us and we had ease:
> Our foreheads felt the wind and rain,
> Our youth returned...

Such smiles, such tears, such restorative energy — 'the freshness of the early world' — are the gifts that John Ford has left us in his films.

Ford and his actors. From top left, clockwise: directing Flesh; *with Madeleine Carroll (*The World Moves On*); with Hoot Gibson, old friend (*The Horse Soldiers*); Four Sons; with Constance Towers (*Sergeant Rutledge*); with Pat Wayne, Tyrone Power and John Wayne (*The Long Gray Line*); dressing McLaglen (*Rio Grande*); and (centre) showing Charles Winninger how (*The Sun Shines Bright*).*

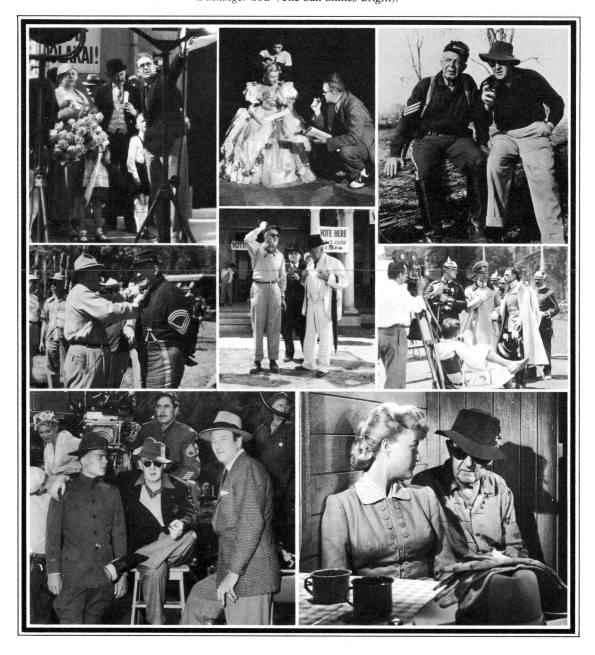

Talking About Ford

Actors

A man can be judged, they say, by his friends: so, and for much the same reasons, can a director be judged by the actors he chooses to work with him. Ford was celebrated for his preference for working with actors and actresses whom he knew, and by whom he could feel sure of being understood. Hence his 'Stock Company', and the famous comradeship of his units. For a director of his temperament it was important to feel this kind of sympathy, and to know he could get the performances he needed without having to explain or justify himself.

Actors, under these conditions especially, see more of the game than is generally appreciated. There may be depths and meanings to a film of which they are unaware; but they are likely to know their director and understand him with a clarity that can often elude his more theoretical critics. Invariably they have good stories to tell.

I am grateful to these four actors who talked with me so freely and so generously: Henry Fonda, who gave substance to the greatest, or at least the most morally memorable of Ford's heroes; Harry Carey Jnr., who carried on his father's part in the Ford legend with such grace, talent and good nature; Donal Donnelly, who came late to the tradition, but whose Irish insights throw light on a particularly sensitive area of Ford's nature, and Robert Montgomery, who played Captain Brickley so memorably in *They Were Expendable*. To these interviews I have appended three anecdotes. Two of them, among the best of hundreds similar, are by fully paid-up members of the Ford Stock Company: they are reprinted from the magazine of the American Screen Directors' Guild. Miss Astor's story, revealing in quite a different way (as one would expect from an actress of such special sensibility) is from her autobiographical *A Life on Film*.

Harry Carey Jnr

Los Angeles, July 1978

HARRY CAREY: Ford was a very sentimental man, and he had a great love for my Dad. No one seems to know how they met, not even my mother, but there wouldn't have been a John Ford if it hadn't been for Harry Carey. Well, — I think he would have made it eventually — he was too bright — but he was only eighteen or nineteen when they began. Ford said it himself; in Peter Bogdanovich's book, a couple of years before he died, he said, 'Harry Carey brought me along, and coached me when I was a young director . . .' Anyway, my father said to Carl Laemmle, 'You know, there's a young Irishman here called Jack Ford. I don't know where he learned it, but he knows a hell of a lot about making movies. I'd like him to direct the next picture.' Laemmle said, 'I'm not going to take some kid.' And Pop said 'I'll watch.' And he talked him into it. Ford had been working as a prop man, and they cut his salary when they made him a director. He got something like thirty-five a week. They made a picture called *The*

Soul Herder: that was the first one. And of the twenty-five pictures he and my Dad made together, only one was preserved, *Straight Shooting*. I think they found it in Czechoslovakia.

LINDSAY ANDERSON: They've got it at the Museum of Modern Art now.

HC: Terrific! . . . Well, they made twenty-five films together and then they split up. Ford said to me a couple of times — only a couple of times — during our association, 'You know, your father got to be such a big actor, he didn't need me any more.' And my Dad used to say, 'Jack got to be such a big-shot director, he didn't want me any more.' When they were both alive, they'd make sarcastic remarks about each other to other people. There were two actors, J. Farrell McDonald, who was in Ford's camp, and an old-timer called Joe Harris, who was in the first *Three Godfathers* when it was called *Marked Men*. My Mom says that Joe Harris would come to my father and tell him things that Jack Ford said about him and J. Farrell McDonald would go to Ford and tell him things that Dad was supposed to have said about him.

Father...Harry Carey in The Outcasts of Poker Flat *(1919)...*

LA: Just like kids.

HC: That's right. So finally they got pissed off with each other. Ford used my Dad again in *Prisoner of Shark Island*, and God he was fantastic in that picture! He played the Commandant of the prison.

LA: He was excellent.

HC: Wonderful. And he got along great with Ford. There wasn't any sarcasm. Because God knows Ford could be sarcastic and cruel. But he was great with my Dad and I thought they'd make some more. And about a year before Pop died, I said, 'Pop, how come you won't work for Jack Ford?' and he said, 'It's simple, he won't ask me.' That's all he said. It surprised the hell out of me, because over the years I'd heard him say disparaging things about Ford, and then always qualified by saying 'Of course the sonofabitch is a genius.' And I asked him once who was the greatest director that ever lived, and he said 'Jack Ford.' Bogdanovich asked Ford in my presence who was the greatest Western star that ever lived. I thought he'd say 'John Wayne', but he said 'Harry Carey', and I don't think Wayne would be a bit surprised at that.

LA: No, he'd be right too.

HC: Of course Wayne idolised my father. So long as they didn't get on to politics. My father was a dyed-in-the-wool democrat. Oh, I remember — when I said to my father, 'How come you don't work for Jack Ford any more?', and he said 'He never asked me.' Well, then he said, 'You will.' And I said 'How do you know?' and he said 'I just know, you will, but not until I croak.'

LA: And you did.

HC: In *Three Godfathers* — right.

LA: Was that your first picture?

HC: No, Raoul Walsh gave me my first picture.

LA: Like he did John Wayne.

HC: That's right. Mine was *Pursued*, with Robert Mitchum and Teresa Wright. Well, I'd done one scene before, just one line in a picture called *Rolling Home*. I count that for sentimental reasons, because of Bill Berke. He was a quickie picture maker: my father did five Westerns for him, and they made them in six days . . . Well, after that I got an agent, and he got me a test at Warner Brothers. They tested twenty-six actors for this role and I did make a good test . . . Raoul Walsh directed it and he was really nice. He didn't tell me a great deal: once in a while he'd say, 'Move a little to your left, so you'll be clear.' I needed help . . . But Ford didn't want to hear about *Pursued* or *Red River*, or any of those. And he was right really. Because *Three Godfathers* was an unforgettable experience.

LA: Had you acted much then?

HC: Only a limited amount of stage experience — a few bits in summer stock. I knew nothing about the camera. And this was a big role, and I didn't know my ass from first base. I didn't know if I was in-camera or off-camera. I had a terrible habit of getting behind somebody all the time, and if you can't see a person through the finder it drives a director mad! I didn't know where my mark was, and I'd miss it and I'd look down at it, and he'd yell 'Don't-you-look-at-your-Goddam-mark!' I really don't blame him getting mad. He'd threaten to replace me with Audie Murphy all the time . . . He'd say, 'Audie Murphy begged me for this part. Here I am screwing around to get you, and Audie Murphy wanted it.' He was terrible with Duke, too. He'd say, 'Why don't you act like Gary Cooper for Christsake?' He'd just say awful things to him.

LA: And that was the first time you worked for him.

HC: Yeah — I guess I learned a lot on that picture.

LA: What was he like directing actors? Did he go in for any detailed work on the characters — on their feelings and relationships at any particular moment?

HC: No, not in the sense you mean. Of course he'd work to get a scene right. And he'd show you how he wanted it played. He'd get up there and do it himself. And that was a time there'd better not be any photographers around. He didn't care what he looked like; but if anyone tried to take a picture, they'd be out on their ass. He didn't mind how much of a fool he made of himself: he'd do something quite grotesque — but you understood what he meant . . . I remember when we were starting on *She Wore a Yellow Ribbon*, and Ford was trying to show

Ben Johnson how he wanted Tyree. Ben wasn't really an actor then of course. Ford had discovered him punching horses and put him into that weird thing he and Cooper produced about a giant Gorilla . . .

LA: *Mighty Joe Young.*

HC: That's it. Well, we began with that scene when the stage coach drives in and there's a guy's body hanging out with an arrow in his back. We're all there and Ben has to be looking at the arrow. He didn't do it the way Ford wanted it: he was trying too hard, I guess. So Ford goes out and stands there looking completely bored, his mouth hanging open, quite ridiculous. 'Now', he says, 'You're just there. You know it's Arapaho. You're an actor: this is the nine thousandth Indian you've seen with an arrow in his back. It doesn't mean a goddam thing to you'. And he stood there looking absolutely half-witted. But Ben got the idea. And Ford finally got him so loose that he practically stole the picture. In fact when we finally got to the opening in Kansas City, he did steal it.

LA: He shot fast?

HC: Oh he did. On *Three Godfathers* we were about three weeks in Death Valley and about ten days back here, and that was it. *Yellow Ribbon* was twenty-eight shooting days.

LA: That's incredible

HC: Incredible. Of course he shot very spare. He never made unnecessary close-ups. In *Yellow Ribbon* I only remember one: that was Duke at the grave of his wife. He'd say, 'I don't want to see nose-hairs and pores on people's faces on a fifty foot screen.' I remember him saying that. And if he had a three-shot in a dramatic scene, he didn't go from head to head, he kept it in that three-shot to get the contact between the people.

LA: *Rio Grande*, which I think is a very good picture — that seems to have been made in a hurry. Particularly the action-climax where they rescue the kids.

HC: Oh he did that very fast: in fact it wasn't much more than a day.

LA: I suppose that was working on a Republic budget. Republic pictures weren't extravagant, were they?

HC: They weren't, no . . . And I don't know what Wayne's salary was at that time, but I know it was a lot, very high. Even though he'd work for Ford for a quarter of the salary he'd work for anyone else, because he felt he owed it to him.

LA: There's some corny stuff in that picture.

HC: Oh that singing business and everything? He'd got a big thing for the Sons of the Pioneers.

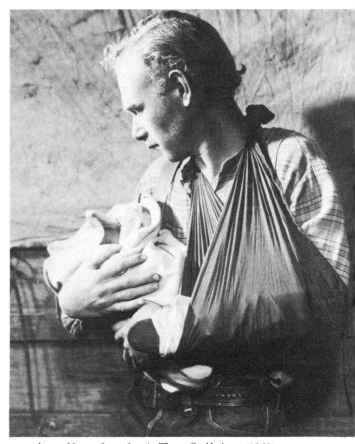

. . . and son. Harry Carey Jnr. in Three Godfathers *(1948).*

LA: The singing shots were obviously all done in the studio: they're so poorly lit . . .

HC: It's true. It always bothered me in *Rio Grande* that scene.

LA: And I always flinch at those close-ups of that idiot stuttering, 'Ber-ber-b-b-ber . . .'

HC: Oh, Shug Fisher, yeah . . .

LA: There were more things like that in the later pictures.

HC: Well I have a theory . . . Ford had this tremendous control and he was total boss of everything on a picture, right down to the little candlestick on the table, everything. He was props-crazy and wardrobe-crazy. In fact he was everything-crazy. He was the cutter, he was the producer, he was the cameraman, he did the set up, he looked through . . . he was as good a cameraman as was ever born. Well, he got old. He had the big drinking bouts and he even had a bout taking all kinds of pills for a while; and towards the end, you know, when the cancer got a hold, and his sight was failing, and his hearing, he just wasn't operating like he was in the past. He needed somebody to say 'Jack, you forgot to cover that thing.' Because he used to have it all in his head and he never missed a beat. 213

Rio Grande. *Harry Carey Jnr. and Ben Johnson as Troopers Daniel Boone and Tyree.*

But when he got old, he needed someone to do what a script-girl is supposed to do, the continuity, because he forgot. You'd see flashes of brilliance, but there was no storyline or anything, no grasp. Of course nobody was going to come along and say 'Look, you're screwing it up here — you haven't got a shot of him coming out of the Courthouse', or whatever it was they needed . . . So he'd miss a lot of stuff, and that's one reason why the pictures were falling off. He got a big thing for Dick Widmark, he was very fond of Dick and he loved working with him, but towards the end, in the last five years or so, Dick and Duke Wayne would avoid him, because they were afraid he was going to say 'I want you to do this picture.' And if he got their okay, he'd get the money. Hawks did the same thing. And it was cruel, but dammit they couldn't afford to make another bomb. Duke said to me one time 'I got to go over and see him. But he's got some story he wants to do and I think I have paid my debt now.'

LA: *Two Rode Together* must have been one of those.

HC: Right, and *that* didn't look like a Ford film. He never cut it, he never touched it. When he got back from location he walked away from it.

LA: *Cheyenne Autumn* was another one.

HC: He got bored with that. I could see him getting bored. He was only out there three weeks and he decided he wanted to come home.

LA: One problem was all those Indian characters. It just didn't work to have Dolores Del Rio and Victor Jory and Sal Mineo dressed up . . .

HC: No, and he would never have done that twelve or fifteen years before. And he didn't get on with Sal Mineo. He was nice to him, but if he was nice to somebody, he wasn't getting along with them. And Gilbert Roland — with the hundred of movies he'd made, he'd still try and upstage people. Ford called him up the first day — I was standing behind him — and he said, 'You've succeeded in putting a nice shadow on Ricardo's face. But that's alright', he said, 'because I'm going to do a close-up on Ricardo and not on you, so it doesn't make any difference.' Of course he was terrified of him, Gilbert Roland was. You'd think he wouldn't try those tricks, but it was a habit.

LA: It's a compulsion!

HC: Ford just sort of horsed around with that picture. Not at all like most of the movies I did with him. It sounds really corny, but when he'd walk on the set of *The Three Godfathers* or *She Wore a Yellow Ribbon* or *The Long Gray Line* . . . well, if you were waiting outside, and the red light went off, it was almost like going into a sacred shrine. There was such a feeling on the set. Yet people weren't all uptight. He was a terrific disciplinarian, but he was never mean to anyone on the crew. He knew every one of their names, and how many children they had, everyone, even up to the guy who swept up the cigar butts. He knew all of them, and he'd never be mean to any of the crew. He'd only be mean to actors — and sometimes the cameraman . . .

LA: That's interesting: because the actors are the sensitive ones.

HC: He never really caught on with me. I can respond better when people are nice: I really can do much better work.

LA: It was a pity he never worked with Fonda again wasn't it?

HC: Yes, I saw all that happen and it wasn't anybody's fault. *Mister Roberts* was a mistake. They should have just shot the play. But instead Warners said 'We're going to do it big. We're going to Midway. We're going to have John Ford direct it.' Well, after two years in the theatre, Fonda was married to that role; he knew every thing, every nuance in that picture. He loved Jack Lemmon as Pulver. But he was very offended about the rest of us. Of course the crew didn't have nearly as much to do in the picture as in the play, so we weren't as important as they were on the stage. But Ford took me for Stefanowsky and I don't think I was right: Stefanowsky was a huge big Polish guy, with muscles all over the place. And the other guys weren't right either. Ken Curtis wasn't right for the Yeoman, and all of these things annoyed Fonda. So Ford would start improvising, like he always did — which is what James Bellah got mad at — and he started changing things, and building the Chief's part up, which was Ward Bond. He started adding dialogue and putting pieces of business in and that upset Fonda and Hayward. Then he realised that they were upset, and when they got to Honolulu, he went on a big toot. Ford started drinking. And then Fonda really got mad with him. And later, when I wasn't there, Ford jumped up and hit Fonda on the jaw and called him a traitor or something. But Henry was at his funeral. I saw him there at the funeral.

LA: Yes I know. I think he was bitter about Ford at one time. And then time passes . . . Anyway, it was total miscasting. You couldn't turn *Mister Roberts* into a Ford picture.

HC: No, no, Josh Logan should have made it.

LA: And I always think Ford's slapstick was one of his weak points, don't you?

HC: When he used the same thing over and over again, which he did. With Victor Maclaglen he did. That slow-burn thing he'd do, you know.

LA: That bar-room brawl in *Yellow Ribbon*, that was funny because it came out like a music-hall turn. And McLaglen was good in that picture wasn't he?

HC: Oh yes, very good. I've got to tell you the story about the dog. Ford used to say some funny things; he could be really funny, as you know. If you were in his bedroom or the den and laughed at him, he loved it. But some crack he made on the set — if you laughed then, oh it was your ass. Anyway we're all lined up on our horses, about ten in the morning. And Victor McLaglen is giving the troops a pep talk before they go out. And Ben Johnson is sitting there. And I'm there in front of my troops. And Agar's sitting there in front of his Company. So Victor's going 'Now men! I want you to do this and that.' And as he's doing this at the rehearsal, a dog, a mutt, a friendly mutt with his tail wagging, wanders on into the middle of the scene. And Ford says 'Victor, pet the dog.' Well, Victor was a little slow on the uptake. So he says 'What?' And Ford says, 'The dog. There's a dog there. Pet it. Say "Whose dog is that? . . . Nice dog. Irish Setter. Nice Dog. Irish Setter."' This was the whole idea, an Irish dog! So they get ready for the take, and we're sitting there. And Ford says 'Action'. And the camera's going, and the dog walks in again. And in the take, McLaglen starts off 'Now men!' and the dog comes in and he says 'Whose dog is that? Whose dog is that? Nice dog. Cocker Spaniel.' And Ford goes: 'No, Russian Wolfhound, you stupid sonofabitch!' Well, when he went 'No, Russian Wolfhound' I started to laugh, and Agar started to laugh and Johnson started to laugh, and the tears were running down my face. Thank God he didn't see it! Of course the take was ruined anyway. He was so goddam mad at Victor he didn't see us laughing. That was so funny. 'Cocker Spaniel' he says! He never got the joke.

LA: A picture I've always wondered about is *Wagonmaster*. It's a lovely film, but it doesn't really have an end.

HC: No it never did have an end, and he knew that, too. There's the shoot-out with the Cleggs, and then he did a reprise . . .

LA: But the big climax should have been the wagons going over the mountain. But there's only one shot: and then we see a group standing, obviously a studio shot, looking into the valley.

HC: He never found the mountain. And they only had a small budget: I think the picture only cost half a million or seven hundred thousand, so they never found the mountain. He had guys going all over,

215

Cliff Lyons, who was second unit, Jim Basevi and everybody, going everywhere looking for a mountain for them to go over. He was in Moab, Utah, so they couldn't move to Monument Valley, because they couldn't afford it. So finally he came back to Hollywood. He used to have lunch in his office there at RKO/Pathe in Culver City, he had a bungalow and he used to send across the street to the delicatessen, and they'd bring in this whole big thing full of sandwiches and pickles and cheese and beer — by God you'd better not drink one, but they'd bring it! And he'd sit there, and say 'I haven't got a damn ending for this'. So finally he called Ray Kellog, who was the Head of Special Effects at Fox, a terrific guy, a big husky guy, who'd also been in his outfit in the services. Now Ray was involved in the *Titanic,* or something, you know — some huge film — doing special effects. And he said 'I want you to do me a little favour' and Ray said 'What do you want and when?' and he said 'I want you to come over.' Ray tells it, 'My God, I was right in the middle of work, but I turn it over to somebody else, I ride over to Pathe, and he says "Ray I want you to do me a favour. We haven't got a mountain in *Wagonmaster* and we got to have a shot of the line of wagons going along this ledge." ' So Ray said 'Yeah, so you want me to shoot it?' He said 'No, no, no, I can't shoot it, I'm through with the picture, but if you could do it in miniature . . .So Ray says 'Who do I see about paying for all this?' Ford said 'For nothing.' He said 'You could put it on Fox over there, fiddle around, give me a shot, just one shot.' In about five minutes he'd talked Ray into it. Ray went home and in his spare time carved these little animals and made the little wagons and shot the damn thing at Fox. On Fox's money . . .

LA: Well, they owed it to him. And it's a beautiful picture anyway.

HC: I think *Wagonmaster* was the only picture I ever went through with Ford without getting my ass chewed out at least one day. He wanted me a goofy, sort of happy-go-lucky kid, and he didn't want me down, so even if I made a mistake he never jumped on me. He might say, 'No, no, wait a minute', or 'Dammit, your're not listening', but he never got cruel. I made twelve or fourteen pictures for him, and the happiest I've even seen him on a film was *Wagonmaster*. That was a happy time for us all.

'A happy time...' Harry Carey Jnr. in Wagonmaster.

John Carradine

'Ford always finds a patsy among the cast of his pictures and rides him with gentle sarcasm. Usually he chooses a stage actor, because he has a certain contempt for those who come from the 'theatuh'. On *The Hurricane* it was Raymond Massey. On *Grapes of Wrath* it was O. Z. Whitehead. On *Stagecoach* it was Tommy Mitchell.

Ford kept needling Tommy throughout the picture. The climax came when we had the scene at the bar when we were celebrating the birth of the baby. It was a difficult scene, because we were standing six feet apart, and all of us had dialogue. Ford sent away the stand-ins so we could work out the scene ourselves. All of us were engaging in badinage, and this annoyed Ford. He bawled out all of us, but mostly Tommy Mitchell. Tommy took it for a while and then replied, 'That's all right, Mr. Ford. Just remember: I saw *Mary of Scotland*.'

Ford left the set for fifteen minutes. When he returned, not another word was said about the incident.'

Andy Devine

The first time I worked for John Ford was in 1919, when he came to Arizona to make *Ace of the Saddle* with Harry Carey. I was working on a ranch then, wrangling cattle and horses, and he gave me a job in the picture. I didn't work for him again until *Dr. Bull*, with Will Rogers, in 1933.

Then he sent for me when he was doing *Stagecoach*. One day he got sore at me and said, 'You big tub of lard. I don't know why the hell I'm using you in this picture.'

I answered him right back: 'Because Ward Bond can't drive six horses.'

Ford didn't talk to me for six years. But I worked for him again, of course. Every time I did, he saw to it that I had a Mexican wife and nine kids.

Sometimes you'd like to kill the son of a bitch. But, God love him, he's a great man.

Right: Stagecoach. *Top: John Carradine as Hatfield. Centre: Thomas Mitchell as Dr. Boone. Bottom: Andy Devine, George Bancroft as Buck and Sheriff Curly Wilcox.*

Henry Fonda
Los Angeles, August 1978

LINDSAY ANDERSON: There are so many stories, aren't there — and so many of them untrue . . .
HENRY FONDA: Oh yes. He was a great bullshitter. There are so many things said about him that *are* true though — he did shoot a minimum of footage on a film, and not give his cutter too much to work with in the cutting room. (At the same time of course the editor could cut his stuff down, he couldn't prevent that.) And he did never want to do more than one take. He'd hate it, get mad if something prevented the first take being good. He liked to print the first take — and very often it wasn't as good as it should have been. In *Roberts* particularly. (Now of course we're going past Ford at his prime.)

For instance, when he did the first scene of *Mister Roberts* on location in Midway. The reason we went to Midway was to get that hot sun and the Pacific Ocean in the background. Of course it cost a lot to take a moving picture company that far away: the crew, a big cast, a Navy ship, and housing the whole lot on that little island. Anyway, we're all there and we're shooting the scene. It's the opening scene in the play, with Roberts writing his letter and Doc coming down the hatch and sitting down and Roberts tells him why he wants to get transferred and how badly he wants to get away . . . It's a long scene, and moving because it meant so much to the man. Bill Powell was playing Doc: he was retired and Leland talked him into coming back. First time he'd been in a film for ten years. He was so nervous that nerves were jumping in his cheek, in spite of the fact that I'd been sitting hours with him, just running lines casually. Ford said 'Is he all right? Does he know them?', and I said 'Well, he's saying them all right in there.' He was insecure, unsure, and soon the timing was all gone, and it's a long scene, about as long as a thousand feet of film will run in the camera. And I'm thinking all the time 'God, I hope Ford isn't going to get on him.' Any other director would have cut before we got too far, because it wasn't going well. But we finally, finally got through the scene. And the camera is right there, and Ford right beside it. And Bill is sitting next to me, and I just kept my head down because I didn't know what Pappy was going to say. And there's the longest, longest pause, and I think 'The sonofabitch, I hope he doesn't say the wrong thing to Bill.' The first thing I heard was Pappy saying 'Did you ever see anything like that?' — he was looking at his cameraman — and the cameraman didn't know what he was talking about, and said no, he never did. Then Pappy looked over his other shoulder at the property man — 'Did you ever see anything like that?' — the property man didn't say anything. 'Print it.' And he got up and walked away, for the next set-up. Now we didn't know for some time that what he was talking about was that during this long scene in the hot Midway sun, a lone cloud came over and cast a shadow, so there was a light change in the middle of the take. And *that* was what Ford bought and loved, that fucking light change! We had to reshoot the scene four months later on a soundstage at Warner Brothers, with the blue cyclorama instead of the hot Pacific sun, because Ford was that sort of a crazy sonofabitch. The stories that you ever heard of him! If an actor wanted to know about a scene . . . There was this actor, Jack something or other, kept bugging him about a scene. He was the Mestiso in *The Fugitive*, the Indian informer . . .
LA: J. Carroll Naish.
HF: That's him — he was that kind of an actor, he liked to put on accents. Well he's really on to Ford, trying to get him to talk about this scene, and Ford finally just took the script, found the scene, tore the pages out and never shot it. That's true, it happened; I was there on the set.
LA: But did those things happen on his good pictures? Say on *Lincoln* or *Clementine*.
HF: On *Grapes of Wrath* or *Clementine*, no.
LA: Or *Lincoln*?
HF: No. *Lincoln* was the first I did with him and that was a totally marvellous experience. So were *Drums Along The Mohawk* and *Grapes of Wrath* and *Clementine*. *The Fugitive* was the first one where he had any kind of disagreement — it wasn't a big one — but he wanted to do a clowny thing on the parade to the priest's execution, and I didn't think it was good, and we talked about it. It was not an argument. I just thought it didn't feel right. And he said, 'Let's do it both ways,' but he didn't, he just shot it the one way. But it's true that on the good ones, and the ones I had good experiences with, no, there weren't those times.
LA: It seems so strange, though I know it's true, that pictures with performances of the subtlety of *Lincoln, Grapes of Wrath* and *Drums Along the Mohawk* (like that scene where you recount the battle, all in one set-up), were achieved without rehearsal.
HF: Yes, he hated to rehearse. As a matter of fact, he just wouldn't. The best example of that is the goodbye scene in *The Grapes of Wrath*. I feel, and I think I knew him pretty well by then, that he

wanted to get it on the first take, partly because he liked the things that could happen first time through. He felt that if you do a scene, particularly an emotional one, over and over again, you're going to begin to dispel or lose the original emotion. Now there was never any conversation about this. He wouldn't say, 'Now look, this is an emotional scene, I don't want you to blow it and leave it in the locker room' — but if you knew him, as I did by this time, you were aware that this was what he was up to. That scene was reasonably difficult for the photographer and the crew. Starting in the tent, and the camera pulling round, and then the long dolly as we walked down past the tent to sit on the bench beside the dancefloor where we'd had the party the night before, going on into the scene itself. It took several hours for Gregg Toland to light it, to get the camera moves, so everyone knew exactly what was to happen. And Jane and I would rehearse the scene — there was never any dialogue, or if there was, it was just a whispered 'Come on Ma', or something like that. Once we got to the bench, Ford would cut rehearsal and talk to Gregg about the moves or something. Jane and I never got to do the scene. We didn't even run it together sitting on the floor. But I knew her well enough, we both knew that we knew the lines, we were aware we had a good scene to play, we wanted to say 'Hey fellas, let's do it.' Now I feel, and I've felt ever since, that Ford knew this was building up in us. And when he finally was ready to go and everybody else was ready, and there was not going to be any mistake to make us do it the second time, he said 'Okay, roll 'em.' And both Jane and I were so charged with the scene we knew we had — I've never talked to Jane about it, before or since, but I'm sure she felt the same way — that when we did get into it, the emotions all came up so that we had to hold them *back*. If they had all come pouring out it would have been embarrassing and no one would have wanted to watch, but both of us had the emotion there charging our voices, and I'm sure our faces, but we were holding it back so it didn't come pouring out, and as a result we got that scene. Ford didn't even say 'Ooh', or 'Look up' or anything, he just got up and walked away. He could have been crying himself, I don't know, I know the script girl was. Never did it again.

LA: Now, that was the two-shot?

HF: Wasn't it one take?

LA: No, actually it's interesting: the last time I saw it I noticed it's a two-shot and there are two singles.

HF: Do you know, I can't remember that at all! That

Left: Fonda as Tom Joad in The Grapes of Wrath.

The Grapes of Wrath. *Top: Fonda and Carradine as Tom and Casey. Above: Fonda and Jane Darwell as Ma Joad.*

shows how much I notice when I look at the film!

LA: For a director who'd worked in the theatre it would be impossible to do that. And, of course, it's all very well, but there are actors who only get to be good on the fourth take. Wouldn't you agree?

HF: Of course, I'm an actor who loves to rehearse. That's one of the reasons I don't get as much satisfaction and joy out of filming as I do from the theatre. You're told by your assistant director 'Tomorrow we're going to do Scene 44 on Stage 11, start at 9 o'clock.' You learn the lines, you go there; and before lunch you have done it. It's gone to the laboratory and you don't ever get to do it again.

LA: When you know the scene, you're all right; but

occasionally you feel 'I'm not ready. This is forever.'

HF: You know the scene, and you can do it well, but you can do it better again. You can do it better the four hundreth time if you're in the theatre.

LA: I suppose it was Ford's background, coming through silent movies and all that, and not being connected with theatre in anyway. So he would feel (and it may be true of a lot of the actors he worked with) that they wouldn't have got better with rehearsal. Do you think?

HF: That's true, yes. But here's a funny thing about Ford, typical Ford too. I'm reminded of it when you say he had no background of theatre. As you well know, he began as a property man and a stuntman for his brother, then assistant director and so on. Another time in *Grapes of Wrath* we were doing a reasonably emotional scene, although there wasn't any dialogue. It was when the family had arrived at the camp, and the truck pulls in down the lines; the camera follows the truck and you can see all the other families already there; and finally they find a place to park and the family all get out and Ma starts to set up supper. When she's ready she calls the family, who all come back to have the stew or whatever she's got. Now there's a half-circle of kids, hungry kids, about twenty or thirty feet away, just watching — which was Ford's touch of course — and as we were walking in to take our places to eat, aware of the kids, the actor who's playing Unc — I can't even remember his name — I wasn't watching, so I don't know what he did, but Ford saw, and he stopped us. And he chewed that guy up in front of the crew and the cast and everything else. But how did he say it? This is the guy who never had a theatre background. He said 'You working with Theresa Helburn last night?' Does that name mean anything to you?

LA: No.

HF: She was the head of The Theatre Guild in New York. Now who knows but me and a few, the Lunts maybe, who Theresa Helburn was? But John Ford, chewing this guy up, that's what he thought of saying — 'Had Theresa Helburn over at your house last night, huh? Working on the scene, huh?' And shamed this poor sonofabitch so that when he did it again there was no emotion, he was drained, which was what Ford wanted of course. Imagine Ford thinking Theresa Helburn out of the blue!

LA: Did you feel that by comparison there was a certain falling off after the war — well after *Clementine?* I don't think *Fort Apache* is really a good picture.

HF: No, it's not. And I didn't like *The Fugitive*.

LA: Was that because he was trying to make Art?

HF: Well it was more than that. It was partly the fact that you couldn't shoot Graham Greene's book, well maybe you could — but Ford wouldn't. I don't know how good a Catholic he was, but he loved Catholicism sentimentally, and he wouldn't make the whisky priest the father of a child by the whore. So many things in Greene's novel wouldn't have been allowed, or Ford wouldn't have done them that way, which took away a lot. And it wasn't just the cameraman . . .

LA: Figueroa.

HF: . . . it was Ford too, because Ford put those images up there, with the door open and the crucifixion poses. I agree with you that it wasn't good; and particularly it wasn't *for me*. We were on this fishing trip, after *The Grapes of Wrath,* getting drunk on this boat down at Mazatlan, when Ford gave me the book. And I read it down there and loved it, and he said 'I want to make this into a film.' I thought what a hell of an idea, and he said 'I want you to be the priest' and I said 'You're out of your mind!' Well the war came along and he went into the Navy, and I went into the Navy, and now four years later we're back and we do *My Darling Clementine,* and now he wants to do *The Fugitive.* I said 'Pappy, it's not for me. Audiences won't accept me, anymore than they would Robert Montgomery. You couldn't put him in that outfit and expect them . . .' Anyway, I went back and I was trying to think who could play it, and I thought Jo Ferrer could. Jo happened to be out here casting, looking for a Rosalind for his stage production of *Cyrano* and he is an old friend of mine, so I took him over to Ford's office. Ford loved him. Made a deal. But Jo had to go back to do *Cyrano.* Then Ford was ready to go, so he turned to me, and in those days when Ford said 'Come' I firmly had to go. But I was reluctant and I never felt I was right. Anyway, I agree with you that it was a mistake for him to have done it. And it was a mistake for me to have done it. And he knew, the perverted sonofabitch, he knew that it wasn't good in the end, but he damn well wouldn't admit it, and he still talked about 'That's my favourite film', you know.

LA: Yes. I can understand about *Mister Roberts* now. And again it wasn't really a Ford subject, was it?

HF: Well you would have thought so. When Leland asked me who should direct, I said 'There's only one. I mean Ford. He's a Navy man, he's a man's director, he's a location director; for almost any reason you can think of, this is a typical Ford picture.' Ford had come back and seen the play four or five times during the three or four years I was doing it. He

didn't really see it. He saw it once, then he'd hang about backstage. But the big mistake, which I didn't think about when I told Leland he should be the director, was that he didn't ever want to reproduce anything that anybody else had done. So he had to take what we felt were liberties. He didn't think they were liberties. If one nurse was funny, he made five nurses. Five nurses weren't funnier than one nurse, of course, but I could go on and on and on. It was not a happy experience.

LA: Don't you think that in certain areas he had coarsened?

HF: No question about it.

LA: And whether it was drink, or age, I don't know . . .

HF: Well, drink isn't going to help anybody. Although in all the pictures I'd done before with him — and this was the eighth — he never had a drink during production. He couldn't have a drink and stop. We'd always go on a drunk when we'd finished. Go down to Mexico on his boat or some place like that. *Roberts* was the *first time,* and he really was, you know, he had to be pulled off and put into a hospital, and wrung out finally.

LA: You can feel it. The work wasn't fine.

HF: When it was fine, there wasn't anybody like him. What an inspiration.

LA: It was Ford that persuaded you to do *Young Mr. Lincoln* in the first place, wasn't it?

HF: No question. The producer and Lamar Trotti, who wrote it, sent it to me and I read it and I said 'Fellas, it's a beautiful script, beautiful, but I can't play Lincoln.' To me it was like playing Jesus Christ or God. Lincoln is a god to me. They persuaded me to do a test. So I allowed myself to go in there and spent three hours in the make-up chair, and they did a nose and a wart and fixed my hair, and put the wardrobe on, and I went on the soundstage and did a scene with a girl, I don't know who she was . . .

LA: Who directed the test?

HF: I think there was a test director who was unknown. Well, the next day I went in with Lamar Trotti and the producer Kenneth McGowan, and I saw the rushes of the test. And it came on the screen, and I remember my first reaction was 'Sonofabitch!' And then he started to talk, and my voice came out and destroyed the whole image. And I said 'No way' and I turned back to Lamar and said 'I'm sorry fellas, but I just can't do it.' Ford was not part of the package then — he had a deal with the studio but he was away somewhere — and it was months later, when he came back, that they assigned him to the picture. They must have shown him the test and told him my reaction, because I got a call to go and see Mr Ford. Now I had stuck around stages and watched when he was doing *Stagecoach* at United Artists when I was over there with Wanger, but I'd never met him. So now I was going to see Mr Ford. I felt like the guy in the white hat and he was the Admiral. I stood and he sat at the desk in a slouch hat, and either a pipe or a handkerchief tugging round his mouth, you know, and the first words he said to me as I walked in were, 'What the fuck is all this shit about you not wanting to do it?' That's the only way he could talk. 'You think he's the goddam Great Emancipator. He's a young jack blag lawyer from Springfield, for chrissake.' And in a way he shamed me into it. He said 'You think you're playing the Great Emancipator. It ain't like that at all.' Anyway, one way or another, I went with this guy, who seemed to make sense, and I could hear what he was saying to me. We went to Sacramento, I think, at the beginning of the film, and he used to tell the story that he only ever saw me in make-up and on the first day we were leaving location to come home, when I came through the lobby without the make-up he didn't know who I was. He loved to tell that story, which wasn't true. But it was a joy from the first moment, with this man who was so inventive. It was a beautiful script, but like in *Clementine* there were things that he'd put in at the moment, just little pieces of business, sometimes little pieces of dialogue, that were so right on. I've often been asked if I didn't want to direct. No way. Because I know those things wouldn't occur to me and if I wasn't that good, I wouldn't want to be a director. It was just total joy.

LA: But did you never get what you'd call direction in the past?

HF: No.

LA: Good God.

HF: Not direction as I think of it. Like Sidney Lumet, who's from theatre: I've done three with Sidney, and he won't shoot a film unless he's got two weeks' rehearsal. And you rehearse the way you would in theatre, with direction. There are very few other directors who do that. Hitchcock in a way didn't direct, if you think of a director as a man who can come up and communicate with an actor and talk about a scene. Ford didn't talk.

LA: It almost makes one wonder — in movies, is it wrong to work on performances?

HF: No way is it wrong, no, no. Ford's genuis was picking a face or an actor — like Victor Mature. Admittedly Mature's not an actor, in the sense that Alfred Lunt or Laurence Olivier are actors — but Ford knew that he could get the performance, because he cut dialogue down to nothing for him.

LA: Did he work with *him* at all?

HF: No. He just photographed him — he just photographed all of us. Where Ford was great was knowing where to put his camera and he hated if it wasn't on a tripod. He was old-fashioned, so he hated the dolly shots — he'd do them, reluctantly — but he loved it if the camera was on a tripod. The guy slung the tripod over his shoulder and Ford said 'Put it right down here.'

LA: When we hear stories about Ford they seem always to be about his most monstrous moments, and of course we know that something conjured up the moments of extraordinary tenderness — which perhaps represented the side of himself that he wanted to hide, don't you think? I've often felt that this great aggressive front which Ford presented was to some degree a kind of screen. Do you think that's true . . .

HF: Well it could be. I've never been analytical, of myself or anybody else, so it's hard for me to say, but I think it's very possible. He was recognisably a sensitive man, but I don't think he liked to be thought of as a sensitive man.

LA: When one thinks of it, it's a sensitive idea — a marvellously poetic idea — to call a film about Wyatt Earp and the gunfight at the O.K. Corral *My Darling Clementine*, isn't it? The whole Clementine element in that film . . .

HF: I wouldn't be surprised if that was pure Ford. I remember when we were back after the war and I was seeing Pappy some place or other — he had screened at the studio a picture about Wyatt Earp that they'd made quite recently, I think with Randolph Scott and Cesar Romero.

LA: *Frontier Marshal* . . .

HF: I didn't see it, but I think that was it. Well, Ford saw it and said 'Shit. I can do better than that. I'm going to do it again. I'm going to make a better one.' And I still owed Zanuck a film, so he said 'Let's do the Wyatt Earp story.' Now when it became *Darling Clementine* I don't know. But he was in it from the beginning.

LA: Did he contribute much to the script?

HF: It's difficult for me to know. He'd throw in lines: it's hard now to remember which . . . I tell you one I do remember was a Ford line. When I go to the barber and get shaved up, and the barber squirts the stuff on me. It's on a Sunday in Tombstone. And I'm out on the boardwalk again, standing looking out over the desert, and Ward Bond comes along and says 'Smell the desert flowers', and I say 'It's me.' That wasn't in the script. Now we didn't know he

Right: Fonda on set for **Young Mr. Lincoln.**

Left: **My Darling Clementine.** *Sheriff Earp and Doc Holliday rescue Granville Thorndyke from the Clanton boys. Doc completes the soliloquy — 'The undiscovered country, from whose bourne no traveller returns...'*

was planning that until just before we shot it. He threw those lines at us just before he rolled.
LA: It's a magical picture.

HF: In many ways this man was a poet — a visual kind of poet. God knows some of his cameramen were great — Gregg Toland was one of the great ones, and Arthur Miller — but he could take a journeyman cameraman and get Academy Awards for him. Because Ford had a picture eye. A poet's eye.

Mary Astor and Aubrey Smith in The Hurricane.

Mary Astor

... While I was playing the Coward shows (*Tonight at Eight Thirty*) I went into a picture for Sam Goldwyn called *The Hurricane*. Dorothy Lamour's first picture with sarong, Jon Hall, and some *good* actors, Thomas Mitchell, Raymond Massey, C. Aubrey Smith, Jerome Cowan, John Carradine. And directed by the greatest, John Ford ...

I saw him do a wonderful piece of direction with a very small Polynesian child playing one of the native boys who were helping in Jon Hall's escape. The boy was being severely, harshly questioned by Ray Massey as to his activities. And Ray could look *very* severe and frightening as he shouted, 'Where were you, boy?'

The close-up of the child was to be all big eyes and a lie in just one word, 'Fishing.' A lie, and a frightened one. And John stood close to the boy and

repeated over and over two musical notes, about a fourth apart — like C to F — 'Fish-*ing.*' 'Fish-*ing.*' And the boy would say it, and then John, and sometimes the camera would be going and sometimes not, according to his hand signals behind his back. And finally it was all big black eyes and the whopper of a lie, 'Fish-*ing.*'

I think 'laconic' is a good word for John Ford and for his technique of direction. No big deal about communication with John. Terse, pithy, to the point. Very Irish, a dark personality, a sensitivity which he did everything to conceal, but once he said to me while I was doing a scene with Ray Massey, 'Make it *scan*, Mary.' And I said to myself, 'Aha! I know you now!'

Robert Montgomery
New York, May 1980.

ROBERT MONTGOMERY: Anything that's good about *They Were Expendable*, in the script, the performance, the editing, the camerawork, was Ford's achievement . . .

LINDSAY ANDERSON: How did you come to play Brickley?

RM: It was a great piece of good fortune. I'd been away from Hollywood, in the Navy, away from acting for four or five years. All that time I'd thought of nothing except how to do my job well: never thought of movies or my profession. Then I found myself back in Hollywood: the war was pretty well wrapped up, the bomb was just about to fall on Japan. Ford was going to make this picture, and he was doing it for M-G-M. He asked me if I'd like to do it. I said yes without reflecton.

LA: Had you known him before?

RM: I'd met him two or three times — never professionally. Strangely enough, during the Normandy landings I was on a destroyer. I saw Bulkely on his PT boat and waved to him. There was another man on the bridge with him. I had no idea then it was Jack Ford. After I'd accepted the role, I hardly thought about it. It just seemed an ideal way to get back to acting. But when we were down in Miami to shoot the first scene — we shot the picture in continuity as far as we could, and we started with the boats going through their manoeuvres, out in Manila bay — that's when it really hit me. I was seized with panic. I realised I'd forgotten everything, forgotten acting, forgotten what the whole thing was about; I felt I couldn't do it any more. I was desperate. At four o'clock in the morning I was up in my hotel room, pacing the floor. There was a knock on the door. It was Ford. 'You in any trouble?' he said. I told him yes, how I had no idea how to set about it. He'd made a big mistake: he's better get himself another actor. Ford listened, then he said would I mind running the boats around a bit? . . . I said 'sure'. So he said: 'You take the boats out and play around with them — and when you're ready to start, we'll start. It may be three days, it may be three weeks, or three months . . . we'll wait till you're ready.' So that's what we did. The next day I took the boats out in the bay and got used to command again. The second day we did the same. At lunchtime on the third day, I suddenly felt it. I walked over to Ford and I said, 'Shoot!' And we started. I never had any difficulty after that. He had that kind of instinct — that intuition.

. . . I had a hard time sometimes on *Expendable*,

though, holding the ring. He had this long-time abrasive relationship with Wayne, like father and son . . . and of course apart from Wayne, everyone in the picture had been in the service. It was hard for him. Right at the start we had an extraordinary scene between them. We were shooting the scene where the Admiral inspects the outfit after he's watched them exercising in the bay. Duke and I had to march with him along the line, then salute and stand by as he drives off in his jeep. We did the shot once, then Ford called out for another take. We didn't know why. After the second take — the same thing again. Duke murmured to me — 'What's wrong with it?' I had no idea: it seemed to me to have gone perfectly well. Half-way through the third take, Ford called 'Cut!' Then — and there must have been at least a thousand people crowding round, watching the shooting — he yelled out at Wayne, for everyone to hear: 'Duke — can't you manage a salute that at least looks as though you've been in the service?' . . . It was outrageous, of course. I walked over to where Ford was sitting and I put my hands on the arms of his chair and leaned over and said: 'Don't you ever speak like that to anyone again . . .'

LA: And Wayne?

RM: Oh — he'd walked off the set. Gone back to the hotel. We had to break shooting and everyone went back. I told Ford he'd have to apologise. He blustered at first — 'I'm not going to apologise to that son of a bitch . . .'; then he came out with a lot of phoney excuses — 'What did I say? I didn't mean to hurt his feelings.' He ended up crying. Of course they made it up in the end. I always thought that was why he gave Duke that poem to recite in the funeral scenes, as a kind of recompense: "Under the Wide and Starry Sky . . ."

LA: Wasn't that in the script?

RM: No, it was one of the things Ford put in.

LA: Did he change the script a lot?

RM: Oh, all the time. He'd done a lot of rewriting on the script M-G-M produced: there was a lot of bad stuff in it.* He got Frank Wead in and they did it together. Then during shooting he was making changes all the time. Sometimes he'd expand a few lines into a page of dialogue. And sometimes he'd take pages of dialogue and reduce them to a few lines. That scene with the young submarine commander from whom Wayne and I extort torpedoes. There were pages of dialogue there in the script. When the poor boy arrived on the set, all prepared, Ford just handed him a sheet of paper

---

* This was presumably Frank Wead's original script as 'polished' by Sidney Franklin. See Dan Ford's *Pappy*, p. 193.

They Were Expendable. *Ford and his unit.*

with about four lines he'd scribbled on it. That was his part. He nearly collapsed.

LA: Did you rehearse at all?

RM: Depended on the scene. Sometimes we'd rehearse; sometimes we'd do it straight off.

LA: Many takes?

RM: Not if we could help it.

LA: Your goodbye, for instance, to the men who have been detailed to join the army on Bataan, before you leave with the boats, and they march away. That's a beautiful scene.

RM: One take.

LA: Was there much improvisation?

RM: Ford would throw in lines, or a piece of business of course. So would we. Don't ask me which.

LA: Another instance: your goodbye to Arthur Walsh, when you look across at the chap standing near him and make a gesture and say 'Watch him!' Was that yours?

RM: I've no idea. I'd like to think so.

LA: A good unit spirit.

RM: Very close . . . When the girl was due to start, Donna Reed playing the Nurse, they brought her on to the set to see Ford, for him to approve her costume. He wouldn't look at her. She was kept standing around for half an hour. He pretended not to notice she was there. Finally they dared to come up and ask him to see her. He just snarled and told them to take her away: 'Who cares about costumes in a picture like this?' She was intruding into the men's game, you see . . .

LA: And she was so good in the part.

RM: She was very intelligent. She didn't let Ford upset her: she used his attitude — played off it. It gave her strength. And she gave a fine performance. After we'd been working with her about three weeks, I took her across the floor and presented her to Ford. I said: 'I think it's time you were introduced to our director.' He took it very well: they got on fine after that.

LA: How did you come to take over the end of the picture?

RM: We were back at the studio, doing cut-ins for the battle sequences. Ford was up on a gantry with the camera and the lamps. He stepped backwards — and fell into the darkness. We ran round and found him lying there. Duke and I found him: he wouldn't let anyone else touch him. He said: 'I've broken a leg.' We lifted him on to a stretcher and took him to hospital. When we were going up in the elevator there was a woman there who kept looking at him.

227

'Looking for the Arizona…' Robert Montgomery, with Harry Tenbrook and Arthur Walsh in They Were Expendable.

She couldn't take her eyes off him for some reason. Finally he looked back at her and growled — 'Alcoholic!'

A day or so later Duke and I were visiting him in hospital when the telephone rang. It was Eddie Mannix from the studio, wanting to know when he'd be back. He said: 'I'm not coming back . . . I'm staying here and getting my leg right. Then I'm going back to the Navy. Montgomery'll finish the picture.' That was the first I heard of it. It was quite a shock.

LA: Did you enjoy it?

RM: Very much. Ford had a great crew; they all knew him and they were fiercely loyal. They'd have defended him to the death. They gave me as good. And by that time I felt so in tune with the way Jack thought and felt that it didn't seem difficult. I just tried to imagine how he'd have done it. When we saw the first edit — all the material strung together — Ford said 'I couldn't tell where I left off and you began.' I couldn't ask for more.

LA: Had you thought of directing before you finished off *Expendable*?

RM: No. That is, not specifically. I suppose I always had it at the back of my mind that I'd go on to it one day. But that started me off . . . So little of what I did in Hollywood gives me any pride of achievement. Three or four pictures out of sixty-odd. It's not very much. Ford was the best I ever worked with: the only one I'd call creative. After *Expendable* I'd cheerfully have signed a contract to work for him exclusively. I don't know that the idea would have appealed to him, of course. But I'd have been happy. He was a genius.

228

Donal Donnelly

London, November 1977

LINDSAY ANDERSON: Do you think Ireland brought out the best or the worst in Ford?

DONAL DONNELLY: Well I don't know whether it was the worst, but I can't believe it was the best. He pretended he was born there, in Galway . . .

LA: And did people believe him?

DD: Well, the technicians were predominantly English and they were in awe of him from the outset. They tremendously admired him. Bob Krasker was his cameraman and from him on down all these people wanted to work with Ford . . . I began to think before I was finished that this only made them more vulnerable to him.

LA: Did he treat them scornfully because they were English?

DD: I'll tell you a story . . . This particular time we were filming in the Queen's Theatre, and we had a vast crowd of extras sitting as audience in the old Abbey Theatre . . . I was playing that fugitive, you remember . . .

LA: I remember . . .

DD: Well, they rushed me in to make me up in the Abbey. I was escaping as a nun and then they got me into the theatre and made me up as a ballad troubador or something ridiculous — so we're shooting this scene. They have the sound van and everything outside in Pearse Street. The guy on the boom is the only sound man in there, and he has one of these walkie-talkies, you know, that go 'beep-beep', 'beep-beep-beep', and he was talking back and forth. So we did this scene with Philip O'Flynn rushing me in there and this Londoner, with a very London accent, operating the boom. Now Ford loved getting what he wanted first time, so we rushed across the stage, talking to each other, a very short scene, and Ford said 'Cut . . . print it.' And this thing on the sound man went 'beep-beep' and he said 'Excuse me Mr Ford . . . excuse me guv.' 'What is it?' 'His brogue's too thick.' Ford said, 'I'm afraid I don't understand you, could you say that again?' 'His brogue, it's too thick.' So Ford goes over, grabs me, takes me up underneath this man, who's now isolated up on a height, all on his own, and he says 'Lift up your foot Darn-al.' (Darn-al he called me, that's one Irish thing he couldn't achieve, the pronunciation of my name.) So I lift up my foot and he gets hold of it and says: 'I don't think that's very thick, I think that's pretty good' (looking at my shoe). 'What do you mean his brogues are too thick, what's wrong with them?' 'No, no', says your man, 'it's his accent, his accent's too thick.' Ford said

'Look, brogues are what we wear on our feet here friend, on our feet, do you understand? Now I find it very difficult to understand you. I'm beginning to wonder whether I ought to get an Irish soundman. What do you think?' And of course the people outside didn't know what was going on and the think kept going 'beep-beep' and Ford said 'What does that mean — "righteo"?' (putting on a terrible English accent). It all went on much longer — it was awful . . .

LA: Of course a thing like that can be done with grace and humour —

DD: We'd just come in from location — we'd been two or three weeks out in Galway — we were all friends by then. We wouldn't have been so distressed if there'd been any grace or humour attached to it at all. Ford was looking back you see for approval; he thought he was fighting the fight for Ireland.

LA: Do you think that this particular kind of behaviour is in fact Irish — however unpleasant . . .? Because Ford wasn't just a phoney Irishman, was he?

DD: I think he was genuinely partisan for Ireland, *genuinely;* but I don't think he was intelligent about Ireland. I think he was *sentimental* about Ireland. Just out of date. You could compare it with the kind of Irishness you get in the pubs on Long Island or in the Bronx, where they pour out so many dollars for arms for Ireland, because they see it in a very simple old-fashioned way — continuing the battle their grandfathers told them about.

LA: How did you start working for him?

DD: I went to be interviewed — with a lot of people for all different parts. The interview was in his suite at the Shelbourne Hotel in Dublin. I went in and he said 'Can you sing?' So I said, 'Well, I'm not a singer. I'm an actor.' 'Can you sing "The Rising of the Moon"?' I said I knew it, so he said 'Sing me a verse of it. I sang a verse of 'The Rising of the Moon' and he said 'great, great, great' and then he got up and said 'Come over here Darn-al', and he took a small table lamp with an ordinary shade on it, and he put me in a corner, and came over with the flex, and held it near my face. He lit me from here with it, lit me from there with it. put it under me, all round my face, and then sent me off . . . And the next thing I knew the casting director left a message at the Gate and said that he wanted me to do it.

LA: Did you think that was all bullshit?

DD: I didn't know.

LA: Would it surprise you if it was?

DD: Not at all.

LA: When you did the picture, did he work with you

Ford and Abbey Theatre players on The Rising of the Moon. *Donal Donnelly centre.*

on the character at all?

DD: No, I found that kind of thing didn't exist. He went for the general *atmosphere* of a scene. But as for talking to an actor, the way I think you mean it, I never saw that.

LA: You rehearsed?

DD: Yes, we rehearsed. For instance: my teeth are crowned now — I used to have a gap between all my teeth if you remember, way back. Well, my first scene on the picture had me kneeling in the prison cell . . . Ford did a long shot of it, and he came in for a close-up: I was supposed to be praying. And he said 'Darn-al, come here, I want to talk to you.' (All secret stuff you see, with the crew all round.) So he takes me in a corner and he says, 'When I'm doing these close-ups now, you just make sure you keep your mouth closed . . . Now this is no offence to you', he said, 'you are a victim of these guys. These are what is known as Famine Teeth . . .' So it was like him and me together, two Irish oppressed people, and I was the living witness to the sufferings of my nation. 'Famine teeth!' Amazing bullshit . . .! (He was quite right about me keeping my mouth shut, I'm not saying that . . .). But overall he treated me very well — I suppose because I kept out of his way and I didn't get too involved. But we had one guy who was absolutely Ford-insane — before Ford

landed at all he was saying 'I'm *going* to be in that film, I'm *going* to be in that film'; this was going to be his big chance to work with John Ford. He was a delightful guy, wonderfully outgoing.

LA: Who was it?

DD; Let's call him Pat Ryan.

LA: And did he get in?

DD: Oh, he did. First of all he *fell* into Ford's room at the Shelbourne, and reeled off all his films, and, you know, just nearly broke down . . . I suppose that was too much for Ford and he cast him as one of the R.I.C. men in *The Rising of The Moon* — Royal Irish Constabulary. Now that was vicious there, making him a policeman, to start with. Then the poor lad fell foul of him when we were night shooting. We had the whole Galway Fire Brigade up all hours of the night, pouring rain. Pat Ryan and another fellow were supposed to be two very frightened R.I.C. men, with their rifles, really terrified, because they didn't know who was coming at them. And Ford kept saying 'Cut for Christsake!' He was getting very tetchy, and he kept saying, 'You're scared, as far as you're concerned this is one of the most dangerous Republicans abroad, and this is the man you are looking.' Well he cut two or three times, then he went in, and he started an harangue of Pat Ryan, his worshipper. The most awful onslaught. There were hundreds of Galwegians there, up all night, with a rope barrier holding them back. And Pat just went to pieces, the tears you know were in his eyes, his lips were gone, he could hardly walk, and Ford said 'Now for Christsake, ROLL 'EM.' And Pat comes out, totters along, stammers his lines, and Ford says, 'PRINT IT. Right. Go on.' He deliberately reduced the man to real fear to get him to get on with it. I'm sure that's absolutely fine, you know, in screen terms, but in terms of human behaviour it's appalling. I know it works, but as an actor I can't stand it.

LA: What's really interesting is that in Ford's good films the performances are incredibly truthful and sensitive — and relaxed . . . You can't imagine him working like that with Fonda. But, of course, he wouldn't need to.

DD: No, he'd know to treat him differently. You remember that famous speech of Henry Fonda's with the mother in The Grapes of Wrath . . . You know, 'Whenever you hear a baby crying I'll be there', that wonderful thing — 'I'll be there' to the mother. I mean that's just this sensitive, incredible actor with this director who instinctively couldn't seem to put a foot wrong.

LA: Did you ever see any evidence of this other side of Ford . . . the sensitive and intuitive?

DD: Well, the whole Galway thing was different, you see . . . There was a terrific no-nonsense ruggedness about the man. And this constant baiting, I was telling you, of the English crew . . . and not only the English. There was a certain Irish actor, whose name I won't mention, because he's an old man and not well now, who was a terrific, God help him, arse-licker and groveller, which Ford couldn't stand. He really couldn't stand anything like that at all. Well before this actor arrived on location, Ford had performed one of his big bullshit acts. He had been driving, looking for locations out in Connemara. He came across a beautiful little church out in the downland, and he said 'Stop the car', so the car stopped, and all the cars behind.

LA: I suppose he said 'This is where my parents were married'?

DD: Just wait. He goes in; they all follow him — they think it's a location you see. They all go in, crowding behind him in this little church. Ford takes off his cap and looks at them, and those with hats bare their heads. So he says, 'If you'll excuse me fellas', he says, 'I'm just going to kneel down here for a few minutes. This is the church where I was baptised.' So they all start whispering: 'This is the church . . .' It's become a shrine already. So he kneels down at the back of the church and they all kneel

down behind him. And he says 'I'm just going to say a prayer for my mother.' Blesses himself. And they all bless themselves. So Ford gets up and into the car and away they go. So this is all over the hotel you see — 'This lovely church where he was baptised . . .' Now our actor — we'll call him Dermot, which wasn't his name — has just arrived, he's in the bar that night, and he's listening to all this — it's all 'this wonderful little church . . . he prayed there . . . we all knelt down.' And Dermot is sucking all this up, you know, the eyes going . . . you see. So he goes up to Ford — and they've been eating and Ford is in the corner — and he says 'Jack', (he called him 'Jack', real native stuff you see) and Ford's just finished his meal and Dermot says, 'I don't know what your plans are Jack, but I know this country very well, and I was thinking, depending on how you feel yourself, you know, that if you're not busy or anything, we could take one of the unit cars, up along the coast, and there's a little church out there . . . Now I don't know how you are yourself, but I personally would like to go to Confession — maybe you would too.' Saturday night, you see, they go to Confession. And Ford says, 'Fuck off.'

LA: He liked a different kind of subservience didn't he?

DD: Oh yes, how right you are.

LA: Now tell me your nice story.

DD: Well my nice story is Gideon's Day. I was unemployed — totally and absolutely and had been for months. Which wasn't as bad as it seems because I used to live on £2.10s a week, but it was demoralising. Well, one day I was going up Wardour Street, and coming out of this big building were Michael Killanin and John Ford, getting into a big car. And quite a few years have gone by now since The Rising of The Moon . . . And Michael Killanin says 'Donal! Do you remember Donal?' Ford says 'Of course I remember him. Yeah, whatya doing? Are you doing anything? Working?' And I say 'No, not at the moment', you see. And Killanin is already waiting to get into the car and Ford goes on 'Listen go up to the whatever-it-was floor, and ask for Paul . . . (What was the name of that old casting director? He's dead now, grey-haired and very nice) . . . 'Tell him I sent you up, that I want you in the movie. Make an appointment. You can be here at eleven tomorrow morning?' I said 'Yes' and he said 'OK, that's great' and got into the car. It was absolutely extraordinary. So I go in and upstairs and this guy is so nice. I said 'I've just met Mr Ford in the street' and he says, 'Yes?' and I said 'I knew him before, you know, I was in The Rising of The Moon', and he says, 'Yes?' and I said 'He told me to tell you that he wants me in the film, and to make an appointment for eleven o'clock tomorrow morning.' And he says 'But the film is cast. Did he say what part?' And I said 'no, I just met him in the street.' And he said 'But it's cast, I don't know what he means. But you'd better come in at eleven if he said so . . .' So I come back the next day at eleven. Your man is there, he recognises me; Ford is inside at a meeting. I wait till quarter past eleven, quarter to twelve, best part of an hour, the door opens and out he comes, Killanin in tow, and he's very conscious of me sitting there. He's a sweet guy.

LA: Killanin or Ford?

DD: No, no, the casting director. And he said 'Mr Ford, Donal Donnelly here, you asked him to come at eleven o'clock.' And Ford said 'Yeah, Darn-al, sorry to keep you waiting.' And he said 'I was explaining to Mr Donnelly that the film is cast. But I thought he ought to be here since you asked him.' 'It isn't cast.' 'Oh, I thought it was, I thought it was cast.' 'It's *not* cast.' (He used to do this a terrible lot. Remind me to tell you the story about the location manager in Galway with the donkey and the ass.) 'I see, well what part is Donal playing?' 'He's going to play one of the Teddy Boys.' 'Oh, but . . .' (He'd told the man to make arrangements in the East End to interview real Teddy Boys.) 'Oh, but you wanted real cockney Teddy Boys . . . and Donal's Irish, and I've made arrangements.' He was getting weaker and weaker all the time. 'He's playing one of the Teddy Boys' Ford said, 'I'm tired of Cockneys screwing up Irish parts. I'm going to have an Irishman screwing up a Cockney part.' And I duly obliged him I must say! I had a cap and a razor blade . . . he made me take a razor blade out of my sleeve . . . and all that kind of crap . . . it was awful. So he put me in. It was three day's work, thirty pounds a day, which was enormous then, when you had nothing at all. And here's what he did. The three days were up. He finished shooting — but no one went, you just hung around and waited . . . And on this evening Ford came out and he said 'Now, I need him and I need him and I need him, and I need Donal, and I need him.' So for ten days he called me. He was giving me three hundred pounds.

LA: Did you get into *Young Cassidy* the same way?

DD: Who really cast me in that was Sean O'Casey. I never met Sean O'Casey, but he had an interview in *The Irish Times* about the filming of his book — which was a deplorable enterprise and Eileen* says now the only good thing about Sean's death was that he died before seeing it . . . They had that guy in it.

That Rod Taylor, you know — the whole thing was appalling. Anyway O'Casey said that he really didn't know much about films and he was glad that so-and-so was in it, but disappointed that Donal Donnelly wasn't in it. Because he's seen me on television as Johnnie Boyle, and told his daughter it was very real.

LA: You should have played Young Cassidy.

DD: Well, it wasn't that kind of movie . . . it's all marquee stuff, typical Irish locations, big names, everything. Eileen was very good about it in her book about Sean, actually. She says that the only bit that had the stench of what an Irishman could be was that awful scene of burying the mother, which is so powerful in the book. Ford did that. Anyway after that interview, someone said 'Let's please the old man.' So they phoned up, could I go over, so I went. When I got there, my first sight of Ford appalled me, he had aged beyond compare. And he stepped, or rather stumbled, out of his caravan, in which he had a fridge, with ice-cold Guinness, which I think is awful anyway. But iced Guinness he was drinking, and his lips were brown with it, and he was unshaved, and his eyes were all watery and I thought 'Oh my God!' It was indescribable the change, really indescribable. There was nothing, nothing. He was like an old, old man being led to the camera. But he came down and he did the scenes with the hearses, where I took the coffin out and everything. But then he was taken off the film, or he left it, and Jack Cardiff took it and it became a nothingness anyway . . . It was a nothingness from the word Go.

LA: Did you ever see *Gideon's Day*?

DD: I did.

LA: I quite enjoyed that.

DD: I came in one day on one of the buckshee calls that he did to subsidise me, I suppose at Columbia's expense. I was just wandering around: I'd never seen such a set, it was a warehouse set . . .

LA: I remember.

DD: And the fog, and the smoke, and the mist . . . And this huge studio filled with the crates and things, and the light coming out through them, it was fantastic. And I'm standing there, and this man, Mr. Wingate Smith, he was always there, and I said 'Fantastic!' And he said 'Yes, I thought that the first four or five times I saw it.' He was terribly despondent; he said Ford wasn't directing any more. He was just repeating, he had no original shots, no original concept, no original anything. The poor man was really down.

LA: Ford certainly wasn't at his best then.

DD: *The Grapes of Wrath* to me was *the* film. It still is.

LA: When you look at a picture like that, do you feel

* Eileen O'Casey, Sean's widow.

On location for The Rising of the Moon. *Ford and Dubliners (Denis O'Dea, left; Eileen Crowe, background right).*

it has Irishness in it?

DD: I hope so. It has that great sense of family. And the family splitting up. And the mother — a tremendous figure. I'd say his mother thing was fierce.

LA: I suppose that's Irish . . .

DD: Well, he was a Feeney, we know that. And his mother came from there, right?

LA: There's a tale that one of his parents came from Galway and the other from the Isle of Aran.

DD: There, you see. The Isle of Aran and Galway intermarriage. That is the peasant Irish marriage of all time. Aran is the last piece of land before Boston. In fact that's where all the Aran emigrants are. They didn't go to New York, they went to Boston. From all down that coastline. That's where they lost a million-and-a-half during the famine. And no doubt he took all this from his father. So all that's there; that's his roots.

LA: Did you ever see *The Sun Shines Bright?*

DD: Oh you see, that's another of my favourites. And that's another one that bears it out — the family idea was wonderfully handled, only there it's the race thing, the human family, the family of man. There's a great strength of compassion there, that feeling for the family of man.

LA: And that changed?

DD: Well I'd say he could handle the question of race in terms of 'We're all children under Christ', or 'God bless America'. But when the children became full-grown human beings, and began to say 'Now listen . . .' I don't think he could fit into that situation at all.

LA: Yes, I think that broke his heart.

DD: Time passed him on. It has to pass everyone on. He was no part of what's happened in the last two decades in America. Or in Ireland either.

LA: Did you feel the stature of Ford when you met him, even though he was no longer in his prime?

DD: I could. You couldn't mistake it.

233

Writer-Producer

When I visited Willis Goldbeck on Bellagio Road in 1978, he shied away from talking to me on the grounds that he had already given a long interview to Kevin Brownlow. He made it sound as though he had seen Kevin quite recently. To my surprise, their meeting had in fact taken place eight years before. Their talk had ranged widely over Mr. Goldbeck's long, remarkable career, with particularly fascinating information about the work and personality of Rex Ingram now remembered almost solely as the director of Valentino in *Four Horsemen of the Apocalypse*. In the twenties, of course, Ingram had been one of Hollywood's leading directors, a far bigger name than John Ford. I am most grateful to Kevin Brownlow for allowing me to print this extract from his conversation with Mr. Goldbeck.

Willis Goldbeck

WILLIS GOLDBECK: I'm sort of bracketed between the Irish directors: started with Ingram, wound up with Ford . . . Ingram had an enormous admiration for him; he said: 'There's nothing there I could do — but I think he's marvellous . . .'

The poor man's lost the sight of one eye now, and he has a curious split vision in the other. He reads like this (*Book held up inches from his eye*). I wondered several times how he could make a picture and yet when you get out on a set he seems to see everything that goes on. I remember when we made *The Man Who Shot Liberty Valance*, he'd sit there in a corner eating ice cream — he never ate anything for lunch except ice cream — and any move on the set, or anything anybody did, a whisper, he was aware of it. He was on top of everything all the time.

KEVIN BROWNLOW: Did you find him easy to work with?

WG: . . . I think there's a tremendous insecurity under Jack Ford. Even in his great days. He came from Maine, the son of a saloon keeper, and he's never forgotten it. If you are the son of an Irish saloon keeper in Maine, you feel you aren't of the upper stratum. He is fascinated by the fact that his wife is blue-blooded Virginian. These things come out every once in a while: there is that insecurity underneath. It's hard to believe when a man has been so dominant in this business; but it is there, and I think it accounts for a great deal of the things he says and does, turning on other people . . . slashing away to keep his own position clear, to keep the people around him reduced . . . Even Wayne was cursing him out . . . But I've always found him such an interesting character that, although I

Left: Shooting The Plough and the Stars. *Preston Foster, with Joe August, Ford and unit reflected in the window.*

know he's been hacking at me occasionally, it never bothers me. It fascinates me a little bit. He finally drove James Bellah out of his mind, and Bellah won't go back to see him — won't speak to him any more. He's so tyrannical and harsh. This invective that comes out is awful. To me it's funny; I laugh at it . . .

KB: He's very uncommunicative about pictures.

WG: He's a brilliant talker if you can get him started . . . I went out with him to U.C.L.A., when he talked to the students — he ran *The Searchers*. He started to answer questions. He had his daughter Barbara with him, who's dynamic and witty and a great foil to him. The two of them got started and the students were absolutely delighted, laughing and fascinated. Jim Bellah and I were there, and we sat a little astonished too. He went on and on talking about pictures. He came alive.

KB: Yet he likes to present the front of a man who doesn't give a damn.

WG: Oh sure he does. But his whole life is pictures. He'd give anything now to get out on the set and do a picture . . . I've got a script on my desk that I wanted to do with him and he said 'I'm your man'. But I cannot get financing for him. I think the man still has a brilliant mind about pictures; if he was given a fine story he would make it. But he got to the point where he was so anxious to make pictures, he'd go out and do anything. He did too many of those, after *Searchers* . . . I can't think of their names . . . Nobody wants to do a Ford picture.

. . . Ford had the classic approach to his pictures. You're not aware of his set-up, but if you weight it carefully, you see he's got one beautiful shot after another. Monument Valley isn't that beautiful. It's a stunning place — but it took Ford to find the approach to it. It was that way with Ingram most of the time. But Ingram was not a very emotional man; he never had the emotional thing that Ford had . . . He was a mental man; Ford is a passionate man. And it shows in his pictures.

Writers

In 1953, when I was starting work on my monograph for the British Film Institute, I wrote to Dudley Nichols and Frank Nugent, asking them if they could give me any information on their experiences of writing for Ford. They answered amiably and generously; I used portions of their letters in my original piece. Here they are reprinted more or less in full.

I had been in touch with Nunnally Johnson earlier, when he had been in London in 1950, producing *The Mudlark* for Fox. I found him (as can here be seen) a vehement proponent of the Writer's Cinema. We agreed, in the friendliest way, to differ. Then I wrote to him again, some five years later, when I was preparing a Ford season for the National Film Theatre. This time he was a little more forthcoming; but he had not changed his mind.

Nunnally Johnson, of course, had never written scripts for Ford — which in itself throws interesting light on the Hollywood studio system — only scripts which Zanuck assigned to Ford, or asked him to direct. Undoubtedly his impatience with the over-exaltation of the director was to some extent justified: it still is. But it is odd to find him so imperceptive of the creative contribution of a great director, unresponsive to the cinematic and poetic values of a film like *She Wore a Yellow Ribbon* (as Dudley Nichols was unresponsive to *The Quiet Man*). Writers, though, are not critics: they are as personal and partial in their judgements as any other artists, and as entitled to them.

Some of these comments or opinions were, when they were written, offered in confidence: clearly neither Mr Nichols and Mr Johnson wished to incur the charge of professional indiscretion, or to risk angering or hurting Ford. However, now that so many years have passed, the interest of what they had to say seems to justify or excuse printing their letters in full. I crave indulgence of their shades.

Dudley Nichols

Dear Mr Anderson,

I could never be 'impatient' with your request concerning John Ford, nor would I ever use the location 'mere critic', for I have a very high opinion of the critic; my only regret is that there are so few of them. The term is loosely used nowadays in every field of expression, applied to all sorts of incompetents and half-literate men who possess neither background nor knowledge of the work they pretend to weigh ... The true critics I value almost above the originators, for certainly they are more rare ... I wish I might be able to sit down with you and give all possible information as to Mr Ford's past work; but I have just finished a long stint for 20th Century-Fox and am too exhausted to do more than rest; and moreover much of what I might say to you personally is too personal, and too much a matter of opinion, and intuition (and perhaps, in some instances, bias) to put on paper ... There are certain aspects of Mr Ford I have never discussed with anyone that I can remember.

He is, it goes without saying, a great man in the history of cinema.

To go back to beginnings, I landed in Hollywood in June

1929. I had earlier finished ten years journalism in New York, reporting, drama criticism, music criticism, columning, one year on a roving assignment in Europe for *The World* (deceased) and cut my journalistic ties to go on with fiction and other writing. I was offered an advance by a publisher to do a book on Spain, which was near to my heart, and Winfield Sheehan, then executive head of Fox Films, had offered me letters of introduction to the American ambassador and others he knew in Spain. While he was getting out these letters, he talked me into coming to Hollywood. Sound had arrived and writers were needed. I knew nothing about film and told him so. My love was the theatre. I had seen one film I remembered and liked, Ford's *The Iron Horse*. So I arrived here rather tentatively and experimentally, intending to leave if I found it dissatisfying. Fortunately Sheehan assigned me to work with Ford. I like him. I am part Irish and we got on. I told him I had not the faintest idea how to write a filmscript.

I had been in the Navy during World War I, overseas two years, and we decided on a submarine story. I told him I could write a play, not a script. In his humorous way he asked if I could write a play in fifty or sixty scenes. Sure. So I did. It was never a script. Then I went on the sets and watched him break it down into filmscript as he shot. I went to rushes, cutting rooms etcetera and began to grasp what it was all about. But I must say I was baffled for many months by the instinctive way Ford could see everything through a camera — and I could not ... Working with Ford closely I fell in love with the cinema. What I found was an exciting new way to tell a story; new to me, old to Ford.

He had grown up in the 'business'. His older brother, Francis Ford, had become a silent film star. He brought Jack in as prop boy. At that time a prop man had to do almost anything that was called for — take falls, double stunts, be a live wire, and resourceful. I imagine Ford was watching the process of making films (or pictures, as they said from the start. He is extremely intelligent and sharp-witted and he has an inner toughness that was absolutely requisite to get a foothold — and keep it. The film world was, and still is as you know, a tough, competitive, cut-throat world, for all its pretensions to the contrary. I myself never had the fibre it takes to make films. The temperament of the writer is wrong for it; if he's a man of action he is usually not a good writer, though there have been exceptions. Ford's Irish heritage gave him the story-telling instinct and he was strong enough to fight his way up.

I warmed to Ford right away, because for one thing he was most generous to me. Right off he told Sheehan I had done a fine 'script'. I know because Sheehan, a tough Irishman, told me so. Most directors of that day — and does it change? — simply loathe telling the writer or anyone else in authority that the writer has done a good script. And mark you, I hadn't even written a filmscript — just a play in many scenes — which I grant you is the approach to a script.

This first script was *Men Without Women*. We had some other title, but the studio bought the final title from Hemingway, who had no connection with the story or film. It was, I believe, a remarkable film for its time, though not very successful — save with other film makers.

I see, glancing above, that my mind jumped over a stage of Ford's development. From prop boy Ford progressed to making shorts and westerns. They were shot in a few days. He teamed up with Harry Carey for these, at Universal, of Papa Laemmle's day. I knew Harry well in his later days, a fine man, and he'd tell me funny stories of how Ford and he worked up their stories and then shot them during 'the balance of the week'. Improvising mostly, as they shot. The old trick was to get one story and shoot it at various studios in succession, using new titles and different actors. I think Ford told me he shot one story about ten times — and no one knew the difference*. They were funny, energetic, catch-as-catch-can days for 'the movies'. Prior to sound-film, Ford rose high in Hollywood prestige with *The Iron Horse* and...I can't remember...something about Sons†. A mother-son story, which was one of his favourites in those days. (We did something of the sort later on, called *Pilgrimage*, in sound-film).

Sound arrived and the established directors, like the studios, were in confusion...Ford first made a short film in sound, using a one-act play by Arthur Caesar called *Napoleon's Barber*. I never saw it, never heard anyone speak of it save Arthur Caesar. Next he made a full-length film called *The Black Watch* — Vic McLaglen, Myrna Loy etc. It was not very good, in my opinion. I recall my laughter when McLaglen kept addressing Myrna Loy, an oriental creature named Yasmine in the script, 'Yes-minny'. Yet it was an advance, something done in the new medium of sound-film. And Ford's brilliant sense of composition, of forcing the camera to record what he wanted, was revealed in it.

Next came *Men Without Women* — where I came in. It was remarkable in many ways. They believed long dolly shots could not be made with the sound camera. He did it — one long shot down a whole street, with men carrying microphones on fishpoles overhead. And there were many astonishing pictorial things in it. I remember, when I started the 'script', I told Ford I feared I would imagine and write scenes which could not be photographed. 'You write it', he said, 'and I'll get it on film.' Well, he did. Even put the camera in a glass box and took it on a dive on the submarine. It is old hat now. Not then.

Our next film together was *Born Reckless*, which was, I believe the first American gangster melodrama in sound-film. Fox had had an earlier success with a silent film of this genre made by Irving Cummings, titled *Born to Kill*. That perhaps influenced the title of ours, which was a study of a gangster named Louis Beretti. It was fairly successful with the public but did not attract the attention of the first film I had written (so unskilfully) for Ford. Gradually, however, I was commencing to see fiction cinematically, to see ideas as Ford saw them instinctively. Everything I learned about film writing in those early years I learned from Ford, though of course I studied every film I could get hold of or find in the theatres. It seems to me now that I was running film in projection rooms half of my time in those days; yet I could learn more from Ford than from other films. From that point on we collaborated on a succession of films, now forgotten. In fact I can hardly remember the titles. I think the next was *The Seas Beneath*, followed by *Pilgrimage* and others I forget. (There is, I suppose, a will to forget unsatisfactory work). I was deeply dissatisfied during that period with the status of the writer in the 'motion picture industry' and was always on the point of quitting and returning to the career of pure writing which I had earlier planned. During this time the 'supervisor', shortly afterwards called the 'producer', was rising into prominence and seizing control of film-making — in my opinion one of the strongest factors in the decline of the American film: the business man, at least a man whose chief goal was to make money with 'product'. When the whole aim is to make money, the end result will be to lose money. Because such a producer is too far from film itself.

In the early 30's Ford and I separated. I worked at Columbia, RKO and other studios, also at the new enlarged studio of Fox Films at Westwood. I had very unhappy experiences with other directors, who worked by rote, whose minds were vulgar and unimaginative, whose only talent seemed to be vigor and the toughness necessary to be held in esteem by studio heads. They had

---

*A typical Ford exaggeration. Almost all Ford's early Westerns starred Harry Carey, and all were made for Universal.
†*Four Sons*, 1928.

know-how, having come up through the mill, but no audacity or experimental desire; they made 'pictures out of pictures'. I noted Ford did not pay much attention to the work of others, he was always trying to find his own way into new effects, and I tried to go that direction myself. I was working at Fox studio again, it must have been around 1933, when Ford, who had gone to RKO to make a modest film from Philip McDonald's war novel, Patrol, called me in some urgency. He said he was to commence shooting in about ten days — and had no script. What had been done he considered a mess and unshootable. Eager to help, I got leave from Fox and we sat down together with the novel, taking a fresh concept and starting from scratch. I wrote and Ford would spend part of the time with me. The script was finished in eight days, very long days I must say. Ford made Lost Patrol from it and the film was again a great critical success. It did much to advance him in critical esteem. During this time Ford had broached to me the idea of filming O'Flaherty's The Informer and I was enthusiastic; but he was unable to get any producer or studio to back the project.

I went back to Fox and finished my stint there, having charged Ford and RKO (it was a percentage film for him, as I remember) for eight days work only. From Fox I went over to Paramount and scripted The Crusades for C.B. de Mille. I was seeking to work with any director who seemed to have a different style, or at least a style of his own; and nobody can deny de Mille had one, no matter how much he derived from the Griffith of Intolerance. (Confidentially, my comment on that aspect of film-making is Ars longa, vita brevis, hokum aeternum est).

I had just completed the script for de Mille, when Ford and a producer at RKO named Cliff Reid called me with enthusiasm. They had obtained approval to film The Informer, against much studio resistance. Reid was a lovable, plump character who had unshakeable confidence in Ford and, I believe I may truthfully say, in myself. I jumped at the chance of course, undertaking it for a fraction of what I had been paid at Paramount. Ford's arrangement was again on a percentage. I wrote the script at white heat in a phenomenally short time and there was never another draft — the only script I can remember in which .there were never any changes or revisions or further drafts. I had of course been mulling the story for a long time and gathering ideas as to how to do it. I had a few talks with Ford beforehand, but nothing specific was discussed. Then we had one fruitful session together with Max Steiner, who was to write the music; Van Nest Polglase who was to do the sets; Joe August was the cameraman; and a couple of technicians. This, to my mind, is the proper way to approach a film production — and it is, alas, the only time in 25 years I have known it to be done: a group discussion before a line of script is written.

You sense in this film a 'deliberate and devoted stylistic experiment' and you are correct. Ford and I both felt that way from the beginning. By this time our two minds worked as one, we could almost talk a shorthand about film ideas. I believe honestly, though I may be mistaken, that it was I who pushed this idea of stylization hardest. I

never heard Ford mention The Last Laugh or Dr Caligari's Cabinet, but it is very likely he had absorbed what they had to give in the way of new film ideas. He wanted some distortion in the sets from the beginning, and I don't think Van Polglase (or the rigid ideas of a major studio itself) gave him as much of this as he desired. But Joe August was a great cameraman, perhaps the most experimental and audacious I have ever known, and he could heighten desired effects with lighting. My idea was to use symbolism that would be felt but not analysed by the audience; fog itself was the first symbol to get us into the region of Gypo's mind; the blind man (used and then dropped by O'Flaherty) I kept in the film as symbol of Gypo's dark conscience, and the tapping of his stick on pavements would suggest the pursuit of conscience — a blind pursuit. The posters were invented to be used as symbols; and I forget the innumberable small, invisible symbolisms I tried to use along the way — the ship as the idea of freedom and escape from misery — the three coins as symbols of guilt (O'Flaherty had them but did not push them as far as I did). Steiner, when I first discussed it, said he could take their ringing sounds, distort and enhance them and use them as a musical symbolic theme at certain moments. Time and clocks became symbolic of fate and guilt. The blowing wind (obviously impossible with fog but used nevertheless) was another symbol of fate, dragging the idea of betrayal (the reward poster) after Gypo; and the last time we see the poster it blackens in the fire before Gypo's eyes and shoots skyward through the chimney before the haunted, guilty Gypo's eyes (this was a brilliant stroke of Ford's during the shooting). But stylized symbolism was the key to the whole thing.

I brought to the script and Ford brought to the shooting of The Informer everything I had learned and all that he knew. Never since have I been able to work so freely or experimentally and I think Ford has not either; something of it was planned later in The Fugitive, but it did not come off.

I had even pushed symbolism and double photography farther than Ford would go. I know he threw out my idea in one scene and shot it straight, and I am sure he was right; because McLaglen had done the scene so astonishingly well that symbolism would have cluttered it up. That was the scene where Gypo is brought before Preston Foster as a suspect and Gypo drinks crazily and accuses the innocent tailor. If you have ever looked at the script you will remember that I had tried by imagined photography to show Gypo's schizoid mind, where in his terrified confusion and drunkenness, he imagines himself innocent, accusing another; and then is shocked to find it is his other self he's accusing, for his own face appears on the dim, hulking, knelt-down figure he charges with guilt. No doubt it was excessive, only useful if McLaglen had not been so perfect for the character.

As for the lighting, it was Ford and Joe August — perhaps influenced by Murnau in one respect, where flashlights point directly at camera and produce eerie halations. August never hesitated to shoot directly at a

239

sun-arc, if Ford wanted to try it — and Ford had an experimental mind. Most studio cameramen refuse to take chances, fearing censure from their 'department heads'. August was a great man. I learned much from him, watching and talking. Yet observe that *all* cameramen are good with Ford; he may not be able to operate a camera but generally he knows more what can be done with it than they do. He has the true film-maker's eye. His physical eyes are not too good, but he has powerful eyes in his mind. I daresay all painters, graphic artists and visual writers have this kind of seeing. Anyone who works in cinema must try to develop it. I say 'perhaps influenced by Murnau' because of that one brilliant scene in *The Last Laugh* where the old nightwatchman comes towards camera with his flashlamp hung on his chest — halations weave and dance — it's entirely unnatural vision and wonderful cinema! That was the first time I saw it. *The Informer* as the second. Hollywood has been half destroyed by its dead-set at 'realism', making everything appear exactly as it does to the average man, or to a goat, instead of sifting it through the feelings of the artist. *The Informer* was not realism at all, but a search for the truth through the use of the artistic lie.

The Informer was a critical success, but not commercially — until after it won the Academy awards, when the studio got behind it. Even after the preview the RKO heads look disgruntled and said, 'We should never have made it!' Ford and I walked out from the preview past glum faces, and we were heading for the nearest pub to drown it all, when we were saved by dear Dudley Digges, who stopped us with outstretched arms and tears of happiness in his eyes. So we never did reach that pub!

After that I worked elsewhere for a while... I went back East, half minded to quit filmwork, for I saw it was a director's field more than the writer's; there must be a dominant personality to make a good film and that person must be the director. And I knew I had not the temperament to be a director in Hollywood, where a man must be tough and determined and commanding to make an individual film — more extrovert than introvert... I loved the film medium but the cost to oneself as a filmwriter was too heavy for me.

I came back to Hollywood to adapt Hemingway's *For Whom The Bell Tolls*, Sam Wood directing, at Paramount. I spent more energy fighting for the integrity of the film (or what I conceived to be its integrity) than I did on the script. I was very dissatisfied with the film, though I learned a good deal from Wood, who knew his medium well.

From there on I sought to work with directors of individual style. First, I believe, I went with Ford and Walter Wanger to script *Stagecoach* and, afterwards, *The Long Voyage Home*. I wrote *Stagecoach*, though consulting with Ford before and after each draft. I have always tried to write three drafts of a filmscript, completely rewriting each one as more cinematic ideas came.

Thereafter I worked with Fritz Lang (*Manhunt* and *Scarlet Street*), with René Clair (*It Happened*

Tomorrow and *And Then There Were None*) and finally with Jean Renoir, whose first script I had written at 20th-Fox, *Swamp Water*... I seem to have forgotten another script I wrote for Ford, *Hurricane*, produced by Sam Goldwyn. There are others I forget at the moment.

The war ended and I dropped my other work to script *The Fugitive* for Ford. This project we had talked about for years, but no studio would back it. Now Ford was independent, with Merian Cooper, and he wanted to do it. I said I thought it was a wonderful tale but I was sure it would not make any profit. Still, I was eager to script it. We soon realized it was impossible to script the Graham Greene novel on account of censorship. Greene's novel was about a guilty priest and we could have no such guilty priest. After I had worked at its impossible problems for a while, I suggested writing an allegory of the Passion Play, in modern terms, laid in Mexico, using as much of Greene's story as we dared. Ford liked the idea. I did a long draft but was dissatisfied and on the point of throwing it over. Yet Ford showed enthusiasm and came to my office at RKO for about a week or ten days and, from what I had written, and from the novel, and from our own ideas, we re-dictated the script.

There are two scripts during our long collaboration on which Ford actually collaborated — *The Fugitive* and *Lost Patrol*. On others I would say I shared his mind and feelings, got about as much help as the filmwriter should get from a conscientious director. As a filmwriter I have always tried to adapt my mind and feelings to those of the director who is to shoot the film. But I always tried to inject the best of myself that I could and to search incessantly for new cinematic ideas. And let me say that Ford was always generous in his praise of everything I did.

He may have been irked by the coupling of my name with his by critics and the praise bestowed occasionally on the script. This is normal. Men of extreme and individual talent (genius, if you wish) must necessarily be men of healthy ego... If a director says he wrote this or that, it does not indicate a grudging or unveracious nature; he has put so much work into making a film that he may quite believe what he says. Ford was a great man for a writer to be associated with, and I have nothing but gratitude for the many things I learned from him. I have worked with directors who never saw the script until it was laid before them in completion, and a few months late seen in print that they wrote the script entirely. Ford is not of that type. He is too good an artist.

I liked the script of *The Fugitive* enormously. I don't know what happened in Mexico, I didn't go down with him. Perhaps he ran into insuperable difficulties. I saw Henry Fonda when he returned here and he was unhappy and perplexed. He said he didn't know what had happened to Ford down there. To me, he seemed to throw away the script. Fonda said the same. There were some brilliant things in the film, but I disliked it intensely — and, confidentially, I don't think Ford ever forgave me for that. (I wondered afterwards whether perhaps he felt free to throw away much of the script because he had participated in its writing).

Later, though, when I was making several films at RKO, he asked me to join him and Cooper (or rather to 'come over with them', which was not the same thing) and said to me that 'we need each other...' No doubt it is true we formed a fruitful collaboration. But then collaborators ever drift apart. I have a great affection for Ford and unlimited admiration, though I am not impressed by the films he has been making in recent years. It seemed to me he was repeating *Stagecoach* and copying himself instead of pushing on to what he should achieve. I hope, confidentially again, he will not take his award for *The Quiet Man* seriously, for to me it is a maudlin film, repeating old gags and worn cinematic ideas he could bring off with one hand twenty years ago. I wish he would be adventurous and go ahead again.

In conclusion, let me accent that Ford has the true film-maker's eye. I recall being on a streetcar many years ago with him, at night. We sat facing a compartment window at the middle of the car and suddenly I noticed Ford was staring at this glass with deep interest. He was seeing a double reflection — the passing lighted street outside and the people in seats behind us — and at the same time looking through at people in the front section of the car. Then he discussed it and I could see him making a mental note to try to catch that with a camera at the next opportunity. There are some film-makers who only use their eyes on the set. Ford used his observation all the time, as a good artist should. He was always on the watch for new things to catch with the camera.

Yours sincerely,
Dudley Nichols

Los Angeles, April 22, 1953

Dear Mr Anderson,

By way of postscript: I woke up remembering three more films on which I collaborated with Ford. One was the ill-fated *Mary of Scotland*, made by RKO. I worked hard on the script, going to historical sources rather than to the Maxwell Anderson play which the studio had purchased, and was of the opinion that I had done a fairly good filmscript. The studio head felt the same way — not that I attach any great value to producers' opinions. Where the film failed utterly was in Mary's relationship with Bothwell, and in lesser degree with Darnley and Rizzio. Casting was partly to blame, but I think (I say this in confidence) that it was another instance of Ford's one blind spot — his inability to deal with the man-woman relationship with feeling and insight, no matter how clearly it may be written in the script — which after all, is only a blueprint for a film... Ford's weakness, if I may stand in the place of critic for a moment, is that he cannot create in his actors the normal man-woman passions, either of love or the hate that is the dark side of impassioned love. I should guess he does not know it, does not understand it. Such blind spots, of one kind or another,

are common in artists and indicate blank spaces in the experience of the artist. Whatever the reason, it was a very disappointing film, and even the great scenes of Mary and Elizabeth, Mary and her judges (the first imaginary, though I believe Schiller first hit on it) did not come off as I had imagined them. Yet there was some brilliant 'Ford-work' along the way.

The other two films were *Judge Priest* and *Steamboat Round The Bend*, both using Will Rogers — comedies. I collaborated with Lamar Trotti on both scripts. Ford later used Trotti on *Young Mr Lincoln* — very successfully. Perhaps it is over-sensitivity on my part, but I had the feeling Ford was always trying to displace me, find another writer who would do just as well or even serve him better; yet it may have been quite proper on his part to seek the very best he could find and he may have been annoyed by limitations in me which I could not perceive or he may have been annoyed by my tendency to stand up against him and quarrel with him at times when I felt he was wrong... I had some sharp conflicts with Ford on occasions — and generally lost the argument. He has a strong personality, as you must know. He learned through the years how to paralyze the opposition of studios and executives, with courage and savage wit, in order to get his own way. Trotti, my good friend who recently died, was a young Southern newspaperman who had gone with the Will Hays office. He wished to learn to write scripts and I liked him so much I undertook to 'break him in' by collaborating, which I have always avoided because I don't believe in collaboration between writers — the true collaboration being writer and director. We did a number of scripts together, among them the two starring Will Rogers, and then Trotti was able to stand on his own feet and go his own way. Very successfully, I am glad to say, though in my frank opinion he never had the 'film sense'. Ford gave *that* to *Young Mr Lincoln*.

There are no doubt other films on which I worked with Ford — but I shall bother you with no more postscripts. I have been very frank in the foregoing and rely on your being discreet with the information. I have tried to answer your general questions, as a matter of friendly duty: I feel there is a true fraternity among film-workers and critics — men who are devoted to what is great in the medium rather than to what profit may be gained from its exploitation. I would not express publicly any critical opinions of Ford for the world; I respect him too much and value my years, on and off, with him. One can never forget one's teachers. I also tried to learn as much from other director's work, past and contemporary during those years, as I could... I think I have seen almost every film of any consequence ever made; but like Ford I do not bother to look at the contemporary run-of-the-mill stuff. Ford never gave a glance at the assembly-line product of Hollywood. He was his own man.

To touch once more on the blind spot, I cannot recall one of his films in which the man-woman relationship came off with any feeling or profundity. Like many fine artists (Herman Melville for instance) his true feeling was for the man-man or man-men relationship. Perhaps that is what has stimulated his passionate (and unfortunate, to my way of thinking) drive to be in military service: he still devotes a lot of time and energy to duties in the naval reserve. Even as a matter of zealous patriotism, it seems to me an error; mine is the artist's view, and I believe one serves one's country best by doing what one does supremely well. He missed War I, in which I served (he is a month older than I) and he may have erroneously counted that a failure of duty in himself. I don't know. I am just guessing. Or perhaps I am taking a less idealistic view of duty than he does... Frankly, Ford's passion for the uniform in recent years — certainly *since* the war — seems to me adolescent. If the experience gained were used for the creation of great true films about men at war, I would approve. But his service films seem to me false and sentimental.

Now please protect me in anything I have said in my desire to place myself at your disposal. I know you would have a hard time drawing any straightforward and self-revealing statements out of Ford himself. He is entertaining in an interview, but his calculated confusion is the method of the squid — he is not one to reveal what really goes on in him. For all this, he is a generous-hearted man who demands more of himself than of others, a high virtue, and he has a gift for arousing intense personal loyalties. In fact, one of the reasons we are not working together now is that I may not be capable of giving the kind of blind loyalty he desires; for I will always say no when I think no...

Sincerely,
Dudley Nichols

Los Angeles. April 24, 1953

Frank S. Nugent

Dear Mr Anderson,

I can appreciate your difficulty attempting to interview Ford. He hates direct questions. To my knowledge he has only once — and then reluctantly — consented to stand still for an extended profile. It was one I did for *The Saturday Evening Post* in 1947, when he was shooting *The Fugitive* in Mexico. I spent two weeks with the company and managed to crowd in a few sessions with Ford after the day's shooting. The title of my piece, as I recall it, was 'Hollywood's Favorite Rebel'.

It is rather difficult to describe my experiences writing for Ford — and some of them are painful to recall. And very funny too. As briefly as I can:

Ford is a great reader. He has not hobbies, no diversions. He has had — still has — two careers: one in the Navy, which he loves, and one as a movie-maker. I've never known anyone so thoroughly dedicated to his craft. Therefore his reading marks time between pictures. I don't think he reads novels much, certainly not the current best-sellers. But he is extremely well-read in history, biography; Irish literature of course; and Americana — southwest, Civil War mostly. With few exceptions, I believe he finds his own stores. *The Informer, Stagecoach (Stage to Lordsburg), The Fugitive, The Quiet Man,* his current *The Sun Shines Bright* from three Irvin Cobb short stories — all these, I know, were stories he had read, loved, brooded over for years and years. He incubates them. I know, for example, that he has been talking of a Lincoln story called *The Perfect Tribute* for the six years I have known him. I don't believe he owns it, but I am reasonably sure that someday he'll get around to it. He was talking of the Cobb stories to Laurence Stallings and me when we were working on *She Wore A Yellow Ribbon*. I never sparked to them; but Laurence knew them and liked them too. I think Ford knew that I'd be no good on the assignment, so he never even discussed it with me.

I had known him slightly when I was motion picture critic of *The New York Times*. Our paths crossed again when I did the *Saturday Evening Post* article in 1947. After the article was finished, I dropped in to see him one day and he started talking about a picture he had in mind. 'The Cavalry. In all westerns, the Cavalry rides in to the rescue of the beleagured wagon train or whatever, and then it rides off again. I've been thinking about it — what it was like at a Cavalry post, remote, people with their own personal problems, over everything the threat of Indians, of death...' I said it sounded great. And then he knocked me right off my seat by asking how I'd like to write it for him. When I stumbled and stammered, he grinned and said he thought it would be fun. He gave me a list of about 50 books to read — memoirs, novels, anything about the period. Later he sent me down into the Old Apache country to nose around, get the smell and the feel of the land. I got an anthropology major at the University of Arizona as a guide and we drove around — out to the ruins of Fort Bowie and through Apache Pass where there still are the markers 'Killed by Apaches' — and the dates. When I got back, Ford asked if I thought I had enough research. I said yes. 'Good,' he said. 'Now just forget eveything you've read and we'll start writing a movie.'

He made me do something that had never occurred to me before — but something I've practised ever since: write out complete biographies of every character in the picture. Where born, educated, politics, drinking habits (if any), quirks. You take your character from his childhood and write out all the salient events in his life leading up to

Nugent for Ford. Top: The Quiet Man.
Bottom: Cavalrymen in She Wore a Yellow Ribbon.

the moment the picture finds him — or her. In some cases a full page or more, single-spaced, was required to describe the character. The advantages are tremendous, because having thought a character out this way, his actions, his speech are thereafter compulsory; you know how he'll react to any given situation. This is in marked contrast, as you must know, to the usual thinking where a character is described as an 'Alan Ladd type' or 'a sort of Humphrey Bogart guy', or a 'Gilda character'. None of this for Ford.

Anyway that was how *Fort Apache* was born. He had James Warner Bellah's short story, *Massacre*, which touched the character and provided the ending. But the first 80% had to be worked back from that ending — and the key to it was in the character development. Ford works very, very closely with the writer or writers. I don't think it would be entirely true to say that he sees his story in its entirety when he begins — although he sometimes pretends to. Sometimes he is groping, like a musician who has a theme but doesn't quite know how to develop it. I've had the feeling often — in story conferences — that he's like a kid whistling a bar of music, and faltering; then if I come up with the next notes and they're what he wanted, he beams and says that's right, that's what he was trying to get over. He has a wonderful ear for dialogue and a lot of it is his own — like Barry Fitzgerald's wonderful line in *The Quiet Man*: 'It's a fine soft night so I think I'll go and talk a little treason with me comrades.'

Usually a script is written scene by scene, gone over, discussed, rewritten maybe, then okayed — and you don't go back over it again — which, again, is good for a writer. So often you run into producers or directors who pass a scene one week, then come back the next and start worrying it, changing their minds, pulling you back from the forward movement to reconsider or revise. This loss of momentum is so horrible in writing. With Jack, once the scene is okayed, you can put it behind you — certainly until the first draft is complete.

His own complete concentration on the script forces the writer to maintain the pace. It isn't slave-driving. Actually the writing hours are short — a few in the morning, a few in the afternoon. There have been times when he felt I was driving too fast. During *The Quiet Man* he actually pulled me to a stop and for three days we just talked over the next bloc — which I felt I knew thoroughly and was eager to write; but he made me tell it and re-tell it, examining it from every angle, professing a skepticism that I still believe was assumed. I don't know why he did this — except, possibly, that he believed my very eagerness to get on with the writing would break the leisurely pace of the story. Actually it was written in 10 weeks, which is pretty good time. Stallings and I did *Three Godfathers* in a bit more than 4 weeks; *Yellow Ribbon* was 7 weeks; *Fort Apache* claimed 15, but at least 7 of those were spent on the research and discussion.

He can be rude and frequently insulting; he can also be affable, charming, genial and generous in his praise. (I prefer not to tell you what the percentage is). But once the script is finished, the writer had better keep out of his way. On rare occasions he will invite you to visit the set; if he

has not invited you, you enter at considerable risk — and then are advised to remain in the background. The finished picture is always Ford's, never the writer's. Only if there is some emergency — such as the need for added narration — will he permit the writer to see the rough cut of the picture; you sense his reluctance even to have the writer attend a studio screening — to which the stunt man and crew have been cordially invited. I don't profess to understand this, but I suppose it is a small price to pay for the privilege of working with the best director in Hollywood.

You asked about the music. I know he was familiar with the old cavalry tune "She Wore a Yellow Ribbon" — just as he knew most of the Irish airs played in *The Quiet Man*. He professes to have a tin ear for music, but he can carry a tune quite well for a man who has no voice. I don't know this, but I suspect that when he begins thinking of a story, he does his own research in a quiet way and sends for music of the period and, in general, enters his office well-armed with a strange miscellany of fact and fancy to toss casually at writer, wardrobe man and everybody else who comes under the gleam of his Celtic eye.

Cordially,
Frank S. Nugent

Los Angeles. May 3, 1953

P.S. I see there is one point I haven't covered: Ford's adherence to the script. This varies. On *Quiet Man* there were remarkably few changes. A line dropped here or there, some cuts in the opening and the elimination of one sequence directly preceding and building to the steeple-chase. (We had to bridge this with narration). Those cuts were made after the film was shot. He was far more ruthless on *Wagonmaster*. That was one picture in which we did not work at all closely. He read our treatment (Patrick Ford's — his son — and mine) and then did not enter the scene again until we turned in the complete first draft. His script cutting — especially of dialogue — was rather harsh... Stallings and I both fought with him over *Yellow Ribbon* where he eliminated what was to us a key scene: an explanation of Brittle's mission when he initially sets out. It had always been a tough scene to write, because it had to be expository — and Ford detests exposition. We trimmed it to the bone and Ford reluctantly accepted it at long last — then threw it out after shooting it. I've always felt the film suffered because no one really knew what Brittles' problems were... I do know, from what I've heard from other writers and from his script girl — that he has been far more brutal on outside scripts, i.e. those in which he has had no part during their creation... One more thing: he never previews his pictures — no sneak previews to test audience reaction. He makes them his own way to suit himself. I'm sure that is the only standard he considers important. F.S.N.

Nunnally Johnson

Dear Mr Anderson,

Many thanks for *Sequence*. I read your story about Ford with great interest, and a good part of the rest of the issue as well, and while a good many of the things you say about him are unquestionably true, my conclusion was that the whole spirit of your editorial policy seems to be that of a cult dedicated to the worship of the director to the exclusion of all other factors in the composition of a film. I'm afraid I can attribute this only to a stubborn blindness to the actual processes of making a picture. Only non-professionals, I have noticed carry this adulation to such lengths . . .

My belief is that the amount of creative ability on the part of anyone making movies is extremely limited . . . In the first place, it is all collaborative, numerously collaborative, and it is nonsense to attribute great distinction to anyone who collaborates. In the second place, nine-tenths of it is not only derivative but sometimes second- and third-hand derivative. In the case of *The Grapes of Wrath*, John Ford worked with material from me, who in turn was working with material from John Steinbeck. Who but an incredibly vain or fatuous person could feel for one second that he had more than a faintly contributory interest in a third reworking of someone else's story? And if you are looking at me, I will tell you immediately that *The Grapes of Wrath* is a work by John Steinbeck and that he and his creation were the sum and substance of the picture of that title.

The contribution of the director, in my opinion, is the least to be proud of. He does not contribute the story and plot, he doesn't provide a character, he does not create a line of dialogue, which I would say are the salient elements of a picture. His contribution to the photography is again collaborative, in varying degrees, and the photography to me is the only element allowing for creative development. But when we speak of photography we are now rather far down the list in the catalogue of ingredients.

I believe I could make an argument that the director does not even provide a great deal of the direction of a picture. If you have read a good script you must have realized that in a very pronounced sense the picture is already directed there. I should say that the writer has provided as much as 85% of the actual direction of the story and film in his construction and scenes. At any rate, I have made many pictures and I have never yet seen a director depart far from the instructions in the script.

In other words, the margin within which a director can exercise his own invention and creative ability seems to me too small to warrant the almost entire credit which *Sequence* gives to him. I think that in the present case, you could with equal validity have examined the work of Dudley Nichols and speculated on when Ford's direction had or had not benefitted him. It seems to me that by almost any standard the body of Nichols' work has called for more of what we generally understand to be creation than the collaboration, of which the director is part, that

has gone to put it on the screen.

I trust my ambitions aren't pretentious but the fact remains that my scripts, as are Nichols', are unusually detailed. If by any chance you read the script of *The Grapes of Wrath* in one of those anthologies, you read one that was greatly pared down to spare readers a lot of purely professional direction. But I must assure you that none of my scripts leaves Ford or any other director the leisure to enrich them indiscriminately as you suggest. In three pictures I have found Ford following the script much more faithfully than many inferior directors. You refer to a court scene in *The Prisoner of Shark Island*. It seems to me to be taking nothing away from Ford to say that this trial was described in detail in the script, even as to the emotions of the spectators, and only a sort of emotional ignorance of the circumstances could have led you to assume otherwise. Again, you form a musical taste and affection for Ford which you base in part on the songs in *Tobacco Road* which I remembered from my own Methodist childhood and wrote in the script before ever Ford saw it.

I have gone through years reading scholarly comments on directorial touches in my pictures which were set down in the script in detail, and I no longer care very much whether this error is made again or not. Because of its complicated collaborations and the derivative nature of nearly all of its accomplishments, the making of films seems to be a very questionable source of any artistic satisfaction whatever. I think one must be very eager in the quest of art to find much of it in pictures . . .

With best wishes,
Nunnally Johnson

Shepperton Studios,
Middlesex. June 7, 1950

Dear Lindsay,

The other day I saw two reels of a picture, all I could take, and while watching it I wondered what you would say of a film of such cheap and vulgar behaviour, of direction which permitted a cute little leading lady to make cute little faces at the hero behind his back, of crude little two-scenes of nothing but interminable bickering, of comedy so drab and corny it was difficult to stomach in mixed company. And just as I was preparing to drop you a line the next day and cite this as an example of what happens to a director when he has a shabby script, I received your copy of *Sequence* and discovered in your story about Ford that you had studied *She Wore a Yellow Ribbon* seriously and with respect.

It's no use. You must be bewitched. Nobody, in all truth admires John more than I do — when he is provided with the strength and support of a script. I thought *When Willie Comes Marching Home* was first-rate, acutely observed and told with fresh, honest humor and comedy. But how could you have sat through *Yellow Ribbon*? What would

you have said of it if Ford hadn't directed it? Or if you hadn't known that Ford directed it? I love Westerns, I love John Wayne, and I love Westerns that are put together by John Ford with John Wayne, but what I saw of that one was too shameful for me to want any more. I am tired of Victor McLaglen stealing slugs of whisky and then bellowing at a line of soldiers who give him the bird behind his back.

The blame for such a picture I put on Ford because this was his company, he had absolute control over every detail of its composition, and in this particular case he assumes responsibility for everything about it, good or bad. He accepted a trashy script from two writers who were little more than amenuenses, if that's the word and spelling I'm thinking of. This, as a matter of fact, was the way Lubitsch worked, but Lubitsch was a great deal better qualified for that kind of operation. He was a very ingenious and amusing concoctor of situations and lines. Ford's approach to lines and situation is what might be politely described as basic.

With best wishes,
Nunnally Johnson

London. June 30, 1950

Dear Lindsay,

Ford again! Or is it still?
Oh, well!
If memory serves then, John was not assigned to the three pictures I did with him. I wrote the scripts without thought of the director to do them and they were offered to him by Zanuck, who selected all the directors for my pictures in those days. All were accepted in the form offered, and though I have worked with directors who made suggestions and contributed ideas, I can't remember that John ever said anything one way or the other about them. Nor can I remember his ever altering or rewriting any of the scripts on the set. It was on the set, I might add, that John made all his contributions to the picture. These were in the staging of the scenes, the shaping of the characters, and his wonderful use of the camera. In any case, the pictures he did with me were, for good or bad, completely faithful to the text of the script.

In *The Grapes of Wrath* and *The Prisoner of Shark Island* his interpretation of the characters through the actors seemed to me perfect. That is, they were either exactly as I had thought of them or in some way more effective. Only in *Tobacco Road* did he seem to me to go off the track. One of the characters, I remember, came out an imbecile, which was something of a shocker. Others seemed to me much too extravagant in their oddities. An explanation for this may be that, being something of a

Nunnally Johnson for Ford. Top: The Prisoner of Shark Island; *Mudd apprehended. Bottom left:* Tobacco Road. *Bottom right:* The Grapes of Wrath.

Tobacco Road boy myself, I was familiar with the kind of eccentricities these people might have, while John knew nothing whatever about them and had to rely on a kind of old-fashioned bed-slat comedy idiom. The result, to me, was a fiasco. I had, and still have, a certain respect for that curious play and its curious people; the play was, in my opinion, a fascinating caricature of the truth; but I'm afraid I found nothing whatever of this in the picture. To me it was just a crude, clumsy fake.

As for the assignment of pictures, I don't believe there is any such thing for a director of John's position and distinction. They are offered to such a director and he is free, out of respect and commonsense, either to accept or reject them ... Lesser directors may be given assignments as a routine matter, but never would a man like Ford be 'assigned' to a picture.

This is not to say that every distinguished director likes every picture he agrees to do, but the decision to do them issues out of himself. He may be anxious to get through a contractual arrangements as quickly as possible, or he may accept out of a friendship connected with the script. But rarely, almost never, would a studio order him to do a picture he disliked...

I hope this answers some of your questions. It is a matter of importance to pictures that writers like yourself examine and consider them seriously.

My best wishes,
Nunnally Johnson

London. January 24, 1955

P.S. About the ending of *The Grapes of Wrath*, I can't understand that French critic's account of what he says he saw. The picture ended with the Joads on their way to another rumour of few days work, and his last words, as I remember them, were when Ma said, 'We're the people.' No such ending as the one the Frenchman described was ever shot or even considered. I agree with you that M'Sieur must have been hitting the cognac* when he wrote that!
N.J.

* I am sure this implication that Jean Mitry, the distinguished French cineaste, had been 'hitting the cognac' was unjust. All the same, it is bizarre that he should write with such certainty in his book on Ford (*John Ford*, Editions Universitaire. 1954. Vol. II, p. 43) of an ending to the film which never existed. 'Ma states her faith in the power of the people which can never be defeated. We find the family later in a barn where they have taken refuge. They are working in the cottonfields. Rosasharn gives birth to a still-born child, and rescues an old man dying of hunger. She gives him her breast to save his life.' The version of the film shown in France, according to Mitry, ends with Tom's departure, omitting even Ma Joad's concluding speech. The scene in the barn, which is in fact the end of the novel, 'was suppressed in almost all the European versions', adds Mitry. He saw it, he says, in Switzerland in 1945. A cautionary tale for all critics. (L.A.)

Films Directed by John Ford

1917
For Universal

The Tornado
With: Jack Ford, Jean Hathaway. (2 reels)

The Scrapper
Camera: Ben Reynolds. With: Jack Ford, Louise Granville. (2 reels)

The Soul Herder
Script: George Hively. Camera: Ben Reynolds. With: Harry Carey, Jean Hersholt, Elizabeth James, Molly Malone, Vester Pegg, Hoot Gibson. (3 reels)

Cheyenne's Pal
Script: Charles J. Wilson Jr., from story by John Ford. Camera: Friend F. Baker. With: Harry Carey, Jim Corey, Gertrude Astor, Vester Pegg, Hoot Gibson. (2 reels)

Straight Shooting
Script: George Hively. Camera: George Scott. With: Harry Carey, Molly Malone, Duke Lee, Vester Pegg, Hoot Gibson. (5 reels)

The Secret Man
Script: George Hively. Camera: Ben Reynolds. With: Harry Carey, Morris Foster, Elizabeth Jones, Vester Pegg, Hoot Gibson. (5 reels)

A Marked Man
Script: George Hively, from a story by John Ford. Camera: John W. Brown. With: Harry Carey, Molly Malone, Vester Pegg, Hoot Gibson. (5 reels)

Bucking Broadway
Script: George Hively. Camera: John W. Brown. With: Harry Carey, Molly Malone, Vester Pegg. (5 reels)

1918
For Universal

The Phantom Riders
Script: George Hively, from a story by Henry McRae. Camera: John W. Brown. With: Harry Carey, Molly Malone, Buck Connors, Vester Pegg. (5 reels)

Wild Women
Script: George Hively. Camera: John W. Brown. With: Harry Carey, Molly Malone, Martha Maddox, Vester Pegg (5 reels)

Thieves' Gold
Script: George Hively, from the story *Back to the Right Trail* by Frederick R. Bechdolt. Camera: John W. Brown. With: Harry Carey, Molly Malone, Vester Pegg, Harry Tenbrook. (5 reels)

The Scarlet Drop
Script: George Hively, from a story by John Ford. Camera: Ben Reynolds. With: Harry Carey, Molly Malone, Vester Pegg. (5 reels)

Hell Bent
Script: John Ford, Harry Carey. Camera: Ben Reynolds. With: Harry Carey, Neva Gerber, Duke Lee, Vester Pegg. (5,700 feet)

A Woman's Fool
Script: George Hively, from the novel *Lin McLean* by Owen Wister. Camera: Ben Reynolds. With: Harry Carey, Betty Schade, Roy Clark, Molly Malone. (60 minutes)

Three Mounted Men
Script: Eugene B. Lewis. Camera: John W. Brown. With: Harry Carey, Joe Harris, Neva Gerber, Harry Carter, Ella Hall. (6 reels)

1919
For Universal

Roped
Script: Eugene B. Lewis. Camera: John W. Brown. With: Harry Carey, Neva Gerber, J. Farrell McDonald. (6 reels)

The Fighting Brothers
Script: George Hively, from a story by George C. Hill. Camera: John W. Brown. With: Pete Morrison, Hoot Gibson, Yvette Mitchell. (2 reels)

A Fight for Love
Script: Eugene B. Lewis. Camera: John W. Brown. With: Harry Carey, Joe Harris, Neva Gerber, J. Farrell McDonald, Princess Neola Mae, Chief Big Tree. (6 reels)

By Indian Post
Script: H. Tipton Steck, from the story *The Trail of the Billy-Doo*, by William Wallace Cook. With: Pete Morrison, Duke Lee, Magda Lane, Hoot Gibson. (2 reels)

The Rustlers
Script: George Hively. Camera: John W. Brown. With: Pete Morrison, Helen Gibson, Hoot Gibson. (2 reels)

Bare Fists
Script: Eugene B. Lewis, from a story by Bernard McConville. Camera: John W. Brown. With: Harry Carey, Molly McConnell, Betty Schade, Vester Pegg. (5,500 feet)

Gun Law
Script: H. Tipton Steck. Camera: John W. Brown. With: Pete Morrison, Hoot Gibson, Helen Gibson. (2 reels)

The Gun Packer
Script: Carl R. Coolidge, from a story by John Ford and Harry Corley. Camera: John W. Brown. With: Ed Jones, Pete Morrison, Magda Lane, Jack Woods, Hoot Gibson. (2 reels)

Riders of Vengeance
Script: John Ford and Harry Carey. Camera: John W. Brown. With: Harry Carey, Seena Owen, Joe Harris, J. Farrell McDonald, Betty Schade, Vester Pegg. (6 reels)

The Last Outlaw
Script: H. Tipton Steck, from a story by Evelyne Murray Campbell. Camera: John W. Brown. With Ed 'King Fisher'. (2 reels)

The Outcasts of Poker Flat
Script: H. Tipton Steck, from stories by Bret Harte. Camera: John W. Brown. With: Harry Carey, Cullen Landis, Gloria Hope, J. Farrell McDonald, Duke R. Lee, Vester Pegg. (6 reels)

The Ace of the Saddle
Script: George Hively, from a story by B. J. Jackson. Camera: John W. Brown. With: Harry Carey, Joe Harris, Duke R. Lee, Peggy Pearce, Vester Pegg. (6 reels)

The Rider of the Law
Script: H. Tipton Steck, from the story *Jim of the Rangers* by G. P. Lancaster. Camera: John W. Brown. With: Harry Carey, Gloria Hope, Vester Pegg. (5 reels)

A Gun Fightin' Gentleman
Script: Hal Hoadley, from a story by John Ford and Harry Carey. Camera: John W. Brown. With: Harry Carey, J. Barney Sherry, Kathleen O'Connor. (5 reels)

Marked Men

Script: H. Tipton Steck from story *The Three Godfathers*, by Peter B. Kyne. Camera: John W. Brown. With: Harry Carey, J. Farrell McDonald, Joe Harris. (5 reels)

1920

For Universal

The Prince of Avenue A

Script: Charles J. Wilson Jnr., from a story by Charles and Frank Dazey. Camera: John W. Brown. With: James J. 'Gentleman Jim' Corbett, Mary Warren. (5 reels)

The Girl in No. 29

Script: Philip J. Hurn, from the story *The Girl in the Mirror* by Elizabeth Jordan. Camera: John W. Brown. With: Frank Mayo, Harry Hilliard, Claire Anderson. (5 reels)

Hitchin' Posts

Script: George C. Hull, from a story by Harold M. Schumate. Camera: Benjamin Kine. With: Frank Mayo, Beatrice Burnham, Joe Harris, J. Farrell McDonald. (5 reels)

For Fox

Just Pals

Script: Paul Schofield, from a story by John McDermott. Camera: George Schneiderman. With: Buck Jones, Helen Ferguson, George E. Stone, Duke R. Lee, William Buckley. (5 reels)

1921

For Fox

The Big Punch

Script: John Ford and Jules Furthman, from the story *Fighting Back* by Jules Furthman. Camera: Jack Good. With: Buck Jones, Barbara Bedford, George Siegmann. (5 reels)

Jackie

Script: Dorothy Yost, from a story by Countess Helena Barcynska. Camera: George Schneiderman. With: Shirley Mason, William Scott, Harrey Carter, George E. Stone (5 reels)

For Universal

The Freeze Out

Script: George C. Hull. Camera: Harry C. Fowler. With: Harry Carey, Helen Ferguson, Joe Harris, J. Farrell McDonald. (4,400 feet)

The Wallop

Script: George C. Hull, from the story *The Girl He Left Behind Him* by Eugene Manlove Rhodes. Camera: Harry C. Fowler. With: Harry Carey, Joe Harris, Charles Lemoyne, J. Farrell McDonald. (5 reels)

Desperate Trails

Script: Elliot J. Clawson, from the story *Christmas Eve at Pilot Butte* by Courtney Riley Cooper. Camera: Harry C. Fowler and Robert DeGrasse. With: Harry Carey, Irene Rich, George E. Stone. (5 reels)

Action

Script: Harvey Gates, from a story by J. Allan Dunn. Camera: John W. Brown. With: Hoot Gibson, Francis Ford, J. Farrell McDonald, Buck Connors, Byron Munson, Clara Horton. (5 reels)

Sure Fire

Script: George C. Hull, from story by Eugene Manlove Rhodes. Camera: Virgil G. Miller. With: Hoot Gibson, Molly Malone, Reeves 'Breezy' Eason Jnr. (5 reels)

1922

For Fox

Little Miss Smiles

Script: Dorothy Yost, from the story by Myra Kelly. Camera: David Abel. With: Shirley Mason, Gaston Glass, George Williams. (5 reels)

The Village Blacksmith

Script: Paul H. Sloane, from a poem by H. W. Longfellow. Camera: George Schneiderman. With: William Walling, Virginia True Boardman, Virginia Valli, David Butler, Tully Marshall, Francis Ford, Bessie Love. (8 reels)

1923

For Fox

The Face on the Bar-Room Floor

Script: Eugene B. Lewis and G. Marion Burton, from a poem by Hugh Antoine D'Arcy. Camera: George Schneiderman. With: Henry B. Walthall, Ruth Clifford, Walter Emerson, Alma Bennett. (5,787 feet)

Three Jumps Ahead

Script: John Ford. Camera: Daniel B. Clark. With: Tom Mix, Alma Bennett, Virginia True Boardman, Francis Ford. (4,854 feet)

Cameo Kirby

Script: Robert N. Lee, from the play by Harry Leon Wilson and Booth Tarkington. Camera: George Schneiderman. With: John Gilbert, Gertrude Olmstead, Alan Hale, Jean Arthur. (7 reels)

North of Hudson Bay

Script: Jules Furthman. Camera: Daniel B. Clark. With: Tom Mix, Kathleen Key, Frank Campeau, Eugene Pallette, Fred Kohler. (4,973 feet)

Hoodman Blind

Script: Charles Kenyon, from a story by Henry Arthur Jones and Wilson Barrett. Camera: George Schneiderman. With: David Butler, Gladys Hulette, Regina Connelly, Frank Campeau. (5,434 feet)

1924

For Fox

The Iron Horse

Script: Charles Kenyon, from a story by Charles Kenyon and John Russell. Camera: George Schneiderman and Burnett Guffey. Music: Erno Rapee. With: George O'Brien, Madge Bellamy, Judge Charles Edward Bull, William Walling, Fred Kohler, J. Farrell McDonald, Jack O'Brien, George Waggner and others. (11,335 feet)

Hearts of Oak

Script: Charles Kenyon, from the play by James A. Herne. Camera: George Schneiderman. With: Hobart Bosworth, Pauline Starke, Theodore von Eltz, Francis Ford. (5,336 feet)

1925

For Fox

Lightnin'

Script: Frances Marion, from the play by Winchell Smith and Frank Bacon. Camera: Joseph H. August. With: Jay Hunt, Madge Bellamy, Edythe Chapman, Wallace McDonald, J. Farrell McDonald. (8,050 feet)

Kentucky Pride
Script: Dorothy Yost. Camera: George Schneiderman. With: Henry B. Walthall, J. Farrell McDonald, Gertrude Astor, Winston Miller. (6,597 feet)

The Fighting Heart
Script: Lillie Hayward, from the novel by Larry Evans. Camera: Joseph H. August. With: George O'Brien, Billie Dove, J. Farrell McDonald, Victor McLaglen, Hank Mann, Francis Ford. (6,978 feet)

Thank You
Script: Frances Marion, from play by Winchell Smith and Tom Cushing. Camera: George Schneiderman. With: George O'Brien, Jacqueline Logan, Alec Francis, J. Farrell McDonald. (75 minutes)

1926
For Fox

The Shamrock Handicap
Script: John Stone, from a story by Peter B. Kyne. Camera: George Schneiderman. With: Janet Gaynor, Leslie Fenton, J. Farrell McDonald. (5,685 feet)

The Blue Eagle
Script: L. G. Rigby, from the story *The Lord's Referee* by Gerald Beaumont. Camera: George Schneiderman. With: George O'Brien, Janet Gaynor, William Russell, Robert Edeson, David Butler, Harry Tenbrook (6,200 feet)

Three Bad Men
Script: John Ford and John Stone, from the novel, *Over the Border* by Herman Whitaker. Camera: George Schneiderman. With: George O'Brien, Olive Borden, J. Farrell McDonald, Tom Santschi, Frank Campeau, Lou Tellegen. (8,000 feet)

1927
For Fox

Upstream
Script: Randall H. Faye, from the novel *The Snake's Wife* by Wallace Smith. Camera: Charles G. Clarke. With: Nancy Nash, Earle, Foxe, Grant Withers. (5,510 feet)

1928
For Fox

Mother Machree
Script: Gertrude Orr, from the novel by Rita Johnson Young. Camera: Chester Lyons. With: Belle Bennett, Neil Hamilton, Philippe De Lacy, Pat Somerset, Victor McLaglen. (75 minutes)

Four Sons
Script: Philip Klein, from novel by I. A. R. Wylie. Camera: George Schneiderman and Charles G. Clarke. Music: S. L. Rothafel, Erno Rapee, Lee Pollack. With: Margaret Mann, James Hall, Charles Morton, George Meeker, Francis X. Bushman Jnr., June Collyer, Earle Foxe. (100 minutes)

Hangman's House
Script: Marion Orth, from a story by Donn Byrne. Camera: George Schneiderman. With: Victor McLaglen, Hobart Bosworth, June Collyer, Larry Kent, Earle Foxe, John Wayne. (7 reels)

Napoleon's Barber
Script: Arthur Caesar, from his play. Camera: George Schneiderman. With: Otto Matiesen, Frank Reicher, Natalie Golitzin. (32 minutes)

Riley The Cop
Script: James Gruen and Fred Stanley. Camera: Charles G. Clarke. Editor: Alex Troffey. With: J. Farrell McDonald, Louise Fazenda, Nancy Drexel, David Rollins, Harry Schultz, Billy Bevan. (67 minutes)

1929
For Fox

Strong Boy
Script: James Kevin McGuinness, Andrew Bennison and John McLain, from story by Frederick Hazlett Brennan. Camera: Joseph August. With: Victor McLaglen, Leatrice Joy, Clyde Cook, Slim Summerville, J. Farrell McDonald, David Torrence. (63 minutes)

The Black Watch
Co-director: Lumsden Hare. Script: James Kevin McGuinness and John Stone, from novel *King of the Khyber Rifles* by Talbot Mundy. Camera: Joseph E. August. With: Victor McLaglen, Myrna Loy, Roy D'Arcy, Pat Somerset, David Rollins, Lumsden Hare, David Torrence, Francis Ford. (93 minutes)

Salute
Script: John Stone, from a story by Tristram Tupper. Camera: Joseph H. August. With: George O'Brien, Helen Chandler, Stepin' Fetchit, Frank Albertson, Joyce Compton, David Butler, Lumsden Hare, Ward Bond, John Wayne. (86 minutes)

1930
For Fox

Men Without Women
Script: Dudley Nichols, from story *Submarine* by Ford and James K. McGuinness. Camera: Joseph August. Editor: Paul Weatherwax. With: Kenneth MacKenna, Frank Albertson, Paul Page, Pat Somerset, Walter McGrail, Stuart Erwin, Warren Hymer, J. Farrell McDonald, Harry Tenbrook, John Wayne, Robert Parrish. (77 minutes)

Born Reckless
Co-director: Andrew Bennison. Script: Dudley Nichols, from novel *Louis Beretti* by Donald Henderson Clarke. Camera: George Schneiderman. Editor: Frank E. Hull. With: Edmund Lowe, Catherine Dale Owen, Lee Tracy, Marguerite Churchill, Warren Hymer, Frank Albertson, Ferike Boros, J. Farrell McDonald, Ward Bond, Jack Pennick. (82 minutes)

Up the River
Script: Maurine Watkins. Camera: Joseph H. August. Editor: Frank E. Hull. With: Spencer Tracy, Warren Hymer, Humphrey Bogart, Claire Luce. (92 minutes)

1931

Seas Beneath (Fox)
Script: Dudley Nichols, from story by James Parker Jnr. Camera: Joseph August. Editor: Frank E. Hull. With: George O'Brien, Marion Lessing, Warren Hymer, William Collier Snr., John Loder, Harry Tenbrook, Francis Ford. (99 minutes)

The Brat (Fox)
Script: Sonya Levien, S. N. Behrman and Maude Fulton. Camera: Joseph August. Editor: Alex Troffey. With: Sally O'Neil, Alan Dinehart, Frank Albertson, Virginia Cherrill, June Collyer, J. Farrell McDonald, Victor McLaglen. (81 minutes)

Arrowsmith (United Artists)
Script: Sidney Howard, from novel by Sinclair Lewis.

Air Mail (Universal)
Script: Dale Van Every and Frank Wead, from story by Frank Wead. Camera: Karl Freund. With: Pat O'Brlen, Ralph Bellamy, Gloria Stuart, Lillian Bond, Russell Hopton, Slim Summerville, Frank Albertson, Leslie Fenton, Jack Pennick. (83 minutes)
Camera: Ray June. Designer: Richard Day. Editor: Hugh Bennett. Music: Alfred Newman. With: Ronald Colman, Helen Hayes, A. E. Anson, Richard Bennett, Claude King, Beulah Bondi, Myrna Loy. (108 minutes)

1932
Flesh (M-G-M)
Script: Leonard Praskins and Edgar Allen Woolf from story by Edmund Goulding. Dialogue: Moss Hart. Camera: Arthur Edeson. With: Wallace Beery, Karen Morley, Ricardo Cortez, Jean Hersholt, John Miljan, Vince Barnett, Greta Meyer, Ed Brophy. (95 minutes)

1933
Pilgrimage (Fox)
Script: Philip Klein and Barry Connors, from story *Gold Star Mother* by I. A. R. Wylie. Dialogue: Dudley Nichols. Camera: George Schneiderman. Editor: Louis R. Loeffler. With: Henrietta Crossman, Heather Angel, Norman Foster, Marion Nixon, Charley Grapewin, Hedda Hopper, Francis Ford. (90 minutes)
Dr. Bull (Fox)
Scrpt: Paul Green, from novel *The Last Adam* by James Gould Cozzens. Camera: George Schneiderman. With: Will Rogers, Marion Nixon, Berton Churchill, Louise Dresser, Rochelle Hudson, Andy Devine, Robert Parrish. (76 minutes)

1934
The Lost Patrol (RKO Radio)
Script: Dudley Nichols and Garrett Ford, from story *Patrol* by Philip MacDonald. Camera: Harold Wenstrom. Editor: Paul Weatherwax. Music: Max Steiner. Design: Van Nest Polglase and Sidney Ullman. With: Victor McLaglen, Boris Karloff, Wallace Ford, Reginald Denny, J. M. Kerrigan, Billy Bevan, Alan Hale, Brandon Hurst. (74 minutes)
The World Moves On (Fox)
Script: Reginald Berkeley. Camera: George Schneiderman. Music: Max Steiner, Louis de Francesco, R. H. Bassett, David Buttolph, Hugo Friedhofer, George Gershwin. With: Madeleine Carroll, Franchot Tone, Lumsden Hare, Paul Roulien, Reginald Denny, Siegfried Rumann, Louise Dresser, Stepin Fetchit, Dudley Diggs. (90 minutes)
Judge Priest (Fox)
Script: Dudley Nichols and Lamar Trotti, from stories by Irvin S. Cobb. Camera: George Schneiderman. With: Will Rogers, Henry B. Walthall, Tom Brown, Anita Louise, Rochelle Hudson, Berton Churchill, David Landau, Brenda Fowler, Hattie McDaniel, Stepin' Fetchit, Charley Grapewin, Francis Ford. (80 minutes)

1935
The Whole Town's Talking (Columbia)
Script: Jo Swerling, from novel by W. R. Burnett. Camera: Joseph August. With: Edward G. Robinson, Jean Arthur,

Wallace Ford, Donald Meek, Edward Brophy, J. Farrell McDonald. (95 minutes)
The Informer (RKO Radio)
Script: Dudley Nichols, from novel by Liam O'Flaherty. Camera: Joseph August. Editor: George Hively. Music: Max Steiner. Design: Van Nest Polglase, Charles Kirk. With: Victor McLaglen, Heather Angel, Preston Foster, Margot Grahame, Wallace Ford, Una O'Connor, J. M. Kerrigan, Joseph Sawyer, Neil Fitzgerald, Donald Meek, Francis Ford, Dennis O'Dea. (91 minutes)
Steamboat Round The Bend (20th Century-Fox)
Script: Dudley Nichols and Lamar Trotti, from story by Ben Lucian Burman. Camera: George Schneiderman. Editor: Alfred De Gaetano. With: Will Rogers, Anne Shirley, Eugene Pallett, John McGuire, Berton Churchill, Stepin' Fetchit, Francis Ford, Irvin S. Cobb, Roger Imhof. (80 minutes)

1936
The Prisoner of Shark Island (20th Century-Fox)
Script: Nunnally Johnson. Camera: Bert Glennon. Editor: Jack Murray. Music: Louis Silvers. Design: William Darling. With: Warner Baxter, Gloria Stuart, Claude Gillingwater, Arthur Byron, O. P. Heggie, Harry Carey, Francis Ford, John Carradine. (95 minutes)
Mary of Scotland (RKO Radio)
Script: Dudley Nichols, from play by Maxwell Anderson. Camera: Joseph August. Editor: Jane Loring. Music: Max Steiner. Design: Van Nest Polglase, Carroll Clark. With: Katharine Hepburn, Fredric March, Florence Eldridge, Douglas Walton, John Carradine, Donald Crisp. (123 minutes)
The Plough and The Stars (RKO Radio)
Script: Dudley Nichols, from the play by Sean O'Casey. Camera: Joseph August. Editor: George Hively. Design: Van Nest Polglase. With: Barbara Stanwyck, Preston Foster, Barry Fitzgerald, Dennis O'Dea, Eileen Crowe, Arthur Shields, Erin O'Brien Moore, Brandon Hurst, Una O'Connor. (72 minutes)

1937
Wee Willie Winkie (20th Century-Fox)
Script: Ernest Pascal, Julian Josephson, from story by Rudyard Kipling. Camera: Arthur Miller. Editor: Walter Thompson. With: Shirley Temple, Victor McLaglen, C. Aubrey Smith, June Lang, Michael Whalen, Cesar Romero, Constance Collier. (99 minutes)
The Hurricane (Samuel Goldwyn—U.A.)
Script: Dudley Nichols, from novel by Charles Nordhoff and James Norman Hall, adapted by Oliver Garrett. Camera: Bert Glennon and Archie Stout. Editor: Lloyd Nosler. Music: Alfred Newman. Design: Richard Day, Alex Golitzen. With: Dorothy Lamour, Jon Hall, Mary Astor, C. Aubrey Smith, Thomas Mitchell, Raymond Massey, John Carradine, Jerome Cowan. (102 minutes)

1938
Four Men and a Prayer (20th Century-Fox)
Script: Richard Sherman, Sonya Levien and Walter Ferris, from novel by David Garth. Camera: Ernest Palmer. With: Loretta Young, Richard Greene, George Sanders, David Niven, William Henry, C. Aubrey Smith, J. Edward Bromberg, Alan Hale, John Carradine, Reginald Denny,

Burton Churchill, Barry Fitzgerald. (85 minutes)

Submarine Patrol (20th Century-Fox)
Script: Rian James, Darrell Ware and Jack Yellen, from novel *The Splinter Fleet* by John Milholland. Camera: Arthur Miller. Editor: Robert Simpson. With: Richard Greene, Nancy Kelly, Preston Foster, George Bancroft, Slim Summerville, John Carradine, Warren Hymer, Henry Armetta, Douglas Fowley, J. Farrell McDonald, Elisha Cook Jnr. (95 minutes)

1939

Stagecoach (Walter Wanger—U.A.)
Script: Dudley Nichols, from story *Stage to Lordsburg* by Ernest Haycox. Camera: Bert Glennon. Editors: Dorothy Spencer and Walter Reynolds. Music: Richard Hageman. Design: Alexander Toluboff. With: John Wayne, Claire Trevor, John Carradine, Thomas Mitchell, Andy Devine, Donald Meek, Louise Platt, Tim Holt, George Bancroft, Berton Churchill, Tom Tyler, Francis Ford. (97 minutes)

Young Mr Lincoln (20th Century-Fox)
Script: Lamar Trotti. Camera: Bert Glennon. Editor: Walter Thompson. Music: Alfred Newman. Design: Richard Day and Mark Lee Kirk. With: Henry Fonda, Alice Brady, Marjorie Weaver, Dorris Bowdon, Arleen Whelan, Eddie Collins, Pauline Moore, Richard Cromwell, Donald Meek, Ward Bond, Francis Ford. (101 minutes)

Drums Along The Mohawk (20th Century-Fox)
Script: Lamar Trotti and Sonya Levien, from novel by Walter D. Edmonds. Camera: Bert Glennon, Ray Rennahan. Editor: Robert Simpson. Music: Alfred Newman. Design: Richard Day and Mark Lee Kirk. With: Henry Fonda, Claudette Colbert, Edna May Oliver, Eddie Collins, John Carradine, Dorris Bowdon, Jessie Ralph, Arthur Shields, Francis Ford, Ward Bond, Roger Imhof. (Colour, 103 minutes)

1940

The Grapes of Wrath (20th Century-Fox)
Script: Nunnally Johnson, from novel by John Steinbeck. Camera: Gregg Toland. Editor: Robert Simpson. Music: Alfred Newman. Design: Richard Day and Mark Lee Kirk. With: Henry Fonda, Jane Darwell, John Carradine, Charley Grapewin, Dorris Bowdon, Russell Simpson, O. Z. Whitehead, John Qualen, Eddie Quillan, Zeffie Tilbury, Frank Sully, Shirley Mills, Ward Bond, Darryl Hickman, Grant Mitchell. (129 minutes)

The Long Voyage Home (Argosy-U.A.)
Script: Dudley Nichols, from four one-act plays by Eugene O'Neill. Camera: Gregg Toland. Editor: Sherman Todd. Music: Richard Hageman. Design: James Basevi. With: Thomas Mitchell, John Wayne, Ian Hunter, Barry Fitzgerald, Wilfred Lawson, Mildred Natwick, John Qualen, Ward Bond, Joe Sawyer, Arthur Shields, J. M. Kerrigan. (105 minutes)

1941

Tobacco Road (20th Century-Fox)
Script: Nunnally Johnson, from play by Jack Kirkland and novel by Erskine Caldwell. Camera: Arthur C. Miller. Editor: Barbara McLean. Music: David Buttolph. Design: Richard Day and James Basevi. With: Charley Grapewin, Marjorie Rameau, Gene Tierney, William Tracy, Eli-

zabeth Patterson, Dana Andrews, Slim Summerville, Ward Bond, Zeffie Tilbury, Russell Simpson, Grant Mitchell. (84 minutes)

How Green Was My Valley (20th Century-Fox)
Script: Philip Dunne, from novel by Richard Llewellyn. Camera: Arthur Miller. Editor: James B. Clark. Music: Alfred Newman. Design: Richard Day and Nathan Juran. With: Walter Pidgeon, Maureen O'Hara, Donald Crisp, Anna Lee, Roddy McDowell, John Loder, Sara Allgood, Barry Fitzgerald, Patrick Knowles, Ann Todd, Rhys Williams. (118 minutes)

1942

The Battle of Midway (U.S. Navy and 20th Century-Fox)
Script: John Ford, Dudley Nichols and James Kevin McGuinness. Camera: John Ford and Jack McKenzie. Editor: Robert Parrish. Music: Alfred Newman. Voices: Henry Fonda, Jane Darwell, Donald Crisp. (Colour, 20 minutes)

1943

December 7th (U.S. Navy)
Co-director: Gregg, Toland. Camera: Gregg Toland. Editor: Robert Parrish. Music: Alfred Newman. (20 minutes)

1945

They Were Expendable (M-G-M)
Script: Frank W. Wead, from book by William L. White. Camera: Joseph August. Editor: Frank E. Hull and Douglas Biggs. Music: Herbert Stothart. Design: Malcolm F. Brown. With: Robert Montgomery, John Wayne, Donna Reed, Jack Holt, Ward Bond, Leon Ames, Arthur Walsh, Cameron Mitchell, Charles Trowbridge, Paul Langton, Harry Tenbrook, Marshall Thompson, Louis Jean Heydt, Russell Simpson, Murray Alper. (136 minutes)

1946

My Darling Clementine (20th Century-Fox)
Script: Samuel G. Engel and Winston Miller, from story by Sam Hellman, based on *Wyatt Earp, Frontier Marshal* by Stuart N. Lake. Camera: Joseph P. MacDonald. Editor: Dorothy Spencer. Music: Cyril M. Mockridge. Design: James Basevi and Lyle R. Wheeler. With: Henry Fonda, Linda Darnell, Victor Mature, Walter Brennan, Tim Holt, Ward Bond, Cathy Downs, Alan Mowbray, John Ireland, Grant Withers, Roy Roberts, Jane Darwell, Francis Ford, Arthur Walsh. (97 minutes)

1947

The Fugitive (Argosy-RKO Radio)
Script: Dudley Nichols from *The Power and the Glory* by Graham Greene. Camera: Gabriel Figueroa. Editor: Jack Murray. Music: Richard Hageman. Design: Alfred Ybarra. With: Henry Fonda, Dolores Del Rio, Pedro Armendariz, Ward Bond, Leo Carrillo, J. Carroll Naish, Robert Armstrong, John Qualen. (104 minutes)

1948

Fort Apache (Argosy-RKO Radio)
Script: Frank S. Nugent, from *Massacre* by James Warner Bellah. Camera: Archie Stout. Music: Richard Hageman.

Design: James Basevi. With: John Wayne, Henry Fonda, Shirley Temple, John Agar, Ward Bond, George O'Brien, Victor McLaglen, Pedro Armendariz, Anna Lee, Irene Rich, Guy Kibbee, Grant Withers, Jack Pennick. (127 minutes)

Three Godfathers (M-G-M)
Script: Laurence Stallings, Frank S. Nugent, from story by Peter B. Kyne. Camera: Winton Hoch. Editor: Joe Kish. Music: Richard Hageman. Design: James Basevi. With: John Wayne, Pedro Armendariz, Harry Carey Jnr., Ward Bond, Mildred Natwick, Charles Halton, Jane Darwell, Mae Marsh, Guy Kibbee, Ben Johnson. (Colour, 106 minutes)

1949
She Wore a Yellow Ribbon (Argosy-RKO Radio)
Script: Frank S. Nugent and Laurence Stallings, from the story *War Party* by James Warner Bellah. Camera: Winton C. Hoch. Editor: Jack Murray. Music: Richard Hageman. Design: James Basevi. With: John Wayne, Joanne Dru, John Agar, Ben Johnson, Harry Carey Jnr., Victor McLaglen, Mildred Natwick, George O'Brien, Arthur Shields, Chief Big Tree, Francis Ford. (Colour, 103 minutes)

1950
When Willie Comes Marching Home (20th Century-Fox)
Script: Mary Loos and Richard Sale, from *When Leo Comes Marching Home* by Sy Gomberg. Camera: Leo Tover. Editor: James B. Clark. Music: Alfred Newman. Design: Lyle R. Wheeler, Chester Gore. With: Dan Dailey, Corinne Calvet, Colleen Townsend, William Demarest, James Lydon, Lloyd Corrigan, Evelyn Varden, Henry Tenbrook. (82 minutes)

Wagon Master (Argosy-RKO Radio)
Script: Frank S. Nugent and Patrick Ford. Camera: Bert Glennon. Editor: Jack Murray. Music: Richard Hageman. Design: James Basevi. With: Ben Johnson, Harry Carey Jnr., Joanne Dru, Ward Bond, Charles Kemper, Alan Mowbray, Jane Darwell, Ruth Clifford, Russell Simpson, James Arness, Kathleen O'Malley, Francis Ford. (86 minutes)

Rio Grande (Argosy-Republic)
Script: James Kevin McGuinness, from *Mission With No Record* by James Warner Bellah. Camera: Bert Glennon. Editor: Jack Murray. Music: Victor Young. Design: Frank Hotaling. With: John Wayne, Maureen O'Hara, Ben Johnson, Claude Jarman Jnr., Harry Carey Jnr., Chill Wills, J. Carroll Naish, Victor McLaglen, Grant Withers. (105 minutes)

1951
This Is Korea! (U.S. Navy)
With (voice over): John Ireland and others. (Colour, 50 minutes)

1952
What Price Glory (20th Century-Fox)
Script: Phoebe and Henry Ephron, from play by Maxwell Anderson, and Laurence Stallings. Camera: Joseph Mac-Donald. Editor: Dorothy Spencer. Music: Alfred Newman. Design: Lyle R. Wheeler and George W. Davis.

With: James Cagney, Corinne Calvet, Dan Dailey, William Demarest, Craig Hill, Robert Wagner, Marisa Pavan, Casey Adams, James Gleason, Paul Fix. (Colour, 111 minutes)

The Quiet Man (Argosy-Republic)
Script: Frank S. Nugent, from story by Maurice Walsh. Camera: Winton C. Hoch. Editor: Jack Murray. Music: Victor Young. Design: Frank Hotaling. With: John Wayne, Maureen O'Hara, Barry Fitzgerald, Ward Bond, Victor McLaglen, Mildred Natwick, Francis Ford, Eileen Crowe, May Craig, Arthur Shields, Charles FitzSimmons, Sean McClory, James Lilburn, Jack MacGowran. (Colour, 129 minutes)

1953
The Sun Shines Bright (Argosy-Republic)
Script: Laurence Stallings, from stories by Irvin S. Cobb. Camea: Archie Stout. Editor: Jack Murray. Music: Victor Young. Design: Frank Hotaling. With: Charles Winninger, Arleen Whelan, John Russell, Stepin' Fetchit, Russell Simpson, Ludwig Stossel, Francis Ford, Paul Hurst, Mitchell Lewis, Dorothy Jordan, Slim Pickens, Jane Darwell. (90 minutes)

Mogambo (M-G-M)
Script: John Lee Mahin, from play, *Red Dust*, by Wilson Collison. Camera: Robert Surtees and Fredrick A. Young. Editor: Frank Clarke. Design: Alfred Junge. With: Clark Gable, Ava Gardner, Grace Kelly, Donald Sinden, Dennis O'Dea. (Colour, 116 minutes)

1955
The Long Gray Line (Columbia)
Script: Edward Hope, from autobiography, *Bringing Up the Brass* by Marty Maher. Camera: Charles Lawton Jnr. Editor: William Lyon. Music: George Duning. with: Tyrone Power, Maureen O'Hara, Robert Francis, Donald Crisp, Ward Bond, Betsy Palmer, Phil Carey, William Leslie, Harry Carey Jnr. (Colour, 138 minutes)

Mister Roberts (Warner Bros.)
Script: Frank S. Nugent and Joshua Logan, from play by Logan, Thomas Heggen, and novel by Heggen. Camera: Winton C. Hoch. Editor: Jack Murray. Music: Frank Waxman. Design: Art Loel. With: Henry Fonda, James Cagney, Jack Lemmon, William Powell, Ward Bond, Betsy Palmer, Phil Carey, Nick Adams, Harry Carey Jnr. (Colour, 123 minutes)

Rookie of the Year (T.V. Screen Directors Playhouse)
Script: Frank S. Nugent. With: Pat Wayne, Vera Miles, Ward Bond, James Gleason, Willis Bouchey, John Wayne. (29 minutes)

The Bamboo Cross (T.V. Fireside Theatre)
Script: Laurence Stallings, from play by Theophane Lee. With: Jane Wyman, Betty Lynn, Soo Yong, Jim Hong, Judy Wong. (27 minutes)

1956
The Searchers (Warner Bros.)
Script: Frank S. Nugent, from the novel by Alan LeMay. Camera: Winton C. Hoch. Editor: Jack Murray. Music: Max Steiner. Design: Frank Hotaling and James Basevi. With: John Wayne, Jeffrey Hunter, Vera Miles, Ward Bond, Natalie Wood, John Qualen, Olive Carey, Henry

Brandon, Ken Curtis, Harry Carey Jnr. (Colour, 119 minutes)

1957
The Wings of Eagles (M-G-M)
Script: Frank Fenton and William Wister Haines. Editor: Gene Ruggiero. With: John Wayne, Maureen O'Hara, Dan Dailey, Ward Bond, Ken Curtis, Edmund Lowe, Kenneth Tobey. (110 minutes)
The Rising of the Moon (Four Provinces-Warner Bros.)
Script: Frank S. Nugent, from story, *The Majesty of the Law* by Frank O'Connor, and plays, *A Minute's Wait* by Michael J. McHugh and *The Rising of the Moon* by Lady Gregory. Camera: Robert Krasker. Editor: Michael Gordon. Music: Eamonn O'Gallagher. Design: Ray Simm. With: Tyrone Power, Noel Purcell, Cyril Cusack, Jack MacGowran, Jimmy O'Dea, Tony Quinn, Donal Donnelly, J. G. Devlin, Dennis O'Dea, Eileen Crowe, Maurice Good, Frank Lawton. (81 minutes)

1958
The Last Hurrah (Columbia)
Script: Frank S. Nugent, from novel by Edwin O'Conner. Camera: Charles Lawton Jnr. Editor: Jack Murray. Design: Robert Peterson. With: Spencer Tracy, Jeffrey Hunter, Dianne Foster, Pat O'Brien, Basil Rathbone, Donald Crisp, James Gleason, Edward Brophy, John Carradine. (121 minutes)

1959
Gideon's Day (U.S.: Gideon of Scotland Yard) (Columbia)
Script: T. E. B. Clarke, from novel, by J. J. Marric (pseudonym for John Creasey). Camera: Frederick A. Young. Design: Ken Adam. With: Jack Hawkins, Dianne Foster, Anna Massey, Cyril Cusack, Andrew Ray, James Hayter, Howard Marion-Crawford, Derek Bond, Griselda Harvey, Miles Malleson, Jack Watling, Donal Donnelly, Billie Whitelaw. (Colour, 91 minutes)
Korea (U.S. Dept. of Defense)
With: George O'Brien. (30 minutes)
The Horse Soldiers (United Artists)
Script: John Lee Mahin and Martin Rackin, from novel by Harold Sinclair. Camera: William H. Clothier. Editor: Jack Murray. Music: David Buttolph. Design: Frank Hotaling. With: John Wayne, William Holden, Constance Towers, Althea Gibson, Hoot Gibson, Anna Lee. (Colour, 119 minutes)

1960
The Colter Craven Story (T.V. Wagon Train series)
Script: Tony Paulson. With: Ward Bond, Carleton Young, Frank McGrath, Terry Wilson, John Carradine, Chuck Hayward, Ken Curtis, Anna Lee, Lon Chaney Jnr., John Wayne (under pseudonym Michael Morris). (53 minutes)
Sergeant Rutledge (Warner Bros.)
Script: Willis Goldbeck and James Warner Bellah. Camera: Bert Glennon. Editor: Jack Murray. Music: Howard Jackson. Design: Eddie Imazu. With: Jeffrey Hunter, Constance Towers, Woody Strode, Billie Burke, Juano Hernandez, Willis Bouchey, Carleton Young. (Colour, 111 minutes)

1961
Two Rode Together (Columbia)
Script: Frank Nugent, from novel, *Comanche Captives*, by Will Cook. Camera: Charles Lawton Jnr. Editor: Jack Murray. Music: George Duning. Design: Robert Peterson. With: James Stewart, Richard Widmark, Shirley Jones, Linda Cristal, Andy Devine, John McIntire, Paul Birch Willis Bouchey, Henry Brandon, Harry Carey Jnr. (Colour, 109 minutes)

1962
The Man Who Shot Liberty Valance (Paramount)
Script: Willis Goldbeck and James Warner Bellah, from story by Dorothy M. Johnson. Camera: William H. Clothier. Editor: Otho Lovering. Music: Cyril J. Mockridge. Design: Hal Pereira and Eddie Imazu. With: James Stewart, John Wayne, Vera Miles, Lee Marvin, Edmond O'Brien, Andy Devine, Ken Murray, John Carradine, Woody Strode, Denver Pyle, Strother Martin, Lee Van Cleef, Robert F. Simon, O. Z. Whitehead. (122 minutes)
Flashing Spikes (T.V. Aloa Premiere series)
Script: Jameson Brewer, from novel by Frank O'Rourke. Camera: William H. Clothier. Editors: Richard Belding and Tony Martinelli. Music: Johnny Williams. Design: Martin Obzina. With: James Stewart, Jack Warden, Pat Wayne, Edgar Buchanan, Tige Andrews, Harry Carey Jnr., John Wayne. (53 minutes)
How the West Was Won (Civil War episode. Cinerama—M-G-M)
Script: James R. Webb. Camera: Joseph La Shelle. Editor: Harold F. Kress. Music: Alfred Newman and Ken Darby. With: John Wayne, George Peppard, Carroll Baker, Henry (Harry) Morgan, Andy Devine, Russ Tamblyn, Willis Bouchey, Claude Johnson. (Colour, 162 minutes)

1963
Donovan's Reef (Paramount)
Script: Frank S. Nugent and James Edward Grant. Camera: William H. Clothier. Editor: Otho Lovering. Music: Cyril J. Mockridge. With: John Wayne, Lee Marvin, Elizabeth Allen, Jack Warden, Cesar Romero, Dorothy Lamour. (Colour, 15 minutes)

1964
Cheyenne Autumn (Warner Bros.)
Script: James R. Webb, from book by Mari Sandoz. Camera: William H. Clothier. Editor: Otho Lovering. Music: Alex North. Design: Richard Day. With: Richard Widmark, Carroll Baker, James Stewart, Edward G. Robinson, Karl Malden, Sal Mineo, Dolores Del Rio, Ricardo Montalban, Arthur Kennedy, Elizabeth Allen, John Carradine, George O'Brien, Sean McClory, Harry Carey Jnr., Ben Johnson. (Colour, 159 minutes)

1966
Seven Women (M-G-M)
Script: Janet Green and John McCormick, from story, *Chinese Finale*, by Norah Lofts. Camera: Joseph La Shelle. Editor: Otho Lovering. Music: Elmer Bernstein. Design: George W. David, Eddie Imazu. With: Anne Bancroft, Sue Lyon, Margaret Leighton, Flora Robson, Mildred Dunnock, Betty Field, Anna Lee, Eddie Albert. (Colour, 87 minutes)